RAEMIL

DARKNESS RISING: BOOK ONE

Printed in Australia

Cover by Jess Chaplin Creative

Internal design by A to B Editing

Second edition 2024

Paperback ISBN 978-1-7637637-1-5

eBook ISBN 978-1-7637637-2-2

Hardback ISBN 978-1-7637637-0-8

The author acknowledges the traditional owners of the land and pays respects to Elders, past, present and emerging.

NATIONAL LIBRARY OF AUSTRALIA — A catalogue record for this work is available from the National Library of Australia

RAEMIL

DARKNESS RISING: BOOK ONE

L. M. PAGE

Dedicated to Elizabeth Parker, for encouraging me to read my first fantasy novel and sparking a lifetime of love for a magical genre where your imagination is the limit. I miss your friendship and that rip-snorting laughter dearly.

To Debra Shaw, for always encouraging me and believing in me. Thank you for the countless pictures you critiqued for me when I was a kid and letting me use your computer late into many nights. Funnily enough, I can't begin to put into words how much you helped me and boosted my confidence when I was growing up. You are a true treasure.

Prologue...

Smoke drifted lazily around her. She could smell burning hair and flesh as she lay in what had been a forest but was now only a collection of blackened twigs reaching into the pale sky. Unable to move, and the sky and burned trees her only view; she waited for the other to stand above her, to gloat before dealing the final blow. They did not come.

Her beautiful red hair was scorched; she could see its shrivelled ends in her peripheral. A silly thing to be worried about now, she supposed. She couldn't move to see her hands, but they felt like they were on fire still. *They very well could be*, she mused. More likely, they would be blackened claws, not dissimilar to the tops of the trees she could now see. Breathing was hard, she couldn't hear anything above her own wheezing gasps; if her opponent was near, she couldn't tell. She wished they would hurry up; she was getting tired.

The sky grew darker and, as she waited, her mind began to wander back to better days, a time when she was at her happiest, surrounded by good friends and wonderous discoveries. It just so happened that these were also her darkest moments, before she lay blackened in a forest, waiting to die.

Her younger years were spent in Otowan, a cursed land, now known as 'The land of the betrayers'. Once, her kind had been accepted in those lands. She was a mage, her pale skin, height and strange coloured eyes ensured that it was known. Humans, mortals as they still habitually called them, all looked the same to her. To be fair to herself, they did all have tanned skin, brown hair and brown or grey eyes. The fact there were varying shades of those colours throughout the human population escaped her.

She and her mage friends went about their daily lives and the mortals went about theirs, and for the most part, their lives did not intersect. She was unaware that outside the bubble of the academy of magic, mortals and mages were beginning to resent one another. Her attitude was no better. It was easy to dismiss mortals as unimportant while living in a school, secluded from the general population and outside world. They spent their days with noses buried in books, time spent on school grounds practising magic with friends.

Those had been glorious days. There had been five students that were classed as 'live-ins'. They either had no family, like her friend Stah or, like herself, Preah, Myla and Bascillium, couldn't journey for every semester break across to Iadron where their families lived. Very few families lived in Iadron at this stage; the reason why only these few students remained.

These girls had become fast friends, and living in a school meant that all five became very good at the art of magic. During the holidays, they had each other, their power and what seemed like infinite resources. There were rules and they were watched to a certain extent, but the girls were young and wild. They found ways to practise magic when they weren't allowed, break into the potions stock and steal into the restricted library to find all kinds of juicy tales and spells.

Laying there, scorched and still smoking, she wished she could go back in time, at least before everything went wrong; before one of their teachers became a fanatic and lost his mind. If it weren't for him, Otowan may have stayed the mainland, mages and mortals may have still been living together. Tensions had always been high between the two races; she just hadn't noticed until it was much, much too late.

A lot of the animosity came from a disagreement on the gods. It was widely believed there were nine gods. The new religion only had room for one. Humans had begun to follow the new god, the 'only' God, as they would have others believe. This one God just so happened to decree that mages and magic were evil.

Otowan quickly became a very dangerous place for mages. She should have listened to Stah. She was a blonde-haired beauty with eyes of amber and a laugh that could lighten even the gloomiest of moods. Stah had been the first to mention that something was afoot outside the academy. If they had listened then, perhaps all the other teachers wouldn't have died in the fire.

She could now appreciate how painful, if not how terrifying, that must have been, trapped in the academy while it burned. How terrible it must have been to watch the doom of your own race, to know it was caused by one of your own.

The five girls didn't stay to heroically fight the flames and try to save the school and hundreds of years' worth of learning and history, like the staff had. Narrowly escaping, they watched from afar as the place they had called home burned to the ground.

Pulling her out of her reflections of the past, she saw a large bird through the break in the burned trees overhead. It dipped and wheeled above the scene, no doubt a bird of prey, looking for small and injured creatures crawling out of the ruined forest. It was directly above her, circling as though deciding whether or not she was too big to eat. Ridiculously, her only fear was that it could shit on her from this position. She didn't want her body to be found after an epic battle, only to have the one thing remembered about it was that she lay dead with a giant bird shit on her face. That would be a cruel and frankly, unacceptable, ending.

The five former students were on the run for a while, only survival on their mind in the beginning. How to get back to their families without being captured and murdered by mortals, came in second. By now, there had been a mass exodus of mages from Otowan into Iadron. Once the humans had realised the mages were fleeing across the sea, they took control of the docks, making it near impossible to get back to Iadron.

Bascillium had been the best at gem spells among them. It was she who convinced them of the power of, not only gems, but the natural stones around them. The most powerful family houses held power stones, a different colour represented a different house. The stones helped mages access their power and boost it if needed, as well as being tools for communication. There were not many great houses and by the time the war would end, only four of those families would remain.

Each of the girls had worn a pendant around their necks, made from their families' power stones; small pieces to carry with them on their journeys away from home. They were to help the young mages learn to control their power, a focal point, and something weaker mages would rely heavily on. All five gave up their house pendants to Bascillium and she made with them a tool they would use against Eldantez, the power-hungry mage that had instigated it all.

Eldantez couldn't see anything but devotion in those mortals. This led him to his doom. His human followers betrayed him, earning Otowan its second name. The combined power of his former students banished him from the mortal plain, but the fighting was not over.

Their world was utterly and irreparably changed after the evacuation of mages from Otowan. So many had died and they had been few in number in comparison to the humans to begin with. Battles raged between mortals and mages, but even powerful mages had their limits; even they became exhausted and overwhelmed.

The bird was gone, leaving her alone in the quiet again. Her opponent was nowhere to be seen; perhaps she was dead or dying too. She and her four friends from the academy had parted ways a long time ago, deciding it was safer that way, until now, that was. Bascillium had reached out to her after such a long time. It seemed that Bascillium had had a change of heart. She wanted to resurrect the academy, to make Otowan a place for mages again and rule the mortals there.

Leaving her family behind and, without explanation, she had stupidly been lured to the land of the betrayers. She went to determine if Bascillium worked alone, if she was just deranged from a long and traumatic life, or if she was in fact dangerous. It turned out to be the latter. She and Bascillium battled through a land full of people that would burn them alive, given the opportunity. Their final battle ground was this forest, where, to both their surprise, they seemed very evenly matched.

The final blast of raw power threw her back so far, she couldn't even see Bascillium and what damage she may or may not have done to her former friend. Since she was still not dead, and it was starting to get dark and cold, she could only assume Bascillium was dead. Internally, she assessed the damage, her mind probing her own body for fatal wounds, she could not see, but could feel. She discovered half cooked organs, burned lungs and trachea, extremities burned to charcoal and tremendous pain.

Sick of waiting for death to come to her, she decided to meet death on her own terms. They had flirted before, she and death. She wondered why it was taking so long for him to take her now. Drawing on what little power and energy she had left to her, she sent her spirit from her body, drifting to the Inbetween. It was a place void of light and sound; it was the small or incredibly large place between places. The veil separating the Inbetween and the Underworld was very thin.

Standing now in the void, she lifted her hands to inspect them. She was glad to see that here, they were not looking like crispy, over-cooked chicken feet as she was sure they looked back on the mortal plain. While she waited for death, she realised, after reflecting back on her long life, a greedy part of her wanted more than this. She had been through so much, and for what? To die pointlessly and alone? There was more to come, she could feel it in her bones. This was not her end, so when death drifted quietly into the void to take her, she lifted her chin and she told him *no*.

He laughed. They all said no: the young; the old; the pretty; the ugly; the poor and the wealthy. What had they to give him? What could they bargain with other than their lives, which were already his to take? But this one was so sure she could be the one to cheat him. She stood there so confident, so strong, her elegant neck craned, her long, red hair pushed back behind her squared shoulders, a defiant look on her fine face. Mage-kind were all the same, all arrogant, all thinking they could just take what they wanted with no consequence.

'I could give you more lives,' she said.

As though he hadn't heard that one before.

'I gain nothing from murders,' he said dismissively.

He accepted lives and housed souls before their crossing, but he could not keep them. He could neither prevent their transformation nor hurry it along. Murder victims were the least interactive and of the least benefit to his existence; a way to discourage such bargains that led to mass killings. Wars were a little different. The definition of murder during war times became a little more ambiguous, and a war was coming; it would be a busy and enjoyable time ahead for him.

'What can you gain from anything here? As Death?' she asked.

Death looked at her in a new light. She was pretty, beautiful even, and very powerful; even in the underworld where he ruled, power was still coveted.

'Now that is a question that is rarely asked.' Death smiled.

The imprudent mage smiled back, arrogance forever the downfall of her kind.

1. Farewell to a kingdom.

A creeping darkness haunted the halls of Caelin, the northernmost kingdom of Otowan. Quietly it crept, stalking from shadow to shadow, ever closer to the page-boy hurrying toward the kitchen. It knew all the places to avoid, stepping lightly over the squeaky boards. The boy had no idea that the important document hanging carelessly from his pocket was going to be snatched into enemy's hands.

Voices drifted from below, accompanied by footsteps. There could be no witnesses. With no more time to waste, the darkness rolled across the floor just as two people came around the curve in the stairs. Coming up onto its feet with its back against the wall, it froze, listening to the uninterrupted chatter, confirming it had not been seen. Unaware of his looming doom, the boy continued to stroll casually down the hall. Darting past the tapestries and into the corridor directly behind the boy, the shadow timed it perfectly. Just as he pushed the kitchen doors open, the shadow snatched the coveted documents and turned to flee... but instead, almost collided with Tarrlyn.

'What did you get this time?' he asked, winking at her.

'Treasonous poison from the enemy.' She offered up the handkerchief she'd snatched from the boy.

Both Tarrlyn and she realised it was a used handkerchief as she held it aloft and quickly flung it over the railing. She tried to muffle her laughter as a sharp protest came from below, clearly unimpressed by the snotty assault.

'Both disgusting... and far too easy,' the old man said as he offered her his arm to escort her away from the imagined scene of the attack.

'Last week, I took the captain's knife,' she whispered in his ear. 'From under the table,' she added with barely contained glee.

'Crawling under tables is no place for a princess.' A stern look wrinkled his face to the point that his eyes almost disappeared.

'No harm was done. Besides, that hardly matters anymore.'

Absently, she adjusted her hood and cast her eyes down as they passed people in the hall going in the opposite direction.

Tarrlyn sighed. He could swear she was aging him faster than he already had. Ever since the king announced he would not go after her brother, who had been captured and taken to the Horsham mountains, the princess was obsessed with going after him.

He glanced at the side of her heavily cowled head, wishing he could shake some sense into her. Sometimes he caught a glimpse of her face: a smile, a flash of her bright eyes, nothing more. It was a shame she was afflicted with such an unsettling appearance. She was sweet and intelligent and one of his favourite people, despite her current, foolish obsession.

The hooded cloak was her constant attire. A comb in her hair and another sewn into the inside of the hood inter-locked, to ensure it would not easily slip. She hadn't complained about it in a while, either a sign of maturity, acceptance, or more likely, she was lying low.

On her name-day, the nobles gathered to hear what the new princess had been called. The Caelinians were never told a name, only that the princess was disfigured and unlikely to survive. Her mother, the queen for such a short time, had fled.

Eventually her name was released – Raemil, daughter of King Farramand of Caelin Castle, sister to Prince Serrin. She was even branded on her thirteenth birthday with the Caelinian sigil under her collar bone, as was her brother and their father, and his siblings and their father before him.

As Tarrlyn escorted Raemil to her rooms, a thrill went up her spine at the thought of her escape. Almost everything was ready, and she could hardly contain her excitement.

Tarrlyn was her most trusted friend, her only friend left, in fact. He was a retired master-at-arms and now an advisor to the king, hardly an appropriate friend for a princess. It was not that she hadn't tried to be friends with the other girls of the court or even the young maids at one point. They were either frightened by her or disgusted or both. Eventually, she came to terms with the fact that she would not be friends with fine ladies and other princes and princesses.

Raemil sat at her dressing table before her mirror, removing her hood and pulling her combs out. She hadn't looked at her reflection in a while. She pulled the sheet from her mirror and waved away the dust-motes. It was true, she would never be beautiful or even pretty. She was ugly, everyone said so, even though lately she'd been careful not to be seen. She combed her hair while wishing she looked like someone else, anybody else. With a frustrated flourish, she threw the sheet back over the mirror.

She was not always so careful to conceal her face and body; in fact, she rebelled against her father and her nanny many times. In the beginning, her father was almost kind toward her. The king procured dyes for her hair and special oils to darken her skin so she could be seen among the people. The dyes washed out, even if she was just caught in the rain; her hair refused to hold any colour that was not her own. The oils for her skin were the same. Some were patchy, some made her itch furiously; the ones that stayed longer than a day made her look speckled and ridiculous.

Eventually her father stopped trying, stopped even looking at her. When Serrin left, the castle became so empty somehow, their father so bitter. Once, during an argument, she followed him into the hall shouting. She had forgotten that she'd not yet donned her cloak. Her father was furious. He told her he would teach her how to be careful, and he hacked all of her offensive hair off. She screamed and cried and fought back, resulting in a patchy and mostly bald head with several cuts in her scalp. Raemil was much more careful after that. At the time, it felt like it took forever for her hair to grow back. Nanny tried her best to console Raemil, but she was a fifteen-year-old girl. Even an ugly girl's hair was still precious to her.

Most princesses had handmaidens after they had outgrown their nannies, but not Raemil. It would only be one more person to have to look upon the princess' face and know King Farramand's shame that he should produce such a thing. Nanny cared for Raemil's scrapes and bruises, taught her how to behave like a princess and a lady, how to dance and what it was to be a woman. Nanny stayed on past her time, and when she died, Raemil was sure her father had not noticed. He never bothered to replace her.

Raemil slid under her bed at the back, where she kept her satchel. It was made of supple leather, beautifully sewn and soft to touch. Inside she kept the things she gathered during her shadow games. She played to practice, determined to master the art of going unnoticed. She still had the captain's knife. She wasn't likely to use it as a weapon, but it would certainly be useful. Tarrlyn had told her she should practise with a knife, that it was more practical for a woman to use as a weapon, but she would have none of it. Her brother played with wooden swords when he was a child, and later he used real ones. She would not settle for less.

She made a mental checklist of the things she still needed, like food that couldn't be stored under her bed. She wanted her sword the most, but she wouldn't dare bring it into the castle. Tarrlyn had it hidden safely away, for it was not for ladies, much less a princess, to wield a sword. Her training with Tarrlyn had all been in secret. She had defied her father in almost everything, even living past her first year. What was one more defiance?

Raemil lay on her bed, staring up at the ceiling. She tried to imagine the places she would see, the friends she might meet on her journey, and ultimately, the day she would rescue her brother. She hadn't realised she'd fallen asleep until music drifted up to her room from below. Her stomach growled; she'd missed dinner.

Using shadows to remain unseen, Raemil took every opportunity to practice. The servants weren't overly vigilant. Raemil almost ran into a couple hiding in one of her shadows. They were busy kissing and didn't notice as she narrowly avoided running into them. Raemil had made it her mission to get to the kitchen and back quickly. The kitchen was a dungeon, the bread she liberated from the counter was her brother, the servants were the vile men from Horsham and the cook – a hideous mage named after the Horsham Mountain, just as the men were.

* * *

A month later, a cloaked figure darted across the deserted courtyard of King Farramand's castle. Red hair escaped her hood, aided by the wind; she quickly brushed it aside and hastened her strides. She passed the huge oak tree that grew in the centre of the courtyard, its roots breaking up the pavement.

She sensed him there before she saw him, and quickly she turned to face the man. He was heavily cowled to conceal his face. His frail grey hands reached for her shoulders. She loved him dearly, and he loved her, but there were no more words left between them that hadn't already been said.

'I wish...' he started, then fell silent, thinking better of whatever he was about to say.

She turned away and hurried to the place she had hidden supplies at the gate the day before. Tarrlyn disappeared into the stable. A tall, grey wall guarded the castle. The big wooden gates that led into the courtyard were old, worn by weather with big cracks marring the surface. She had always looked upon them as a living thing and sometimes she imagined she could hear their heartbeat.

Shod hooves rang on the pavement, as Tarrlyn led her tall, black mount toward the gates. Her horse nickered as he recognised his master and she stroked his nose before moving to the stirrup and turning her back to mount.

'Raemil...'

She turned back to Tarrlyn with tears in her eyes.

'Bring him home safe.'

Nodding, Raemil brushed an escaped tear from her cheek and leapt onto her horse's back. Tarrlyn handed Raemil her sword, which she hung at her hip. Anxious, her horse sprang forward as Tarrlyn opened the gate, but she reined him back to stand beside her old friend.

'I will miss you so very much.' Her voice wavered with emotion, before she laid heels to the Black, fearing her resolve might break.

Determined, Raemil did not look back to the place she had spent all seventeen years of her life. Knowing that she only rode to war and famine in most places, she forced herself to think only of her brother's freedom and, if she was honest, her own.

2. Harsh reality.

She had never known what lay beyond the grassy fields and soft, sloping hills of Caelin. To her, it was forbidden. As a child, she could only watch people come and go. She watched wistfully as her brother travelled out of Caelin, while her freedom was denied.

Freedom was what Raemil sought, but it was her brother's captivity that drove her. Raemil had been fifteen when her brother, Serrin, left with a great portion of their father's army. Serrin had been twenty; he had dark brown hair and deep brown eyes. He strode into the courtyard and out of Raemil's life two years ago.

Her brother and his army, together with the Korran, had fought the Horsham warriors for a full season. Eventually, she and her father received the news that most of the Korran and Caelinians had perished. It was rumoured that a small number of survivors were taken to Horsham itself, Serrin among them.

Raemil had no army at her back like her brother, but foolishly or not, she was determined to free him. Her father would spare no more Caelinian men for a journey that seemed both costly and dangerous. He mourned the loss of his son and moved on. The king's sour disposition toward the princess, his remaining heir, only deepened.

Raemil could see the thin orange line of dawn on the horizon. Soon her father would find the drugged guards slumped against her door and find her room empty. She knew the king himself would pursue her this time, knowing full well what she meant to do. It likely wouldn't have mattered if she hadn't been branded, effectively being named heir. He would forever regret that decision and wonder what had come over him. He couldn't very well have his disfigured daughter-heir running around the country side, spreading false hope of rescuing the prince.

She walked her black mount steadily through the fields as the sun crept over the horizon and slowly flooded the land, awash with sunlight. From the crest of a sloping hill, she could see yet more of Caelin's lush, green meadows, and beyond. She spotted a small village not far in the distance. Despite her weariness of Caelin's people, loyal to their king, Raemil longed to experience her world and know its people.

She whipped her cloak from her shoulders and tucked it into a saddle bag. The sun's warmth touched her pale, white skin and glinted from her red curls, flowing down her lower back. Her white cotton skirts were spread about her horse's back. Despite her excitement, she felt exposed and guilty. It was like she was standing outside naked for the world to see. Taking a steadying breath, she reminded herself she was free now. She could go where she pleased and could reveal her red hair and pale complexion if that was her want. She tapped her heels to the Black's flanks and he sprang down the slope.

Only moments later, her mount skidded to a sudden halt and reared. Raemil kept her seat and laid hands on his neck, trying to calm him. It worked only briefly, and, with a snort, he startled and swung around.

Hearing a rustle in the hay, Raemil forced him around to face the noise. There, on the ground, sat a wide-eyed peasant. Her woven basket was on its side on the ground, its contents of pink and white wild flowers were scattered amidst the hay. Raemil gazed into her wide, brown eyes, staring in sheer terror. Her golden skin had turned sickly and pale, almost matching Raemil's.

'You've nothing to fear of me.' Raemil tried to sound, and appear, non-threatening.

The woman continued to stare; her knees huddled protectively against her chest. She wore a white apron, long since turned brown from dust and hard labour, tied over a yellow dress.

The Black stamped his hoof impatiently. Instantly, the woman gathered her skirts about her knees and ran, leaving the spilled wild flowers and basket behind. Raemil's gaze followed to where the woman sought sanctuary. She urged the Black into a trot and trailed at a distance. The woman looked back and assumed she was being pursued. She screamed in terror and ran yet faster from the woman with flames for hair.

Were all of Caelin's folk this afraid of strangers? Raemil was annoyed to think she was a stranger to her father's own people, locked away in the castle for so many years. So what if she looked a little different? She had never hurt anyone; she had never even been cruel to anyone. She hadn't had the chance.

The fleeing woman reached the village and disappeared into a hut. Raemil spurred her horse on faster. She didn't consider that it might look to someone else that she was chasing someone down. The Black burst from the field and onto a road running through the centre of the small cluster of houses. He pranced shyly forward, not accustomed to the rocky road beneath his hooves.

For a moment, Raemil paid no heed to the dancing horse beneath her as she looked upon their surroundings. These were hard-earned homes on hard-worked land. All seemed silent and deserted, save for the few clucking hens that roamed unafraid beside the road. Fluffy, yellow chicks followed closely at their mother's side, cheeping noisily, without a care for any predators they might attract.

Momentarily distracted, she hadn't noticed the village people crowding their doorways, staring at her in both wonder and fear. Raemil scanned their faces until her eyes fell upon the woman in the yellow dress. There were small children huddled about her skirts, seeking reassurance from their frightened mother.

Suddenly there was a harsh cry from what looked like a priest's wife, breaking the silence.

'Serlyn!' the old woman cried, clutching a cross to her heart and pointing accusingly at Raemil.

Raemil was shocked by the sudden anger surging through the gathered people like a wave of hatred. The Black bolted as a rock sailed by his wither and Raemil only just managed to rein him back.

'Serlyn, be gone!' shouted the priest, and another rock was hurled, falling short.

Raemil was dumbstruck, and she could not tear her eyes away from the woman in the yellow dress. All timidness had vanished; now angry eyes bore into Raemil's. Hate was like a contagion spreading through the crowd. A rock struck her horse hard on the rump. He jumped free of Raemil's tight rein, causing her to topple as rocks rained down. She tried to stand, but a stone struck her temple and she was knocked senseless.

Raemil's vision blurred and she felt heat run down the side of her face. She feared for her life as everything went white and the world seemed to go silent. Almost instantly, she was back in the noise and projectiles again. People were running at her. Fear and desperation took a hold of Raemil and she leapt to her feet. She drew her sword and thrust it point first into the ground at the feet of her first assailant. The cries of anger turned to those of fear, as everything around her and the villagers started to crumble. Though the very ground quivered and shifted beneath her, she managed to stay upright. The projectiles stopped midway from their destination and dropped heavily to the ground.

Everything settled just as suddenly, and a calmness washed over her. She yanked her sword from the ground and turned her back to walk away. The people had been knocked from their feet and sprawled on the ground. She left them dazed and confused, and, most of all, terrified.

Raemil felt numb as she surveyed the scene. The small earthquake had caused stones to tumble from houses, leaving unsightly and unwanted windows into people's homes. One house, in particular, was reduced to a pile of rubble. The priest's wife looked upon the ruin and wailed into her apron. In a daze, Raemil went the direction her horse had fled, sliding her sword safely into its sheath at her hip. No one dared to pursue her.

Sometime later, Raemil heard the soft and familiar nicker of the Black. He emerged from the meadow beside the road. She stroked his nose in greeting, and the Black buried his head low in her skirts, as if feeling shame for running.

The day was nearly gone when they reached a small, fast flowing creek. She stopped her horse there and they both drank deeply. Leaving the Black to graze by the road, she walked up the creek a way to where the water flowed slower. She remembered the likeness of the village people, the same as the people of her father's castle. They all had varying shades of brown hair, but it was brown nonetheless. Their eyes were all shades of brown, and their skin was golden. All the same.

Raemil leaned over the bank and frowned at her reflection. Aside from her white skin and red hair, her eyes were green – like mould or algae. *It is all so wrong*, she thought and swiped away the offensive image. She leaned back on her heels, staring into oblivion. Her thoughts turned inward.

Raemil felt a sickening fear, as she looked past the creek and across the vast landscape. She feared that perhaps she was the only soul alive that did not have golden skin or brown hair. She had hoped there were others out there like her, others that had been born deformed. Despite being told by one of the maids that had she not been a princess, she'd have been dropped off a cliff like common people did with their failed children; she needed to believe she was not alone.

She couldn't remember what 'Serlyn' meant, save that it was of ancient Caelinian tongue. Suddenly she was overwhelmed. *Why were they afraid? Why did they call me that name? What was that disaster in the village?* She tried to shake her mind free of such wild thoughts, but she could not. *Was it my doing that shook the foundations? Did I direct this disaster mostly at the priest and his wife, because they were first to threaten me? No. No.*

'NO!' Raemil suddenly cried, and, gathering her skirts, she fled her thoughts as she ran for her horse.

The Black thundered down the creek, splashed through the water and back up onto the continuing road. It was well into the night before Raemil stopped. The horse was tired and Raemil wished she hadn't been so cruel to him; he who had been nothing but loyal to her.

After her meagre dinner, Raemil lay back on the hard ground and looked up at the winking stars. Both moons had risen, the blue moon and the red. The red moon only graced the sky when marking a month's passing. Raemil exhaled a sigh as she looked dreamily up at the red moon. This night that only happened once a month was called Bloodnight, for the moon cast a light to the earth that gave everything a red glow. Her eyes lowered from the moons and soon she fell into a deep and much needed sleep.

The red moon had chased the blue moon from its position directly above the planet, and the Bloodnight grew yet bloodier. The night was astir with nocturnal animals, but they failed to wake Raemil from her slumber.

A shrill cry rang out into the night, not far from where Raemil slept, but still she did not wake. The Black whickered softly as he smelled the familiar scent of his stablemates approaching. A second cry went up, much closer than before and caused Raemil to jump awake this time. She knew the call of her horse well enough to know this sound did not come from him. This cried warning of her father's approach. Sparing no time to put her fire out, she ran for the Black.

Raemil mounted the nervous horse as the rumble of hooves sounded on the road. Wheeling the Black around to see, her fears were confirmed. Around the bend in the road, came six Caelinian soldiers; her father, distinctly dressed in blue, rode ahead of them. She whirled the Black around again and laid heels to his flanks, galloping into the Bloodnight.

The Black stumbled on a loose stone and quickly regained his footing, only to find the soldiers at their heels. A young member of the Caelinian army reined in beside Raemil and snatched at the reins. She pulled the Black hard to the left, darting away from the man astride a bay, war-trained horse. She directed her horse into the field.

A dark crack split the meadow, and, in the dim Bloodnight, it went unnoticed by all. Suddenly, there was no soil beneath the Black's hooves. He screamed in terror as his side hit the bank and he rolled. Raemil was half crushed by her rolling mount. She tumbled free from him, but was struck in her ribs by a flailing, shod hoof. Both the Black and Raemil splashed into the ice-cold water. Raemil's breath had all but left her from the shock of the water as much as the impact of a hoof to her side. The creek had turned back on its self and was much deeper than it had been earlier. She could not swim; her fear of drowning became more urgent than her imminent capture.

Out the corner of her eye, she saw the Black gain his footing and reached for his wet tail, holding on tight as her horse bounded awkwardly up the opposite bank. Raemil was dragged roughly aground. Before she could gain her bearings, she heard the splash of hooves in water and her father, on his grey mare, appeared in front of her.

The king laid eyes upon Raemil as though she was a filthy rat. This angered her, and she scrambled to her feet and fixed him with her best approximation of a glower. One of the men seized the Black's reins roughly as if to punish the horse for obeying his rider.

She turned her glare to the man who held the frightened Black. Her hair was a sodden weight that strained her neck, her once white skirts were dripping a muddy brown, and her leather vest was chafing her underarms. Raemil's green eyes cast loathing at her father, but he didn't seem to notice, nor would he have particularly cared if he had.

'End this madness, Raemil. Come home.'

'I will not.' She held her head high, despite the state of her.

'I am not asking this of you.'

'You can no longer deny me my freedom,' she said, staring, unblinking, at her father.

'Can't I?' he nodded toward her exhausted and injured horse.

She shook with rage; her father was more than happy to forever have her locked within the walls of Caelin's castle.

'I shall never forgive you, *Father*' – she spat the word as though it tasted foul – 'if I must gain my freedom by force.'

He laughed mockingly.

'Dear Raemil, you are no match for a small child, let alone seven men.' He chuckled again, his men taking up the laughter. 'You are careless with your words as you are careless with your horse.'

Her cheeks flushed hot with a mixture of embarrassment and rage. She sprang toward the man holding the Black and rolled, coming to her feet in a crouching position while drawing her stolen knife. She cut the girth of the bay mare, trying her best not to harm the horse, but it was near impossible. Before anyone could react, the horse screamed and jumped forward, causing both man and saddle to slide to the ground. Raemil leapt onto the mare's bare back, seizing the reins of her own black steed. Hearing the smooth slither of a sword being unsheathed at her back, she twisted on the mare's back, swapping knife for sword. Metal struck metal and sparks flew between them, then the Caelinian soldier's sword was thrust from his hand. He was taken completely by surprise.

The king reached for the Black's reins and Raemil turned with sword ready again. She pointed it to his throat.

'You underestimated me once, Father. Do not try me again.'

Raemil spun the mare and galloped away with the Black stumbling behind.

It wasn't long before the Black slowed, clearly injured from his fall into the creek. She slowed and cursed her father for his persistence, as she heard the men approaching again. She noted the change in the sound as several horses dropped back and her father continued alone.

'End this now!' He was angrier than she had ever witnessed.

He snatched at the bay mare's reins, but Raemil pulled away.

'It is you who is careless with your words, as you *care less* about your son who lies imprisoned in Horsham.'

Her words cut deep, but her father returned with anger. The Caelin king reached for his sword, but with youth on her side, Raemil was quicker. The king held his reins taut, keeping in pace with the bay that Raemil rode. She took advantage and drew her sword, cutting the rein between the bit and her father's grip. Caught off guard, his right arm snapped back, wrenching his poor grey mare's head to the right. The mare did as the bit told her, and she spun around sharply, unseating the king. Raemil spurred the stolen horse on faster, desperate to put some distance between herself and her father.

Eventually, the sounds of pursuit disappeared. She found her way back to the road and continued on, this road being the only landmark she knew. After a while, Raemil stopped and let the horses graze. She knew the Black would not stray far, but she also feared he couldn't, even if he wanted to. Raemil was not concerned whether the mare stayed; she didn't particularly need the extra mouth to feed.

The morning found the mare gone. Raemil winced as she rose, her injuries from the previous night had gone stiff and hurt more now than they had in flight. She found the Black sitting down and unwilling to get back up, she tugged on the reins a third time before he rose with a groan and unsteady legs. As she led him, she realised he was in no better state than she, if not worse.

By noon, Raemil shook with fever. Having slept in her wet clothes and eating little food, her energy had long since been spent. She and her horse both clumsily stumbled, as neither of them could find even the energy to lift their feet. She stopped once to change into trousers and a man's shirt, glad to be rid of skirt and chafing leather. She unpacked her white wolf-fur cloak and wrapped it around herself, concealing her features again.

A cool breeze whispered through the meadow hay, and in her fevered mind, she thought the wind spoke to her. It told her to run, to run home to safety. Raemil tripped and fell for what only seemed like a second, but when she got up, night had fallen, and the Black was nuzzling her gently with his nose.

3. The mind of a beast.

Gorran had crept from his sleeping household to tend his lame pony. He had turned eleven several months ago and finally received the pony as a gift after at least a year of begging. His large family lived in poverty and could ill afford a stable. The pony was tethered across the road from their house, where no one had disputed its presence so far.

He stroked its mane and spoke softly, its ears twitching this way and that. Suddenly, the pony whinnied and looked west. Gorran thought nothing of this until he heard the noticeably deeper reply. He turned to see on the rise of the road a magnificent black horse, almost camouflaged into the night. The Black's head suddenly dropped low and he stumbled and almost fell.

A woman was slung over the horse's neck; she appeared to be dead. Gorran approached cautiously. As the horse walked unguided through the village, he seemed not to notice the boy until the last moment and his head shot up and he shied away. Gorran jumped back and the woman in white furs toppled to the ground, dangerously close to the horse's hooves.

'Shh, easy... easy now.' Gorran tried to calm the horse as lights began to appear in the windows of the houses.

He stretched for the horse's reins to lead him from the woman, but the Black snorted and stumbled away. The horse went down, falling on his knees and grazing them badly on the gravel road. Gorran ran to the woman, hoping she was alive.

He shook her gently, then rougher and more urgent.

'Lady, you have to wake up!'

He stared at the shadowed face in the white hood, willing her to rise. He shook her shoulders so her hood fell back and tangled red curls spilled out to frame a white face. Her green eyes flew open. Gorran yelped with surprise. This woman had cat eyes! The woman yanked her hood back over her head and rose unsteadily. Gorran watched as she swayed, dangerously close to falling again. People had emerged from their homes now, most stood back and watched, a few dared to come closer.

The black horse staggered to his feet; globules of blood dripped from its torn chin. The woman in white furs suddenly came to her senses. Walking into the path of the mad horse, she offered her hand, beckoning him to her. The horse shied and stopped, swaying unsteadily, before making a noise resembling a whicker. A sigh of relief went through the crowd as they watched the horse go to its master.

Gorran, forgetting all fear, ran to the woman's side.

'Are you hurt?'

She eyed Gorran from beneath her cowl. 'Please, say nothing of my appearance,' she said in an urgent whisper. She searched his face for his answer, satisfied when the boy nodded.

An angry-looking man approached, giving the horse a wide berth.

'What brings you here at this hour, causing havoc with this... this creature?'

'I ask only a night's shelter for my horse and me.' She spoke softly, she herself now swaying from the effort of standing.

The man strode away toward another. He spoke quietly to a short, thin man, before they both came back. The short, thin man studied her a moment, no doubt trying to guess if she had money.

'I am Thenysies. I am the master of both the inn and stables. Where do you come from? And who do you flee to inflict such injuries on that animal?'

'Again, I only ask shelter. I ride on a journey and flee no one.'

She wanted to offer money, but she also had the presence of mind to be cautious. They could just rob her if they thought she had anything of value, and she was in no state to even attempt to defend herself. He eyed her suspiciously.

'No. You will find no shelter here; away with you,' he simply said, dismissing her with a swish of his hand.

A stocky woman barged through the crowd at that moment.

'Thenysies,' the woman snapped, 'how could you cast this girl out? She is clearly exhausted. Look at the poor dear. I won't have it, and I say she may shelter here as long as she wishes.' She grabbed Raemil's hand. 'I am Thysirra. I am mistress of the inn and stables; I am also a healer. Come now, you need to rest.' The woman beckoned, taking no notice of her embarrassed husband.

'My horse...'

'Gorran will take him to the stable and tend to his needs. Come,' she repeated, looking over her shoulder and eyeing the young boy to make sure he did just that.

'If there be trouble, Thysirra, let it be on your head,' Thenysies called after her.

Ignoring the man, Thysirra whisked the hooded girl inside.

Gorran took the horse by the reins and led him to the barn. He seemed all out of energy and willing enough to follow the boy now. Restless ponies moved about in the half-lit stalls. Some whickered softly to the Black, but the animal seemed not to notice. Gorran took a rag and gently bathed his wounds. He stayed with the horse most of the night.

Raemil sat up in alarm, thinking her father had taken her back, then she dizzied and fell back into the soft pillows again. The night before was difficult to remember, like a fading dream. Her hood was still on, she found with relief, and she vaguely remembered telling someone time and time again to leave it. The combs she used to keep her hood secure were so badly tangled in her hair that she doubted she could pull it back without cutting it free.

The door to the room opened very slowly, and a short, plump woman, carrying a tray backed in. She set a broth down on the bedside table, brushing grey hair from her face as she straightened.

'Ah, you're awake. Do you remember me?'

Raemil shook her head in confusion. The face was vaguely familiar, but she couldn't recall a name.

'I am Thysirra. You didn't have the chance to tell me your name.'

'Raemil.'

'Raemil...' the woman repeated. 'How fare you this morning, my dear?'

'I'm worried about my horse; what news of him?' Raemil asked anxiously.

'I must admit at this point, I do not know; I will see. You must drink this broth; it will help with the fever. Now eat, my dear, before it gets cold.'

With that, the woman strode from the room.

Raemil had no appetite, but she drank the broth anyway, eager to be well enough to leave. She slept little and was soon restless of this small room. The thought of her injured horse nagged at her, until she could stand it no longer. She drew the sheets back and staggered to her feet, swaying as dizziness overwhelmed her. She leaned against the wall for a time, until she was sure she could manage with no support.

Raemil emerged from her room and was faced with a long hallway. She counted six other rooms. The house was old, the wooden frames were cracked, there were stains on the ceiling from past or current leaks and the floorboards were uneven and more squeaked than didn't. She wandered down the hall until bumping into Thysirra, who was possibly alerted by the noisome floor.

'Where do you think you are going? You mustn't be out of bed.'

'I have to see my horse.'

The woman's face softened and Raemil's unease grew.

'Come then, you will see.' Thysirra took Raemil by the arm and helped her outside.

The day was still warm, though dusk was settling in fast. Children still laughed and played outside, and farmer's wives and mothers busied themselves around a huge black pot that was set over a fire in a cleared area. Raemil was intrigued. It appeared as though they were cooking; a strange thing to do out in the open in Raemil's, albeit limited, experience.

Thysirra, who was supporting Raemil, noticed her intrigue and nodded toward the activities.

'Birth celebrations. Tonight we eat together under the stars. You may join us if you like, but not for too long; you really shouldn't have left your bed.'

Raemil only nodded distractedly, watching as a band of people and animals came down the road toward the centre of the village. Despite her worry for the Black, she was fascinated by these people and their customs, amazed that she would be invited to join such a gathering.

She felt light-headed as they stopped at the red doors to the barn. She heard a pony snort from within and the restless shifting of another. Thysirra pushed the doors open and they swung noisily on their hinges, startling a pony in the opposite stall. The musty smell of horse, mixed with the sweet smell of hay, wafted out.

A crow startled Raemil as it squawked and fluttered out, perching itself on a nearby post. It preened its feathers, pushing them neatly back into place with its beak, before fixing her with a beady eye.

'Come,' said the crow, 'you need not be afraid. Come fly south with me, and I shall tell you all that awaits you.'

'Excuse me?' she gawked at the bird.

'Hmm?' Thysirra looked up at Raemil, puzzled.

The crow squawked and flew away.

'Did you hear it?'

'Hear what?'

'That crow, it...'

'Crow? Where?' Thysirra ducked and looked about.

'Never mind,' Raemil said, a little confused herself.

Raemil mentally filed this encounter away with the growing list of unsettling experiences since she had left the castle.

It was dark inside, and as her eyes adjusted, she could see the darker shadows of ponies shifting about. Her breath caught as she spotted the largest shadow in the second-to-last stall. She didn't realise how tense she had been and she had to fight the urge to run to him and fling her arms around his neck.

Thysirra busied herself looking for a lamp whilst Raemil went to the Black. She leaned on the rails of his stall and watched him. His head hung low, seeming despondent. Thysirra found her lamp and came down the aisle, greeting each pony as she went. The Black shied as the light flooded his stall. Raemil reached out, but he stood back frightened and hurt. Raemil took the offered lamp from Thysirra and brought it to inspect him.

Raemil slowly and carefully climbed over the rail so as not to startle him further. The Black's chin was torn across the front and ran an inch and a half long down the left side. Hay and straw had stuck to the blood. The left side of his face was grazed from the eyebrow to his cheek. A flap of flesh hung from his cheek and on closer inspection the flesh seemed to be undulating.

Raemil gasped and took an involuntary step back. The Black spooked and rushed at her with his ears flat back. The stall was too small for him to gain any speed, but he was certainly heavy enough to crush her. She had no time to climb the rail. Raemil heard Thysirra scream for help as she ducked and covered her head. A leg brushed past her and knocked her off balance. She fell on her side and waited for further assault. There was none. She could feel his hooves stomping around her. Opening her eyes, she looked up and saw his belly above her. Raemil crawled out from under him, causing him to shy wildly to the left. Out of the corner of her eye she saw someone throw a rope.

'No!' she tried to shout, but the word was caught in her throat and she was too late. The Black reared, but the noose looped over his neck and was pulled taut, choking the cry to an abrupt strangled cough. He leapt sideways into Raemil and squashed her against the rail. The person who held the rope was now on the ground and had slammed into the wooden skirting of the stall. The Black's rump was right up against Raemil's body, as three men struggled to pull him away.

There was sudden relief as the Black took a step forward, and Raemil crumpled to the ground, gasping for air. Altogether, the three men heaved on the rope. The Black only pulled back, sweeping them all from their feet. A boy around Raemil's age jumped into the pony stall behind her to try and rescue her. She was distracted by this momentarily, but when she turned back to the Black, she saw his back hunch, his hind quarters bunch up, and instantly both shod hooves thrashed out toward the sounds behind him. She ducked and heard a loud *thwack* above her as his hooves pounded against the dividing rail between him and a dappled colt in the next stall. Raemil felt arms around her waist and she was swept off her feet and over the rail.

The Black's hooves hit the rail twice more as the boy put Raemil down and steadied her on her feet. There was a loud snap, and she was pushed to the ground as a large piece of the railing broke off. It was sent spinning through the air, just missing them both. The Black stumbled over the broken rail and tripped over the remaining divider. The rope dangled from his neck, now unmanned, and his hocks bleeding. The dappled colt raced wildly around in his stall, terrified of the huge black beast invading his space.

The Black's sides heaved and he focused on nothing in particular. His hind legs were in one stall and his front legs in the other. The unknown boy lifted Raemil off her feet again in an attempt to lift her out of harm's way.

'No.' She struggled from his grip.

The movement startled the Black and he backed fully into the dapple's stall, breaking the rest of the divider with his front hooves as he went. He faced them both now, his big, brown eyes studying them. Raemil reached out and sought in his eyes the fear that had taken hold of him.

She concentrated, oblivious now to everything but the Black, her field of vision faded to only the warm brown of his large eyes. She saw a flash of something unfamiliar, and she delved deeper, trying to rediscover her horse's sanity. She had known and loved this horse for the majority of his life.

Suddenly, it was like something reached out and grabbed her. She fell to her knees and gasped. Unaware of the boy who knelt beside her, or even the Black that was in front of her, she was blind to everything but what she saw in her mind and felt.

The night was glowing red, her vision was wide and she felt exposed. The rocks under her feet made her slide. She could hear horses behind her and something nagging at her back, always pushing and demanding of her, but she did as she was asked, because she loved this thing.

A horse sprung into her vision and her head was suddenly pulled hard to the side. The cruel metal bit wrenched the corner of her mouth and it stung. Her legs were whipped and tiny cuts bled and itched. She could smell the sweat and the fear of the other horses behind her. Her lungs felt as though they were going to burst, and her head pounded with the rush of blood.

There was suddenly nothing under her feet. Something hit her hard. She screamed for her master's guidance, but there was no answer. She rolled and tumbled. A lump tumbled away from her side – what was it? The world spun in a blur and it surrounded her, all whirling toward her, hitting her on all sides – what is it?! She kicked out her legs, desperately trying to find the ground. She was frustrated and alone; the presence of her master was lost somewhere below…

Raemil found herself back in the stable, on her hands and knees, a boy she didn't know beside her, and the Black still standing in front of her. Her vision went dark around the edges and she felt herself sinking again. She fought to remain here in the stable.

Either she had lost her mind, or somehow something had opened between her and the Black. She was seeing and feeling the fear he was struggling with. Raemil fought hard against his memories, his feelings, his senses, but she sunk back to that night, suffocating in his memory.

Gathering her own slippery thoughts back to herself, she managed to push back until the image altered. The vision took shape and she no longer felt what the Black felt; instead she concentrated on the memory and the feelings she wanted him to feel instead.

'Come with me and I shall bring you into the light.'

And with that, the darkness of that night faded.

Raemil was now just fifteen. She laughed and smiled as the Black ran around her on light feet; he was only a colt and was not yet trained for riding. Raemil laughed and patted him on the rump. He spun around, and she followed him; they were dancing, twirling and twirling.

It was evident Raemil had been crying earlier, as often she did. She cried for her loneliness and she cried because she missed someone dear to her heart, and mostly she cried because she wanted to be free. But now she was with the black colt nothing else mattered. She pretended the guards weren't nearby watching them closely.

Raemil climbed on the black colt's back. At first, he was afraid, but then she petted him and moved on his bare back. It was the first time something really clicked between them. He felt what she wanted, instead of seeing what she wanted. And so, he turned for her. He turned and he turned, and now they danced as one. He was an extension of her, and she was an extension of him.

'I love you, Black,' she whispered, as she slid from his back and hugged his neck.

He didn't know what those words meant, but it sounded nice. The black colt nudged the small of her back, and she laughed and ran from him. This was how they played: he chased her in the field until she was tired. They both sat down in the shade, and she read a tattered old book to him until he slept and she slept against him. He enjoyed hearing her voice and her laugh because it meant she was happy, and that made him happy. It made him feel safe.

Raemil let the Black out of her mind, or she got out of his, and the connection wavered, then it was gone. They were both back in the broken stall amongst strangers. No one else had dared come in, but the boy was holding her in his arms.

All her energy had been sapped from her body. Finally, she gave in and asked the boy to take her out of the stall. The Black made no move to protest their actions. He simply stood and watched. Raemil was taken back to her room, though she was unaware, her consciousness had left, and she was dreaming before she had entered the inn.

Gorran watched as the older boy, Jakarn, carried Raemil from the stable. There was something about the woman, neither good nor evil, but something strange that nagged at him. He didn't know whether he should be afraid of her or befriend her, but he felt that he had to satisfy his curiosity either way.

4. A lost soul.

He was hot and tired and definitely not in the mood to deal with people, let alone hostiles. He rubbed his face and tried to muster the energy. The Horsham men were trying to raise an even bigger army. The peasants were given a choice to either join their forces or die. It was rumoured the surviving wives were used as whores and the children would be slaves until they were old enough to join their mothers; or old enough to fight beside their fathers. He knew he could never make a difference. This plague of Horsham men was too strong and too many; but he could at least vent his anger on the two that approached him now.

He put his foot in the stirrup and swung into the saddle. His eyes stayed glued on the two Horsham men. He could smell them already; they reeked of body odour. No doubt the blood of their last victim was still smeared on their filthy clothes. He waited for them to approach him.

They were slightly shorter than the average man, but they made up for it in brawn; their necks were thick and their skin tough. He watched as one pulled out a long piece of rope; it boded ill for him that they showed their hand so early. He tilted his head toward the trees, the only cover out here. He was suspicious of an odd shape that might be an archer sitting in the high branches of a tree. He wondered why they even bothered trying to hide.

They stood silently either side of his horse, as though they expected him to offer his wrists to be bound. *Not likely*, he thought. Without warning, he swung his horse around, knocking one down. At the same time, he drew his sword and thrust it in the other's neck. He only just managed to hit the jugular. He wrenched his sword from the half-severed neck and sheathed it. His horse squealed and he had to pull an arrow from her neck. He was then tackled by the other Horsham man, who had regained his footing. A rope was stretched across his throat, choking him. He turned his horse's rump to the archer, using the Horsham man on his back as a human shield.

Managing to unsheathe his short sword again, he thrust it under his arm and into the Horsham man's stomach. He forgot the archer for that split second as he let the body slide from his back. Searing heat shot down his arm, quickly reminding him that he was not out of danger, as an arrow lodged high in his right shoulder muscle. He ducked before the next arrow came and thanked the gods that he was out of range for a fatal shot. He spurred his horse on, clinging awkwardly to her side to block a clear shot.

Lestadt was travelling to a small village just inside the perimeter of Horsham's wastelands. His goal was to raise an army, seeking revenge for his mother and sister's brutal rape and murders.

He stopped his horse beside a drying lake and let his paint mare drink whilst he steeled himself to remove the arrow from his shoulder. It was deep but not so deep that it would significantly delay him. He dropped to his knees as he pulled the bloody arrowhead out and tossed it in the water.

Lestadt surveyed the area. It was ugly and dead and the ground was cracked and dry. The lake once covered kilometres, but now it was little more than a stagnant pool. Trying to distract himself from the pain, he gazed south-east, the direction he must go to get to Irramai.

He had been assured he would find an army at Irramai that resisted Horsham and had loyalty to no one but themselves. It was once a small and humble village, but when Horsham rose, the refugees took over the abandoned castle and, in time, it grew a band of rebels. These rebels were who Lestadt sought to become his army. He was confident he could convince them his cause was also theirs. At the very least, he was a good swordsman and he could find a purpose among them.

Lestadt turned his attention back to the water; a stick-tongue fish flew above the surface. They were hideous creatures, with small wings and big heads filled with sharp teeth. They did not actually fly. A thin, long fin was located ventrally, which constantly vibrated from side to side, pushing its body just above the water. It could keep itself suspended in short bursts while looking for birds to eat. Drinking birds would often be caught, quite literally, by surprise. Even its scales were patterned to mimic feathers.

A brown bird flew past Lestadt's head and the fish licked at it but missed, catching Lestadt on the neck. The fish was also equipped with a sticky tongue that could stretch deceptively far. Lestadt pulled back in surprise and the fish was dragged to the shallow edge of the water. He grabbed its tongue and yanked, ripping it from his neck and taking skin with it. No sooner had he released the tongue, the fish snapped it back up and flopped itself back into the deeper water. He wiped the blood from his neck in disgust. If it appeared again, he was in a mood to stomp on it. It had been a shit enough day already without losing skin to a fish.

As night fell, Lestadt rode his mare through the dead forest of Kannakor. The skeletons of trees were so tightly packed together it was hard to see around the next turn. Shadows cast from the moonlight through the dead sticks peppered the eerie forest floor.

The creatures that lived in this particular forest were shy but savage. It was the only cover for a while. According to the older people in his village, the forest's inhabitants once lived in the trees, using the leaves as shelter, but since the trees died, they sought sanctuary underground in deep burrows. These creatures were called kannaks and were human-like, with slender, hairy bodies and taloned toes and fingers.

Tales of mutilated human bodies turning up on the edges of the dead forest were favourites among campfires. Though humans were much bigger than the kannaks, the creatures were fast and flexible and rumoured to work in packs. He only hoped if they were real they weren't nocturnal.

His mare suddenly shied and Lestadt nearly lost his balance. He glanced down to find himself staring into a black hole, a burrow in fact. Sweeping his gaze ahead, he could see a whole network of burrows. Dread constricted his chest as he contemplated manoeuvring his way safely around the kannaks' city that he had unwittingly walked right into. As the mare moved, a shadow came over Lestadt. The sharp snapping of a twig came from above, shattering the silence, but as soon as he looked up, the shadow left him. A shiver went up his spine.

He set up a small camp a good distance away from the burrows and tried to get some sleep. For Lestadt, it was never hard to fall asleep; the difficulty lay in staying asleep. He dreamed of his mother dying in his arms and his sister's naked and bloody body hanging by her neck in their living room. It was more or less the same dream every time.

At twenty-one, Lestadt should have still had a mother and father and his sister; he should have been courting young women and maybe even considering settling down. Instead, he was alone, bitter and lived only for revenge. Lestadt was lost in hatred and he had buried his grief so deep that it only fuelled a reckless anger.

Lestadt was woken by his screaming mare. His sleep-addled brain and bleary eyes were confronted with a humanoid face covered in hair. It hung upside down by its feet from a branch before hissing and leaping at him.

The kannak hissed and raked its claws across his cheek. Lestadt's wrists were bound by rope; he was surprised to discover such a form of intelligence in the kannaks. A large group of them took turns hissing and grunting at him until they would get frustrated and claw him. Lestadt could do nothing but try and communicate with them; it only got him clawed more fiercely.

A dark brown kannak stalked around, hissing and grunting at the others. It was clear to him they communicated, but Lestadt could not pick up any patterns in their behaviour or the shrieks and grunts. He could see the leader didn't like the others near his back, and, on closer inspection, he discovered why. The kannak had an arrowhead stuck in its back that it obviously could not dislodge and didn't want anyone else near. He could sympathise, given his own injury.

Lestadt waited for the leader to come near again and turn its back, and as it did, he reached out his bound hands and grabbed the broken shaft. The kannak screamed, both enraged and in pain; its arms flailed wildly in the air. Lestadt yanked the arrow, wrenching it from the creature's back. The others were in uproar, thinking their leader was taken hostage. The leader rolled away then hissed at Lestadt. He offered the arrowhead to the critter. It was a peace offering that he hoped would give him clemency for his trespass.

The kannak bit Lestadt's hand instead. He snatched his hand back, his limited patience already worn thin. He turned the arrowhead toward himself and slipped it under the bonds. It was difficult to cut with his hands bound as they were, and, as he sawed through the rope, the kannaks took it in turns to lunge and attack. He dodged them as best as he could while on his knees, his ankles also bound. Once he cut through the rope, he kept his hands together while he started on the rope around his ankles. The kannaks were too focused on their assault to realise he was cutting himself free.

Once free, Lestadt jumped up and ran for the horse. It was a credit to the mare that she hadn't turned tail and fled at the sight of him running at her with predators on his heels. The kannaks screamed in rage and took to the trees in pursuit. A couple jumped on him, biting and scratching, but heedless of the gouges left in his skin, he tore them off and battered them against the tree trunks where he could. His mare was at a gallop, twisting and skidding through the dead trees. The kannaks moved fast through the treetops and had no trouble in keeping up. It was dawn when Lestadt and his mare burst through the trees. The kannaks remained in their branches screeching while watching the man flee.

Some of his scratches were deep, but Lestadt was relieved to have gotten away without being mauled too badly. He wiped his face clean of the blood with his shirt. He could see in the distance the village that he knew should be Witchgrave.

'I'll need a strong drink after that. How about you?' he asked his horse as he reached forward and scratched the mare's ears.

There was a tavern in Witchgrave where he longed to quench his thirst and rest in the blessed cool of an actual building. Lestadt laid heels to the mare in hopes they might reach the Witchgrave tavern by nightfall.

5. A window into a normal life.

Raemil woke, alone in her dark room. She wanted to see anything but the dark right now. The fading remnants of a dream still filled her with a sense of dread and hopelessness. She had been alone in the sense that she was living and whatever was with her had been dead for millennia. Its face was twisted in an expression she could only describe as torment.

'I walk amongst the dead, the living memory of my soul, so shall you walk beside me.'

Its voice had been akin to the whisper of dry leaves blowing in a deserted wasteland.

She had never thought that dreams were significant, but the lingering sense of doom felt so real. A tentative knock at the door interrupted her analysis; a welcome distraction.

'Come in.' Raemil patted the top of her head out of habit to ensure her hood was in place. She still hadn't addressed that knot; it was starting to ache.

After a brief pause, the door slowly opened and a glowing light floated in. Raemil squinted at the boy who held the lantern. She knew him, not by name but by his face. He had taken the Black to the stable for her that first night.

'Forgive me, Thysirra sent me to ask if you felt well enough to join the celebrations.'

Raemil didn't really know how to talk to children. She hadn't had the opportunity, or the courage. She felt awkward and nervous.

'What is your name?'

'I am Gorran of the Kannan house. What is yours?'

'Raemil.'

'Of what house?'

Raemil became very still. She hoped he couldn't tell that internally she was panicking. She could hardly tell him she was the king's runaway daughter. She probably should have thought of that before she left; she probably should have come up with a plausible reason for her to be travelling alone and made up a realistic identity for herself.

Having had no reply, the boy suddenly began to fidget with his sleeves and his nervous eyes darted around the room.

'I apologise, that was rude of me to ask. It's none of my business.' His words tumbled out anxiously.

Raemil smiled. Aware he wouldn't see it, she hoped the smile would reach her voice. 'I would be honoured to join the celebrations.'

Before the party, Raemil scrubbed an alarming amount of filth from herself in a tub. She winced as she stepped into her skirt, her body aching in several places. She had no clean cloaks and was disappointed to have to choose which of the two were the least dirty. She went with the black one.

Raemil finally brushed out the giant knot that had kept her hood on rather too securely. Confronted with a mirror, she studied herself. Her green eyes were shaded when she pulled her hood forward. The unusual colour wasn't obvious if she kept her head lowered. She fixed her hair by tying it behind her head, and once she was sure no one would catch a glimpse of her face, she was as ready as she could be.

It was still warm outside and the delicious smell of food hung in the air, reminding Raemil how hungry she was. The fire blazed brightly in the middle of the clearing, and the cooking pot had been removed. She could hear laughter and see shadows of children running fearlessly in the dark, just out of reach of the circle of light the fire emitted.

Spotting Thysirra, Raemil took the space beside her. The chatter ceased and all eyes turned to her. Raemil avoided eye contact, fearing she would see in their eyes what she had seen in the eyes of the woman in the yellow dress before Raemil, or something, shook their village. She stared so hard at the fire she thought the image would be burnt onto the inside of her eyelids forever. Someone began to speak, then another person was talking, until they all spoke and laughed again.

They ate and drank wine and some people began to sing while others danced. Raemil watched them dance and laugh together; this was as close to being a part of a community she had ever been.

'Do you dance?' came a voice from beside her.

Raemil was startled. She had been watching Thysirra dance with Thenysies, and was unaware the boy had been standing beside her.

'I-I don't think I know this dance,' she replied shyly as she turned to see the boy who had carried her from the stalls earlier.

'I will teach you; it's not difficult.' He offered his arm.

Panic took hold again; she had never danced with a boy that was not her brother. She was afraid something would give her away.

'I'm sorry, I can't. I still feel quite weak,' she declined, angling her head so the firelight cast more shadow over her hooded face.

He shrugged, undeterred. 'May I sit then?'

Raemil nodded. She could hardly say no without being impolite, though she was baffled by his persistence. The boy produced a flask and offered it to her. She took it hesitantly at first; it tasted like wine. She had only had a glass or two at special occasions. They sat in awkward silence for a while and passed the flask back and forth. By the time they finished most of the wine, Raemil's anxiety had eased. Her stomach was warm and her head was swimming with drunken thoughts.

'I could never think of leaving my birth place, I don't know why anyone would want to,' the boy, Jakarn, said after Raemil had explained she was travelling to go stay with some relatives.

'How can you stay in the same...' Raemil hiccupped, then continued, '...place for your whole life and never see what is beyond that hill or that mountain or that field? Never knowing what people you might meet or the discoveries you might make.'

'Why leave your family and friends behind for something as uncertain as all that is out there?' Jakarn argued.

'Because out there,' she gestured with a wide, exaggerated sweep of her arm, 'is everything and anything. It's freedom to live by your own rules, not by some king in a grand castle.'

'King Farramand is a good king. We've never come to any harm under his rule.' Jakarn was suddenly defensive.

'No, I didn't mean to speak ill of the king. I just meant to say that out there, I can make my own rules.' Seeing that the boy was not convinced by her logic, she decided to change the subject.

'Why all the animals?' She'd noticed a small pen of animals that the farmers had gathered earlier.

'They are gifts for the new baby. The animals may choose if they wish to stay with the baby or go back to the fields.' He looked puzzled, as if she should know this already.

'How do you know what they have chosen?'

'The gate will be opened, and if they stay in, then they have chosen the baby.'

Raemil was about to argue the flaw in his understanding of choice, but she thought better of it. She still had enough wits about her to know that anything said out of place could give her away and turn these people on her.

'Come with me,' he said and led her into the dark.

They walked for a while, tripping and laughing, before they reached a small group of trees. He stopped there and leaned her against a tree.

'Where did you come from Raemil?'

'I came from over there by the fire.' She giggled.

'You know what I mean. Where is your family?'

'I'm going to find my brother – he's lost,' she blurted.

She was a terrible liar it turned out, and the wine wasn't doing her any favours.

'I'm sorry.'

'It's okay, I know I'll find him.'

Jakarn eased her hood back. Raemil didn't even think to stop him. He frowned as he shimmied it back from the comb in her hair. She braced for a reaction but then realised he would not see the colour of her hair in the poor light. To her, he was all shades of grey; any colour had leeched away in the dark of night.

'You are lovely, Raemil. Why do you cover your face?'

Caught by surprise, she didn't have an answer. She was frozen to the spot momentarily as he moved in to kiss her. At the last second, she awkwardly sidestepped as though casually moving out of the way of a passerby. Raemil's anxiety returned instantly. No one had ever treated her like this, certainly no one had ever tried to kiss her. She wasn't even attracted to him; the romantic notion maybe, but not the boy himself. This was the wine's fault.

'We should not be doing this.'

'I was only going to kiss you,' he said awkwardly, looking a little embarrassed now.

She could only imagine his cheeks were likely as hot and red as hers.

'We just shouldn't.' And brushing past him, she headed back toward the fire, leaving Jakarn standing alone and rejected in the dark.

When Raemil arrived back at the celebrations, the animals were 'choosing' whether they wanted to stay or go. She was tired and no longer interested, so she headed back to the inn.

In the morning, Raemil had a throbbing headache. She crawled out of bed and went down stairs.

'Raemil, how are you feeling?' Thysirra was cheerily stirring a pot.

'I have a headache,' Raemil complained as she plonked down on a stool.

'Too much wine last night... here.' And chuckling, she handed Raemil a cup. 'It will help, but it'll leave an unpleasant taste.'

Raemil thanked her and took a sip. It was bitter and she wanted to spit it out, but she forced it down. Thysirra laughed as she saw the girl hold her nose and chug it down.

Raemil went outside, already feeling much better for the day and night of rest. She hoped she could leave soon. The sun was out and it was already mid-morning. The children were out playing loudly but were soon scolded by a sore-headed adult. Not many people were around but Raemil noticed the ones that were had all found a job to do that was quiet.

She opened the door to the stables and was greeted by Gorran as he was coming out with a pail of water.

'Your horse is still in a bad mood. I tried to coax him over with a carrot, but he turned his back to me.'

Raemil went to the Black's stall and called softly to him. He whickered and hobbled to her; she noticed the wound on his cheek was festering with maggots. Raemil left the stables again and passed Gorran on his way inside this time.

'Gorran, do you think you could help me in a moment?'

'Of course,' he said, eager to please.

Raemil went back to the inn and found Thysirra hammering some lose nails in on the floor boards whilst Thenysies held his head and groaned.

'Thysirra?'

'Yes, dear?' she asked around the nails held in her pursed lips.

'Do you have some sort of medical kit that I could use on the Black?'

'For a horse? I've never fixed a horse before,' she said, standing and dusting her knees off.

'It's the Black. His wound is deep and I think there are maggots.'

Thenysies covered his mouth and ran outside.

'We had better take a look then.' Thysirra followed Raemil, ignoring her rather green-looking husband.

Raemil held the Black steady as best she could whilst Gorran washed the festering wound. Thysirra mixed up a pulpy solution in a wooden bowl.

'I need you to put this on his tongue. It should make him numb, so you can work easier.'

'Me?' Raemil's voice squeaked, as she took the bowl.

She hadn't done anything like this before.

'*I'm* certainly not getting in there with that horse. I'll tell you what to do. Besides, if you are going to travel alone, you should learn these things.'

Raemil had never seen anything so gruesome. Thankfully, it didn't make her ill despite the delicate state she had woken up in. Gorran spoke softly to the Black while Raemil tended to the horse's wounds under Thysirra's direction. When they were done, Raemil thanked Thysirra before the woman left to go back to her morning tasks at the inn.

'And thank you, Gorran, you did a good job holding him.'

He grinned up at her, encouraged by her kindness.

'Would you like to see my pony?'

'I'd love to.'

Raemil and Gorran walked beside each other to the tethered piebald. She petted the pony and commented on his sturdy legs and sweet nature.

'He was lame, but I think he is okay now. His name is Patch. Do you want to go for a ride?'

'I cannot ride the Black.'

'What about a pony...?' Gorran glanced up at her and suddenly looked crestfallen. 'You probably wouldn't want to ride a pony; they aren't as graceful as a horse.'

'Nonsense. I would love to ride a pony.'

'Really?' he asked excitedly. 'I will ask Jakarn if you could ride his.' And before Raemil could stop him, Gorran raced off.

Perfect, she thought, the same boy she had left standing alone in the dark the night earlier. Jakarn emerged from one of the huts, holding his head. Gorran ran ahead of him. They walked to the stable in strained silence. Raemil felt awkward and embarrassed, and she wondered if Jakarn did too. They stopped at a chestnut mare's stall. She trotted to Jakarn and he produced a carrot and ruffled her forelock.

'She doesn't have a saddle; I hope you don't mind riding bareback?'

'That will be fine.' Raemil's face felt like it was on fire. She wanted this exchange to end quickly.

They led the mare outside and Gorran ran ahead to get his pony, leaving Raemil and Jakarn alone. Raemil never knew she could sweat from her palms instantaneously.

'Look, Raemil, I'm sorry for last night – I...'

'It is okay, Jakarn. Let's put it behind us.' She couldn't let him finish; she just needed a swift end to both of their misery.

Gorran returned, astride his little pony, providing a welcome interruption.

'Thank you for letting me ride the mare,' she said brusquely.

She swung her leg over, eager to ride away as fast as possible from this awkwardness; even if it was gracelessly bobbing up and down on a pony who had shorter legs than her own.

'You can ride her whenever you like.' His voice was over-bright and he, too, looked eager to escape.

Gorran, being much younger than both Raemil and Jakarn, was oblivious to the intensely awkward exchange.

As Gorran rode beside Raemil in the field, he decided he liked this woman. He couldn't deny she was strange, but that couldn't mean that she was a bad person. He watched her bouncing on the pony's back, her feet almost touching the ground.

'Have you ridden a pony before?' He wanted to know everything about her.

'No. I have only ever had the Black, can you tell?'

Gorran grinned at her, brushing his mop of hair out of his dark brown eyes.

'Yes,' he said, cheerful and brutal. 'What happened to him, the night you came?'

'During the Bloodnight, we fell into a creek. What were you doing out so late?' She tried to deflect the attention back onto him.

'Patch was lame, my brother rides him too hard. I wanted to stay with him.'

Gorran and Raemil talked for a long time, letting the ponies wander, grazing as they went. Raemil hadn't had a real friend before. She liked Gorran and hoped he would be her first one. Even though he was much younger than her, it didn't feel like she was talking to a kid – for the most part.

'Raemil, why do you look different? I have never seen anyone like you.'

Raemil checked their surroundings before removing her hood, revealing her long red curls and green eyes.

'I have asked myself that question so many times, but I honestly don't know.'

Gorran didn't question her sincerity, he believed her with the innocence of a young boy.

'Where did you come from?'

Raemil looked out across the fields, contemplating the risks of being honest with the boy. She liked him, trusted him even; he had that wide-eyed innocence. She could tell he wanted to be her friend and it was a nice feeling. She wanted to be his friend too, but she wasn't sure if it was wise.

'Can you keep a secret?'

'Yes,' he said solemnly, clearly taking this conversation very seriously.

'Promise? If anyone finds out, I could die.' She fixed him with a serious gaze of her own.

Gorran nodded again, his dark eyes fixed on hers.

'I am King Farramand's daughter. I lied to Thenysies when I told him I flee no one. I flee the king, Gorran. I have to get away. I would sooner die than go back.'

She looked at him with wild desperation in her eyes, instantly scared that she had made the wrong choice; but she could not take back the words now.

'I won't tell a soul, Raemil.'

They were silent for a while, both thinking about what they had just said and wondering if they would regret it.

'Was it the king that chased you into the creek?'

Raemil nodded.

Gorran remembered the story told to the public. The princess that never left the castle was Raemil, and the prince had been killed in battle against Horsham.

'I'm sorry about your brother.'

'I will find him. I know that Serrin will be alright; he has to be.'

He looked at her quizzically. 'You will find him? King Farramand announced that he'd been killed...'

'Serrin isn't dead. I was there when we received news, he was captured...'

'Maybe I misunderstood.' Gorran puzzled over this as they rode back.

It was dusk when Raemil and Gorran re-entered the village. They put the ponies away and said nothing of Raemil's shared secrets.

6. Fallen grace.

The dungeon was cold and damp; the stone floor was covered in congealed blood and dirt. The Horsham men would often walk by, rattling the hilts of their swords along the bars. They said little to him. His wrists were bruised and the skin was raw from constant chafing from the cuffs, and his ankles were always swollen so his skin had begun to grow over the shackles.

Sometimes Serrin would cry at night when the guards weren't close enough to hear. The rats were his only company. Sometimes he was thankful for it, but mostly he was not; for they were hungry creatures and were not above eating human flesh. Serrin would rather have been killed on the battlefield like a man than be rotting in this dungeon. His dignity diminished every time he sobbed when he could not sleep because the rats were hungry.

A Horsham man approached his cell, pausing to eye Serrin before sliding a bowl of water under the barred door. Serrin moved as close to the bars as the shackles would allow. The guard laughed and pulled the water just out of Serrin's reach and walked away. Serrin was so thirsty, he licked his dry, cracked lips and strained against his bonds. His outstretched fingers barely brushed against the bowl. Sitting back on his heels, he could almost smell the water. If his mouth hadn't been so dry, he might have been salivating. It had been two days since he had been given water and he couldn't remember the last time he'd eaten.

He closed his eyes and pictured the lush, green fields of Caelin and his father and little Raemil, though he suspected she wasn't so little anymore. These were the thoughts that kept him sane: that there was something beautiful out there still, that not all was lost. He opened his eyes in time to spy a rat drinking from his water bowl.

'NO! Filthy piece of shit!' Serrin screamed hoarsely and lunged for the creature.

The rat knocked the water bowl over and scampered away. Serrin looked at the spilled water creating mud on the floor just inches from him in utter despair.

'You fucking bastards! Arseholes! I hope you all fucking rot in hell... Fuckers!'

In a stupid, blind rage, he threw himself at the bars. He came up short and landed hard on the floor, ripping the skin open on his wrists and ankles.

There on the floor in the dust and mud of his dungeon, Serrin cried aloud. No longer could he sob quietly in shame; he had nothing left to be dignified for. He cursed the Horsham men, trying to think of the most offensive and vilest things to say, and secretly he hoped someone would take offence then take his life. All hope of being rescued was gone; he hoped for any kind of death to end his suffering. As night fell, he begged for them to kill him, but no one came.

* * *

Raemil contemplated the last few days as she entered the inn. She liked Gorran, he seemed very mature for his eleven years, but she still wondered whether it was a mistake to confide in him. In truth, she was glad to have someone to confide in, even if it had been a selfish impulse on her part.

Entering the main living room, she saw Thenysies trying to string a bow, but he didn't quite know how to hold it. Raemil offered her assistance, but he turned away, as though he couldn't bear the thought of her stringing it for him.

'Is it yours?'

'It is now. Someone left it here. Let that be a lesson: don't go leaving anything of yours here when you leave.'

'Would you sell it?'

She had only just started training with a bow and wasn't very skilled. She might be able to practise on the road. It could be useful for hunting since her trapping wasn't too great either.

'Depends. What have you got that I might want?' Thenysies said as he studied her up and down with a lecherous smile.

He couldn't see her face; her cloak still hugged her figure. Disgusted, Raemil turned away.

'I will see what I have,' she muttered.

She had not experienced this kind of attention before and hadn't considered that life outside of Farramand's castle might be very different.

She suddenly questioned her behaviour; she stood out so much already – remaining hooded as she was – but what of her behaviour? The way she spoke? This was not something she had studied under Tarrlyn's tutelage.

Raemil gathered some of the gold she had stolen from her father and went back down to Thenysies. Setting two pieces on the table, she watched as his greedy eyes lit up.

'Where did you get them?' His excitement was quickly overshadowed by suspicion.

'Do you want to sell or not?' she snapped.

After feigned consideration, Thenysies nodded and handed her the bow. Raemil all but snatched it from his hands.

Two weeks had passed since Raemil had come to the village. She knew most of the people's names now and most knew hers. Gorran and Raemil had ridden the ponies on numerous occasions. They went on their own and often talked of her past and of his dreams for his future. If Raemil wasn't with Gorran, she was in the stable with the Black. She spent long hours talking to her horse and had even found a book to read to him; Thysirra had loaned her a book on healing medicines.

The season was changing. Over the last few days there had been dark clouds in the sky, heavy with the threat of rain. Raemil opened the doors to the stables and made her way to the Black. He whickered and moved to the front of his stall. His wounds were now scarring and his knee wasn't so swollen. She handed him an apple and stroked his nose; she thought that maybe today she should try to ride him.

As it turned out, the Black was not overly keen on being ridden. He dumped Raemil on the ground several times. Raemil daren't try to go into his mind again. She wasn't sure what had happened, or how it happened, but whatever it was, she didn't like the way that it drained her and left her feeling vulnerable. Raemil didn't know whether it was the Black or her, or whether it was the both of them that connected in such a strange way. Was it her? Were all these strange things that had happened because of her? She didn't understand. Could anyone do this if they put their minds to it or was she odd? Was she so different on the inside as well?

After failing to use the bridle and saddle numerous times, Raemil tried one last time with no tack at all, remembering the days when he wasn't properly broken and she would ride bareback. The Black seemed to tolerate this and Raemil decided to construct something simple to hold her saddlebags on the Black. The device would need to be put on in a hurry and in the dark easily; it also needed to make the Black feel less restricted.

She found some old scraps of leather Thysirra was happy to part with. Raemil puzzled over her ideas all afternoon. Gorran helped her too. Finally, they had made a saddlebag harness. Raemil wanted the bags behind her and out of her way should she need to use her sword whilst riding. It took a few tries before the Black would accept the contraption.

After a long day with the Black, Raemil lay in her room for some time. She was saddened to leave these people that had, for the most part, accepted her into their lives. She knew it was time to go. These last few days, she had begun to feel an itch to leave. She still hadn't struck up the courage to tell Gorran. The next morning, she would be leaving, but she kept putting off her farewell to the young boy.

Raemil packed her belongings, leaving her clothes out on the bed for the morning. She had just set her new bow on top of her saddlebag when there was a loud crack and rumble above the inn. Neither she nor the Black liked storms. She went outside to check on him. It was dusk now, but visibility was somewhat poorer than usual due to the heavy clouds. Children were still running about in excitement as the storm gathered above, charging the air with electricity.

The Black roamed free of the stables now and Raemil whistled for him. He whickered and nuzzled her with his nose. There was a loud clap of thunder above the field, and a streak of light forked down dangerously close to the drying meadow hay. The Black shied and galloped to the stable doors, trying to seek comfort from the ponies.

A nervous mother called her children, and Raemil turned to see the little ones running back to their parents. The Black called out to the west, his ears pricked forward in interest rather than fear. Raemil turned to where every other creature looked and held their breath.

Descending the rise in the road were three men draped in blue and displaying the royal Caelinian emblem. Raemil forgot to breathe. She knew she needed to run, but she was paralysed with dread. Raemil spied Thysirra and Thenysies among the people emerging from their homes. The women clutched to their husbands and the men stood in front of them protectively.

Gorran stood beside his mother and was deeply afraid. His stomach was twisted into a knot as he searched the crowd. His eyes picked the cloaked woman out with ease, confirming his fears; she stood out.

Raemil was his friend and she had said she would sooner die than go back to the castle, and he believed her. She turned and her desperate face captured his; her green eyes glowed from the shadow of her hood like they never had before. There was a distinct numbing feeling that came over him and a nagging nausea. Something pulled at every nerve and every sense. He was certain that it was her. She had done something that day to the horse when they were in the stables and she was doing this thing to him now. Gorran felt helpless, torn between his loyalty to his friend and a nurtured fear of what she was. Forcing down his terror, he surrendered to her, trusting that she was his friend and she would not hurt him.

He began to only see her; her bright green eyes were intense with concentration. The urgent whispering of the crowd faded and the vision of Raemil wavered and disappeared.

He was in a house; the sheep skin rugs were worn and tattered and the wooden doorframes were cracked with age. A whisper called him to the stairs, he was about to ascend...

He was pulled out of the vision and back into the crowd beside his mother. The transition was harsh and he grasped his head as his thoughts strained to comprehend what happened and where he was. His vision blurred, his nasal passage burned and his ears were ringing. It was as though his senses couldn't keep up with the instant change from one place to the other.

Raemil was desperate. She needed to run, but if she ran to get what she needed, she would be trapped. She didn't know if she could commune with Gorran, but she had to try. Just as she was showing him what she needed, a man had cried her name, and she pulled out of Gorran's mind.

'You defy the king,' one of the royal guards shouted over the crowd.

Raemil glanced around; the villagers were staring at her with mixed emotions. Even Thysirra looked confused, undecided if she were angry at Raemil or angry at the soldiers. Raemil touched the hilt of her sword. It gave her comfort.

She was caught by surprise as a man grabbed her roughly from behind.

'Who are you?' he demanded as he wrenched her hood back from her head, ripping the combs painfully from her hair.

The man leapt back from her with a yelp of surprise, as did the people standing close to her. Raemil's red hair tumbled down her back, and her treacherous skin practically glowed white in the near dark. Another low rumble sounded its warning and lightning cracked across the sky.

The soldiers made no advance, appearing to enjoy watching her exposed and helpless. Raemil looked to Gorran as the first accusations flew. The people called her a liar and again – 'serlyn'. Raemil tried to block out the taunts as she reached for Gorran's mind again.

He was running up the stairs now and the voice, her voice, guided him into her room. There was a flash of another vision, it was Thenysies; then it was gone and Gorran was in the bedroom again. Her saddlebag harness, her bow and her clothes were on the bed. A word was shouted; it was out of place in the otherwise quiet house. He knew that it came from the real world. Gorran felt the urgency and her fear; he understood what she was asking of him.

The picture failed and dropped from his eyes like a veil, revealing the monsters that were his kin. His feet were running beneath him before his senses had adjusted; he had to get to the inn. He couldn't understand the viciousness of his family and the rest of the village, but then he had known from the start who she was and what lay beneath her hood.

The first sleet of rain came down hard as a soldier rushed her, seizing her by her hair and winding it tightly in his fist. He kicked his horse and Raemil was yanked backward then dragged in the dirt. All she could see were angry faces through the rain. She could hear the steady beat of the horse's hooves mixed with the taunts of the village people. All she could think was she had shared meals with and slept amongst these people, and while she'd only hidden her face, they had hidden something much uglier.

Raemil struggled to reach her sword as she tumbled through the dirt. Eventually, she pulled it awkwardly from its sheath and swung the sword up in desperation. Raemil felt her hair give and she hit the ground fully, hearing the horse cry out. The guard's curse was drowned out by another roll of thunder. He spun the cut horse around, still holding the rest of Raemil's sacrificed hair enclosed in his fist.

Crawling to her feet, with sword still in hand, an angry mob at her back and an armed soldier in front, she raised her head and planted her feet. Two soldiers had stayed well back, initially content to watch, but now they reined in beside the lead soldier.

'Should you refuse us now, let it be known that there will be a bounty on your head, dead or alive. The king has disowned you as daughter-heir.'

'Princess?' someone behind her asked.

The crowd of people shuffled back, confused and afraid. Raemil whistled for the Black and edged back, her eyes never leaving the lead soldier. The people made way for the Black as he charged through the crowd. Raemil didn't think twice about retreating. She swung onto the horse's back before the soldiers laid heels to their own steeds. As lightning lit up the darkening sky, she spotted Gorran emerging from the inn. She felt guilty as the Black belted toward him and she snatched up her belongings on her way past. Raemil had hoped for a short but heart-felt goodbye, and she could not even give Gorran that.

Raemil continued east. She had to pass through Caelin's gates, for the physical reassurance of leaving this place. She and the Black had been on the run all night, but the soldiers never caught up.

Raemil could see two sharp objects spearing into the sky ahead: the gates of Caelin. She stopped between the two stone structures, almost afraid to step over the threshold. They towered above her. Painted at eye level, on the inner sides of the structures, was the royal Caelin emblem. A sword pointed to the earth with a black snake coiled around the hilt, its head hanging part-way down the blade. Raemil looked upon this emblem, absently touching her right collar bone. As a potential heir to the throne, Raemil had been tattooed with the very same image.

Raemil was apprehensive; she would be alone out there, no father to run home to, no home to even go home to. Fearing she might be struck down any second by some unseen force, she took a deep breath and urged the Black over the threshold.

Glancing back often, she almost couldn't believe it. She had really gotten away; she was finally free. Though the land ahead was anything but welcoming, Raemil could not help but smile.

The soil beneath the Black's hooves was dry and the thin layer of weed was anything but green. It contrasted greatly to Caelin. It had been a day since Raemil had fled from the village and she was consumed by the idea she had been disowned by her own father. How could he do this to her? All she wanted was her freedom and to find her brother. King Farramand was not worth her tears, she knew this, but she could not help but feel unloved and very alone. She wiped her eyes and tried to think only of what lay ahead.

She came across a wooden post stuck crookedly in the ground and a pile of both animal and human skulls placed around the base. Someone had painted the words 'Deadlands' on the post. The Black was skittish, his hooves kicking up the dust around them and forming a red cloud around his legs.

Heat rose off the ground ahead and she could see distorted shapes floating and shifting in the heatwaves. It was dusk when Raemil and the Black came upon the remains of a village. She could see huts and stables gutted by fire. Most of the huts were completely burnt to the ground. The stable looked as though it could fall at any moment. The walls were stained black from smoke and inside what used to be a stall were the charred bodies of three horses. The bodies were piled as though they were all trying to climb over each other and out of the remains of a window.

The Black skittered away from the stables, jumping over a cow's skeleton as he fled. She passed a relatively intact house and saw, burned into the wood of the front door, the shape of a hand, with a red circle painted in the palm. She couldn't take her eyes from the strange brand as she rode by – what did it mean?

As they left the burnt village, she could see a charred post. The flames had licked at the sign and turned some of it black. She stopped and scratched the soot away, revealing its name before the village had become part of the Deadlands.

'Verramoi'.

Raemil was about to urge the Black on, when she heard the flutter of wings close by her head. Sitting on the sign was a crow; it cawed and ruffled its feathers.

'Death is the dream you will not wake from; life is the death you will dream,' it said.

She wondered if she had gone delirious from dehydration.

'Death is the dream you will not wake from; life is the death you will dream,' it repeated.

Raemil shook her head and tried to shoo it away.

'Leave me alone.'

The bird took flight and swooped her, beating its wings and scratching her with its claws.

'Death is the dream you will not wake from; life is the death you will dream! You live it! You live it!' The crow shrieked again and again.

Blood trickled down her arms as the Black sprung away from the raving creature. Raemil was dizzy as she rode on the galloping black horse. She closed her eyes briefly, and when she opened them, they were in a desert; the Black's hooves beat tirelessly beneath them.

7. And so, it begins.

Sergo had just tied his horse outside; the gelding stomped his hoof impatiently. Sergo was nervous about the coming festival. It had crept up so fast; already a decade since the first. He was always jumpier at this time of year and he had every reason to be. It was *his* life that had been threatened for his part in the ceremony ten years before.

He rolled his shirt sleeves up and wiped his sweaty brow as he looked toward the lowering sun. It was always hot; it would not cool until full dark. He'd stay in the tavern until it cooled off.

He turned to enter the tavern when a moving figure caught his eye. A sense of doom washed over him as he watched the approaching stranger. This man was tall with broad shoulders and the lean build of a youth. Sergo didn't like strangers coming to his village.

A decade ago, the villagers killed a young woman that had been living among them. Her name was Tannagan. From when she was a child, she had been disliked for her odd appearance. Her hair was not any shade of brown like normal people, it was dark blue and her eyes were orange. When she became a woman, things began to happen, things that *she* made happen. The day after she was confronted, there was a massive plague of deadly spiders; ten people had been killed.

It was Sergo that convinced the villagers that she must die. He had been the only one that dared say the word 'witch' out loud, even though they all thought it. She knew he had instigated the attack. The village people hunted her down, believing their luck would change if she was sacrificed. The villagers believed it was a lucky day still – ten years later, and every year they would mark the anniversary with a festival. They believed it was good luck to dance around Tannagan's grave performing their rituals.

The memory of Tannagan's death was still fresh in his mind; his paranoia had kept it that way. He could hear her words even now. She had looked directly at him when she spoke as her body burned.

'A stranger will come with war on his shoulders. He shall release me; that is when it begins for most, but this night it will end for you.'

Sergo shivered as he remembered the words. He had expressed his fear to many, but they all laughed at him. They could all believe she was a witch, but it was impossible for them to believe she could rise again. So, every year, Sergo feared for his life quietly at the back of the crowds.

He could not help but fear the stranger that approached him now. Tannagan had not stipulated when this time would come, but he could feel it in his bones. She would rise soon. The man approaching him was at least ten years younger than he. He carried fresh scratches across his face, arms and, judging by his ripped shirt, on his torso as well. Sergo watched him suspiciously as he climbed stiffly from his horse and tied her beside Sergo's gelding. The man headed for the tavern door; Sergo moved to block him.

'A stranger in our midst? Do you come for the festival?' He tried to sound jovial, but he may have come on a bit too strong.

The young man's head snapped up. He had been looking down at his ripped shirt as he came up the steps, likely debating whether or not he should change. Now his bright blue, and decidedly hostile, eyes locked onto Sergo's.

Sergo was taken by surprise. Though he couldn't say that the young man was completely alien, not like Tannagan had been, but his dark, almost black hair and bright blue eyes were uncommon.

'I've come for a drink, if you don't mind.' The man rudely dismissed him and moved around Sergo into the tavern.

Lestadt sat at the bar brooding over the events of the last couple of days. The scratches on his body cracked and bled every time he moved, and the mare had thrown a shoe on his way into Witchgrave. His shoulder still ached abominably where he'd been hit with the arrow, forcing him to sleep only on one side on the hard ground, and now that shoulder ached too. The man that had blocked him outside the tavern hadn't helped his mood. He finished his second glass of beer to numb the pain, when a jolly drunk sat beside him.

'I am Delgar. I don't believe we have met?' He had dusty brown hair, bushy eyebrows and was slightly overweight.

'No, I don't believe we have,' Lestadt said and went back to spinning his empty glass on the bar.

He was in no mood for pleasantries, his disposition was decidedly *un*pleasant at the moment. Delgar apparently didn't pick up such social cues.

'Are you just passing through or have you come for the festival?' He continued before Lestadt could answer, 'I'll bet you are here for the festival. We get some strangers through here at this time of the year. Most come because in Witchgrave we consider it good luck to celebrate the death of the witch.'

This piqued Lestadt's interest. He had never heard of any such festival, and he assumed Witchgrave was just a name.

'Witch?' he prompted.

'There's a witch buried here. We have a festival to celebrate her death every year. She brought bad luck on us; now for ten years it has been changed.'

The man that blocked Lestadt at the door was suddenly beside him. Lestadt stood from his stool – his back itched when sitting – while this stranger was behind him.

'Delgar, that's enough – he doesn't need to know our business.'

'I think the man should be free to speak to whomever he likes.' This man was beginning to get on Lestadt's nerves.

Lestadt did not care if Delgar was silenced with a gag. He just didn't like the other man now standing beside him and he wanted to make a point of it.

'Who are you?' demanded the large man.

'I am Lestadt of Hewter.'

'Then you are a long way from home. What brings you here?'

'Nothing that concerns you.' Lestadt's gaze was unwavering.

'I shall make it my business to know.' The man took a step nearer. He stood slightly taller and much heavier than Lestadt.

'Sergo, what has come over you? Leave him be,' said Delgar, stepping between them.

'Perhaps I *will* stay for the festival.' Lestadt was never one to walk away from a disagreement. Sergo glared at Lestadt before grudgingly turning away.

As the night went on, the tavern at Witchgrave became lively. Though Lestadt was not one for socialising, unless it benefited him in some way, he began to enjoy the atmosphere. People toasted to meaningless nothings and they laughed and talked of old times. Lestadt's trained ear fell upon an interesting conversation. They spoke of the witch called Tannagan. This person that spoke of her was more sympathetic to the dead witch. According to the speaker, Tannagan's parents had seen her at birth and fled, and an old woman had taken her in. The death of the old woman seemed to trigger a series of horrible events.

He listened as families reunited and thought it odd that this would be an occasion to do so. He listened to the gossips in the dark corners speaking of the evil magic and prospects for good luck this year if all went well at the ritual. Lestadt concluded that Witchgrave was a superstitious, weird, little village. These people acted as though their very lives depended on the outcome of the festival. He didn't think there were many witches around anymore. People were afraid and drove them away or killed them. Lestadt supposed there still could be witches and wizards in hiding, but most had likely fled across the Sapphire Seas where the people with magic ruled.

Several beers later, Lestadt was ready to call it a night. He'd rented a room in the inn above the tavern. During the night, the noise from the tavern drifted up through the floor. Lestadt heard the scuffle of a fight before, finally, his exhausted body and mind succumbed to sleep. His dreams were troubled with his painful past and sleep became exhausting in itself by the time morning came.

Waking late the next morning, he stepped outside and squinted at the bright sun. He checked his horse was alright and could reach the water trough still. Part of him wished he hadn't threatened to stay. He didn't like this place, almost as much as he didn't like to lose face.

Sergo saw Lestadt check on his horse. He had the urge to remind Lestadt that his presence was unwelcome. He'd been talking to the blacksmith about the stranger while he put new shoes on Sergo's gelding. There were still a few sympathetic ears in town.

Leaving the blacksmith to do his work, Sergo headed to the tavern. He was in the mood to encourage the young man right out of town. Lestadt was still grooming his mare, checking over her legs and feet. As Sergo approached, Lestadt looked up at him and Sergo smiled a crooked smile.

'How is your horse?' he asked as he nodded at the contented animal.

'She seems fine. Thanks for your concern.' Lestadt smiled just as falsely, before turning away and heading inside.

Lestadt heard Sergo following him through the door and he felt dread sink into his belly. He could tell from the start that this guy was going to be a pain in the arse. He chose a seat at the centre of the bar and sat down stiffly. Sergo casually pulled up a stool beside Lestadt and childishly ensured that he ordered his beer first. Sergo seemed to have taken an immediate disliking to him.

Lestadt ignored the man and quietly drank his beer, but the silence was not to last.

'It is possible that I have been too subtle. I'll be blunt with you; I want you out of Witchgrave by tonight,' Sergo said without looking at him.

Lestadt laughed, but the humour never reached those cold blue eyes. Lestadt could see Sergo's rage was kept barely in check, but Lestadt was cocky and remained undaunted.

'I don't give a damn about what you want,' Lestadt said, turning his attention back to the woman behind the bar.

'I'll have another, thank you,' he said as he finished the last dregs of his first beer.

Sergo chewed over this for a heartbeat. 'What if I were to give you six silver pieces to disappear?'

Lestadt raised his eyebrows out of amusement. He couldn't understand why Sergo was so desperate for him to leave, but it pleased Lestadt to get under his skin. He remained silent.

After a time, Sergo's price went higher. 'Seven.' He watched for a response, but there was none. 'Eight pieces of silver... name your damned price then,' he said as he slammed his fist angrily on the bar.

There were a few people in the tavern who looked up, and Lestadt waited for them to begin talking again.

'I neither want nor need your money, so I'll let you imagine where you can stick your silver pieces.'

That was a lie; he could use the silver pieces, but he wasn't about to take them from Sergo. He stood and turned to leave. He heard the stool grate on the floor behind him and he spun arburd to see Sergo standing and looking to fight.

Lestadt dodged a fist and flung his arms out. Sergo glanced at the silenced people; all eyes were on hirh. Lestadt had made sure he did not throw a punch and had moved his arms away from his body, almost beckoning Sergo to try again. Lestadt wasn't above violence, but times were hard. People were edgy and he was new to the area. He was not stupid.

Sergo cursed. The man had cleverly protected himself and coaxed Sergo's rage into the spotlight.

'You will get yours, you little bastard,' he said loud enough for only him to hear, as Lestadt brushed past him and walked out.

Sergo sat down again, brooding over what had just taken place.

Now he despised this stranger; the man knew just what buttons to press, and Sergo admitted that he pressed them well. He had been fair, he had tried to resolve this without incident, but Lestadt just would not budge. Sergo wanted him gone. He had worked himself into a frenzy, believing Tannagan was coming back for him, unless he could escape his fate for at least another year by getting rid of Lestadt.

Lestadt didn't want to show his temper whilst he was in the tavern and, most importantly, in front of Sergo, but as he mounted the mare, his hands shook with rage. He didn't appreciate being intimidated or bribed. He'd done nothing wrong, and Lestadt didn't see why he shouldn't be allowed to stay for the festival. He felt he would be showing weakness if he left now; his hand was forced, in a way.

He kicked the mare on harder than he had meant to, and she jumped into a gallop. Lestadt needed some space, so he rode to the limits of the village and visited the witch's grave himself.

Lestadt stopped near the milling crowd around Tannagan's grave. There was no cross to mark her grave, nor were there grieving relatives or friends. The grave was marked with a ring of limestones and the ground was bare. It appeared nothing had grown in that place for years. There were people laughing and gossiping and some women were cooking a feast. There seemed to be no young people around the grave; he felt very out of place. He could not bring himself to stay too long. Lestadt was not overly fond of the idea of witches or anything magic either, but he felt that surely, though a menace she must have been, Tannagan should still have the right to rest in death.

It was after dusk when Lestadt re-emerged from the inn, still curious and determined to witness the festival. Where the buildings cast shadows, it was near impossible for his eyes to pierce the darkness. He strolled past his mare and greeted her briefly, before heading toward the orange glow of the event. There were rows of huts that lined each side of the road.

Lestadt turned to walk between two of the small homes when he heard the slightest of sounds. It was probably just the wind. He hesitated only a moment, before continuing through the shadows. As Lestadt was about to move back into the light, he made the mistake of letting his guard down just a second too early. He felt a heavy hand shove him in the back, and as he stumbled forward, he tripped over someone's foot.

The right side of his face and body was ground into the dirt. Before he could get up, he felt a huge hand enclose around his neck, pushing his face harder into the gritty soil. He heard the approach of another on his right. Lestadt could see the shadow of a tall, skinny man, but the one that held him down was still a mystery. He was kicked hard in the ribs by the skinny man. Lestadt could do little but curl over his stomach in a feeble attempt to protect himself.

'I believe that you were asked to leave on numerous occasions, were you not?' asked the skinny man.

Lestadt said nothing.

'What say you, Lestadt of Hewter?'

Still, he remained silent, weighing up his options.

'It's polite to answer when you are spoken to. Perhaps we should beat some manners into this young man.'

Lestadt heard the skinny man leave his side, and he knew that if he was going to escape them, this was his chance.

The large man on his left was still holding him. He moved so that his legs were in front of the man's feet, then quickly he hooked his right knee over the man's right shin. Using the heel of his left foot he kicked the man's shin as hard as he could. Lestadt used his weight and the strength in his legs to his advantage, pulling the man's legs out from under him. His captor had to release Lestadt's neck in order to brace his own fall.

As Lestadt rolled away from the man on his left, the skinny man ran at him with a lump of wood. He saw him coming and rolled backward and up onto his feet in a crouching position. As Lestadt stood, he felt the other man's arms wrap around his chest and arms. It wasn't until now that he realised this man was massive and stood several inches above Lestadt's own near six feet. The skinny man jabbed Lestadt hard in the stomach with the wood before swinging it into his ribs. The skinny man and the giant exchanged a few words, or perhaps they spoke to him, but Lestadt's mind reeled with pain and he struggled to register anything else.

He regained as much breath as he could and looked up to see the skinny man standing close to him. He was saying something and, though Lestadt could hear it, he wasn't actively listening. He gathered all his strength and leapt up and back, kicking the skinny man in the groin and, using him as a launch point, he flung his head back, smashing the giant's nose. The skinny man fell backwards and was laying on the ground clutching his groin, whilst the other man clutched his face. Lestadt drew his sword and held it to the big man's throat.

'I want you out of my sight, or I will split you from navel to neck. As for Sergo, tell him to do his own dirty work next time. Am I understood?' He stood very slightly bent over, but his voice carried every bit of authority that he could muster.

The man nodded but was obviously enraged. Lestadt heard the skinny man approaching from behind. He pulled out his short sword in a flash and aimed it so carefully for his throat that the skinny man almost walked right into it. Lestadt stepped back and lowered his swords marginally to sweep both men with his hard gaze.

'Go.' He nodded in the opposite direction that he was going.

Instead, the skinny man drew his sword. Lestadt lashed out, slicing a diagonal line across his attacker's face. The man dropped his sword and fell howling to the ground. Lestadt once again turned and faced the giant, ignoring the screaming man on the ground.

'Take him and go.'

The giant moved past Lestadt's watchful eye, grabbed the skinny man and hauled him away.

'Arrogant shit,' he heard the giant say under his breath.

He watched them leave before sheathing his swords and continuing to the festival. He walked slightly hunched. It hurt to breathe if he straightened completely. Lestadt wiped his face clean of the dirt and stepped into the outskirts of the fire's glow.

There were many people circling the grave. Some were finishing a meal and almost every person was drinking wine or beer. A fire blazed over the grave. He circled the crowd to the other side, feeling too vulnerable with his back to the shadowy huts.

The people were silenced as an oddly dressed man entered the circle and stood before the fire. The man was dressed in a blue, silk cloak; he had long hair with a halo of feathers and bones crowning his head. There were strips of dyed red material tied around his arms that streamed down to the ground. He raised his arms to the heavens.

'And so it begins!'

The crowd cheered loudly, but quickly fell silent when the music began.

A small group of people sat behind the fire, playing instruments that produced a unique but pleasant sound. Lestadt could see the crowd breaking away over the other side, making way for a dozen or more small children. The children were dressed plainly enough, but they were also draped in red streamers of material. The music was light and cheerful as these children danced happily. Soon, another child entered the circle and the music escalated to a much heavier sound. This young girl was draped in blue streamers and also had blue streamers tied in her hair.

Lestadt was drawn into the dramatic dance of sacrifice that the children performed. The music came to a new height as the dancing climaxed into a fight. The young girl, representing Tannagan, threw small black beads over the children who represented the village people. Some died dramatically, but others picked up pretend swords and chased the witch. The children looked to be no older than ten, yet they danced gracefully and silently.

As the young witch danced and twirled in front of the fire, she changed. Lestadt saw a young woman with dark blue hair. He looked around at the other people, but they smiled and laughed. When he looked back to the dance, she was only a little girl with streamers in her hair again. He saw a flash of the witch once more and then, just as quickly, she was the little girl again.

The dancers jabbed the little witch with their pretend swords and members of the crowd threw pig blood into the air and it splattered on the grave. The music became more urgent, dramatising the dance. The girl was held in the air in front of the fire and she went limp. Lestadt dizzied as he looked at the child. She looked up and again it was a woman smiling wickedly at him, her blue hair flowing like a river behind her before she went limp and she was a child again. Still, the crowd did not react. He could only assume he was the only one seeing the real witch. Lestadt did not see the end of the dance. He was busy searching for a beer or even wine, anything to warm the cold chill that ran down his spine and to relax the raised hairs on the back of his neck.

When Lestadt had slaked his thirst, he pushed his way to the front of the crowd to see the children taking their bows. He spotted Sergo and his two henchmen, all staring angrily at him from the other side of the fire. He returned what he hoped was a malicious glare, despite his sweating palms and tingling spine, and looked away as more activities began on the grave. Young women were handing out long pikes to people in the crowd. As each person was given a pike, they went to the centre of the grave and thrust them into the ground before taking them out and returning them to the young women. Lestadt spied Sergo and his men moving through the crowd toward him.

A young woman approached him with a pike.

'Would you like to enter the grave?'

'Hopefully not yet.' Lestadt laughed half-heartedly, immediately hating himself for making such an obvious joke.

Even so, the girl gave him an astonishing smile, as though she had never heard that one before.

'It is considered good luck to strike her grave. Please, you have nothing to lose.'

Lestadt glanced at Sergo who was almost beside him, and he grabbed the pike and entered the circle.

There were several people in the circle with him, each taking a stab at their so-called good luck. Lestadt raised his pike and thrust it into the ground, which cracked and broke away too easily for his liking. As he slowly drew it from the ground, he could see something dark smeared on the end. He dropped it in surprise as blood dripped onto the parched ground. He glanced around nervously, but no one was paying him any particular interest, except Sergo, who could not see the pike from where he stood.

Lestadt couldn't move. Initially, he thought it was his crippling fear, but it was more than that; he really couldn't move anything below his neck. He studied the hole before him and saw movement within, causing his heart to feel like it had plummeted to his feet. He saw three grey fingers, smeared with blood, reach out toward him. The fingernails were a sickly yellow-brown colour and were more like talons than fingernails. He felt sweat break out on his forehead anew as he watched the fingers search the edges of the hole. His knees went weak. The fingers disappeared as a girl put her hand on his shoulder. He could have jumped out of his own skin at the touch if he could move, of course.

'Are you alright?' she asked, but he didn't hear her. He only heard his name being whispered from the dark depths of the hole.

The girl moved to pick up the pike, then stopped short and let out a piercing scream.

'Blood!' she cried as she raced into the safety of the crowd.

The villagers quickly retreated to the other side of the white stones.

They watched Lestadt standing frozen at the centre of Tannagan's grave. His name was whispered again, yet this time it was much louder, trickling through the crowd. The people glanced around in terror.

Sergo grasped his head. He did not hear the girl's scream or the whispered name. He was trapped in his own torment inside his head.

'Get out!' he screamed as he twisted around, searching for someone he recognised, but there was only Tannagan in every face.

'Get out, get out, get out!' he continued to scream, while she whispered in his mind the things she was going to do to him.

Suddenly, Sergo leapt at a limestone. He picked it up and started to bash his own skull in. Some jumped back in utter horror, others dived at him to stop him from spilling his own brains. By the time the rock had been wrestled from him, the men's hands were slick with blood. Sergo had disfigured one side of his face into a hideous pulpy mess that spewed a river of blood. Sergo looked around as though it was the only logical option he had left. He spat blood from his mangled lips as he spoke. 'She won't leave, she won't... get her out!' He half sobbed and half screamed as his mind was driven far beyond the boundaries of sanity.

He shrieked and ran off, half blind into the night, with hundreds of Tannagans laughing at him in his deranged mind.

Lestadt was shaking, listening to Sergo's ravings behind him; but he dared not take his eyes from the hole. More soil crumbled away and up came the searching grey hand.

'Lestadt...'

Suddenly the whole grave collapsed before him as though the inside had been hollow the whole time.

And Tannagan rose from the earth. She was grey and decayed to the bone in places. Her blue hair hung below her shoulders and her orange eyes bore right into Lestadt. She stood naked, mere inches from him. He wanted to vomit, he wanted to run, but he could do neither.

'Lestadt...'

Her voice seemed to echo far across the lands and bounce back, louder than before.

'It has begun, and you have done this.'

* * *

Kilometres away, a young red-haired woman woke from her sleep and heard the name of a man she had never met, from a voice she could not have heard.

'What has begun?' she whispered to herself, and an involuntary tear rolled down her cheek as an inexplicable dread gripped her heart.

8. A bloody end.

Tannagan glided past Lestadt, and relief, though short-lived, flooded him as he felt the movement come back to his limbs. He turned and would have stepped back from her if there hadn't been a recently vacated grave behind him.

She addressed the crowd, speaking in a raspy, dry voice. 'It is I who shall celebrate *your* deaths for the next ten years.'

Tannagan leapt at the man wearing the blue-silk cloak. She snapped his neck before he could voice a scream and whipped the cloak from his crumpling body. She slipped into the garment and paused, her concentration elsewhere. Lestadt could not see what she was doing, but the villagers watched on, terrified.

From the ground at her feet burst a creature made entirely of shifting insects. Using tentacle-like arms, it crawled from beneath Tannagan's feet and stood upright, its shape vaguely human. It paused for a heartbeat, turning what one could only assume was its head to the witch, who nodded in return. The creature exploded into thousands of wasps.

The villagers tried to flee, but many stumbled into each other, swatting and screaming. Tannagan turned to Lestadt and beckoned him; he didn't think he really had a choice, so he fell in behind her.

'I'm feeling generous. For your part in my release, I will spare you,' she simply said as she walked through the swarm and the crowd.

The wasps parted for her and Lestadt. He looked down to see a small girl who had given up. She cried for her mother, but there was no reply; she was covered from head to toe. He felt sick as he crouched beside the girl and looked up at Tannagan.

'Won't you spare the children? They don't understand this; they had no part in your death.'

'I will spare no other.'

She kept walking, heading between the huts and towards the inn.

Lestadt lifted the girl and ran past Tannagan with her in his arms. He was stung several times on his arms and chest as he ran toward the tavern. He put the girl in the water trough and told her to hold her breath. Sprinting up to his room, he hastily packed his belongings before coming back out to his mare.

The girl watched him solemnly from the trough with teary eyes and a red face. The welts were coming up all over her body. He could hear distant screams and shouts from the people at Tannagan's grave.

As Lestadt turned to mount his mare, he was again faced with Tannagan. He jumped back in surprise. He still had the urge to lose his dinner every time he looked at her partially rotting face. She looked like a young girl masquerading as a very old, and very dead, body.

'Why leave so soon? My festival has only just begun.' She laughed and turned her attention to the tavern.

Despite his better judgement, Lestadt followed her gaze. There was a loud groan. It almost sounded mournful and it came from the very walls of the tavern. Blood began to weep from the wooden panels. Lestadt's mare began to jump around on the end of her tether; he could see the whites in her eyes.

He untied her and held fast to her reins as he mounted. She needed no encouragement to make a hasty retreat. She galloped in wild fear, away from Tannagan the witch, away from the screaming people and away from the bleeding walls of the inn. As they thundered down the road and out of the village, Lestadt heard the tavern at Witchgrave fall.

A cloud shifted and the red moon cast its glow to the earth. Sergo looked up briefly before stumbling on. His head had stopped bleeding long ago and half of his face was a bloody scab. It was near midnight; he was weak and his mad flight had slowed to a crawl. Brain-damaged and raving mad, he took turns crying and shrieking as he crawled like an insect away from Witchgrave.

Sergo was steadily climbing a small hill; limestone was scattered on the ground and a dead tree stood at the top. He looked up and saw a figure standing beside the tree, and he breathed a sigh of relief.

'Thank the gods. Can you help me?' he begged as he reached for salvation.

The figure turned.

'I will help you, Sergo.' And she laughed.

Sergo looked up at her and was puzzled, but she took his hand.

He cried out as that hand tightened and her nails dug deep into his wrist. She flung her hood back, blue hair streamed in the wind and her grey, dead flesh cracked into a wicked smile. She pulled him up fast and with her other taloned hand she ripped into his stomach. Sergo screamed a blood curdling scream as he felt her fingers digging and tearing inside. She pulled out his intestine and wrapped it around his neck. He died clutching at his own slippery insides, clawing and ripping to get air.

Lestadt was heading slowly south. The road had ended a few yards back, and the ground was fairly rocky where his mare walked. The clouds were low in the sky. They kept the mountains that Horsham sat atop hidden from view far off in the distance. He took his sweat-soaked shirt off and put it in his saddlebag, letting the breeze cool his damp skin. The season had changed to autumn some weeks ago, and Lestadt was looking forward to the approaching winter.

Earlier in the morning, Lestadt had caught himself a rabbit, which hung from the saddle behind him. On the edge of a forest, not far from a lake, he stopped to prepare his catch. The cool breeze rattled the leaves above him and the green treetops were a welcome sight. It had been a while since Lestadt had seen fertile land. His home in Hewter was not as green as some places, but it certainly wasn't as dead as the last few leagues he had travelled.

He made an incision down the rabbit's gut, cutting through the layer of skin and fat. He pulled out its insides and hung the rabbit from a tree to let it bleed. He tried not to think about the blood and the way it dripped, like it dripped from the pike, like it dripped from Sergo's smashed face. He rested himself against a tree and watched the mare eat small shoots of grass and weeds beneath the shade. Eventually he relaxed enough to doze off.

Lestadt woke to the sound of a screaming horse. He jumped to his feet, looking around for the mare. *What now?* he thought disbelievingly. Hearing another strangled cry, he turned to see his horse rolling on the ground with a great mountain lion on top of her. It had a black head, and the rest of its body was a fawny-brown colour, save a thin black stripe that came from its head, running down its spine and onto its black tail. Its paws were crimson with blood.

Lestadt drew his sword and charged, but as he ran, he less than gracefully tripped and fell over a rock, dropping his weapon in the grass. The lion was distracted momentarily by his clumsiness and the mare took the opportunity to kick the predator off. The large cat rolled once before it was back on its feet, but the mare had already fled. Lestadt moved to pick up his sword, and the lion's attention immediately snapped to him. Before he could reach the weapon, the great feline was on him.

He was flat on his back as the lion's claws raked his legs. He only had the strength to hold its head back from his throat. The lion growled and dug its claws deeper; he could feel its long claws push between ribs. Lestadt could voice little more than a moan. If he wasted anymore breath, he would not have the strength to hold the massive head at bay. The lion's head was at least twice the size of Lestadt's; its mouth was open wide, bearing rows of sharp teeth just inches from his face.

He turned his head momentarily for some reprieve from the lion's stinking breath. His arms were shaking with fatigue. His sword lay tantalisingly out of reach. If he let go to grab at it, he risked missing the sword and letting those massive fangs tear into his throat.

Lestadt strained and shifted his weight under the lion's crushing power so that he was just that bit closer to the weapon. Resenting its prey's struggle for freedom, it moved its front paws to Lestadt's shoulders and raked a long gash into his chest. Lestadt could see his own blood pooling on the ground around him, and he choked back a sob, knowing that his end was so very near.

9. The fear she incites.

Raemil yawned and crawled to her feet, thinking about the whispering voice that had woken her during the night.

'It has begun, and you have done this.'

Now she couldn't be sure if it was real or a dream. Seeing that she was awake, the Black whickered and nuzzled her as she reached for the harness that held her bags. She pulled out some dry meat and chewed the tasteless, leathery stuff. Soon she'd have no food, forcing her to learn to hunt. She sat down beside the Black and surveyed her surroundings. She was in a forest, but there was not a living tree to be seen.

The Black suddenly leapt sideways past Raemil, snorting and skittish. Raemil couldn't see anything threatening, but she heard a hissing sound. Looking up, she spied dozens of brown, hairy creatures perched in the trees. A dark brown creature leapt to the ground in front of her, hissing and spitting like a feral cat. Raemil crawled backwards away from it, afraid to turn her back on the nasty little beast. Its face looked human, but as Raemil looked into those black, soulless eyes, she knew it was far from it.

More of them jumped to the ground, all watching the darker one, waiting for him to make a move. Raemil tried to get up and run, and the dark one leapt on her, pushing her onto her back. As she fell, her hood dropped back just enough to remove the shadow from her face. The creature stopped, its claws raised in the air. It had a look of such surprise on its ugly little face. Raemil lay perfectly still, afraid to move a muscle. It leaned close to her face and sniffed her; the others crowded around, all with the same intense curiosity.

The dark brown beast suddenly screamed and leapt off Raemil. The others mimicked their leader, hissing and screaming in confusion. Raemil took the opportunity to get to her feet, eyeing the strange creatures. A few that were in front of her cowered, covering their heads with their spindly little arms. Raemil feigned an attack and they screamed and shot into the trees with their fur raised. Climbing onto the nervous Black, she moved him very slowly past the predator-filled trees. She eyed them as she rode. Some huddled close to each other, hiding their faces, and others took one look and leapt through the branches and out of sight.

It took Raemil the better part of the day to navigate her way out of the dead forest. Admittedly, she may have gotten lost and got herself turned about at one point. The sun was setting when she stopped beside the last trees. She glanced back to the wall of grey trees, and all was silent; the forest seemed gloomy and lonely. She decided to sleep under the shelter of the last trees, sure that the hairy creatures would not bother her again.

The Black shifted restlessly on the bark-littered forest floor. Raemil was aware of his restlessness somewhere in the back of her mind, but she was largely preoccupied. She stared for long hours into the dancing flames of the fire, thinking about the strange things she had seen on her journey so far, wondering what her future held.

Her eyes became heavy, but she made no move for the cowhide that was her bed. She blinked lazily at the fire and as she looked into its depths, shapes began to form. At first, they were nothing, but as the figures danced and reached for the sky, they turned into brown, hairy creatures with black eyes.

The creatures were attacking a woman. She faced the other way and Raemil could not see her countenance, but she assumed that it was her, as the woman had long red hair. The forest was alive in this apparition. Raemil could see there was another figure that was fighting with her. The two fought whilst the hairy creatures wanted them both gone. There was a mighty white blast that suddenly came from Raemil, the other figure was blasted backward and the trees were set alight. The figure regained its footing and a black storm brewed up fast over the forest and soon the trees were wracked with wind, hail and lightning. Raemil was blasted by a bolt of lightning and she fell to the ground. As she rolled over, her, or rather the woman's, face was revealed... and it wasn't Raemil at all.

Her face was slender with high cheekbones, whereas Raemil's face was a little more rounded. The woman's eyes were golden, but her lips and chin and skin complexion were the same as Raemil's.

Some of the creatures had been scalded, others had been killed and the rest fled.

The image faded and Raemil looked around. Suddenly she was alert again; she was still on the edge of the dead forest. There were no creatures in sight and the Black had settled for the night. It dawned on Raemil that this woman in the fire could be her mother; who else could resemble her so closely? The king had spoken little of her mother and was not inclined to answer Raemil's questions about her. She began to think about the strange white blast and her hands trembled. She had no way of answering questions that were forming. Closing her mind off from what she had just seen, she crawled to her bed. She spent the rest of the night tossing and turning, trying to avoid coming to terms with what she might be.

Raemil and the Black set off early the next morning. She was beginning to feel lonely. At the castle, she could rely on Tarrlyn to talk to when she needed human company, and Serrin before that. Now she had no one. She had so many secrets and questions that needed answering.

The day dragged on and the sun beat mercilessly down on her, making her sticky with sweat. There was no landmark besides the road; the scenery was so repetitive that Raemil dozed on the Black. A yellow snake slithered across the road in front of the Black. Spooked, he shied away. It startled Raemil, forcing her to sit up straight in the saddle. Ahead she could see a village stretched across the red and dusty land like a wound. She pulled her hood forward and urged the Black into a gallop, desperate to find civilisation.

As the dusk of another day was settling, Raemil rode into Witchgrave. There were people wandering the village dazed and confused. Raemil rode past a building that was in ruin; the ground around the broken shafts and cracked timber was stained dark red. A girl wandered out in front of the Black; he stopped suddenly to avoid trampling her. Her face slowly tilted up at the horse, as though she was not quite all there. Raemil was distraught by the emptiness in the child's sad, brown eyes. Her face and hands were covered in big, red welts, and her hair was a tangled mess. There was also a dark red rash that seemed to cover her whole body. As Raemil looked on the sickly child, a small and frightened voice inside her mind told her to flee.

Raemil took her eyes away from the child to see a woman approach; she had the same vacant look. Her eyes fell on Raemil with a sudden desperation.

'It burns,' she wailed. 'Will you not help us?'

Raemil was speechless. She didn't know what comfort she could offer. The woman began to scratch furiously at her rash. Raemil was sickened by the amounts of dead skin the woman clawed from her cheek.

'We are burning, please, help us,' the woman sobbed, reaching for Raemil.

Raemil kicked the Black into a gallop away from the people. Though she felt guilty, there was nothing she could do for them, and admittedly, they frightened her.

The words came to her again – 'It has begun' – and she found herself asking the same question: 'What has begun?'

Raemil pulled the Black to a sudden halt about a kilometre out of Witchgrave. He skidded in the dust and stones. Snorting loudly, he pawed the road impatiently, eager to get as far away from the village as Raemil had been.

Raemil could see a hill of red soil dappled with white and the tree sitting atop it caught her attention. It looked as though something was hanging from one of its limbs. Going against her better judgement, morbid curiosity got the better of her and she turned the Black from the road and cantered him toward the hill. The Black stepped high and pranced shyly. He tried to turn away, but Raemil urged him on. She could not yet smell what he could.

Once they began to walk up the hill, the strong odour hit Raemil and she nearly heaved. Now she could see what, or rather who, hung from the tree. The Black stopped with his front legs splayed before him. He would go no further. Raemil understood his reluctance and dismounted, continuing up the hill.

The body swayed with the slight wind and the bough creaked eerily. The rope was slowly spinning, causing the body to eventually face Raemil. She gasped and turned to flee, tripping and grazing her shin before getting back up and running down the hill. She heard the body fall and hit the ground and, to her horror, the corpse began to roll down the hill after her. Raemil reached to mount her horse, but the Black saw the mutilated body tumbling after her and bolted.

Tears streamed down her face. She sobbed and choked on the red dust that was kicked up from the Black's heels. The Black stopped at the road and stood with his head high and his nostrils flared. Raemil ran to him, and with one last strangled sob, she leapt onto the Black and urged him into a gallop.

Raemil barely noticed her surroundings as she rode away. All she could see were horrific images of the man she had just seen. She heard the taunting whispers of a woman. She was not whispering sweet nothings into a lover's ear, nor did she spare details of what her intentions were.

'You will die, your screams of torment will be heard in hell, and those screams will comfort me to sleep at night.'

The whispering was loud in her mind as Raemil caught glimpses of a tall, slender figure standing on the very same hill.

'You will die a thousand slow deaths before I am satisfied with your suffering.'

The figure turned. The face was neither feminine nor masculine; it was grey and dead, some places were devoid of flesh. She smiled with great pleasure and her blue hair flowed free behind her hideous head.

'I will drink of your blood as you stand before me, choking on your insides.'

And Raemil saw that the decaying woman had done just that.

Closing her eyes, she could still see the victim as though the image was burned there. A shrivelled tube extended from his stomach, deflated by the sun and crawling with insect larvae, mostly maggots. It was wrapped around his throat. Carved in his flesh were the words *'Zset 'cae fol ztisda'*. Raemil did not know the language and had never seen it before, but somehow she knew, as though a voice whispered in her ear, *dying for eternity*.

Written on the tree in blood was this message:

> *You who walk on mortal lands,*
> *Shall die in my wake,*
> *With your blood in your hands.*
>
> *Time will cease, and the dark will rise,*
> *'Tis the last thing you'll see,*
> *As you tear out your eyes.*
>
> *The dark lord will rise,*
> *We will become one,*
> *Flee now into madness,*
> *For the end has begun.*

Raemil shuddered and dug her fingers into the Black's mane.

Someone cried out in pain, and Raemil finally took stock of her surroundings. She had passed a small cluster of trees and the road had ended long ago. She spun the Black, and there on the ground was a man in a pool of blood, struggling against a huge cat.

* * *

Lestadt heard hooves beating on the ground, but the rider didn't even look. He cried out in defeat and was about to accept his end, when he heard the horse skid on the loose stones, and the rider turned.

The figure was hidden in the shadow that their hood cast, green eyes burned brightly. For that instant, their eyes locked, and Lestadt's grip on the lion's head faltered. The hood on the figure slipped as the horse galloped toward Lestadt and the lion, revealing red hair streaming behind a woman. The warrior drew her sword and clung to the side of her black mount. There was a hushed moment as the lion looked up at the warrior, as the horse leapt over Lestadt and the beast, and then there was the sound of metal slicing through flesh.

A headless lion now sat on Lestadt. The warrior drew her mount to a halt before his bleeding body and sheathed her sword. Their eyes locked again. He saw fear, confusion and concern on the lovely, red-haired warrior's face. Then time ceased to exist, the dark surrounded him and death took him as his head struck the bloodstained ground.

10. The stranger.

Raemil leapt from the Black, astonished by what she had just done. Without a second thought, she'd killed that huge lion with deadly accuracy and strength enough to remove the head with just one swing. She knelt beside the man and, after several attempts, rolled the body of the beast off him. She was on her hands and knees, panting from exertion; her amazing strength all too quickly gone. Blood still ran in rivulets through the sand, man and beast's mixing together in a crimson pool. There was no steady rise and fall of the man's chest. It appeared that he was already dead. Had she risked herself to save a corpse?

She panicked. She didn't want to see another slain body; she couldn't bear it after the scene at the tree on the hill. She closed her eyes and tried to picture Thysirra's medicine book. She had read it to the Black on numerous occasions. Raemil could see in her mind the brown leather front cover with its gold writing. The edges were worn and there was a small tear in the leather below the title, the evidence of a well-used book.

Inspired, Raemil leaned over the man and began to breathe life back into him. Eventually, she was rewarded with a few of his own shuddering gasps. His eyes remained closed and he made no attempt to move. Raemil was relieved and her hands trembled as she checked over his body.

He wore no shirt and the flesh on his chest was badly torn. Four claw marks ran several inches from his right pectoral and nearly reached his navel. His trousers were shredded and a gaping wound on his left thigh still bled into the soil. He was very pale.

Raemil went to her horse and removed the harness that held her saddlebags. She now owned three saddlebags, the third containing her small medical kit. Thysirra had insisted she start collecting tools and herbs for a medical kit since Raemil was determined to travel alone.

As she began to clean the deep wound on the man's chest, she found herself staring at his well-formed biceps and stomach muscles. She had not been close to a near-naked man before. He was both fascinating and oddly pleasing to look at. She studied his face; he had a square jaw and his brow was furrowed with pain. Before his eyes had closed, they had been a magnificent blue. She had never seen eyes as bright as his, nor as blue. It was like looking at a cloudless sky on a summer day. His hair was dark brown, almost black, and cut short. The man's skin was tanned from days in the sun, and what was left of his trousers were stained with both new and old blood.

By the time Raemil finished bandaging, cleaning and suturing the stranger's wounds, dusk was settling. Raemil got a fire going and made a spit to roast the stranger's rabbit that she'd found hanging from a low branch. She mounted the Black, leaving her harness and saddlebags behind and going in search of water.

There was a lake nearby of considerable size; the view was breath-taking. The sky was giving its evening show of beautiful colours; pinks, oranges and purples swirled in the sky and reflected off the lake, mixing with its own greens and blues. A doe and her fawn looked up as the horse approached. They stood with their ears erect for a moment before prettily bounding away. The birds cooed softly to each other from the trees, their last communications before the quiet of the night. Fish splashed in the lake while their nightly feed of mosquitoes and various species of insects hummed above the water.

Raemil dismounted and filled her waterskin at the lake's edge. Once she had her fill and taken what she needed, she headed back to camp. The Black plodded dutifully behind. As Raemil reached her camp, the rich aroma of cooking meat made her mouth water and her stomach churned in anticipation.

Though she was loath to delay her journey yet again, Raemil could not in good conscience leave the man to fend for himself. She'd been lonely of late and feared that if she had no one to talk to she might very well go mad. At least if the stranger survived, he might provide her with company if only for a while.

After dragging the unconscious stranger onto her wolf-fur cloak to make him more comfortable, Raemil picked up her medicine satchel to take stock of what she had. She sifted through her meagre supplies to see what she might be able to give him for pain. A delay to her journey wouldn't be so bad in a place like this; she needed to restock food, medicine and she desperately needed to learn to hunt.

Sitting by the fire while her broth heated through, she watched the steady rise and fall of the stranger's chest. She began to wonder who he was and entertained her thoughts by imagining his identity. She thought that perhaps he carried a very important message to the king of a faraway palace, or perhaps he was a lost soldier from Caelin, who had lost his memory and had been wandering, helpless and alone until now. Perhaps he had come from the village she just passed, only narrowly escaping whatever horror had befallen them, only to be attacked by a wild beast. Raemil thought that he looked important; maybe he was a general, betrayed and deserted by his men in this cruel land, fighting a lion for his next meal.

Raemil's romanticising was cut-short by a pitiful moan. She removed the pot from its position above the fire and went to him. His face was twisted in pain, his breathing fast, and he whimpered as he buried his head in the fur cloak.

'No...' he moaned and mumbled something, but Raemil missed what he said. She didn't know how to comfort him or if she even could.

'Gods, no, don't...' He shuddered, his face still hidden in the cloak.

He started speaking rapidly and in a different tongue into the furs. Raemil's heart went out to him. She didn't understand his sorrow or what he was saying, but she wanted to comfort him nonetheless. Moving closer, she gently stroked his cheek and absently began to hum a lullaby, a song her brother had sung to her when she was a child. The stranger lapsed back into his comatose state, and soon Raemil dozed off beside him.

During the night scavengers sniffed out the dead mountain lion. The Black squealed and ran off into the forest, away from the sounds of predators tearing into the carcass. Neither Raemil, nor her mysterious patient, woke. Eventually the carcass was dragged off into the shelter of the forest.

The mid-morning sun was already burning brightly when Raemil woke. She rubbed her eyes and yawned. The first thing she saw was that her harness had been dragged away from the fire. She glanced to where the dead lion had been.

All that was left was the long black tail and even that had small bites taken out of it. The Black was nowhere to be seen. She whistled loudly and waited for a reply, but there was none. She pawed through her saddlebags to make sure nothing was missing. She was surprised and a little offended to find her broth had not been touched.

11. The hunter, or the hunted?

Raemil left the sleeping man, praying that nothing would happen to him while she was gone. Strapping her quiver over her left shoulder and hanging the bow over her right, she headed to the lake.

Raemil had been educated by Tarrlyn in many things and botany had been one of her favourite subjects. It was mostly because it meant she could be outside with Tarrlyn instead of in the castle's dark and dust-filled library. Raemil could identify a vast variety of plants and trees, and she knew what parts of certain plants could be eaten and what was poisonous. Thysirra had taught her the medicinal value of many of the plants. On her way to the lake, Raemil collected useful herbs and roots.

As Raemil walked to the edge of the lake, she startled what looked like a pig. She had little to no experience with wild animals, and she didn't think to be wary. It stood at just above knee level. It had bristly hair running down its spine, its feet had four toes, much like a dog's paw, and its forelegs seemed longer than its muscular hind legs. Raemil studied its ugly head. There were horns on its snout that looked sharp and pointed back toward its ears. Before it wandered any further away, she knocked an arrow, the way Tarrlyn had shown her.

Raemil drew back as hard as she could, until her arm began to shake. She aimed for the pig's heart and let fly. The arrow went wide and clattered against a tree before falling impotently to the ground. The pig briefly glanced in the direction the arrow had fallen before ambling off. The casualness of the animal that she had just tried to kill infuriated her, so she tried twice more, her anger making her aim increasingly worse. By the time Raemil had her fourth arrow in place, the pig had strolled out of sight. Raemil spent the next half an hour angrily looking for her arrows.

Raemil washed in the lake before she attempted to hunt in the forest. She already felt naked without her cloak. It didn't make her any more uncomfortable to remove the rest of her clothes to bathe. She lathered up some soap-weed and washed her hair and skin. She hadn't realised the birds were singing so noisily until they stopped abruptly. There was a flutter of wings when a flock was disturbed.

With her heart pounding as though it were going to burst from her ribcage at any moment, she scanned the area. Raemil heard snapping of twigs and she moved away from the rock she had been resting against to peer behind it. Minutes passed and there was no further noise, so she relaxed when the birds began to chatter again. It was likely just the pig foraging in the leaf litter.

Once Raemil was dressed and in the shade, she felt more at ease. She walked for a while, taking note of the plants around her. Raemil had not seen anything worth hunting and she was beginning to feel defeated. It was near dusk when she found an old boar laying on its side already dying. She killed it with the stolen captain's knife and dragged it back to camp. Raemil's arms were aching from dragging the carcass all the way and she was miserable that she still hadn't come close to learning how to hunt.

With relief, Raemil found the Black waiting back at the camp. She hugged him close and ruffled his forelock playfully before setting herself to task. She spent a long time gutting the old boar. She had read about it, knew the theory behind doing such gruesome work, but she hadn't realised that it would be so difficult and messy. She was aware that his meat would be tough, but with her low skill-set in hunting, she couldn't afford to be choosey. There was a chill in the air and clouds covered the moon. Raemil pulled her hood over her head and wrapped the cloak tighter around her body. She washed the sticky blood from her hands and went to check on the stranger. She wrapped some of the fur cloak over his body and managed to drag him a little closer to the fire, despite her aching arms.

He groaned and his eyes fluttered open. Raemil froze. Grabbing the waterskin, she held it aloft in a silent question. He nodded and attempted to sit up before wincing and dropping his head back down into the furs. Raemil carefully lifted his head so he could drink. He only took a sip before he seemed to grow tired and Raemil laid him back down on the furs.

'Who are you?' he finally asked in a voice weak from disuse.

'Raemil. Who are you?'

He closed his eyes for a moment and his brow furrowed as though he were trying to remember.

'Lestadt. What happened to me?'

'You were attacked by something. You need to drink this; it will numb the pain.' She poured the broth into her wooden cup and supported his head again.

Lestadt drank half before his head went limp in Raemil's arms and he was asleep again. He slept fitfully and she was torn between comforting him and staying well away, in case those bright eyes caught hers again and took away her courage.

Riding the Black through the forest the next day, she was thinking about her patient instead of paying attention to her surroundings. She wondered what disturbed his dreams, and furthermore, what would she say when he asked her about her past? And how to explain why she hid her face?

Raemil was so preoccupied that she did not hear the occasional footfall or the snapping of twigs that followed her. She didn't notice the Black snorting and twitching in irritation or the birds nervous stopping and starting of their chatter.

By the end of the day Raemil hadn't seen any animals to hunt. She spent some time firing arrows at a tree and had only once hit it. When Raemil returned from her expedition, she spent some time preparing her herbs. She found a flat slate stone to dry some apples on then washed and chopped up one of her carrots and put it in her little pot. Her drying rock was long and thin. She thought if she could find two big rocks to prop the slate up over the fire, she could cook a fish on it.

The next few days passed quickly. Raemil kept herself occupied with gathering food and practising her hunting. She was still hopeless with her bow; luckily the old pig had lasted through the week. Lestadt often moaned in his sleep and shifted restlessly, but he had not cried or spoken in his dreams since the first night. When Raemil gave him his broth or water, they rarely spoke.

Often Lestadt would drink and fall asleep right away. Once, he had asked Raemil where she came from, but she remained silent, knowing he was likely to fall asleep and forget anyway.

Raemil tried to be silent as she moved through the forest. Only now realising that for days she had been stomping her way through bark and leaf litter, loud enough to wake the dead and warn every animal in Otowan that she was here. She was pleased Lestadt seemed to be awake more often now, and he had started to sit up on his own.

Hearing a low mumble like a voice behind her, she twisted with her sword ready but could see nothing through the trees. The Black stood grazing a few paces behind her. He had one ear trained on something she could not hear. Raemil didn't know what she heard and started to doubt that she had heard a voice at all; even so, she didn't want to leave Lestadt on his own while there was potentially something lurking in the forest.

Lestadt was still sleeping when she arrived back at the camp. She had left her harness and waterskin beside him in case he woke and needed to drink or eat some dried apple. She leaned the bow and quiver against one of her bags and went to her rock pile where she stored the pig meat to deter scavengers.

Raemil moved some of the rocks and pulled out the cloth bundle the meat was wrapped in. Selecting two strips of the rump, she placed them on her flat stone sitting above the firepit. She was about to start cutting them into bite-sized pieces when she saw movement between the trees. Raemil checked behind her and saw the Black with his head up and his ears pricked. When she turned back, she saw men moving toward her. One carried a rope; the other unsheathed his sword.

She presumed she was looking at the dirty-skinned, brawny and beastly Horsham men. They grinned. Even their yellowed teeth were bright within their filthy faces. They advanced on her, moving past the fire. The sleeping body went unnoticed in the bundles of fur by the Horsham brutes. Raemil drew her sword, but her shaking hands betrayed her, and she instinctively walked backward.

'Woman,' one of them grunted. 'Do not resist us or you will die.'

Raemil could not reply. Her mouth was dry and her terrified eyes stayed glued to them both. Was she destined to die at the hands of these creatures before she had barely begun her rescue mission? Raemil's hands shook violently with fear. She had never killed someone or even entertained the thought, until now, and she wasn't sure she could do it.

There came a whistle from behind the Horsham men. They all three turned in the direction the noise had come from. She was stunned. There stood the man she had rescued, his leg bandaged and his wounded chest bare, holding Raemil's bow, trained on the first Horsham man. Before there was any time for a reaction, an arrow was fired and the first Horsham man stumbled backward toward Raemil and fell at her feet with an arrow protruding from his eye. The next tumbled to the ground, with the same fatal wound.

As the adrenalin wore off, Raemil's knees buckled beneath her and the world went silent and dark.

Raemil shot bolt upright. Her hood was still on, and she had to catch it before it fell back. She looked down and saw that she was on her fur cloak. It was night and the fire was spitting and crackling beside her.

'My... how the tables have turned.'

Lestadt was sitting by her feet, grinning at her and feeding twigs into the fire. She couldn't say anything; she suddenly felt embarrassed and nervous. It was one thing to think about him while he was sleeping, it was quite another to be faced with the full force of that stare, those eyes.

'Are you going to reveal yourself or should I have removed your hood while you were unconscious?' He grinned again.

His teeth were perfect and white. Raemil could see he was, in fact, a very handsome man. She suddenly felt sick – surely that was not a normal response to being face to face with such a man?

'I am Lestadt. Who are you?'

Obviously, he remembered little or nothing of the past week.

'Raemil,' she said in a barely audible voice.

'Raemil... will you not reveal yourself?'

Raemil's heart was pounding. She didn't know what to say, and her mouth was still terribly dry. She was grateful for her hood for once. Not only would he have seen how odd she looked, he would also have seen her cheeks flushed bright red and a stupid, stunned look on her face.

She said nothing and retreated backward awkwardly before getting to her feet and going for her saddlebags to retrieve her waterskin, but it was not there.

When she turned, Lestadt was staring at her with a puzzled expression before diverting his attention back to the fire. Raemil moved closer to the fire and found the waterskin sitting beside him. He saw that she wanted it, and he picked it up and studied it as though he looked at it for the first time.

'I will trade the waterskin for your cloak.'

There wasn't exactly hostility in his expression, but there was no hint of the friendliness that had been there only moments before.

'No.' Finally finding her voice, she sounded harsher than she'd meant to.

A thick and tense silence filled the air between them.

'I'm sorry... here.' He eventually handed her the waterskin, though he was still watching her carefully.

Raemil greedily drank the remaining water. She retrieved the last two shrivelling carrots from her storage. She placed one carrot on the flat stone then whistled for the Black while Lestadt watched her guardedly.

The steady beat of cantering hooves sounded in the dark. Afraid to be trampled, Lestadt struggled to his feet beside Raemil. The Black appeared in the firelight; he showed no signs of slowing and Lestadt stumbled backward. Raemil stayed still, and at the last second, the large black horse skidded to a halt. With a satisfied smirk that Lestadt would never see, she casually fed the Black the carrot and stroked his nose.

'I will be back soon; we need more water.'

Lestadt was bewildered as he watched her ride off into the night with no tack on her horse.

Raemil sat by the lake for a while; the sounds of the forest's nocturnal creatures calmed her. She took comfort in the Black's presence beside her, as though he would keep her safe from harm. She still didn't know what she could say to the man; she couldn't tell him she was king Farramand's disowned, runaway daughter. She couldn't tell him she was wearing the hood to cover her weird and ugly appearance. Raemil had often felt uncomfortable around people, and now she could not help but be afraid. Too many people had betrayed her trust or been cruel. She feared he would not like her, or worse, that he could really hurt her if he wanted to.

Dangling her fingertips in the cold lake, she felt some of her tension ease. After a time, small fish began to dart up and nibble at her fingers. She smiled.

She liked the lake, it soothed her rattled nerves and seemed very much alive compared to the last few kilometres she had travelled. Raemil had to remind herself to not get too comfortable as she longed to see Serrin and hear his voice. She needed her big brother back.

Waking up to the smell of roasting pork, Lestadt climbed stiffly from his bed and moved cautiously over to his rescuer, not wanting to frighten her away again. Raemil looked up from the fire and smiled. He caught a glimpse of a mouth, nothing more. It was as though night itself was captured beneath the hood to keep her face shadowed just so.

'Did you sleep well, Lestadt?'

'I did.'

'I trust that you are hungry?'

'What gave it away?' He grinned.

Removing the meat from the fire, she faltered as she caught sight of his charming smile. She started hacking at the meat aggressively and with intense interest. Raemil handed him a plate of food and began to eat her own, glad she could look at her breakfast for a while instead of him.

'Tell me, did you pass through Witchgrave?' Raemil eventually asked, her curiosity exceeding her awkwardness.

Lestadt felt a chill. Suddenly the night at Witchgrave came back to him, and he pictured Tannagan. What did this woman know of Witchgrave? he wondered. Did she witness the horrific happenings that dreadful night? The hairs stood up on the back of his neck. Perhaps he was speaking to Tannagan now; *perhaps that was why she was so reluctant to remove her hood.*

He edged away from her, and, standing, he drew his sword. Raemil supressed the urge to run, dropping her plate and crawling backward away from him.

'Reveal yourself,' Lestadt demanded.

Raemil was shocked into silence and frozen dumb. Absently, she thought that she really ought to find a better response to danger.

'Did you not hear me? I said reveal yourself,' he said stepping closer, his voice low and intense.

Raemil crawled further away from him, still unable to swallow her fear and answer.

'Who are you? Why did you save me?'

'I—I told you who I am, I am Raemil. I rescued you because you needed help.'

Realising his mistake, he slowly sheathed his sword. If she were Tannagan, she would surely have killed him by now. He realised he had just frightened her even more, and she may just run from him and leave him to fend for himself.

'I am so sorry; I've made a mistake. Why do you ask of Witchgrave? Were you there?'

Raemil gathered her thoughts. She didn't know if Lestadt was honestly sorry, or if he was not to be trusted.

'Please, don't be frightened, I didn't mean to scare you. It's just that...' He stopped, as though he were searching for the words. 'I was there, the night of the festival.'

'You *were* there?' Raemil said, pushing aside her unease. She moved back to the fire and sat beside him. 'What happened? I passed through just before I found you, the people looked... terrible.'

Lestadt took a deep breath. 'You will think I am a mad man, but I know what I saw.'

'Please, go on.'

'I was only going to pass through Witchgrave. I knew there was a tavern there and I was only going to stop for one drink...' Lestadt began.

He told Raemil of his troubles with Sergo and of the silly beliefs the village people held. Lestadt told her of Tannagan's hand poking through the hole in the ground his pike had created. He told her every detail, even Sergo's mad ravings and screams.

'When she came out of the grave, her body looked as though she was halfway through decomposing. She looked at me and said, "Lestadt, it has..."'

'...It has begun, and you have done this,' Raemil finished for him, remembering waking one night and hearing those same, whispered words despite the distance between herself and Witchgrave.

'*You* were there?' he asked, leaning forward, almost excitedly.

'No, I was in a forest of dead trees that night...'

'The dead forest of Kannakor. How could you have possibly heard Tannagan's words from there?' Lestadt was baffled.

'I don't know.'

He leaned back, trying to make sense of it.

Raemil thought over the details of his story, remembering something. 'Lestadt?'

He looked up at her from his puzzled thoughts.

'Tell me of this Sergo. What did he look like?'

'He was tall, heavily set, red nose and cheeks from heavy drinking. Much older than I... thinning hair... Why?'

'I have seen him. He's dead.'

Though the man's face was half mangled, she had a feeling he was the same man Lestadt spoke of.

'Where? How did he die?'

She told Lestadt the gruesome details of the body she found and recited the poem that had been painted on the tree. When Raemil finished, they both looked at each other and asked simultaneously:

'What has begun?'

Raemil glanced up to the sky; the sun had moved well past noon. Lestadt had extinguished the fire long before the morning had ended and they both sat, drinking tea that Raemil had made. She was both relieved and distraught at the same time. Glad she wasn't the only one that had seen and heard some strange things lately, but she was also afraid this Tannagan woman had not finished her destruction.

'Why do you travel alone? It's unusual for a woman to be out here by herself,' Lestadt asked, breaking the silence.

'I don't understand, why wouldn't I be alone?'

Lestadt chuckled. 'I don't understand you either. It's dangerous out here,' he said as though the answer were obvious.

'It's no more dangerous out here for a woman than it is for a man.'

'That's rarely true and especially not in your case.' He scoffed, seeming to find genuine humour in Raemil's innocence.

'What is that supposed to mean?' she demanded, feeling a little offended at Lestadt's implications.

'I saw you with the Horsham men; you are hardly a competent swordswoman!'

Raemil laughed and battered him playfully with the shrivelled carrot she'd forgotten on the flat rock. 'I will show you competent!' Raemil challenged him with her limp carrot.

'No, not the dreaded carrot! I surrender.' Lestadt laughed, holding his arms up.

Raemil tossed the offending vegetable to the Black and sat back down.

'How do you ride him with no bridle or saddle?' He changed the subject.

'I just can. Why do you ask so many questions?'

'Because I can.'

'What are you doing out here alone, fighting lions?' Raemil reached for the waterskin, only to find it empty.

'I am going to Irramai – the free lands. I go alone because no one would go with me.'

'The free lands? Are not all lands free?'

Lestadt laughed, wondering again how she had come to be out in the middle of nowhere and on her own. Had she fallen from the back of a turnip cart? Bumped her head? Was she some farmer's not-quite-all-there daughter?

'What? What's so funny?' She got the feeling he was laughing *at* her, not *with* her.

'You were being serious?' he said, studying her. 'The lands have not been free for a long time. Where have you been? How could you not know that Horsham is taking everything?'

'I know that Horsham is a menace, but...'

'A *menace?!* That's an understatement. Horsham men are being sent out by the dozen to every village, taking men, women and children. What little land left free of Horsham is uninhabitable or ruled by a greedy king. Horsham will soon take those kingdoms too,' he said passionately.

'And Irramai? Who rules there?'

'They mostly rule themselves.'

'People don't just rule themselves.'

Lestadt fixed her with a look, one eyebrow raised, his mouth pressed into a thin line. He looked suspiciously condescending.

Raemil blushed. Luckily, he wouldn't know. Why had she been arguing with him anyway? She only knew what she read in books, old history, nothing of current events, especially since her father kept her sheltered, or, more accurately, imprisoned.

'Where have you travelled from?' She wasn't very good at subtly changing the subject, something she was going to have to get better at.

'My home village, Hewter.' Lestadt waved an arm vaguely to the west.

'You left your family and home?'

Lestadt avoided the question by simply shrugging his shoulders.

'Where is your family? I do not see them here, so it is obvious that *you* left yours.'

'No. My only family left me. I go now to free my brother,' Raemil replied.

'Free him from where?'

'Horsham.'

Lestadt became very still, fixing her with another intense stare. He waited for her to laugh and tell him she was jesting. Raemil didn't elaborate, she innocently sipped her tea as though it were no big issue.

'Are you mad?! Horsham! Of all places! Were you not listening? You will die before even reaching Horsham! Where is your army of ten thousand? Where are all your weapons – Gods! Where is your magic? Because you would need it all to even get close to Horsham!'

Lestadt's outburst had him standing on his unsteady feet looking down at her as though he were scolding a child.

'Would you stand by and let him rot in prison if he were your brother? Could you live with yourself knowing that you gave up when your only family needed you the most and you weren't even there?' Raemil countered defiantly.

This hit Lestadt right where it hurt and he fell into a deep and brooding silence. He knew he would have given his life for his mother and sister to be free of their horrific fates.

Raemil was right, he knew, but for her to face Horsham alone and with no apparent skill with weapons was nothing short of insanity. He closed his eyes and the image of his mother's last moment sprang to life; it played out on the backs of his eyelids all too readily. She'd been in so much pain, but she held on long enough to see him, to know that he was there. Lestadt sighed and tried to shake his head free of those memories, but it was not so easy. He couldn't forget that he had not been there to save them.

Providing a welcome distraction, he watched Raemil stand and touch her hood, as though to reassure herself that it was still there. She was a complete mystery to him. The hood confused him the most. Why did she hide? Surely she was too kind to be a wanted criminal; she certainly wasn't someone he knew or had met, so why hide her face from him? Perhaps she was disfigured? This seemed to make the most sense.

'Where are you going?'

'We need more water and we also need food.'

'I will come; perhaps I could help?' he offered, needing a distraction.

Raemil nodded and smiled to herself. She had forgotten what it was like to have the company of someone her age.

12. Peace and brutality.

Horsham stroked the crow that sat perched on the balcony rails of her private chamber. Outside, the men were gathering below in the courtyard. She looked down on them in disgust; they were hideous and fairly stupid, though they served her well.

The castle was in ill repair and boasted no wealth to the ruler; rats crawled along the kitchen floors and wooden support beams. The West tower was collapsing, no one had been inside since the castle was taken, and most tried to avoid going near it. The East tower still stood, but it was forbidden for anyone to enter; this was Horsham's domain. Of course, there were servants, but they were mutes. After employing them by force, Horsham personally saw to it they became that way.

'Come, Arramaou, it is time.'

The crow obediently hopped onto Horsham's right hand and perched himself on the ruler's shoulder. He preened his feathers and answered with a shrill squawk. Horsham slowly descended the spiralling stairs, dragging a long, blue cape behind. Servants saw her coming and bowed their heads, before scuttling away like frightened rodents. Reaching the next chamber, Horsham opened the door to an empty room. On the far side, was a balcony, the window was wide open and the curtains flapped in the wind. They danced and coiled around each other like serpents.

The Horsham men milled outside in the pitiful courtyard. Some jostled each other like beasts in anticipation of food, sometimes they seemed less than men.

They craved power and were anxious to hear from their ruler. They wanted their revenge on the world, and Horsham promised it to them.

A woman ran through the crowd to catch her child. The young boy had seen his father tethered in the ranks of Horsham men and slave-soldiers, and he was desperate to get to him. The woman was close to tears as she raced to catch the child before one of the vicious, mountain-dwelling men hurt him. Argané, Horsham's general, watched the boy run by and saw the woman in pursuit. As she raced by, he reached out and grabbed her, throwing her to the ground.

'Can you not control your stupid offspring? Perhaps I should solve that problem for you,' he growled, touching the hilt of his curved blade.

'No!' she sobbed.

'Then we will discuss it tonight in my camp – human whore.' Argané laughed to his fellow warriors.

The woman leapt to her feet and slapped him.

Enraged, Argané hurled her to the ground again and unsheathed his curved blade. Grasping her wrist, he pinned it to the ground. Ahead, the woman could see Horsham men stepping aside to reveal her son, standing alone in the clearing. He didn't understand what was happening; tears rolled down his rosy cheeks.

'Mamma,' he cried and turned back for her.

Another Horsham warrior stepped in and grabbed the boy, holding him so he could only watch his terrified mother struggle. A shout came from a slave-soldier in the crowd that could have only been her husband. The woman could see the huge, curved blade poised above her. She screamed and clawed the ground with her free hand in a desperate attempt to get free, but Argané's grip was too strong. The boy howled as he watched the blade flash down.

Her hand was sliced clean off. The Horsham man let the woman's wrist go and stood back to watch. She looked at the stump, spurting forth crimson gore. Clasping it, she screamed, her torment bouncing off the courtyard walls. The boy looked on in horror and struggled harder and screamed even louder. A mournful wail from someone in the crowd was cut short. The child went into a frenzy of biting and scratching his captor before slipping free and racing for his mother.

A hurled rock hit the boy squarely in the face. He fell to the ground before his mother. The woman was dragged away from her fallen child, still screaming. And Horsham's cruel lips formed a smile; she watched from the balcony and was pleased that her warriors were so hungry for violence.

* * *

Raemil and Lestadt sat by the lake. The birds were cooing from the treetops and the sun was setting as pastel pinks, oranges and greys mingled in the sky and lake.

'This is Tagrahan Lake.' Lestadt breathed. 'I heard that it was beautiful, but I never imagined this.'

Raemil nodded.

'I love it here. Whenever I come here, and see all of this, it's like... like nothing else in the world matters but this moment of peace.'

They smiled and held up their water flasks.

'A toast.' Raemil grinned. 'To finally finding someone that can hunt.' She gestured to the fowl that roasted over a small fire. 'And to my rescuer who brought me to this place of peace.'

They knocked their flasks together and laughed.

* * *

Leagues away on the snow-capped peaks of Horsham, war was declared, and preparations would soon begin. The courtyard was cleared and all that was left was a severed hand in a dark pool on the cracked pavers. Arramaou the crow swooped down to the hand and pecked at the fingers. He pulled off a shiny ring that glistened in places with blood. Once, he'd have found this whole scene and his own actions abhorrent, but that was a lifetime ago, in another body with a less polluted mind. He played the part of Horsham's creature well, so well that sometimes he forgot that he wasn't.

* * *

Raemil walked quietly through the forest. The animals remained silent and she feared her presence had been detected, yet again. She ducked under a branch and crouched behind a thick bush. In a small clearing, scattered with leaf litter and twigs, was a foraging pig. Raemil reached for her bow. The animal seemed unaware of her presence and it kept its long nose down, sifting through the detritus for food. Raemil drew back and launched her arrow.

The arrow lodged in its thigh, causing the pig to squeal. It frantically twisted and circled in an attempt to pull it free. Raemil drew her sword and charged into the clearing, ready to strike the killing blow. The pig froze and fixed her with a threatening glare before shrieking at the top of its lungs. This sound was awful and, without thinking, Raemil dropped her sword and covered her ears.

The bushes ahead shook; something was moving through them fast. She had no time to react before a dozen huge pigs burst through the growth and into the clearing. The one that Raemil had injured moved into the safety of the pack.

Raemil bent to reach for her sword, and the largest pig bellowed a challenge. It charged and bit down on her wrist. She gasped and tried to pull back, but it hung on. Whilst Raemil was trying to free her wrist, the others circled her. Raemil kicked its head and yanked free, scraping skin from her hand as she did.

The metallic smell of blood drove the pack into a frenzy and they rushed in from all sides. A tusk tore into Raemil's leg. One rushed at her from behind and knocked her to the ground. The impact forced the breath from her lungs; she was certain she was going to die.

Lestadt was boiling water for his tea. Raemil had left tea leaves by his cup, beside the fire. It felt odd to be cared for by someone else. He smiled at how thoughtful she was and laughed to himself at the notion of her being Tannagan. He sat the cup on the flat rock by the fire and watched the Black as he grazed.

Lestadt's thoughts were suddenly scattered by a prickling feeling running up the length of his spine, making the hair on the back of his neck stand up. It felt like something was crawling in the back of his skull. He began to panic and thought he was going to pass out, then it stopped abruptly. Lestadt was breathless and, in his panic, he kicked his tea over.

'What the hell was that?' he asked out loud, as though the Black might answer.

The horse seemed to be untouched by whatever came over Lestadt and barely looked up from his grazing. Shaking himself off, he walked toward the forest to gather some firewood. It looked like it was going to rain soon.

Just as a pig looked as though it was going to tear into her face, Raemil dug her fingers into its eyes. Miraculously, she managed to scramble to her feet as she shoved the thing's head aside. Half-running and half-limping in a wild panic through the trees, she found herself at the lake's edge. The pack followed close behind, and before Raemil had time enough to decide which way she was going, one of the pigs rammed her and sent her tumbling face-first into the shallow water. She spluttered and choked. She could hear splashing and grunting as they waded in after her.

Raemil rolled over and could see their huge bodies jostling around her. The water seemed to smother the scent of her blood and they were less frenzied, but they still nudged and bit her. With heart thumping, she lay still, not sure what her next move should be. She watched dumbly as the water slowly turned pink around her.

As Lestadt bent to lift a heavy log, he felt it again. It was as though something had awakened in him and it slithered around in the back of his mind. His stomach twisted and he fell to his knees as though he had been physically hit. A vision sprang into his mind, of hairy bodies shifting around a form that he could not quite see. Then it was gone and Lestadt was kneeling at the forest's edge again. He looked around in utter confusion.

Raemil scrambled to her feet and made a run for the large flat rocks that were piled in and around a section of the lake. A large boar jostled her and she slid back down. With some desperate scrabbling, resulting in some broken fingernails, she managed to get back up. Reaching the first boulder, she began to climb, but she could hear the scrabble of hooves as the pigs followed.

As she ran across the flat rock, she slipped in some pooled water and her foot got caught in a crack. Raemil turned and could see a pig coming straight at her. She looked over the edge at the water below. It was deeper than she had ever gone. Raemil had never waded out past waist height because she could not swim. She turned her attention back to the animal and knew he was going to charge her.

Lestadt thought maybe he was getting a fever and was making his way back to his bed to rest when it happened again. It was more urgent this time, slamming into him like a blow as the tingling uneasiness reached a new height and sent his nerves haywire. Suddenly a vision captured and smothered him. *A cloaked woman on a mound of boulders; she was trapped. There was a bristling wild pig barrelling straight for her.* The vision lifted like a veil from his eyes and he knew where he needed to go.

In her desperation, Raemil tried to pull her foot free, managing to tear more skin from her already bleeding ankle. As the pig hit her shoulder, she used her waning strength and helped the pig over the edge using its own momentum. She heard it squeal and splash into the water, but she didn't chance a look as she finally freed her foot and turned to flee from the rest of the frenzied pack.

Raemil's ankle was throbbing, but she couldn't let it slow her. She climbed until she was on the topmost boulder. Breathing heavily, she peered over the edge at the deep water. Thunder rolled above and seemed to shake the earth. A spot of rain dropped at Raemil's feet, then another, and another, until it poured.

Raemil cringed, watching as a pig leapt and scrambled up onto the top boulder with her. She backed away until her heels met the edge, below her was nothing but the deep water. The rain was coming down hard and she was soaked to the bone.

The pig charged and Raemil tried to sidestep, but the rock was slippery. She flipped backward over the edge, and, unable to stop, the pig came tumbling after her. It felt as though a giant hand slapped her as she hit the water. She was winded and floundering hopelessly, quickly realising she couldn't touch the bottom. Unlike Raemil, the pig could swim. It paddled up beside her and tried to hook her with its tusks.

She gasped and spluttered while her drenched hood hung over her eyes, making it impossible for her to see. The comb was firmly tangled in her wet hair now, hindering her attempts at shoving it out of her face. She heard the splashing and grunting and knew others had jumped into the water.

The rest of the pigs were getting closer; one of them latched onto her shoulder. She only had enough strength to keep herself above the water. Going into a frenzy of her own, she screamed in wild panic and thrashed.

There was a loud crack above her head and a tingling heat infused her arms. She looked down to see glimmering white rivulets of light running down to her fingertips. Her veins pulsed with a prickly sensation and there was a buzzing noise in her head that made her eyes water. The light flowed into the water and spread across the whole lake like a living thing.

The pigs that saw it ran for the bank, but others weren't so lucky. The light shot through the water and skipped up into the puddles on the bank from the rain. It touched an unsuspecting pig on the bank and it took off into the forest, squealing and tossing its head with others following suit. The white light continued to stream from her fingertips, but Raemil felt her strength go with it. She sank into the water and the light snuffed out.

'Raemil?' Lestadt shook her gently.

He'd limped into the clearing to find her face down in the mud on the edge of the water. Coughing and gagging, she crawled to her feet.

'Are you okay?' he grasped her shoulders, trying to see her face to gauge how injured she was.

She twisted out of his grip awkwardly.

'I think I am alright.'

Lestadt's eyes widened when he looked past her to the lake. 'What...?'

Raemil turned toward the water then briefly back to Lestadt, unable to find any words to explain. There were scores of bodies floating in the water, both large and small. Lestadt bent down and picked up a dead fish. There were so many bobbing on the surface of the lake. Two pigs floated amongst them.

Raemil sobbed. The adrenalin had worn off, leaving her shaken and exhausted. Lestadt held her as she cried, completely baffled, but he couldn't bring himself to press her on what happened when she was so clearly upset. It wasn't until now that it dawned on him that Raemil was only a girl. Again, he found himself wondering what the hell she was doing out here alone before she found him; she was way out of her depth. As Lestadt stood in the pouring rain holding Raemil, he resolved to convince her to abandon her foolish quest and go home, wherever that was.

13. Secrets.

Raemil and Lestadt both limped back to the camp, coming across the Black standing in the shelter of the trees along the way. By the time they reached camp, the rain had stopped. Thankfully, Lestadt had covered the wood he'd gathered earlier, so he made a fire while Raemil hung everything else out on the trees to dry. They both sat before the cheerily crackling fire, completely exhausted.

'What happened?' he finally asked, breaking the silence.

'I've killed everything,' she whispered.

'Raemil... I don't understand, explain it to me.' He moved to put a reassuring hand on her shoulder.

Raemil shrank from his touch.

'The lake. Everything is dead because of me.'

Trying not to feel awkward and rejected, he dropped his hand back to his side.

'No. You didn't kill those animals. I've seen you hunt,' he tried to joke.

Raemil laughed a little then sniffed and gave him a nudge. She wanted them to be friends, she just didn't know how; he wasn't like Gorran. He was a man, and a very pleasant one to look at. She hadn't come across this situation at home. It was all new and uncomfortable.

Raemil retrieved her medical kit and sat back down beside Lestadt, placing the pouch in her lap. She pulled her cloak and skirt up to expose one leg, hoping he'd assume her white skin was due to shock and pain. He didn't seem to notice, or if he did, he kept his mouth shut on the matter.

Raemil wiped a deep gash from a pig tusk clean with a damp cloth, then carefully selected one of her needles to suture it. Lestadt looked a little uneasy when he realised she was going to suture her own wound.

He watched silently, hearing her breath hiss between her teeth as she started and her hand trembled as she made the first pass through the skin. He was becoming more and more intrigued the more time he spent with her. What little information he knew about her mostly came from observations, rather than information she had volunteered.

He was sure she was only very young, judging by her emotional reaction to seeing the lake destroyed, yet here she was taking to her wounded leg with a needle and thread as though she were sewing a hem. She had obviously taken care of his wounds – they were healing very well – yet what young lady learned healing as a skill among their daily chores? Unless she was indeed a healer in training, but carrying weapons and going on quests to the most dangerous place in Otowan didn't exactly fit that description.

'Where are you from, Raemil?'

She removed the wad of material she had placed between her teeth and considered his question.

Could she tell him? Should she tell him? Raemil thought she might be able to trust Lestadt, but she also felt she would be safer if no one knew she was even from Caelin. She didn't want anyone to figure out that she was King Farramand's daughter. She wasn't sure how serious the threat was when the soldiers said she was disowned and a bounty was on her head. She wondered why. *Why go to such extremes for a runaway daughter?*

'I come from a small village, not far from Callin.' She purposely mispronounced the name.

'Caelin?' Lestadt corrected dryly.

Was that distaste she saw on his face for just a split second?

'Yes, that's it... I never went there,' she added hastily, already feeling guilty for lying.

'And you have travelled all this way? Alone?'

Raemil nodded and put the wad of material between her teeth again. She bent her head back to her task in hopes that he wouldn't ask any more questions.

This seemed to work as he stayed quiet after that.

When Raemil had finished with her leg, she left Lestadt sitting by the fire and limped over to where she normally slept. There was no bedding for them this night due to the rain. She watched him from the shadows. Orange light from the fire danced in his blue eyes, perhaps making his mood seem darker than it was, but she couldn't be sure.

Raemil closed her eyes and was about to doze off when he spoke again. She felt her heart sink. She didn't want him prying into her past any more than he already had.

'Raemil?'

'Hmm?' She feigned a sleepy mumble in hopes of deterring further interrogation.

'Thank you. I'm sure you would rather be rescuing your brother, but instead you're here, taking care of me. So... thanks.'

'You have probably taken care of me more than I you,' she said around a yawn.

She experienced a warm feeling in her heart at the thought of his gratitude. It was going to be difficult to give him up.

Raemil woke in the early hours of the morning as the sun was only just beginning to rise. The Black whickered, noticing Raemil moving around the fire.

'I am sorry, Black. I've not been attentive to you, have I?' She ruffled his forelock and stroked his nose.

She looked over at Lestadt to see him still sleeping before putting her hand on the Black's wither and leaping onto his back. She winced as pain pulsed up her leg and the stitches pulled. She laid heels to the Black anyway and he excitedly took off in a gallop alongside the forest.

Raemil enjoyed the ride with wild abandon, despite her wounds. She was rested and was starting to think about her brother again. Reaching the once beautiful Tagrahan Lake, she blanched. Now it was more like a graveyard. The fish and wild pigs still floated lazily on the surface of the water, their blank eyes almost accusing.

Raemil was angry and confused. She had ruined the lake but didn't understand how. She hardly wanted to remember. She hopped off the Black and walked to the water's edge, deciding she may as well collect some of the fish to eat before they turned rancid. The Black sniffed the water and snorted, turning away.

Lestadt was still sleeping when she came back, so she went about preparing one of the fish for breakfast. A sound disturbed Raemil's hungry thoughts, and she looked over to where Lestadt slept. He rolled over and Raemil saw that same pained look that creased his brow often when he slept. She bent to wake him when he shifted again, startling her with the sudden movement. Raemil was almost going to leave him, but there was anguish written all over his sleeping face. Sweat was beading on his forehead. He mumbled something she couldn't quite hear.

'Herinan.' It was almost a sob; he was speaking an unfamiliar language again.

She could almost feel its meaning, like a familiar taste or sound; it was on the tip of her tongue. Raemil shook him gently to wake him, causing him to sit bolt upright, gasping from the surprise. He avoided looking at her until he gathered his wits.

When he did turn to her, Raemil caught the last few traces of sadness in his eyes and she understood why he had turned away. When next their eyes met, he had a blank expression she was starting to recognise was entirely on purpose, a mask almost.

He turned that charming smile on again, the one she imagined melted most women into simpering idiots. She had to admit: she wasn't entirely immune, but this time she knew it was a façade.

'What's wrong?' she probed.

His smile faltered. 'Nothing, just a dream, I guess.' He shrugged it off.

Deciding to let him be for now, she checked on the fish. She was certain if she pushed him on his private demons, he would push right back about hers.

From the corner of her eye, she watched him get up and walk away. She wanted to follow and comfort him, but she managed to refrain. She felt torn between wanting his attention and being on the receiving end of that smile, and wanting to run from him and all the things that he could and, most devastatingly, couldn't be for her. *Was this what the young girls at Caelin would gather and whisper and giggle about? While I was being shunned like a leper, were they excitedly gossiping and dreaming of boys and young men they wished would lavish attention on them? Idiots, all of them... and me.* No one was going to want that from her. It was silly of her to even entertain such thoughts.

Lestadt sat alone for a while. He was embarrassed and didn't particularly want to discuss his past with Raemil. Being vulnerable didn't suit him. He limped to the lake and sat for some time on the topmost boulder above the water. He looked down at the dead fish and wondered what actually happened, since Raemil had avoided telling him.

He tossed loose pebbles into the water, frustrated that dreams of his mother and sister had started again. He hadn't had one for a while and he was hoping they had stopped now he was on his way to avenge them.

'I thought you might be hungry?'

The voice from below startled him and he turned to see Raemil. She was standing at the bottom of the first boulder, holding a bundle wrapped in cloth and gesturing for him to come down.

'You come up here. The scenery is... Well, it's terrible, but we can look beyond that.'

Looking up at the platform she had fallen from the day before, she shook her head vigorously, just in case he couldn't see just how much she hated the idea.

'Do not tell me you are afraid of heights?'

'No. Water. I can't swim.'

'Come up. I won't let you fall, I promise.'

He climbed down to the boulder in front of Raemil and offered his hand. She hated that she couldn't resist him. Sighing in defeat, she took his hand and he helped her up. Though the events of the previous day proved she was perfectly capable of climbing on her own, he was not to know. Raemil laid the cloth between them and Lestadt eagerly tucked into the fish, but Raemil looked on the scene below and instantly lost her appetite.

'Not the best place for a picnic,' Lestadt observed.

'I have a feeling I will see worse where I am going.'

'True. Horsham is the last place I would want to visit,' he said around a mouthful.

'What is it like?' Raemil asked, despite knowing his answer wouldn't change her mind.

'I haven't actually been, but–'

'You've never been?' She cut him off. 'How is it that you are so angry about me going there if you don't even know what it's like?'

'I have seen the twisted creatures that come out of Horsham; it's enough for me to form a conclusion,' Lestadt said defensively.

Raemil eventually conceded. Though she had not personally seen what the Horsham men were capable of, she could imagine their brutality if she were caught trying to rescue her brother.

'What actually happened here?' He nodded his head toward the lake.

'I was attacked...'

'By wild pigs?'

'How did you know?' Raemil felt a chill go down her spine. Was he there? Did he see the white light spark from her fingertips?

'It was the strangest thing. I saw it, but from the camp.' He looked up at her as though he wanted her to explain it.

She had guided Gorran and communed with the Black the same way. In her panic-stricken state yesterday had she done the same to Lestadt? She didn't understand how. From her limited experiences, she needed eye contact to make the connection with Gorran and the Black, and she certainly couldn't see Lestadt with half a forest between them.

Raemil was relieved. Maybe it was not her doing that let her connect with the Black and Gorran. Perhaps she wasn't so strange after all. Something else was.

'Are you even listening?' There was a hint of irritation in his voice.

'Of course I was listening...' She was caught off guard, thinking about her own experiences.

'How is it that you don't seem surprised? Or have questions, if not answers?'

'I don't know how to feel... I don't understand anything anymore,' she said truthfully.

'That makes two of us.'

'On a semi-related topic, what happened this morning?' Raemil was guiltily curious about his nightmares.

'How is that a semi-related topic?'

'You asked me about something that I didn't want to discuss, so now I ask you.' Raemil shrugged. 'And stop changing the subject.'

'That's about as related a subject as I am to the king... and I wouldn't change the subject if we spoke about things that were more interesting.'

'You did it again,' she readily pointed out, ignoring the fact she was being hypocritical.

'It was a dream, that's all.' He avoided looking at her, though they rarely actually made eye contact.

The hood cast a shadow over most of her face and she often avoided looking up at him, though he was lucky to catch a glimpse of her smile every so often.

A flash of her eyes was rarer still. He couldn't say what colour they were, only that they were bright and usually crinkled with laughter. Those were the times that she let her guard down enough to forget about shadowing and angles and all the things that kept her face so well hidden from the world.

'You don't want to talk about it?'

'Does it look as though I want to talk about it?' Lestadt was irritated again.

He was just as eager to find out what Raemil hid, but not at the cost of his own secrets.

The silence grew tense between them, and Lestadt wondered if his tone had been a little harsh.

'I will trade you: a nightmare for a hood,' he joked, knowing full well she would refuse.

'What is your fixation with my hood?' Raemil snapped.

'What is my fixation?! It's frustrating talking to someone when I don't know who is under there – most people look at each other's faces when they speak. Me? I'm just looking at a shadow or the side of your hood for something different...'

He hadn't realised just how annoyed he was by it until now.

'You know who I am. What I look like does not change that,' Raemil said angrily, feeling her cheeks flush hot.

'That's not what I meant. Besides, I haven't the slightest clue about who you are.'

'Nor I you.'

'Well, fine. We will play it like a game. You know where I came from, and I know where you came from. So, other than what we have already discussed, I will answer any question you want, but keep in mind you then have to answer my question.'

'Fine. I'll start. What was your dream about?' Raemil cheekily asked.

'Okay, I will tell you, but then you have to take your hood off.'

'That is not part of the game. You specifically said questions. That is a demand!'

'Will you take your hood off, *then*?' he snapped.

'No. That is my answer. Now you have to tell me about the dream, and for skipping my turn, you can answer another one.' She could barely contain her laughter. This was fun.

'What?! That isn't a part of the game either. I didn't mean for that to be my question!'

'Well, you should have said so first.' She hadn't grinned so hard or tried to hold in laughter like this for such a long time, delighting in how flustered

Lestadt was becoming.

'You are impossible!' he said, shaking his head.

'Let's start again. Maybe I should go first. Why do you keep your face hidden?' Lestadt asked.

They had both decided from the start they would ask questions they knew would annoy the other.

'Why shouldn't I?' She challenged the rules.

It was her fault. She had set the tone of the game from the start, but she was enjoying seeing him more human. Normally he was so calm and collected – it annoyed her sometimes.

'That isn't an answer. You cannot answer my question with a question.'

'Why not? You never said that I couldn't.'

The laughter she had been doing so well at holding in came trickling out at the sight of his flushed cheeks.

Lestadt was about to retort when Raemil leaned backward over the edge too far and fell off the boulder. She screamed and landed in the deep water for the second time. Lestadt peered over the edge, laughing, until he remembered her earlier confession that she could not swim. He took his shirt and shoes off and dove in after her. Raemil was floundering in the water. Again the hood was like a flapping, wet blindfold over her eyes. She managed to glimpse Lestadt swimming for her and was simultaneously relieved and deeply embarrassed.

Lestadt put his arm around her waist and swam her back to safety. When Raemil's feet touched the bottom, she tore away from his grip and squelched off in her soggy cloak. She heard a chuckle from behind and her embarrassment suddenly boiled into rage.

'You're laughing?! You think that was funny?' Raemil demanded, turning to see Lestadt bent over in hysterics. Apparently, he did.

'Are you kidding?' he managed to gasp. 'That was the funniest thing I've seen in a long time!'

Raemil resisted the urge to march over and kick him. Instead, she picked up a clump of soggy sand and threw it at him before attempting to storm off toward the camp. Before she could get far, she felt something splatter against the back of her head. She turned to see Lestadt with an amused expression and a huge grin. Raemil didn't say a word; she turned back around, exposing the brown patch on the back of her hood as she stormed away to the sound of his howling laughter. Despite herself, she grinned to hear him laugh so hard.

Raemil walked through the forest for some time, trying to put some distance between herself and her embarrassment, but it didn't work that way. To distract herself, she began the search for her sword. She had been too shaken to retrieve it after she had dropped it the previous day and hadn't had any luck on her way to the lake earlier.

She watched the ground for any sign of pig faeces or prints. There were a few scuff marks, making her nervous. She didn't really know what she was looking for; a good reason why she was a terrible hunter. Treading lightly, she tried to avoid walking on brittle twigs and dried leaves, but she found it virtually impossible with a canopy of leaves above her head.

She found her sword covered in leaf litter scattered by the wind; it was in the centre of the clearing. The sun crept past the barricade of leaves and glinted off the steel that protruded from the debris. It was dusk when Raemil returned from the forest. She could not see Lestadt or the Black, but she was unconcerned. Lestadt was getting stronger and stronger by the day and it seemed he was quite capable of taking care of himself.

Lestadt had gone to gather more firewood, with the Black accompanying him. Though Lestadt enjoyed Raemil's company, he was beginning to depend on her, and it made him uneasy. He woke every morning knowing she was already up, cooking breakfast and preparing his morning cup of tea. It was getting hard to think about the journey without her, which was a problem.

He pictured the rare glimpses of her smile and grinned to himself. She had a beautiful smile. He still wondered what lay beneath her hood that she guarded so fiercely. He hoped she would reveal herself in time. Her face was a mystery as much as her past.

He rubbed the Black's ears and picked up his stack of wood to carry back to the camp. His leg was so much stronger and the wounds on his chest were little more than scabs. He was disappointed in a way. He enjoyed the rest at Tagrahan Lake, but he needed to reach Irramai.

When Lestadt returned, he found Raemil warming her hands by the fire. They both began to speak an apology then went silent, realising they were interrupting one another.

'Lestadt, I'm sorry.' Raemil tried again. 'We let a silly game get out of control.'

'I am too,' he said as he put the wood down in a pile and sat beside Raemil. 'It was good to laugh again though. I had almost forgotten what it was like to have the time to laugh, to play games.' He smirked. 'Even to bicker about stupid things.' He was thinking of the numerous times he and his sister had fought.

'It *was* good to feel so carefree for a time,' she agreed.

'What has you so worried now?' He needed to tread carefully here; he didn't want to start another argument.

'Lots of things, I guess. My brother... Things that I cannot even find words to describe.' Raemil's voice wavered.

'What's wrong?' Lestadt moved to comfort her, but she leaned away instantly, uneasy about being touched. He didn't advance further.

'Have you ever felt alone in a room full of people? Like you don't belong anywhere at all? I feel like I will just fade away, out of sight and out of mind, like I never existed at all.'

'I'm sure you belong, Raemil. You may not yet know where, but you will find your place. As for your existence, I won't forget you in a hurry.' *That sounded too sentimental.* 'Your arms and legs flailing like a beetle stuck on its back as you fell off the rock... that will stay with me forever,' he added quickly.

Raemil wondered if one could hear someone's eyes roll. She hoped that he could. *What a jerk.* But she couldn't help but laugh; his happiness was infectious.

His face became serious. 'Raemil, have you not thought that maybe you should go home?'

'About as much as you have,' she said dismissively.

'I am capable of taking care of myself, of fighting and hunting.'

'It didn't seem that way when I found you dying with a lion trying to rip your head off.' Her tone became snappy again.

Lestadt rubbed a hand along the back of his neck and stared up at the stars, trying to think of a better way to convince her to give up on her suicide mission.

'You think that just because I am a woman, I can't take care of myself?'

So far, that had been his thoughts exactly, but he wasn't about to take the bait. He sighed heavily; he was only trying to save her.

'Raemil, how old are you exactly?'

'What has that to do with anything?' Her head turned sharply toward him, but she seemed to remember herself and just as quickly angled her face away.

He stepped closer to her and the fire. 'Because you sound like a girl, not a woman.'

That was mean, he knew, but he was sure that it was also true. Raemil's cheeks instantly burned hot with embarrassment from his casual and brutal observation. She was also extremely aware of the fact she had no clever retort. Unfortunately for her, he wasn't finished.

'What were you thinking? I saw you with those Horsham men. You were just a scared little girl. You've no idea what they would have done to you before hauling you back to Horsham – was that your plan? To become a prisoner? They *rape* and torture girls and women. They don't care if you are alive or not after.'

'Stop!' she shouted, not wanting to hear the gory details.

'No. You don't seem to realise how naïve you are being, marching off with a sword and a bow – one you can't even use! What are you? Fifteen? Sixteen? I think you've gotten carried away with bedtime stories.'

He was surprised at how strongly he felt about it, but he couldn't help but think of the fact she was someone's sister, someone's daughter, marching off to die a stupid death.

'Seventeen!' she snapped. 'And I don't care what you think. I will find my brother, even if it's the last thing I do. You've no right to speak to me like that. You don't know me and you don't know everything,' she said coldly.

He let out the breath he hadn't realised he was holding. Deflated and defeated, he sat down next to her, not sure if he was happy that he was right or horrified. This time, he didn't have anything to say to that.

'You aren't so old,' she said, facing him, confident it was dark enough now that her face was shadowed.

His mouth was pressed into a thin line, an expression she hadn't seen on him.

'No, I am not so old, but I am older than you... and wiser,' he added quickly.

'Oh, please.' She laughed as she noted the corner of his mouth twitch like he wanted to smile.

The tension between them finally broke, lifting like a heavy fog they hadn't realised was there until now. Lestadt and Raemil sat in comfortable silence for some time, both mesmerised by the dancing flames.

'Lestadt, what does the word "Herinan" mean?'

Raemil couldn't help herself. She wanted to know what he had said in his dream.

Lestadt looked a little surprised. 'It's my home village language, a word children sometimes call their mothers. Where did you hear it?'

She felt immense guilt, even though he had just humiliated her.

'You said it in your sleep. I'm sorry, I didn't mean to pry, it's just that, you spoke often in your sleep when I first found you and often to me in that same language.' Raemil expected to see anger, but he didn't react. His expression was blank; he had put on his mask again.

'I heard a woman speak the word "Serlyn". Do you know that word?' Raemil was almost afraid to ask, but she had to know what the village people called her. It remained annoyingly on the tip of her tongue.

'It can have many meanings. Sometimes it means "evil one", a bad person, but usually it means witch or magic one,' Lestadt said distractedly.

She could tell she had pushed her luck; he was not going to continue this line of discussion, and not long after, he removed himself from the fireside and went to bed.

Raemil lingered for a while. Picturing the angry crowd at the first village, she was both saddened and scared that people thought this of her just on sight. She could never show Lestadt what lay beneath her hood. She could not bear to have him look at her like that. It was bad enough that he thought of her as just a girl and not a woman.

Trying to distract herself from her melancholic thoughts, she watched Lestadt as he lowered himself onto his bed. He moved his leg a little stiffly, but it was mostly healed and he would be able to travel now. The thought suddenly hit her: they could leave Tagrahan Lake.

She had a fresh burst of excitement at the thought of continuing her journey to her brother. Her mood sobered only moments later as she realised Lestadt, too, had his own journey to complete. They would part here at Tagrahan Lake and vanish from each other's lives. Raemil could hardly bear the thought of being without him now that she was so used to his company and friendship.

14. Goodbye.

Raemil woke in a cold sweat in the middle of the night, breathless as though she had been a long time without breathing. She surveyed her surroundings nervously to confirm she was indeed back at her campsite. Her nightmare replayed in her mind as she tried to come to grips with what she had seen or known?

She looked up from her resting place and was suddenly blanketed in darkness. As she reached up to dispel it, it crumbled and grains of dirt fell onto her face and body. She frantically clawed at the earth above her, choking on the dry soil that crumbled into her mouth and sucked into her lungs. In her desperation she ignored the falling debris and clawed frantically, trying to escape her grave. She screamed and thrashed as worms and grubs began to crawl in her hair and under her clothes. There was a writhing mass of insects on her stomach and she froze, stunned into motionlessness. The dirt above her twisted into a face that was vaguely human-like. Raemil tried to scream, but her mouth disappeared. Her eyes grew wide with terror.

The soil-face grinned as it spoke. 'You are mine.'

Raemil shook her worm-covered head.

The face twisted into anger. 'You lay in our wedding bed, my love, in dream only, but soon it will be your reality. You are mine,' he stated again. 'This was promised to me.'

Through it all was the noise of something rattling, louder and louder, like a locked door rattling against a frame. Something was trying to get in, or out. It rattled so loud she was sure it was what woke her up.

Now Raemil sat in her sweat-soaked clothes, still feeling the cold touch of her grave. The fire still burned at the centre of the camp and she could see a hunched form silhouetted against it. Shaking in her damp clothes, she moved toward the figure. As she approached, she was afraid they would turn and it would be the soil-face of her nightmare, but it was only Lestadt. He had his back to the cold wind.

Lestadt had been avoiding his own demons in the waking world when Raemil's ghostly form drifted from the shadows and sat beside him. She almost caused him to jump out of his skin.

'Raemil, are you alright?' He eyed her dishevelled cloak that clung to her figure.

A young woman, he mentally conceded before diverting his attention away from her and her body and whatever he was going to think about it.

She said nothing for a time. Lestadt continued to look into the flames, waiting patiently.

'I had a terrible dream. What about you?'

'The very same,' he replied, now staring past the fire and into the depths of the night.

The nocturnal sounds of the nearby forest seemed to seep into the space between them. It created a heavy silence, reminding them of the loneliness that would soon consume them both as they parted ways.

'My injuries have healed well enough for me to travel. I really am grateful, Raemil.' He smiled affectionately.

Raemil thought her heart might stop, but she managed to calm herself.

'I should be thanking you, Lestadt. I have found a friend in you when I needed one the most.'

'And I in you, but unfortunately we both have our separate journeys to complete and...' Lestadt stopped, at a loss for words.

A thought occurred to Raemil at just that moment.

'Perhaps our journeys are not so separate.'

'How so?'

'You travel to a village just outside the borders of Horsham?'

Lestadt nodded. His expression suggested he had realised where she was going with this.

'And I, to Horsham itself. We both, in fact, will be leaving to mostly walk the same path. So, at least until you have your own horse, it would be silly not to just ride with me.'

'Yes.' He grinned. 'I suppose you're right.'

Into the night, Raemil and Lestadt discussed a travel plan. Lestadt drew maps in the dirt of where he planned to stop. He wanted to travel to a place called Vagamore where there was a market, tavern and an inn, in which they could both sleep on real beds.

Despite the late night both Lestadt and Raemil had, they were up at sunrise, walking through the forest with the Black by their side. They walked at a leisurely pace, enjoying the serenity for the last time.

'Are you afraid?' Lestadt broke the peaceful silence.

'I'm afraid of many things, not just Horsham,' Raemil admitted, pulling her cloak tighter against the chill of the morning.

'Is that so? What do you fear, Raemil?' He caught a fleeting glimpse of her smile as she turned to him.

'That is for me to know. Are *you* afraid?'

'I fear nothing,' Lestadt said, puffing out his chest and raising his chin in mock bravado, causing Raemil to chuckle.

Raemil collected herbs as they walked. She told Lestadt about some of the plants, explaining medicinal values and which could be eaten. She thought fondly of Tarrlyn, who had taught her many of those things.

'I should take this opportunity to teach you to wield a weapon. You can hardly go to Horsham with no training,' Lestadt suggested, breaking Raemil's reverie.

'I *can* wield a sword,' she stated, then chuckled. 'Just not that damned bow.'

'Oh really? Care to demonstrate?' he challenged, shifting his stance.

Raemil risked flashing a grin as she drew her sword, and he did the same. They circled each other once in a silent dance of battle before, slowly and deliberately, Lestadt took his first swing. Raemil met with his sword and the steel clinked together. As they began twisting and turning, each meeting the other's attack, they started moving faster and faster. Raemil was enjoying herself immensely and suddenly wanted to prove herself, remembering her lack of confidence when Lestadt rescued her from the Horsham men. His gibe at her about the incident had not been forgotten.

Raemil struck Lestadt's sword harder than she had previously, jarring his grip. Using his surprise to her advantage, she spun and hooked her leg around his, pulling him from his feet. He fell backward and that split second of shock on his face was her reward. With one final blow, she knocked his sword from his hand.

Lestadt landed with a thud on his back. His sword clattered to the ground beside him. Raemil stood triumphant over him, one foot planted either side of his midriff, and her sword pointing to his heart.

'You think to teach *me*?' She laughed, sheathing her sword and offering her hand to help him to his feet.

Lestadt laughed with her and took her hand. As he was being hauled to his feet, Lestadt snatched her sword from its sheath. In one quick movement, he spun her around and held her arm at her back with her own blade against her throat.

'Lesson one: do not underestimate your foe. Never let your guard down,' he said quietly into her ear.

Still holding her hand, he spun her around and flashed her one of his charming grins.

Raemil took her sword back and once again sheathed it at her hip.

'Perhaps we should call it a draw... for now.' Raemil smiled wryly, though she had a distinct feeling that underestimating her was precisely what he had just done and the last manoeuvre was a cheap shot at saving face.

'Are you ready?'

Raemil sighed. She felt at home in this forest. It had sheltered her and provided her with both food and medicine.

As if in silent farewell, she placed her hand on the sturdy trunk of a tree and let her hand linger there for a moment. Eventually, she nodded to Lestadt and called for the Black.

Lestadt and Raemil became lost in memory of their travels so far. Lestadt mostly thought of the good times both he and Raemil had shared. He felt a fierce protectiveness of her that he wasn't sure was entirely due to her young age. He quickly brushed the feeling off. What lay ahead for the both of them was not going to be nearly as pleasant as Tagrahan Lake had been, even after the massacre of the wildlife. It would not do to get distracted.

Lestadt sat awkwardly behind Raemil. He was not used to having no control over a horse nor was he used to sitting behind someone. He didn't know where to place his hands. They felt useless and awkward hanging limp by his sides, but he would feel far more awkward having them wrapped around Raemil's waist.

She had rejected his touch many times; he was not looking to have it rejected again, innocent though it would be. Lestadt remained uncomfortable with his dangling arms for the rest of the day.

15. Hunters in the south.

Lestadt and Raemil rode late into the night. Everything seemed eerily calm and quiet; even the wind did not stir. Ahead lay open plains. The few trees they saw were stunted and starved of nutrients. They were both exhausted and unsettled by the silence of the day by the time they set up camp. No cicada chirped, no cricket sang, tension lay thick in the air.

Lestadt suggested they avoid making a fire, fearing it would draw unwanted attention. He returned Raemil's wolf-fur cloak to keep her warm. He insisted on standing watch, unwilling to sleep out here unguarded.

The morning found Lestadt sound asleep on the hard ground beside Raemil. She smirked and rolled her eyes; she placed the fur cloak over him. She had packed some dry tea leaves for her journey and busied herself by making a fire.

She surveyed their surroundings and saw a group of trees in the distance and a small farm not much further on. She could make out the shapes of horses in paddocks or perhaps cows; it was hard to be sure from this distance. She could also see crops; they were pitiful and would provide little to see a family through until the next harvest. Beyond the farmhouse, the land began to rise. Both fear and excitement tingled up her spine. Just ahead was the beginning of the ranges and foothills that lay at Horsham's doorstep.

The water boiled over and sizzled on the fire. Raemil quickly removed the pot just as Lestadt stirred and rolled over. His gaze lingered on her for a heartbeat, and a grin broadened on his handsome face.

'Your timing is always spot on.'

'Comfortable sleep, Lestadt?'

'I cannot wait to have a soft mattress beneath me,' he said as he gingerly stretched.

They sat with steaming mugs in their hands, relaxed in each other's company. Raemil was relieved at the thought of having her brother back, but it quickly faded, along with her inner peace.

What then? Go back to King Farramand? No. Wander the lands alone for the rest of her life? She would be miserable. Find a humble farmer and wed? Have children and live to obey her man? She could never be content with that. What then?

She realised she needed answers. There were questions that ate away at Raemil's soul. She needed to find herself before she would ever be happy. She was not just the disinherited and disowned daughter of Farramand, nor just the sister of a lost prince. There was something more, and this she had to discover.

Raemil turned to Lestadt and wondered what motivated him. They had never spoken of his mission. They only fought about hers.

'Why are you so determined to get to Irramai?'

Lestadt seemed to consider the question for some time.

'I'm seeking men to build an army,' he said hesitantly.

'An army? What for?'

Lestadt rubbed the bridge of his nose between his thumb and index finger, reluctant to give her any more than that.

'You must have known of the war that Horsham fought against the Korran and the Caelinians that came to their aid?'

Of course she knew. This had been her brother's doom. She nodded and looked to him to continue his story.

'A year ago, a group of Caelinian soldiers were forced back toward my village. They were defeated. They had no food and had nowhere to go. They could have asked the people for aid; they could have just asked, but they didn't. They were angry and knew the battle was lost, so they took it out on Hewter.' Lestadt's voice hardened. 'They stole food, burnt homes and terrorised livestock. They'd stolen wine and were drunk and angry so they fought with the men of the village and then, once they had tired of that...' Lestadt's voice wavered with emotion and he turned his head aside.

'They went to the women of the village. They beat them and raped them... and... and then they murdered them, tossing their bodies aside like rubbish. My mother and sister among them.' Lestadt took a steadying breath. 'For this, they will pay.'

Raemil was stricken with horror. Caelinian soldiers? Was her brother a part of this unspeakable act? She felt overwhelming grief for Lestadt, but she had no words to comfort him. She was a princess of the people that had done this to him and his family. Suddenly she felt horribly ashamed and guilty.

'I am so sorry, Lestadt,' she said lamely.

How could she comfort someone that had lost his family in such a brutal attack? A brutal attack led by her people! She sat in silence for a long time. Not knowing what else to do with herself and needing a distraction, she decided to go hunting.

'We will need food; I'll see what I can find.' She turned her back and called the Black, unable to look him in the eye or shake the immense guilt for what the Caelinian soldiers had done.

Lestadt only nodded and became very busy stoking the fire.

Raemil rode the Black fast across the plain. There was little to see but dwarfed trees and dry and brittle bushes. The grass was thin and weedy and mostly shades of yellows and browns. She blocked guilty thoughts from her mind and focused entirely on the task at hand.

She frightened a flock of birds from their feeding place amidst the weeds. As she watched them disappear, she wished she could use a bow, but she'd grown impatient and never learned before she left Caelin. She turned the Black and galloped him through a cluster of knee-high bushes, hoping that she might flush something out, but the wasteland offered her nothing.

Lestadt could find nothing to cure his boredom with Raemil gone. Eventually, her bow caught his eye. It seemed to always be at his side now; he grabbed it and set off on foot. There would be no harm in them both hunting, he figured. He set off in the opposite direction Raemil had gone.

He wandered back the way they had come but could not recognise any landmarks, as it had been night when they had ridden through. He noticed some distance away there was a deep depression in the land and decided to check it out.

The ground was rocky under his feet and he stumbled often when he was not watching where he was going. He looked up at the sky and shaded his eyes. The sun was directly above him now and he wondered if Raemil had caught anything yet. He lost the thought as he tripped on a particularly big rock and fell. He grazed the palms of his hands and swore loudly. How he longed for his own horse.

Raemil threw her sword to the ground in a fit of rage and kicked a clump of weeds, sending a ball of dust scattering into the wind. The dust blew back in her face, infuriating her even more. She stood with her back to a group of trees and at her feet was a small burrow, no wider than her handspan. She had chased a mangey, grey rabbit for nearly an hour. It had twisted and turned and leapt and squealed in terror. Just as Raemil moved into the position to make the kill, it had leapt down its blasted hole!

The Black stood back, watching her with half interest, but was largely unmoved by the lost rabbit or Raemil's subsequent rage. Muttering to herself, she was angry that this place had offered her nothing but a half-starved rabbit and a hole for it to escape into. She took a deep breath and tried to calm down. They would not starve, she reassured herself. It had out-manoeuvred her and won its freedom, she reasoned. She turned the Black to face the cluster of trees. Perhaps she could find something in the shelter of the stunted trees.

Lestadt found himself at the remnants of a long-dead lake. There was little to see, so he moved around the edge of the lake bed and found himself in a field of wheat. He'd scarcely taken two steps when a flock of fruit-pigeons fluttered out in front of him. Quick to act, he knocked his arrows and fired one after the other in quick succession toward the retreating birds. One dropped only a few metres in front of him; the others followed shortly after.

Just as he bent down to pick up the last pigeon, he heard a shout. He looked around, his heart hammering at the sudden harsh cry that shattered the silence. He couldn't see anything but the sway of the wheat and the dead bird at his feet. Assuming it was nothing, he reached again for the dead bird.

'Hey, you! Git off o' me land!'

Lestadt held two dead pigeons at his side and froze as a farmer waded through the field toward him, shaking his fist threateningly.

'I was only...' Lestadt began in his defence but didn't get very far.

'You was only huntin' on my land! Them's my birds!' the farmer angrily stabbed his finger in the direction of the stolen goods.

'Now wait a minute...' Lestadt said, a little angry that this man was making such a claim.

A slow smile formed on the farmer's weathered face.

'Zen! Butch! Walt!' the man called back toward the way he had come.

There was a bark and a howl from somewhere in the distance, and Lestadt's heart plummeted. He snatched up the other fruit-pigeon then took off through the field in the direction of the camp. He reached the lake bed and glanced behind him. To his horror, there were three rather large dogs moving fast through the field. They barked and salivated, loping along at present, intent to let their prey run ahead for now.

Lestadt jumped into the lake bed and cursed as his feet sank into silt. It would have been quicker to go around. He blundered through the sand and climbed the other side, just as the trio of dogs reached the far edge. The foremost hound howled and jumped down into the lake bed while a large black dog and a patchy mongrel split up and raced around opposite sides of the bowl.

'Fuck!!!' Lestadt shouted and ran harder, but he could almost feel the dogs' hot breath on him.

The two dogs flew around the circular lake bed, great big tongues lolling from their mouths as though they were thoroughly enjoying the chase. Lestadt turned to his left and saw the black dog, so he ran to his right and fell straight over the patchy one. Both dogs leapt on him and began growling and tearing viciously at his flailing limbs.

The black dog had a firm grip on his left shoulder whilst the other mongrel tore at his feet. He could hear the hound howling as he was still trying to climb out of the silt, clearly upset that the attack was going on without him. Lestadt battered one dog repeatedly over the head with the dead pigeons, but it did little to deter it. He punched the large black dog squarely in the nose. It yelped and backed off. He dislodged the patchy mongrel from his right foot with a hard kick. Lestadt scrambled to his feet, momentarily unsure where he should go.

Seeing a lone tree ahead, he made a run for it. Determined to keep dinner, he held on tight to the dead pigeons. The black dog pawed at his bloody nose and the mongrel yelped, holding up an injured paw as the hound finally climbed to the top where the rest of his pack was. With a triumphant howl, it set off after the fleeing man. The other two ran behind, the thrill of the chase far too exciting for them to pause and nurse their wounds.

Lestadt heard the hound close behind and wished he had just used the bow and shot the dogs dead when he had had the chance. He leapt into the tree and climbed onto a branch above the hound. It leapt and grabbed Lestadt's foot, almost yanking him down with its weight. He pulled the bow from his shoulder and cracked the dog over the head with it. The hound snarled and let go, only to snatch the bow from his grasp as Lestadt over balanced and nearly fell.

'Fuck!' Lestadt shouted again as he watched the dogs toss the bow aside and leap at him again.

He scrambled higher into the tree and watched the three dogs circling below. Cursing himself, he settled back against the trunk, hoping they would lose interest soon.

Raemil was chasing a giant ground weasel out of the group of trees. Carefully nestled in her pocket beside her medicine pouch were three large, speckled eggs. The giant weasel twisted and turned; its short, stubby legs propelled its extra long body, surprisingly fast, along the ground. Raemil was determined to not let this one escape.

She chased it toward a large log that lay felled on the ground. The weasel tried to crawl over it but toppled. Luckily for Raemil, giant weasels could not jump. She drew her sword and wrapped her legs around the Black's heaving sides, hanging over his shoulder. With one determined swing, the giant weasel's head was lopped clean off. She tied the body by its feet and swung the corpse over her shoulder then headed for the camp, smiling triumphantly. *I will be a skilled hunter yet*, she mused proudly.

Raemil walked the Black for a long time before realising she was lost. Turning him around, she surveyed the area. Where was the camp? She saw a black smudge on the ground a hundred yards back. Previously she had overlooked it; now she wondered if it wasn't the coal from a fire. As she reached the place, she recognised the view from the camp, but where were their belongings? And where was Lestadt? She dismounted, pulling out her knife to gut the giant weasel.

Raemil waited and waited, but as the sun set, there was still no sign of Lestadt or their belongings. Why would he take their things? And where did he go? Raemil studied the ground, hoping for some sort of clue as to where Lestadt was. She suddenly crawled forward on her hands and knees, staring first at the mark of Lestadt's boot then at small footprints of bare feet around the camp. It appeared that Lestadt hadn't taken their belongings at all. Children had.

So, where was Lestadt whilst we were being robbed? Taken hostage by barefooted children? Nay, stupidly wandering off somewhere, she angrily thought. *How could he be so thoughtless?* What was she to do now?

Having no idea of even the direction he had gone, or how long for, Raemil waited. She paced the camp, her anger toward Lestadt building with every passing minute. She looked up from her angry thoughts to see the Black's harness hanging from a tree. The thieves apparently had no use for the odd contraption.

Night descended and Raemil sat by the fire, both worried about Lestadt and furious with him. She hoped he was only lost and perhaps the light of her fire would bring him back, but the night was still and silent thus far.

Lestadt could still see the restless shadows of the dogs beneath him, and he stared longingly at the bow laying close by on the ground. He still had the arrows, but they were of little use to him now without the bow. The dogs had ceased their barking, but they still periodically leapt at him snapping, as though suddenly remembering why they were there.

He didn't particularly like his chances of escape, but he hoped to sacrifice one of his pigeons for the chance to get the bow.

'Here, boys, a nice, delicious bird,' Lestadt cooed to them, dangling the pigeon dangerously close to raised snouts.

They immediately erupted into a frenzy of barking and snapping. Grinning, he swung it back and forth a few more times, making sure the three of them were watching.

Lestadt threw the bird far into the night. The dogs' heads followed, then looked back at Lestadt and began leaping at him, snarling and barking anew.

'No! You stupid, stupid animals! Over there!' He pointed hopelessly toward the discarded bird, but nearly lost his hand to the black dog.

'Argh!' Lestadt groaned and threw his hands helplessly in the air.

He stared desolately at the mayhem below. The hound began its painful wailing again and Lestadt found himself hoping the farmer would come to collect them. The night was cold and his teeth were chattering. *Why did I leave the camp?* he wondered miserably.

Suddenly there was a flash of metal, the thunder of hooves and the yelping of a dog.

Raemil woke from dozing to the sound of frenzied dogs barking. Lestadt still hadn't returned. *Damn him*, she thought. She could not get back to sleep.

'Oh! Must everything piss me off today?!'

Her head began pounding with fury to the beat of the barking. Unable to stand it any longer, Raemil urged the Black into a gallop toward the racket. She was surprised to find Lestadt sitting in the tree with three dogs circling him, but not surprised enough to negate her anger. It didn't take her long to send the dogs yelping into the night. *And now for Lestadt,* she thought to herself.

'Thank the gods. I thought I'd never get down!' Lestadt made a move to climb down.

'And *who* do you think is going to save you from *me*?!'

He froze in the tree at the harsh sound of her voice, one leg dangling down toward the ground.

'What in the gods' names were you doing?' Before Lestadt could answer, she went on. 'You left our camp unattended, now our clothes and blankets and cowhides are gone! Stolen!' she cried.

'I... I didn't think that...'

'No,' Raemil snapped, 'you didn't think at all. What were you doing?'

'I caught pigeons,' he offered lamely to the hooded face of pure fury.

'Pigeons!' she exclaimed sarcastically, 'Well, thank the gods, because we have fucking pigeons!'

Lestadt flinched. He'd never heard Raemil swear nor use such an angry tone with him.

'I thought I'd hunt; I thought our chances better...'

Ignoring his excuses, Raemil grabbed his dangling leg and, with surprising strength, she yanked him to the ground. He only just managed to land on his feet.

'We cannot wear pigeons! We cannot wrap ourselves up at night, keeping warm with good intentions!'

'I am sorry! I made a mistake, a stupid, stupid mistake! I have been in this tree for hours! I have been bitten and bruised and I don't need this now!

Okay?!' he snapped back.

Raemil had run out of steam for the moment, and, with nothing more to say, she turned and started back toward the camp. The Black followed behind Raemil, and then Lestadt hobbled behind them both, carrying the pigeons and retrieving the bow on his way.

Once back at the camp, which was really just a fire, Raemil untied the weasel from the harness. She tore a length of material from her petticoat and wrapped the meat. Lestadt might have told her that people didn't eat weasel, but decided not to provoke her further.

He plucked his fruit-pigeons once he realised Raemil was going to store the weasel meat. She built up the fire again and provided eggs to stuff the birds. They had effectively prepared the meal, cooked and ate without saying a word.

Raemil curled up on the hard ground beside the fire with her back to Lestadt. He rolled over to sleep and murmured an apology, but Raemil was already fast asleep.

16. Insane.

Raemil woke in the mid-morning sun, curled in a tight ball. She had been so desperately cold, even with the fire at her back. Shivering, she rolled over to see Lestadt with his ankle exposed. He was delicately poking at inflamed wounds reaching halfway up his calf.

She crawled to her feet and removed her medicine bag from her pocket. *That's what was so uncomfortable,* she thought. She stood watching Lestadt for a moment; he did not notice her presence. Raemil felt bad. She had been so angry with him, not even caring that he was hurt.

'Stop poking at them, you'll only make it worse. Here, let me...'

'Not until you forgive me and end this silent treatment.'

'It's *your* leg. You're only hurting yourself by not letting me help.' Raemil half laughed. 'Besides, it is me that should be asking for your forgiveness. How could you have known there were people out here?'

'If you say so. I forgive you, Raemil.'

There was that grin again.

Doing her best to remain unaffected by his charm, she cleaned the wounds on both of his ankles before catching him scratching at his shoulder.

'Your shoulder too?' Raemil asked, hoping he didn't hear the squeak in her voice at the end as her throat became suddenly dry.

Lestadt nodded, gazing down at her. He could only see a shadow, as still as a statue.

Raemil felt incredibly awkward.

'You will have to take your shirt off.' She tried her best to sound nonchalant.

Her cheeks were flaming as she watched him unbutton his shirt and slide his arms out. She couldn't make sense of her body's betrayal, the hot cheeks, fluttering heart. It wasn't as though she hadn't seen him nearly naked before, when she tended his wounds the first time. She sat very close as she worked on his wound, glad to stand behind him instead of facing him. It was much less distracting this way.

Lestadt stared at the ground. He shifted uncomfortably, leaning away from her but not out of reach.

'Sorry, did that hurt?' Raemil asked, moving her hand away.

He shook his head.

'Well, you are mister talkative this morning, aren't you? Even one syllable would suffice.' Raemil laughed.

Lestadt caught a glimpse of her pink, full, lips as she laughed while bending down to rinse her cloth in the water by his feet. Distracted and highly uncomfortable, he didn't respond to her attempt at conversation to relieve the tension.

He felt like he could finally breathe again once Raemil finished tending his wounds for the second time since they met. She busied herself, brushing the Black's coat with a spiny, leafed twig. Watching her, he tried to deny an attraction, justify it even, in some way. He didn't even know what she looked like. All he really knew was she was young, too young to be out here, and too young for him to be thinking about anything other than protecting her as best he could.

'We should be going. We missed a whole day's travel yesterday,' Raemil said as she fastened the meat to the harness and the harness to the Black.

Lestadt only nodded in reply. He was deep in thought, a frown creasing his brow.

'Would you stop that?' Raemil laughed, pushing him playfully aside.

'Sorry,' he said distractedly.

They rode for a long time without saying much, and Lestadt remained with his hands at his sides. Feeling Raemil tense in front of him, he looked where she was looking but could see nothing of great interest.

'That is my cloak and my trousers... and that is my dress!' she cried, pointing at the washing-line standing beside a run-down farmhouse.

Raemil urged the Black straight toward the house.

'Raemil, what do you plan to do? I very much doubt they will apologise and hand them back to you without incident.'

'I will take them. I would like to see them try and stop me,' she said boldly.

As they neared the house, all seemed quiet.

'Perhaps they are raiding someone else's camp today,' Raemil said with a touch of resentment.

'Or waiting inside, with arrows already pointed at us,' Lestadt offered.

Most of the windows were broken and the front door was off its hinges. There were three steps leading up to the porch, but only one looked safe to use. Children's toys were scattered around the skeletal remains of a garden.

Raemil dismounted and headed for the clothesline. Lestadt, feeling unease on a horse that only Raemil could control, jumped down and followed her. She pulled the clothes down and bundled them up in the crook of her elbow. As Lestadt moved to pull some of his clothes down, there was a sharp bark and a whine. Behind a flapping sheet on the line, they could both see the silhouette of a large dog.

'Not another dog,' Lestadt groaned.

They backed away slowly, watching as it crawled out from behind the sheet. Her belly was low to the ground, her ears flat against her head and her eyes lowered. She appeared to be a shepherd, likely for working the animals. Her coat was mangey and she was emaciated. The dog let out a whine that turned into a howl. It was not looking at Raemil and Lestadt but behind them. Lestadt was reluctant to take his eyes from the dog, but Raemil turned, then froze.

She covered her mouth, supressing a scream as she looked on the scene before her. She grabbed at Lestadt's arm and turned him around.

'Gods...' he stammered.

Four bodies hung on the porch. Three were children's bodies and one a woman, presumably the mother. They were headless, bound by their wrists and tied to the support beams. Their feet had also been hacked off and placed neatly on the ground under its rightful owner's bleeding ankles. Two children had been given the wrong feet; one had two right feet beneath it, and the other had two left. Carved into the bare chest of the middle child was a message written in an unfamiliar language. Raemil seemed to recognise it.

'In the beginning...' Raemil started reading then peered closer at the smeared blood, ignoring Lestadt's startled expression.

'We died for your fears... Now you shall die in them.'

Raemil looked at Lestadt. They were both confused and sickened. The shepherd whined again; it had wriggled close enough to grovel at their feet. Lestadt grabbed Raemil and, in his haste to protect her, roughly pulled her behind him. Raemil peered over his shoulder to see a man standing, covered in blood, apparently admiring the work that hung from his porch.

He giggled. It was child-like, and in his bloodied hands, he held the four heads by their hair. Gore dripped down his trousers and pattered onto the ground like soft rain.

Laughing madly and nearly out of breath, it was apparently quite hilarious that his family was hanging, mutilated in front of their home. He stopped abruptly and spun to face Raemil and Lestadt, revealing the axe he held in his other fist.

Raemil and Lestadt remained completely motionless, glued to the spot by sheer horror.

'You,' said the crazed man. 'Who are you?'

Lestadt said nothing. Raemil felt sick to the stomach and couldn't answer. The man gasped, his own expression changed to fear, then he screamed, a mixture of terror and excitement. He ran at them, causing Lestadt and Raemil to stumble backward. The dog yelped and darted between Lestadt's legs for safety.

The man suddenly stopped his mad dash for them, and his face went slack, expressionless.

'Murderer!' he said pointing a fat finger at them. 'I know you. You killed hundreds. Murderer! That hood won't hide you from me! You will die, die, die!' he shouted then laughed again, before dropping dead for no apparent reason.

The man's wrist was encircled with something akin to a daisy-chain. It wasn't a flower Lestadt had ever seen. It was oddly sweet and out of place in this massacre.

Lestadt looked at Raemil, at a complete loss for words. Raemil was shaking, unable to speak, and, in a daze, she turned away from the horrific scene and mounted the Black without a word. Lestadt climbed on behind. Finally, he wrapped his arms around her to offer comfort, and he felt her slowly ease into his arms. Neither of them noticed the shepherd slinking along behind the Black.

'What is going on?' Lestadt asked once some of the shock had worn off, his arms still wrapped around her waist.

Raemil didn't respond. Lestadt was spooked. Who was this woman he travelled with? He could not believe for one second that Raemil was a murderer, but who was she? What lay beneath her hood? And how did the mad man recognise her?

'Raemil, did you know that man?'

'No.'

'Who are you?' he asked, removing his arms from around her waist.

'It does not matter. The man was obviously mad, he doesn't – *didn't* know me.'

'Of course it matters!' Lestadt said, leaning further away from her.

He knew he could just remove her hood, but she would have it back on before he could see her face, and he would have lost any trust she had for him, as minimal as it was.

'It does not matter! I am no one, my past is irrelevant and it certainly does not include killing hundreds of people.'

'I don't believe you killed anyone. I'm just a little concerned about the death threat.' Lestadt's tone softened.

A loud bark and a growl interrupted them. Lestadt looked down to see the shepherd.

'Great! That mutt has followed us.'

Raemil looked down with pity on the canine. Her ribs poked out as though at any minute they would burst through her skin. Yet the dog looked up at Raemil and wagged her shaggy tail as though she didn't have a care in the world.

'Go home!' Lestadt growled, kicking at her, but she took no notice of the feigned attack and continued to bark and growl at the ground, just ahead of the Black's hooves.

Ignoring Lestadt's grumbling, Raemil leaned over, looking to where the shepherd was staring. The dirt began to break up in front of them where a hole was forming. There was something pointed and white poking through the soil. She leaned down yet further to peer at it. Lestadt suddenly found himself shuffling backward in a hurry on the Black, since, without thinking, Raemil backed into his lap. Lestadt's wits were scattered momentarily, the dog's whining finally bringing him back to his senses. It looked like crystal. Just as Raemil was about to dismount, it moved.

'What is that?' she whispered, more to herself than Lestadt, but he heard nonetheless.

Lestadt couldn't find the words, disbelieving, even Raemil's very close proximity forgotten for the moment. Suddenly, two great crystal horns erupted from the soil. Raemil leaned back in surprise, nearly hitting Lestadt as she came up. The Black reared, then pawed the ground, trying to portray his extreme displeasure at being made to stay near this monstrosity.

The creature's head was quite small but carried two massive horns. It had eight beady eyes, possibly some kind of arachnid. It hissed, revealing a gaping mouth full of pointy teeth and a spiny, orange tongue. Its neck was long and impossibly thick for a creature that had such a tiny head. It had no fur, no feathers or scales but had transparent skin, revealing multiple hearts. The Black bucked, his skin crawling as he looked into the creature's many eyes. The horse began to sink to his knees. He seemed unaware of Raemil commanding him to run.

Suddenly, the dog was on the creature, growling and tearing. The hideous thing screeched and slashed the dog's flank open with its spear-tongue. With its gaze directed elsewhere, the Black regained his wits and took off at a gallop. The shepherd hobbled after them, determined to not be left behind.

It was a wild and reckless gallop. The shepherd was lost somewhere behind them in the closing darkness of night. Raemil could make out a shifting mass of red and white ahead; she could not distinguish any shape or form. The ground was shaking. Choking and coughing, they burst through a cloud of thick dust that hung in the air. The horse grunted and skidded to a halt, almost sitting down on his haunches.

Deer stampeded past them. They were nearly climbing on top of each other to get to wherever they were going. Mothers were trampling their own fawns in their desperation. There were all kinds of deer: springboks, red deer, snow deer, blackhorns and even the rarely seen giant krull deer. All running and all desperate to escape something terrible.

Lestadt and Raemil stared, their eyes wide, their nostrils clogged with dust. As the deer passed, they left behind a path of destruction. Logs and boulders had been overturned, vegetation was pummelled into the ground, branches had been snapped off by the sheer force of a leaping buck or the rush of writhing bodies. Worse yet were scores of trampled fawns. Their necks and backs broken, they bled from their noses and mouths from lungs pierced by broken ribs. The fawns and miniature breeds had little chance in the force of thousands of frightened deer.

Raemil could not believe it. In the most dangerous of times, the fawns were always a doe's priority. Yet here they lay, hundreds of broken fawns, forgotten in the panic of the stampede. Lestadt jumped down from the Black, beginning the grisly task of breaking the necks of the deer that still struggled hopelessly on the ground. Grateful for Lestadt's mercy, Raemil turned away, unable to watch.

Raemil followed a movement from the bushes beside them. Without thinking to be frightened, she pushed leaves and twigs aside and there, quivering with fear, stood a tiny blackhorn fawn. Raemil extended her hand to the terrified animal, gently touching its shoulder. She could feel fear rippling through its body as it stepped away from her. Its leg appeared to be injured, otherwise, it seemed fine.

She scooped the tiny fawn into her arms and walked back to the Black while Lestadt turned to her with two miniature deer carcasses slung over his shoulder. He raised his eyebrows and attempted to protest, but Raemil fiercely hugged the fawn to her, effectively silencing him.

It was not for the first time, nor would it be the last, that he wondered just what she was thinking coming out here all alone, ill prepared for the things she might face in Horsham.

Raemil woke in the cold, early hours of the morning, but she was strangely warm. Stretched out under her arm was not the fawn but a big, shaggy shepherd with a blood-stained muzzle and large pot belly. Panic surged through Raemil, thinking the dog had eaten the blackhorn fawn until she felt the warmth at the backs of her knees. Raemil lifted the blanket to see the fawn curled into a tight ball behind her.

Frowning, she struggled out of her bed. There were wounds to be treated and mouths to be fed and she knew Lestadt would have something to say about the dog and probably the fawn too. Raemil carefully wrapped the fawn up in the blanket and walked over to stir the coals of the fire. The shepherd jumped up, stretched, and padded her way over to Raemil's side as though she had already claimed the young woman as her own. She smiled and ruffled the fur on the dog's head. The dog grinned then yawned, stretching out her bony body once again. Raemil prepared some of the weasel meat for breakfast and tossed a leg to the dog.

Lestadt woke to the pungent aroma of a weasel stew.

'I was freezing last night. What about you?' He was already warming his hands by the fire.

Raemil shook her head guiltily and glanced over her shoulder at the shepherd.

'Oh no, that dog is not staying! Get out of here!' he snapped, flinging his arms toward her in a shooing motion.

Raemil giggled as the dog watched him, tilting her head to the side as though questioning his intelligence and, most likely, his importance to the odd pack she had joined.

'We aren't a bloody travelling circus, you know. We have no use for a deer or a mangey dog, nor the food to spare.'

'Settle down, Lestadt. The fawn is harmless and is hardly going to eat all our food. And the dog... well, she apparently wants us.' Raemil shrugged, handing a steaming bowl of stew to him.

'She wants *us*? Well, *I* don't want *her*.'

'Don't have her then. I will take care of her.'

'Fine, but if she gets in my way, I will tie her somewhere and leave her there for someone else to find,' he threatened.

Raemil rolled her eyes and went to tend to the wounds of the shepherd and the fawn. Raemil picked some grass for the deer and retrieved her medicine pouch. While Raemil fixed a splint to the fawn's injured leg, the fawn nibbled at the grass. Raemil wasn't sure if it was meant to still be having milk but was encouraged to see it eating the grass.

When she finished tending the dog's wounds, Raemil studied the two animals curled up on her bed. The shepherd was sniffing at the fawn. She licked it then began to chew its head, the fawn braying as its head disappeared into the dog's mouth.

'No!' Raemil said firmly.

The dog let the fawn go then looked at Raemil, wagging her tail happily as though she had done nothing wrong. Moments later, the shepherd resumed her chewing on the fawn, so Raemil jumped up and shouted at her. The dog immediately whined and rolled over, submissively exposing her round belly to Raemil.

Lestadt didn't seem amused by the situation, but Raemil didn't care. The fawn brayed again and bounded awkwardly to her; its head was wet with dog saliva. Raemil turned and gave a withering look to the dog who then whined and laid her head to rest on her front paws.

Raemil gave the fawn a pat on its slobbery head.

'I think I shall call you... Lylah.'

Lestadt rolled his eyes, but refrained from comment.

'I don't know about the dog. What do you think?'

'Pest?' he offered with sarcasm.

Raemil laughed. 'I'm not calling her "Pest".'

Raemil patted her leg and the shepherd leapt up and ran to Raemil's side enthusiastically. Lylah was barged out of the way, already struggling to balance with her leg splinted. Lestadt laughed and bent to help Lylah to her feet. The fawn sprang in the air and tried to headbutt him but fell awkwardly with her legs splayed. Laughing again, he lifted her into his arms and petted her, before placing Lylah back on the ground.

Raemil grinned. 'I knew it; you aren't so tough.'

'Don't tell anyone.'

Raemil knelt in front of the dog, holding the shepherd's head between her hands and looking into her brown, sad eyes. She growled playfully and wagged her tail.

'Bonnie,' Raemil said finally.

The dog barked and jumped onto Raemil, knocking her to the ground.

'Get off.' Raemil laughed while trying to dodge Bonnie's huge pink tongue.

Lestadt offered no assistance. He gave the trio a disapproving look as Lylah, eager to please, copied the dog and leapt on Raemil.

Once Raemil coaxed the animals off her, with no help from Lestadt, they packed up the camp and set off again. Bonnie trotted behind the Black, and Lylah slept in Raemil's arms.

It was mid-morning when Lylah began to struggle in Raemil's arms. Raemil stopped the Black and jumped to the ground to put Lylah down. With a wag of her little tail, Lylah hobbled after Bonnie, who had stopped to scratch her ear.

Raemil searched through her saddlebags for a rope.

'What are you doing?'

'I need a rope, so I can tie Lylah to the harness so she won't get left behind.'

'Won't she get trampled by the Black?' Lestadt asked, dismounting to dislodge Lylah's head from Bonnie's mouth again.

'He won't step on her. She'll be fine.' Raemil pulled a rope from one of the bags.

Lylah continued to cause havoc trying to follow Bonnie whilst tethered to the Black. Raemil tried to pretend it didn't bother her.

Lestadt sighed heavily behind Raemil but held his tongue. It was going to be a long journey and Raemil was acutely aware of Lestadt's disapproval of the situation.

17. The General.

The Horsham men trained in the barren, rocky paddocks beyond the castle's crumbling walls. The slave-soldiers were used for target practice mostly, but some were able to train against other humans. Three men had targets painted on their bellies and were tied to each other so their only chance at survival was to overpower the others and use the weakest as a shield. The Horsham men tied friends and brothers together and enjoyed the fear, desperation and defeat sweep across their faces.

Argané and three others stood at the gates, or what was left of them, and they waited. A figure on horseback rode fast toward the castle. The rider was reckless, jumping over deep crags in the mountain and racing wildly along paths that were no wider than goat's tracks.

The rider and horse disappeared under the overhang at the castle's gate, and a minute later, they skidded to a stop before the general and his men. The horse's legs were bleeding, its sides heaved and blood trickled from the corner of its mouth from cruel use of the bit.

The woman jumped down from the horse, brushing a tangle of blue hair away from her orange eyes. She wore a blue cloak that was stained with mud and blood. Judging from the state of her and the horse, it seemed they had been riding incredibly hard for some time.

'I must see Horsham,' she demanded, handing one of the Horsham men the reins to her terrified and exhausted mount.

'No one sees the ruler. Who are you and what is your business here?' Argané said, stepping to the fore as his men inched back from her.

'Ridiculous! Is she a ghost? Someone must see her or who would tell you idiots what you are doing? I will see Horsham now or I shall tear your ugly heads off and make a snack of your tiny brains.'

'No one sees...' Argané was not given the chance to finish.

An impossibly strong gust blasted all three backwards. They were slammed against the stone wall, which then crumbled on top of them. It seemed she had passed the test, Argané conceded from beneath the rubble. He watched as she confidently strode through the gates unhindered, barely inconvenienced by the guards.

Horsham watched from her window, grinning as she stroked the crow's head. Arramaou's beady, black eyes watched the intruder with interest. *Who is she?* he asked into the minds of the flock. He listened and watched as their voices came back to him. They were mostly confused and disorganised thoughts. Many had lost their wits long ago and shared images of worms and their shiny collections for Arramaou. One image came back to him of a fallen tavern and diseased people wandering aimlessly in the streets. They were covered in boils and rashes. Arramaou cocked his head. *Ah*, he thought. *I know who you are.*

The blue-haired woman climbed the stairs of the East tower, shoving servants down the steps as she went. She opened the door to Horsham's chamber and found the old woman standing in an empty room in front of a balcony.

'You look old,' was all she said in way of greeting.

'Great power tends to take its toll in one way or another. But what a pleasant surprise. I thought you dead, Tannagan.'

'And why would you think that?'

'Because I left you to die.' Horsham shrugged.

'Oh, Mother.' Tannagan embraced the old woman. 'It takes more than death to keep me from getting my revenge.'

'And that you will have and more.'

Outside in the pouring rain, the slave-soldiers and Horsham men fought. They practised most days and some nights too. The Horsham men were hungry for blood and for the spoils of war.

Once they had been a reasonably peaceful race, living in tribes all over Otowan; the civilised men had never bothered them. Then the people got greedy. They wanted the mountain men's land. The mountain men had the brawn but lacked the brains and the numbers to defeat organised men. They were pushed further back into the freezing cold climate of the mountains. And there they stayed for several generations, full of resentment for the human race that had banished them from their own lands. Their hearts turned black, their minds warped, the harsh climate turning them into strong but bitter survivors.

Kyler came to The Land of The Betrayers to battle their ruler; the red-haired bitch had succeeded in wounding Horsham. The mage was forced to retreat back into the mountains for a time. Horsham waited years before she emerged again, laying low this time and going virtually unnoticed; even when she took the castle at the top of the peaks. The mountains were known as the Horsham mountains. The mage that rose from beneath them claimed the name for herself and for the men that she claimed and ruled. They shared a common hate of man, and Horsham promised them their revenge, the price being their loyalty and obedience.

Serrin was freezing as he stood half-naked in the cold, the rain hitting like ice-needles into his flesh. The weakest had been weeded out in the first few months of training. The remaining men were given wooden swords for practice.

Serrin had given up on self-pity and longing for death; now he craved revenge. The soldiers were fed more generously now – the captives would be of no use in a war if they were malnourished. Serrin had gained back some muscle, but he was still very lean compared to what he had been before marching off to war.

In the beginning, to amuse themselves, the Horsham men played games. They pitted man against man with real swords, forcing them to fight. Serrin excelled at this game and defeated many. When forced to choose between his own life and another's, he found courage to live and chose himself. Serrin slowly won the respect of the other slave-soldiers. They no longer cared whether he was Caelin's prince; they cared that he finally acted like a leader.

'General,' Bennagon said in greeting to Serrin and sitting down beside him.

The men had begun to call him 'General', a nickname only used out of earshot from the Horsham men.

'Bennagon, any news on Galten?' Serrin asked, his eyes never leaving the men as they practised.

Bennagon was a humble farmer before his wife and children were murdered and he was taken to the Horsham mountains. He stood taller than Serrin and much broader. Serrin gained his respect and friendship when they had been pitted against each other, and Serrin won.

'I've not heard, people have been quiet on the matter. Something's wrong. The Horsham men have made a point of not talking about it.'

He passed a waterskin between them. Both men kept their eyes on the fighting.

Galten, the man of which they spoke, had been a merchant. He'd been an important tradesman in his village, until he and his wife were taken. Galten impressed both Serrin and Bennagon with his cunning. Soon the three of them began to conspire against Horsham; they had rarely been seen apart. The three of them put together were mutinous, and soon the whispers down the dark stretch of cell blocks inspired others. The spirits of the men were raised. They no longer secretly contemplated suicide as they were ready and willing to believe they could make a difference; all they had needed was a leader.

A week ago, Galten had seen his wife for the first time in months. She was in a crowd of women at the far side of the training yard being herded to their cells like cattle. When Galten saw her, he dropped his sword and went to her like a man in a dream. It had been a long time since he had laid eyes on her. An angry Horsham man began to beat her viciously for trying to stray from the group to her husband. Galten pushed past all who got in his way. He took the Horsham man by surprise. His fist made contact again and again with the brawny warrior's face, before Galten seized the Horsham man's sword and killed him.

Galten was restrained while his wife was executed in front of him. They were reluctant to dispose of a slave-soldier's life, but the women only had one use. Galten was taken to the West tower, the most dreaded of places in the compound. Not only did the tower look as though it would collapse at any moment, but the men were convinced that something evil resided there, something possibly worse than Horsham.

They hadn't seen or heard of their friend since. Usually, information was easily gained in Horsham. The Horsham men didn't seem overly intelligent and often let things slip; usually a slave-soldier had carefully positioned himself to be there when it happened.

At night, the men dared not speak aloud their mutiny. They passed on small messages, carved into their wooden bowls using sharp stones often smuggled from the training yards. They rolled the bowls down the passage for fellow slave-soldiers to collect through the cell bars. It was all coded, and once the message was read, it would be scratched off. Sometimes they were lucky enough to find paper floating around the yard, but ink was impossible to come by.

Despite their methods of gathering information, they had heard nothing of their friend Galten. Though none of them admitted it, they were all beginning to worry. What if they had underestimated the Horsham men? What if they could see the men grouping together? After all, it was taking place right under their noses. What if they were torturing Galten for information?

'If they knew anything, we would already be in our cells starving.' Serrin tried to portray a confidence he didn't feel.

He took up his wooden sword and went back to training. Bennagon watched him as he fought. Being here had changed a lot of men, but none more than the former Caelinian prince, or so he had heard.

A man emerged from the West tower across the training yard. He was in his forties, his brown hair greying, his grey eyes dull and sunken. Out the corner of his eye, Bennagon saw Serrin pause. The slave-soldiers that were paying attention stopped, first looking to Serrin then to the West tower. The man that emerged was Galten, pale and wounded.

Galten felt the heavy iron ring around his wrist and shuddered, remembering the pain. When he was taken to the West tower, stricken with grief and anger, he was violent with grief and rage, until the iron ring was forced onto his wrist. When next he tried to attack his captors, the ring glowed white hot, burning and melting his flesh. It was bad, but nowhere near as painful as the fire inside. Searing heat shot up into his veins, burning its way into his heart. He passed out from the tremendous pain. Each and every time he raised even a fist to a Horsham man, he was punished by the bracelet.

This was a major setback in the world of a slave-soldier. He would wait until nightfall when they were all back in their cells to send word to the General and Bennagon. He was dismayed at the new development, but eager to see what the General and Bennagon had to say about it before accepting failure. Now more than ever he wanted his revenge; the death of his wife was unbearable, but instead of succumbing to despair, he hungered for revenge.

* * *

In the crooked West tower, an equally crooked old man capered about a dark and nearly deserted room. Shreds of a filthy garment brushed against his knobbly, bare knees while he traipsed barefooted and kicking up thick dust from the floor. He lifted his arms to the ceiling; his saggy flesh draped on his bones like a skin-sweater made too large for the man inside. He wore several blackened daisy-chains on both wrists and one on his head, a bizarre flower-crown for the wicked.

His filthy feet shuffled past the sightless eyes of his recent meal. She hadn't tasted very good, the now empty being that lay sprawled in the middle of the floor. The longer he stayed here, the more tasteless the souls. Someone else had tortured this one, someone else had enjoyed the exquisite suffering. If he wasn't the one causing the anguish, it was like eating food with no seasoning. She was the human equivalent of a boiled vegetable. The most delicious souls were coaxed from a living being, one scream at a time.

There was a pile of shining rings in the corner of the room, his repayment in full to Horsham. Finally, his debt was paid and he was going to go free. Horsham had released him; he was the first of many demons. Her hand in his release meant he was indentured to her for a time until he had earned his freedom. Personally, he preferred the daisy-chains. For him, they were easy to make and he could make them anywhere, but she wanted something hardier.

He clapped his gnarled hands with glee. Soon he would be free to find and torture his own souls. He was cursed with an insatiable hunger for them.

18. Words on the wind.

The night was calm and cloudless. Bonnie had grown tired of Raemil's restlessness and went to sleep with Lestadt. Little Lylah, immediately noticing the dog was gone, bounded after her. In his sleep, Lestadt remained unaware of the animals that now shared his blankets.

Turning over again, Raemil released a frustrated groan. It was so quiet and she was so tired. They had said little of the incident with the axe wielding madman and seeing the strange horned creature had somehow been forgotten in the confusion of that night. What was happening?

Raemil looked past the dying coals of the fire to where Lestadt slept. She wondered what he thought about it all. Was he as afraid as she was? Then she felt guilt stir. Or was he too consumed by the grief of losing his family? And what of her father? How should she feel? How should she react, knowing that should Lestadt succeed, her father's kingdom would fall and he would possibly die? And sweet Tarrlyn, her greatest friend and teacher, would he be killed? No, surely Lestadt would not harm him...?

Raemil could not stop Lestadt from bringing war to Caelin, and she could not warn her father. She wouldn't risk Lestadt's life over her father's, not now. She was no longer a part of that kingdom. In her mind, she had disowned her right as princess as much as her father had disowned her.

Bonnie woke with a start. The fawn was curled beside her, apparently undisturbed by whatever it was that had woken the shepherd so suddenly.

Bonnie whined. She could feel something wrong but didn't know what and it made her uneasy. The wind picked up and Bonnie sniffed the air, but this was not a physical thing waiting in the night.

Raemil felt the cool wind caress her face and felt oddly comforted. Closing her eyes again, she listened as leaves rattled in a nearby tree. Bonnie barked and whined. Raemil's smile vanished and she leapt to her feet.

Did someone call her? She looked around but saw nothing.

Hearing her name again, it whispered all around her and the wind seemed to whip around her feet, casting leaf litter into the night.

'Raemil.'

Raemil was scared. Was this another nightmare? Bonnie whined in answer.

'We know where you are,' said the wind as it continued to swirl around her.

'Who are you?'

'Come home. It's not safe here.'

'Who are you?!' Raemil repeated into the night.

'Come home, Raemil. Come home to us,' said the wind before it died away into stillness and silence.

Raemil turned, searching for a figure in the darkness. She only found Lestadt's puzzled face staring at her from his bed.

'Did you hear it?'

Lestadt shook his head, concern and confusion dominating his expression.

* * *

Hundreds of leagues away, across the sea to Iadron, a young woman sat on the floor of a great chamber and wept tears of frustration.

'Reenah, you work too hard. Come, sit.'

The young woman ran her fingers through her long, black hair and stared disappointedly at the stone in front of her. The stone was a deep forest green and round, but its surface was jagged and uneven. It sat securely in a solid silver stand that was shaped like a tree, its roots reaching into the chamber's floor.

The chamber, though it was midnight, was well lit. Tall arched windows surrounded them and gave the illusion of looking out into a bright summer's day. The high domed ceiling appeared to have no end. The polished floors were orange, yellow and blue, forming a pattern that reached into the middle of the huge room toward the stone. The room stood empty of furniture, save four grand, high-backed chairs farthest from the windows.

The sharp clicking of heels echoed around the chamber as Reenah stood to face the other three women. Her knees creaked and her spine cracked. She'd lost count of the many hours spent on the unforgiving floor in front of the sacred stone since she'd learned the name of the lost daughter. She hastily dusted off her red and cream gown, absent-mindedly smoothing out the creases before brushing her dark hair from her shoulders and wiping her tears away.

Two women sat in the high-backed chairs. They smiled lovingly at Reenah. The third stopped her restless pacing to sit beside the others, patting the empty seat and replacing her worried frown with a smile for the young woman.

Reenah smiled wearily, and, though she wanted nothing more than to fall into her bed and sleep for a decade, she straightened her back and squared her shoulders. The chairs shifted on the floor, arranging themselves so the four women could face each other.

'What news, my dear?' asked the woman who had just been pacing moments before. Her face was pale, but her cheeks were rosy with health. Her hair was silver and straight and she wore a blue gown that flowed elegantly to the floor. Her name was Isran, the middle sister of the trio that now faced Reenah.

'I made contact. I believe she heard my warning, but I could neither see nor hear a reply.'

'Then why look so upset?' asked Elyr, the youngest sister. Her hair was bronze. She was tall and thin, similar to her two sisters.

'You have been trying for months with little success, surely this is good news?' added Oesyth, the oldest of the three. Her hair was a brilliant gold colour. Reenah often joked that the women were her treasures.

'It isn't enough.' Reenah struggled to keep her tone even. 'You said she's in danger. She is moving further away from us each day and closer to her doom.'

'We have to keep trying to make contact.' Isran glanced hopefully between her two sisters. 'We must keep trying.'

'Reenah has been trying for months! Our power is not as strong as it used to be,' Oesyth answered.

Reenah looked at the three women. Not for the first time, she noticed how tense and worried they all were.

Elyr had remained silent on the issue until now. She took a deep breath and turned to Isran. 'I agree with Oesyth, we aren't what we used to be. She can face the threat, she...'

'She does not know who she is; she does not know there *is* a threat!' Reenah snapped.

'There are other methods of contact. We just have to find the right way,' Oesyth suggested.

'Perhaps Kyler...' Isran started but was silenced by the angry glares she received from her two sisters.

Reenah missed the looks from Oesyth and Elyr; she stared in puzzlement at Isran.

'My mother? What of her?' Reenah questioned.

The stone in the centre of the room flared and the sisters stared at each other in silence. They spoke in their minds now. Reenah tried to probe their thoughts, but she'd been shut out.

'She must be told. Reenah would have felt the disturbance as much as we have; we lied to her once, I'll not do it again,' Isran said angrily.

They retreated to a shared space in their minds to speak in private, a particularly strong skill in their family.

'You had no right to bring that up without discussing it with us!' Oesyth shouted, pushing back the imagined chair and slamming her palms down on the table that Elyr rested her elbows on.

Isran stalked the room like a caged tiger.

'I had every right to be true to our niece!'

'I agree, Reenah is no longer a child; she has to know the truth. However, I would have liked for you to discuss this with us.' Elyr, as always, struggled to pick a clear side to any argument. She was forever stuck in the middle, despite being the youngest.

'And what of our half-sister? We know nothing, save that she is no longer concealing her magic. Kyler wanted it this way. Reenah will only be hurt by this.' Oesyth's golden eyes softened.

'Oesyth, the girl thinks her mother to be dead! I don't see how this could make her anything but happy,' Isran replied.

'Do you not think it would hurt her to know we have lied to her? Do you not think it will upset her to discover that for years she thought her mother was dead when in truth she is alive and has not bothered to contact her?' Oesyth was always the voice of reason.

'I didn't think...' Isran's voice trailed off.

'No, you didn't, and now it must be said.'

'We must tell her the whole story. Perhaps she will understand, perhaps not. We can no longer lie for our sister,' Elyr said gravely, and within an instant, they were back in the chamber with Reenah.

Reenah's yellow-gold eyes were full of anger when the sisters returned from their closeted discussion.

'What's going on? What were you saying about my mother?' she demanded.

'There is much we have to tell you, but we are all weary. This is not the time for lengthy discussions,' said Oesyth.

'Tomorrow, we will tell you all that we know,' Elyr added.

'I want to know now! Don't do this to me!' Reenah practically whined.

With grave expressions, and a look from Oesyth that told Reenah a tantrum was not going to get her the results she wanted, the sisters filed out of the room. Reenah looked to Isran in hopes of an explanation, but Isran only placed an apologetic hand on her niece's shoulder.

19. Vagamore.

They arrived at the busy markets of Vagamore as the sun rose. There were people everywhere – on horseback, in carts and on foot – all rushing about with pots, jars, foods, silks, cotton, shirts, trousers, dresses, scarves, boots, jewels or anything that could be sold.

Raemil was overwhelmed by the sight of so many people and with so little consideration for someone who might get in their path. Lestadt kept a watchful eye on the crowd. Several people had noticed he and Raemil rode a horse with no saddle or bridle and there was a shepherd and a fawn following behind them.

'We should get a room at the inn before we look around. Dragging this menagerie through this crowd is drawing too much attention.'

'Yes, I'm in need of a bath, and clean clothes,' Raemil murmured, more to herself than Lestadt.

'You sure are!' he teased, jumping down from the Black and beckoning Raemil to follow.

Raemil watched him fondly as he made his way toward the inn.

The inn was above the tavern, as was the one at Witchgrave. Raemil remained outside with Lylah and Bonnie whilst Lestadt booked their rooms. The porch was large with oak-planked flooring. The twelve steps leading down to the streets were wide and busy. A waist-height fence circled the deck. In the left corner, beside a small round table and two short stools, Raemil fussed over Lylah. Bonnie padded over to Lestadt as he walked back out. Despite having a dislike for the impracticality of traveling with so many animals, Lestadt absently petted Bonnie.

'Tonight, we have a room each, but tomorrow and the next, we'll have to share.' He tossed her the key to her room.

'What will we do with these two?' She frowned at the fawn.

Lestadt shrugged. 'They will have to be tied up on the porch, I suppose. One of the rooms has a window.'

Raemil tied Bonnie to the table and Lylah to Bonnie.

The two rooms were opposite each other. Lestadt was not prepared to sleep with the fawn, so they swapped keys and Raemil had the room with the window out to the porch. She threw her saddlebags on the floor and marvelled at the feel of the carpeted rug beneath her feet. It had been too long since she'd had the comforts of a room to sleep in. The large bed beckoned her. Raemil couldn't wait to dive in and sprawl herself out under the quilts.

Moving to the window to let some fresh air in, she found it stuck and was unable to budge it. With a defeated sigh, she left to find Lestadt.

He opened the door as though expecting her.

'Raemil. Have you seen the washrooms yet? They've hot water!' he exclaimed excitedly. 'I've never seen anything like it!'

She shook her head at the silent invitation to come in.

'My window is stuck; can you see if you can open it for me?'

Lestadt followed her out, closing his door and locking it behind him.

'I'll see about buying a horse while we're here,' Lestadt mentioned as he jimmied the window open.

'They sell horses here too?'

'They would sell their own limbs if they could get a good price in this place, which reminds me, make sure you lock your window and door, even if you are in the wash room. This place attracts thieves like nothing else.'

'How do you know? Have you been here?'

'No, just stories from people that have. I did some asking around and some research before I left.'

Raemil couldn't help but feel the last comment was a dig at her and her poorly planned journey. She stopped herself from starting an argument by climbing out the window to retrieve Bonnie and Lylah.

As Raemil stepped out onto the porch, she heard a loud clattering noise and shouts from the street. The table and both animals were gone. Racing to the top of the steps, she saw Bonnie and Lylah running into the crowded street, the table bounced and tumbled behind them. Bonnie snarled and barked, Lylah leapt and bounded with joy, and a horse called out somewhere below.

Looking to where all the commotion was, she could see two young men heaving on a rope looped around the Black's neck. Raemil leapt down the steps and shoved viciously through the crowd. Bonnie reached the horse first. She leapt at one of the men's feet, snapping and snarling. The young man cried out and fell, with Bonnie shaking his foot. Lylah wagged her tail and pounced, thinking it was all a big game. The table continued to bounce and roll behind them.

A bystander grabbed a broken table leg and hit Bonnie over her back, causing Bonnie to yelp and release the other man's foot. Raemil shoved past the ring of people that surrounded the scene and leapt to Bonnie's defence.

'NO! stop!' she yelled at the man who hit the shepherd, at the two young men trying to steal her horse and at Bonnie, who was intent on savaging anyone who stepped a foot in the circle.

Silence momentarily hushed the crowd. The Black dislodged his captor and trotted to Raemil with the rope swinging from his neck. Bonnie whined and moved to Raemil's side to lick her fingers apologetically, dragging the table and Lylah with her.

'This is my horse, my dog, and that is my deer,' she said, snatching the fawn into her arms.

'Says who?' demanded one of the young men, dusting himself off as he stepped closer to Raemil threateningly. 'That horse was wandering around with no rope or nuthin', could o' been anyone's.'

'Says I,' Raemil snapped.

'And I,' said a familiar voice behind her, and she saw Lestadt step into her field of vision.

The Black snorted and stomped his foot, as though adding emphasis to her claim. The man eyed Raemil and then Lestadt.

'Fine, take 'im, it's bloody crazy anyhow.' He turned and pushed through the crowd with his accomplice.

'Come on,' Lestadt said, placing a hand on Raemil's shoulder.

Raemil nodded and turned away, holding Lylah in her arms with the Black following behind. Lestadt untied Bonnie from the table and lead her with the tattered rope. Seconds after they turned their backs, someone made off with the broken table.

Once the Black was put in a stable, and Lylah and Bonnie were tied securely to the iron fence outside Raemil's window, Raemil could finally go inside and wash. She and Lestadt walked to their rooms together.

'Did I not mention that animals are a bad idea?' Lestadt smirked, despite the situation.

Raemil turned to him to reply then she chuckled. She reached out and wiped a blob of shaving cream from the corner of his mouth.

Lestadt wiped her finger clean with his own and, taking a guess, his hand darted under her hood and placed the cream on the side of her nose. They laughed as Raemil pushed him playfully into the wall. He turned to grab her in retaliation, but she was already unlocking her door and slipping inside. She closed the door in his face.

'I'll be out in an hour.'

'I will get you.' He laughed as he went to his own room. Just as he closed his door, he heard Raemil's muffled reply.

'No, you won't.'

Gods, can this woman go anywhere without causing a commotion? And she thought she could just sneak into Horsham? Lestadt mused as he waited at the bar.

'I thought I would never see you again,' he said as Raemil's familiar hooded figure caught his eye.

Emerging from the tavern, they headed for the stalls and stands at one end of the street. Lestadt had already been to the markets while Raemil had been in the tub. He was anxious to look at the horses now. They parted ways, each with their own list of supplies and errands.

Lestadt walked at a leisurely pace around the market stockyards. There were cattle, pigs, sheep and horses. The first horse yard he went to housed some very fine looking thoroughbreds that were way over his budget.

Eventually he came to a large stockyard that housed less desirable horses. There was a white horse that walked with a limp and looked well past its prime. Lestadt didn't give it another look. There were bays, blacks, roans and chestnuts; all were thin and most were old.

'Can I help you, sir?' asked a man in his fifties. His hair was greying and he was sweaty and unshaven.

'How much for a horse?'

'Three silver pieces and two coppers.'

'That's ridiculous! The horses over there are in much better condition and they only cost a gold piece more.'

The man just shrugged. Lestadt walked around looking at the horse's feet and checking over their scarred and knobbly legs. He heard a whinny and looked to the back of the stables to see another horse. It was obviously some sort of cart horse. It had a deep chest and thick legs ending in feathered fetlocks and large hooves. The yard it was in was built sturdy and the fences were overly high for a horse.

'What about that one?'

'He come in a few days ago. He's feisty, needs some work.'

The man grinned a little too enthusiastically, but Lestadt didn't notice.

Lestadt climbed under the railing and the horse tossed his head and bolted for the far corner of the paddock. The gelding's mane and tail were white and his coat was a blue-grey colour. Lestadt approached him slowly, but he arched his thick neck and took off, bucking and kicking. He watched the horse as it moved. There were no obvious problems with his gait that Lestadt could see.

'How much?'

The man grinned his slimy grin again. 'I'll give him to you for four silver pieces.'

Lestadt watched the horse for a bit. It was temperamental for sure, but he was not ancient like the others. While the grey gelding cost more, he was still cheaper than the other yards. The horse was a gamble, he knew, but he was anxious about spending so much of his coin on a horse. He didn't know how much he would need and wasn't overly keen on postponing his journey to the Freelands by stopping to work.

He paid the man and Lestadt named his new horse Steel, since he was the colour of steel and, at the price he paid, he was also a 'steal', something he was still mildly concerned about, but the bargain was struck now. Other names he'd contemplated had been far less kind.

Steel plodded along, oddly quiet for a horse that put up so much fuss when being saddled. As Lestadt directed him through the gate, the man waved good riddance to the grey, masking it as a wave to his departing customer.

Raemil wandered the stalls perusing the wares. She was struggling to cope in a large crowd. People rudely jostled past her with armfuls of items, children wound through people's legs, men cursed as they tripped and dropped things, only for thieves to snatch them up.

A dress caught Raemil's eye and she was immediately drawn to the stall. It was white with a cream sash that tied around the waist. It laced up at the front and the skirt was long and flowing with a slit up one side. Raemil paid a handsome price, but she loved it too much to leave it. Even though she wore a cloak that concealed everything from the public, dresses still gave her a feeling of beauty. In this way she indulged herself.

After putting her things away, she rode the Black to the yards and saw Lestadt smiling as he spotted her riding toward him.

With a gentle tap of his heels to the grey horse's flank, Lestadt urged his new mount into a trot. Steel tossed his head, but Lestadt kept a tight rein. Unexpectedly, the grey squealed, tossed his head, sidestepped then whipped around so fast that Lestadt nearly lost his seat. Steel took off at a gallop toward the open plains.

Raemil urged the Black after the bolting horse. Lestadt clung to the crazed animal as best he could as it raced for freedom. Steel bucked and leapt incredibly high into the air; he twisted and kicked his legs out to the side before landing and spinning in circles. Lestadt lost one of the stirrups and couldn't get his foot back in. As the grey bucked and leapt again, he was nearly thrown over the horse's head.

Bending to place his foot back in the stirrup, the horse bucked again. In panic, Lestadt dropped the reins and grabbed the saddle, his free leg almost going over the pommel. The reins flicked up and tangled themselves around Lestadt's foot. Steel kicked his legs out to the side, tucked his forelegs in and came down on his flank, crushing Lestadt's leg. As the grey turned to roll, he aimed for Lestadt and struck out. Lestadt was hit with a solid blow to his shoulder. Raemil was there in an instant. Ignoring the rising horse, she reached to disentangle Lestadt's foot.

The horse took off, dragging both Raemil and Lestadt with him. Raemil, determined not to let the horse take Lestadt, grabbed her sword and cut the reins. They rolled in the dust, coughing and spluttering.

'Don't let him get away,' Lestadt wheezed.

'What?!'

'Catch him!' he repeated as he sat up.

Raemil leapt onto the Black and raced after the grey. Catching him quickly, she led him back by his broken reins. The grey horse was not pleased. He bit the Black's rump and kicked out at him. Unimpressed herself, Raemil led the grey back to Lestadt, who was still sitting on the ground where the horse had dumped him.

'I cannot see why you would want this ill-tempered thing back.'

'Because I'm not likely to get my money back and I need a horse.'

'But...' Raemil tried to protest.

'He just needs to be worked, that's all,' Lestadt said stubbornly, barely concealing his pain as he staggered awkwardly to his feet.

'That horse should have broken your leg and its back when it landed.'

'Well, here's to looking on the bright side.' He half smiled, failing miserably at making her laugh.

Lestadt climbed back in the saddle, causing Steel to squeal and rear, but Raemil had a firm grip on the broken reins this time.

20. Shoreline kingdoms.

The castle sat in the middle of the lake; no visible bridges led across. Reenah recited a spell and gestured with her hands, summoning a white bridge that arched from her feet to the far side of the lake at the beginning of West Sirron city. The castle was an inaccessible island unless the sisters, Reenah, or close friends of the mage-kind brought the bridge across.

The houses of West Sirron were white with silver trims. People bustled in the streets while others were only just emerging from their homes. Reenah glanced around, pulling the shawl tighter against the chill of the morning. The common folk stopped to bow to her as she walked by. Reenah smiled at the first few people, but after a while, she grew weary and settled for a small nod.

Her thoughts were troubled; there was so much worry and uncertainty. Being a princess wasn't as glamorous as one might think, and being a sorceress princess added an entirely different element of stress. The common folk had no idea how taxing wielding magic could be. They would never know what it was to worry about the fate of the world. Currently, the general public had been shielded from the knowledge of what threatened from beyond the sea.

A long line of riders and carriages were breaking through the crowd ahead. Reenah's heart skipped a beat as she recognised the symbol on the martingale of the first horse. The symbol was a simple emerald circle with a golden arrow inside. This was the mark of Byrass. The mage king and queen rode in one of those carriages. Reenah found herself wondering if their son, Prince Tylon, rode with them.

Several soldiers rode past, greeting Reenah as they went, before the line was called to a halt. The mage king and queen hailed Reenah from their carriage. Reenah bowed and greeted them warmly before the line moved on. As the carriages and horses rumbled past, Reenah's spirits dropped. She had not seen Prince Tylon.

She hurried back to the palace, not wanting to miss out on the Byrassian visit. This visit would have to be of great importance for the king and queen to come in person instead of spirit travel.

The sisters and the king and queen of Byrass spent the day talking of taxes and laws. It was polite conversation about things that could be said in the dining room. Reenah was on the edge of her seat, waiting for someone to get to the point. She had no interest in the running of the palace or city; she wanted to hear the real discussion that would take place behind closed doors and magical barriers that kept others from hearing.

Reenah had been interested enough in the beginning to hear that Prince Tylon was indeed coming but had been held up with other duties. Reenah had been infatuated with Prince Tylon for many years now, but he had been a busy prince and had little time to notice her. More recently, they had struck up a friendship, but she wished it could be more.

Reenah knew she was never going to have the prince that she wanted, for Prince Tylon was betrothed to Princess Yaeli of Thornbroke. It had been arranged years ago, and the wedding would be at the end of this year. Knowing this did not still the butterflies in Reenah's stomach every time she saw him.

West Sirron and Byrass were the two kingdoms whose territories ran along the shorelines of the Sapphire Sea that joined Centre Point Ocean. Though the kingdoms were leagues apart, they shared the problem that threatened them from across the seas. The other kingdoms didn't believe there was a threat, refusing to waste their time or resources on what they deemed an unfounded fear.

Everyone felt the bridge appear and the conversation paused as Prince Tylon rode onto the island. Reenah's stomach flipped and she suddenly had the urge to flee.

The last time Reenah saw Tylon was on the Sapphire coast, where he had celebrated his twenty-sixth birthday. Reenah and Tylon had escaped the celebrations and shared the evening by a small fire. They had spoken nothing of royalty or magic or the governing of any city, just everyday things, as though they were two commoners. If only it could be so simple.

Once the Prince joined them, the mages rose as one and swept from the dining room, down a hallway and then into a chamber behind the third door on the right. The chamber was small and appeared to be a study with books and maps all placed neatly on shelves. Elyr went to a bookcase on the far wall behind a cluttered desk and waved King Herald and Queen Loree through. The Byrassians stepped through the bookcase and disappeared. Prince Tylon hung back; Isran noticed and urged both Elyr and Oesyth through before stepping through herself. Reenah moved to follow but felt a gentle hand on her shoulder.

'Have I done something to upset you?' Tylon asked, turning her to face him.

Reenah refused to meet his stare, but he placed his hand under her chin and tilted her head back to look at her, sending her heart into a flutter.

'No. Nothing,' she managed to utter, staring into his blue eyes, flecked through with yellow.

'Then why have you not even so much as looked at me tonight? You've been really quiet.'

Reenah turned and headed for the bookcase.

'We must join the others,' she said, stepping quickly through the illusion.

The room behind the bookcase was not imagined into existence; it was real, only hidden by magic. There were seven chairs arranged around a table. Elyr, Oesyth, Isran, King Herald and Queen Loree were already seated. Reenah sat down beside Isran, and Prince Tylon sat opposite her.

'I think we can all agree there has been enough delay,' said King Herald before anyone could query Reenah's and Tylon's tardy entrance.

'Very well,' Oesyth began, 'we are all aware of the disturbances in our power in the past few weeks. We know that this is mostly to do with Horsham, but obviously the other houses disagree. We know it is *she* causing this disruption and we know she is strong to be able to disturb us from across the Sapphire Sea. What we don't know is how we can prevent her from coming across.'

'What of the people across the sea? Do they not have the means to stop her before she gets to us?' asked Queen Loree.

Isran shifted on her seat uncomfortably.

'We have no allies there; they are mostly mortals. We have scried across the lands and have seen that it is beginning already and mortal men have not realised the extent of it.'

'Just how powerful is she?' Queen Loree looked nervous.

'Horsham is old. There is much power to be gained from knowledge alone and over a long lifetime. She could be powerful enough to destroy us all,' Elyr said, finishing her glass of wine with a determination that hinted of uncomfortable conversations to come.

'We can't face her alone. We need every mage and wizard in both lands, but there are few who will believe. What can we do? Oesyth, please tell me that you have a plan.' The king looked hopefully between the sisters.

Isran gave Oesyth a meaningful glance. Oesyth nodded her permission for Isran to speak of their secret. Isran stood and tucked her chair in before looking gravely around the room.

'We said that the disturbances have been *mostly* due to Horsham but not entirely.' Her eyes fell on Reenah before darting away again.

'You all knew of our sister Kyler, killed in a battle with Bascillium.'

There were nods around the table. Kyler was legendary for her battle against the powerful mage Bascillium years ago. Bascillium was a disturbed mage living in the land of the betrayers. Kyler had gone alone to meet with the mage but it was reported that she was killed and Bascillium had vanished, presumed dead also.

'Our sister, Kyler...' Isran looked into Reenah's eyes and suddenly could not find the words.

'We have been keeping a secret from all, as was Kyler's wish. However, it is time that we tell you. Kyler lives,' Oesyth admitted.

There was shocked silence.

The king and queen of Byrass had met Kyler briefly when she was younger but knew little of her as an adult save what had become publicly known. Prince Tylon knew only legend, but his shock was for Reenah. Her mother had been alive for all these years and Reenah had been denied both the truth and a mother.

'How? Why would she want people to think she was dead? Where is she?' the king demanded.

'We don't know where she is or how she survived or why she wanted the world to think her dead. She asked us to forget her for Reenah's sake. We respected her wishes and raised Reenah for her,' Elyr said, unable to look at her niece.

Reenah stared at the table in front of her. She could not speak; her cheeks were flushed and her hands shook as she placed them into her lap. Prince Tylon wanted to comfort her, but decorum forced him to only watch as the other mages went on talking around her. He itched to reach across the table and take her hand, or even embrace her.

'What relevance does this have to the situation at hand? She is your sister. What could she do that none of you can?' asked the king, still shocked from the news.

'Kyler shares the same mother as I and my sisters, but not our father. Our blood is dilute; Kyler is full-blood.' Isran's voice was low, as though even here, behind enchantment, she was afraid to be overheard.

'A full-blood? How could we have not known?' Queen Loree exclaimed.

'We aren't sure of the extent of her power; she was very secretive. However, we know that she has come out of hiding. We felt her presence. She could be powerful enough to defeat Horsham,' Oesyth suggested.

'Have you contacted her?'

'No. We thought it best if this was out in the open first.'

'If Horsham is as powerful as you say, what makes you think that Kyler can stop her?'

'Alone, we aren't sure she could. But with the lost daughter, perhaps,' Isran said, as she walked over to the fire, staring into the flames. She hated herself for withholding the truth from Reenah.

'The lost daughter? I thought that was just a rumour. Does Kyler *really* have another daughter?' The Byrassian queen looked from sister to sister.

'Yes, but we have had trouble finding her. She truly is lost.'

There was a loud rumbling and the table began to shake violently. The mages glanced from one to the other.

'Kyler has no daughters! She is not my mother. Mothers do not just leave their children!' Reenah leapt to her feet, knocking her chair over.

'Reenah, please...' Elyr moved to put her hand on Reenah's shoulder, but Reenah pushed her back and Elyr was sent sprawling to the back of the room.

All were shocked that the princess had used her power on Elyr.

'Stay away from me! You all lied to me. How could you? And now you sit here and tell me she is alive after all these years and think nothing of it? Are you that heartless that you couldn't see how this would affect me?!'

Reenah stormed out of the chamber. Isran tried to follow but was met with a cold, icy wind that forced her backward.

Discussions were cut short after Reenah's outburst; the rest of the mages retired to bed early. Prince Tylon lay awake in his bed worrying about Reenah. Remembering his birthday celebrations at the beach when they had spent the night in each other's company, he felt he owed her. Prince Tylon had had an awful day, and Reenah had been there to offer uncomplicated company.

Sick of tossing and turning, he eventually gave in and slipped from his chambers to find Reenah. He walked down the long hall, wondering which door led to her room. He couldn't knock on just any door; how could he explain that to one of the sisters? He couldn't admit that in the middle of the night he was looking for Princess Reenah's room.

'Can I help you, Prince?' asked a soft voice from behind, and Tylon turned to see a young maid standing there.

'I'm hoping to find Princess Reenah.' Tylon was acutely aware of how wildly inappropriate this would appear at this time of night.

'She's not come back inside the palace.'

Prince Tylon nodded and turned away, heading down the stairs to outside. It was not a large island; he would find her sooner or later.

'Might I suggest the gardens at the back of the palace?' the maid added.

'Thank you.'

The garden was Reenah's refuge. Three gravel paths meandered toward the middle of the garden featuring a water fountain and pond. The hedges were beginning to grow out of shape and weeds were starting to appear in some places, but these imperfections failed to come to Reenah's attention. She sat on a low stone wall surrounding a statue of a horse that had lavender planted at its base. This place overlooked the water fountain, which usually calmed her, but not this night.

How could the sisters lie to her like that? And for so long? Reenah was mostly hurt by Isran. She had told Isran everything, even about her feelings for Prince Tylon, yet Isran kept such a huge secret from her. Warm tears slid down her cheeks and she didn't bother wiping them away. There was no one here to see them, and she didn't much care right now if they did.

She watched from the shadows as Prince Tylon walked past the water fountain and headed down another path. The third time she saw him go past, she thought she'd better intervene.

'Are you lost, Prince?' She hastily wiped her eyes, deciding after all that she cared if *he* saw her tears.

'Reenah, I've been looking for you. I was worried.' He sat beside her on the stone wall. 'Are you alright?' he asked, knowing she wasn't.

'I am fine,' she lied.

'Reenah, it's only you and me now; you can trust me.'

Reenah remained silent.

'Are you mad at me too? I didn't know either.'

Reenah didn't want to open up to anyone again, least of all to the man that stole her heart and couldn't give her his in return. Tylon reached for her hand and cupped it in his. Reenah looked down to their joined hands, feeling the tears welling again.

'I am not angry at you. Just... just everything and everyone else.' Reenah sobbed as Tylon wrapped his arms around her.

'The sisters are planning to contact Kyler. You will have to meet her sooner or later, you know that, right?'

'I know,' she said, reluctantly pulling away from him. 'They will need my help. I will do it because it is our only hope.'

'What of the lost daughter? Did you know of her?'

'Yes, they at least informed me that I have a half-sister. I knew Kyler had left me with the sisters to go on some kind of mission. I was told she died after my sister was born.'

'Half?'

'I don't know who the father is, but the sisters and I have been close to contact. She is very powerful, perhaps even a full-blood herself.'

'All this talk of full-bloods, it worries me. There could be hundreds out there, all capable of destroying life as we know it.'

'Listen to you.' Reenah grinned despite her sadness. 'Sounding more and more like a prince every time I see you... but have you considered that if they *are* out there, wouldn't we know of more by now? I mean, that is if they meant us any harm, and why should they?'

'Sure, but it all starts somewhere, starting with just one full-blood coming out of hiding?'

'You think Kyler is dangerous?' She raised an eyebrow at him.

'Well, she could be. Parents have a knack for destroying lives,' he said the last under his breath, but Reenah heard it anyway.

'The wedding?' she prompted, welcoming the change in subject.

It was surprising how often a mage forgot that muttering under one's breath was pointless around another mage.

'The castle is a nightmare; they're still fighting over where we'll build.'

'Still? Will they not let you have your dream castle by the sea?'

Though she knew it was wrong, she couldn't help but find a small joy in knowing he wasn't happy about certain aspects of his upcoming nuptials.

'I am afraid not. Princess Yaeli wishes to be inland, close to her parents' territory.'

'This will test the strength of your love.'

Tylon's eyes narrowed. 'Reenah, we are royals, love has absolutely nothing to do with it.'

'But how can you marry someone that you do not love?' She struggled to keep her happiness in check. After all, it changed nothing.

'With great hesitation.' He laughed.

'You have been betrothed for a long time now. I'd have thought something would have formed between you,' she pressed, despite herself.

'Only the pain in my backside, which is soon to be my wife!' He scoffed.

'So why not tell the king and queen that you do not wish to marry her?' Reenah asked, then instantly felt embarrassed about her forwardness.

If Prince Tylon had thought it too forward, he did not say so.

'Believe me, I think about it every day, but after several years of planning, it would probably create a war and I would be disinherited.'

'That would not be so bad,' she said wistfully.

'War?'

'No. Being disinherited, being free from the politics and stress of governing a territory.'

'You know, it wouldn't be so bad. I would take my peasant wife, who I would love more than life itself, build a house by the sea, maybe have some cattle and sheep. Have children and a lazy old dog sleeping on my porch beside my favourite chair.'

Reenah sighed. 'If only.' She smirked. 'I'll bet somewhere a peasant is dreaming of our lives as we dream of theirs.'

21. The dead of the night.

Come one,
Come all,
From the darkest depths,
Shall you crawl.

Come now as they sleep,
In the dark of the night,
But the hand that does feed,
You shall not bite.

Crawl and fly,
Slither and cry.
Come now for the evil,
Of which you defend,
This shall be tonight,
In the beginning of the end.

* * *

A little girl hummed as she skipped to the well at the back of the garden. She was sleepy and already longing for dreams of castles and ponies. Her singing drifted sweetly through the night as she hoisted the bucket of water to the edge of the well. As she leaned over, she was met with two huge, yellow eyes that shone like beacons in the pitch black of the well.

Her song was suddenly cut short. In its place an eerie silence greeted the night, momentarily broken by the splash of the bucket as it fell back down into the well. The child writhed and choked on blood in the dust on the ground beside the well. The morning would find a mother screaming as she stood before the tiny, bloodless body of her daughter.

* * *

'I can too!' said the little boy.

'Scaredy, you're afraid of the dark,' taunted his older brother.

'Come back inside,' the father called, watching his boys from the patio.

'I'm not scared of the dark! I'll prove it! I can run to that hill over there and back,' the little boy cried defiantly, wanting to be brave in front of his father.

'Fine. Let's see then,' the brother said smugly.

As the little boy sprinted into the night, the father stepped forth, peering into the darkness. He heard a loud screech, followed by his son's scream. Without hesitation he raced toward the sound. The younger boy raced for his father, screaming all the way and continuing right past him. The father spun around, puzzled, watching his sons run for safety.

'What's going on here?'

In answer, there was a great whooshing sound from behind. Slowly turning, he was faced with a great winged beast. It screeched and opened its mouth wide, razor-sharp teeth glinting in the dark. The man shrieked as massive talons ripped into his belly. He could hear his sons echoing his screams. It was the last thing he heard.

The boys watched as their father was torn to pieces in a bloody tangle of wing, torn limbs and bodily fluids. Both boys would forever be afraid of the dark with the picture of their father's bloody end waiting in the night.

* * *

She nervously smoothed out the creases in her dress. He had been gone only a moment to get them both a drink, but to her it had felt like an age before he returned. The young man smiled as he sat beside her. His teeth were less than perfect, but she didn't mind.

'You're so beautiful,' he whispered, inching closer.

A sharp pain in her side caused her to leap to her feet, both hands grasping at her waist. She began franticly pounding her fists against herself. The young man tried to help while she screamed hysterically. He managed to grab her flailing arms and pull her against him in an effort to calm her down.

'What's wrong?!'

He watched in disbelieving horror as something wormed its way inside her flesh on her neck. He jumped back as the girl crumpled and began to fit. She shook violently. Blood began to trickle from her nose, mouth and eyes. A small worm-like creature burst from her eye socket in a gout of blood. The young man shrieked and fled. Later he was found wandering the village, crazed and alone, speaking of worms and bleeding eyes.

* * *

No one had seen them coming. They had crept and slithered and flown from far below the ground in the deepest chasms and caves. They came with teeth and claws and insatiable appetites for the young and old and, particularly, the innocent.

Many men, women and children were caught unawares; most, if not all, died in utter panic, their screams only attracting other prey for the creatures of the dark. They moved through the shadows of the night, finally free to feed on the flesh of innocence. The dawn revealed the dead and left little explanation as to what had befallen the people.

* * *

The people would weep,
And so shall the lord,
Take their souls to keep.

The unsuspecting and the brave,
Would now lay to rest,
In their dark, shallow grave.

The mad and the scarred,
Would travel the lands,
Forever trying,
To wash the blood from their hands.

Weep not for the dead,
Pray for the promise of tomorrow,
Where with your kin,
You shall bury your sorrow.

Succumb to the pain,
For the deed has been done,
Care not for your sanity,
Now that the end has begun.

22. Ugly.

Raemil rolled on the ground, laughing so hard that her insides hurt. Lestadt dusted himself off for the third time that day. He shook his head at her while she continued to laugh with complete abandon.

Steel stood several paces away, looking rather pleased with himself. In the beginning, the grey horse would dump Lestadt, then run, heading for freedom. Raemil and the Black brought him back every time. Now Steel stuck around, as though he relished the man's bewilderment.

'It's been a long day. I think Steel needs a break,' Lestadt said, grasping the grey horse's reins.

They kept Steel in the stable while the Black roamed free. It was their second day in Vagamore and much of their time had been spent trying to break Steel, but mostly Steel just broke Lestadt.

Lestadt watched the hooded woman as she walked beside him. She stepped lightly and seemed happy; this place seemed to bring the best out in her. He thought that being with Raemil had brought out the best in him too.

'Lestadt?'

'Hmm?'

'What do you make of that death in the next village?'

Earlier that day, Raemil and Lestadt had overheard a conversation about a gruesome death that happened not far from Vagamore. The general consensus was some kind of animal had caused it, but no one could be certain.

'I don't know. We'll go by that village; it's not exactly comforting knowing there's something out there that could kill us like that.'

Lestadt opened the door to the stall for Steel. On his way in, the grey nipped his shoulder. 'Hey!'

'What of that strange creature we encountered before Vagamore? Do you think it could have something to do with it? What was it anyway?'

In the back of their minds the question still remained: *What has begun?* Hearing the concern in her voice, he frowned. Absently, he placed his hand on the small of her back to guide her back toward the inn.

'I've never seen anything like it before, but I've heard stories with fitting descriptions. I thought it only traveller's tales. Some people called them crystal worms; they live underground. A traveller I knew was in a village east of Horsham when he wandered down into the mines. He travelled days down there. As he got deeper, the walls began to appear glassy. Eventually, he wandered into a huge lair that was encased entirely in crystal. He found the creature there. As soon as he saw the thing, he turned and ran. He never knew what it was capable of.' Lestadt shrugged his shoulders, not sure what to make of the story.

'If they live so far underground, what do you think would bring them to the surface?' Raemil asked as they walked up the wide steps to the inn. 'And why now?'

'I don't know. It could have just been a chance encounter. It probably has nothing to do with the death.'

Raemil and Lestadt now shared a room, making things considerably awkward for Raemil to keep her face and hair concealed. She knew Lestadt wasn't looking forward to a night spent sleeping on the floor either.

The sun was setting outside, and a soft, orange light filtered in from the window. Raemil let Bonnie and Lylah in through her sticky window. She'd removed the bandage from Lylah's leg since it proved to be more of a hinderance than anything else. Bonnie jumped on the bed, wagging her tail happily, but was soon scolded by Lestadt. Bonnie and Lylah dashed around the room playing before eventually settling on the floor in front of the fireplace.

'What's wrong?'

She hadn't realised he'd been watching her and that she'd been frowning, and he could see part of her face. She quickly angled her face away from the light.

'I don't know. I guess I'm still thinking of the man, Sergo? His murder was... horrific. And the message on the tree, I think it's all somehow connected.'

'And the voices you heard? Where does that fall into the scheme of things?' Had the trauma of the last few weeks caused her to have a mental break?

'Do not mock me, Lestadt. I know what I heard. You don't have to believe me, but my mind is perfectly sound,' Raemil said angrily.

'I didn't suggest there was anything wrong with your mind,' Lestadt said defensively. He had thought it, yes, but he hadn't vocalised it.

'I heard you, just now.' Raemil eyed him, sure she'd heard or felt it.

Lestadt shook his head. 'I can assure you, I did not say it, but I'll admit I'd thought it. I'm just worried about you.'

'But... I...' A chill prickled her spine and she shut her mouth.

An uncomfortable silence lingered between them. Raemil distracted herself by looking out the window and Lestadt sat heavily on the end of the bed.

Lestadt watched the dog and deer curled up by the fire, his mind wandering to Bonnie's former family, in particular, the brutality in which they had died. He had put Raemil behind him, trying to steer her from harm's way. Even in that moment, as the madman rushed toward them, he hadn't even a plan himself. Raemil was deeply disturbed by it all. He could see it in her body language, feel it in the quietness of her and the way she hugged that fawn to her afterward. She was not cut out for this journey; he'd known it at Tagrahan Lake and it was only becoming more apparent.

Watching her now, he wished he could pull that stupid hood from her head and see her face, to have some idea of what was going through her mind. He could see her fingertips protruding from the voluminous sleeves, worrying at the frayed hem, obviously deep in thought herself.

'Are you going to sleep in that?' He hadn't meant to think aloud, but it had been verbalised now.

Raemil turned from the window and faced him. The sun filtering through almost seemed to cause a halo around her, throwing her face into more shadow.

'I suppose so. I have every night thus far.'

'Don't you think it's time to take that thing off? It's only me. Can't you trust me?' All he wanted was to know her face.

Raemil was taken by surprise. She suddenly realised it was much easier to say no when they were yelling at each other. To have him ask so quietly, so gently, left her mind scrambling for a response. To her horror, he stood and walked toward her. Even though she was certain he couldn't see her face, it seemed like he was staring right at her. She felt like a trapped animal and her palms began to sweat and her heart felt like it was going to beat its way out of her chest. He stopped before her. She was hyper-aware of just how close he was. She stared at her feet so hard she thought her gaze might burn a hole through her boot.

'I am deformed,' she blurted, a mixture of humiliation and relief rushed over her and she thought she might just faint to escape him and this awful situation.

It wasn't an image or a thought that she wanted to leave him with. She'd hoped that she could remain a mystery to him, not some hideous misshapen thing. It wasn't exactly true, but it was an easy explanation for her covered face. It was an easy lie that her father told the servants, then the court, then all of Caelin, once they realised she wasn't going to make his life easier by just dying.

'Nobody sees me because of it. It has naught to do with you and whether or not I trust you. I never want to look at anyone's face again as they see mine for the first time. So please stop asking.' She said it all to her feet.

Moments passed in silence. Eventually, she looked up to see he was gone. She didn't know if he'd heard her last confession or not.

Lestadt sat alone at the bar with a drink in hand, replaying the awful conversation. He could have kicked himself for pushing her. He wasn't sure if he really believed her. A part of him thought she was lying, yet the more sensible part of him believed that he just didn't want it to be true.

She couldn't even face him when she was telling him. He had turned to leave, annoyed that she was so defensive, so distrusting of him, and then he had heard the last comment. To think she'd seen so many terrible reactions to her own face that caused her to cover it was incredibly sad. He didn't know what to say to that. He didn't want her to see the pity he felt for her at that moment either, so he left the room without saying anything, not sure if a pitying face or silence was worse. He downed his drink and ordered another, hoping that becoming drunk may somehow fix the situation.

Raemil sat in the tub. The water had long since gone tepid, but she barely noticed. Her mind refused to think of the incident with Lestadt. She dredged up other awful memories, trying to get some perspective. Over and over in her mind played the things that she had seen and heard and felt and done. How could a bird speak to her? What would drive a man to behead his wife and children? Where did the voices come from? Why did they want her to go home? There were so many questions to be answered and no one to answer them.

Now more than ever she wanted to discover more about her mother and her heritage, but she had to find Serrin first. Raemil snapped out of it as she felt the goose bumps, realising the water was cold. She was in need of something to cheer her up and make herself feel human again, and her new dress might just give her that.

After her bath, she spun before the mirror, the dress complementing her figure. *At least this one part of me is well made,* she thought as she pulled her cowl over her eyes and hair. On rare occasions, she wanted everyone to see her and accept her, but she knew it was silly to buy nice things that no one would see. She'd never be one of *them.*

'Finally. I thought you were lost.' Lestadt was overly cheerful as he pulled a wooden stool out for her.

Raemil had finally found the courage to come down stairs. She'd have to face him eventually. She appreciated the attempt at forgetting the conversation they'd had earlier and was all too glad to pretend it never happened. Raemil took the offered stool and ordered herself a wine.

A band was set up in the far corner of the room and were playing merry tunes while people danced. Some of the drunkards began singing; it wasn't a particularly pleasant sound. The words were at times incomprehensible, the crowd slurring heavily until reaching the chorus, which the whole room seemed to shout. The good cheer was almost contagious, or perhaps the wine was. It seemed to go straight to her head.

Seeing her foot tapping to the beat, Lestadt rose and offered his hand.

'Would you like to dance, Raemil?' His grin set to maximum charm.

Mesmerised, she could not resist. She found herself standing as though her feet moved of their own accord.

They danced at a brusque pace around the floor. Raemil was pleasantly surprised that Lestadt wasn't a bad dancer. He tripped once, but she figured it had more to do with the liquor he'd consumed rather than his skill. She hadn't had a male partner to dance with since Serrin. After a particularly lonely first ball, she had stopped going.

'Where did you learn to dance? I'm surprised. You don't seem like the type,' she said as he whirled her.

'Nor do you. I learnt at village parties. And *you?*'

'In ballrooms.' Raemil laughed as he spun her around and nearly let go.

She felt as though she would have flown around the room like a wooden spinning top. He flashed that smile again, assuming she had made a joke.

Raemil and Lestadt sat back down at the bar when the song ended. Both were a little out of breath. Feeling mischievous, Raemil ordered another wine. She'd gotten away with the truth in the guise of a lie.

'I never thought you would be a drinker,' Lestadt said, watching her gulp down the wine.

'No? What do you think I am?'

Lestadt laughed. 'Incredibly complicated, it seems.'

As the night progressed, Lestadt and Raemil became more intoxicated. Raemil wasn't exactly a seasoned drinker, her mind felt fuzzy, but she was enjoying herself. Both of their inhibitions decreased, and, hearing a slow song start up, Lestadt couldn't resist the chance to hold her close.

He took Raemil's hand in his and led her away from the bar. In the beginning, Raemil was reluctant to come too close, but as they danced, inch by inch, Lestadt drew her in. She was disarmed by his dimples as he grinned while pulling her closer.

He so rarely had an excuse to have her this close, especially now he had his own horse. He had resisted his impulses many times, but now there was no stopping. He pulled her body firmly against his.

Reaching beneath her hood, he cupped her soft cheek in his hand. She froze but did not move away. He ran his thumb across her lips, and he felt them part as she drew in a breath, but still she did not move away from him. In fact, he was sure she leaned in just that bit closer. Without further hesitation, he leaned right in and kissed her. It was a slow and gentle kiss, hesitant at first, neither of them sure of the other. He could feel a slow burn of yearning as they became more confident and held each other tighter.

It was over too quickly. A fight broke out behind them and the crowd ran back toward Lestadt and Raemil. They were forced apart as people rudely pushed between them, eager to stay clear of the violence. In the rush of bodies and confusion, Raemil disappeared. He leaned against the bar, suddenly feeling quite stupid for stealing a kiss. Her disappearance did nothing to bolster his confidence.

Raemil slipped from the room; there were too many people crowding. She stood before the large mirror in the washroom, glaring at her hooded face for a long time. She had an odd feeling in the pit of her stomach. Her cheeks were hot and if she peered closely, they were two round circles of ruby red on a pale face.

She wondered why Lestadt had kissed her, especially after she had practically yelled in his face that she was deformed. It seemed an odd time to want to kiss her. *Was it the liquor?* She had been attracted to him the moment that she had met him, *but what did it mean to him? Was it pity? Some kind of cruel joke?* After several minutes of confused and drunken reasoning, Raemil left the washroom, still confused and drunk.

She didn't look up as she re-entered the bar and ordered a shot of whiskey. She'd seen others do it and thought it might help. She practically coughed it up in the bar-keep's face. Embarrassed, she turned away, and realised the whole bar room was in an uproar. She had just weaved her way through a massive fight without noticing. People were shouting so loud that words lost all meaning in the din. There were bottles being smashed and people being beaten with the wooden stools. She stood on her tip-toes to see if she could spy Lestadt.

He was in the far corner of the room. He'd even managed to get into an argument and at present, had his hand tangled in the man's shirt-collar. Raemil tried to get his attention by waving her arms, but there were too many projectiles flying around the room to gain his attention that way.

A large man tapped her on the shoulder. Raemil turned to face him as he started bellowing at her like a stuck pig. She couldn't hear what he was saying. He blasted stinky beer-breath and spittle at her. Unappreciative of his stench, and the saliva that came with it, she turned away again.

The man caught Raemil from behind and swung her around to face him again. A surge of utter panic went through her and she tried to squirm away. He started bellowing again. She could see the veins sticking out of his neck, obviously furious about some insult he'd imagined. Desperate to escape, Raemil kicked him in the shin, but he didn't even flinch. He only became angrier and grabbed a bottle that had been sitting on the bar, smashing it against the edge. Raemil was sure he was going to stab her. She struggled desperately and heard a ripping sound, but at that point nothing mattered but her escape. Something gave and she fell to the bloody floor on her knees.

Suddenly the room went silent and still.

Lestadt caught sight of the man threatening Raemil with a broken bottle and tried to break through the crowd. By the time he reached halfway, Raemil was on the ground. He stood there shocked, unable to move or think, much like every other person in the room. He watched as Raemil slowly looked down, almost as though she didn't want to see herself. She realised she was no longer wearing her cloak. Their eyes locked. She was absolutely mortified, laid bare for all to see.

Lestadt gazed into her bright green eyes and remembered. He remembered lying on the ground in a pool of his own blood, a huge mountain lion on top of him and there was the hooded woman, Raemil. As she raced to his defence, her hood blew back, revealing the same long red hair and brilliant green eyes. She was the warrior woman he had seen and then forgotten as he lay dying.

Raemil was trembling. He had seen. They were all seeing her, exposed for what she was: a freak. The room erupted again, but this time, all the hate, all the vicious energy, was all directed at her.

'Witch!' cried one woman.

'Evil! Disgusting!' cried a man behind her.

There were shouts and taunts coming from all over the room. People picked up their pieces of splintered wood, the stools, broken bottles or whatever they could find, and heaved forward as one. Lestadt was knocked down and lost somewhere in the surge of bodies.

Raemil could feel a strange tingling sensation run through her body and out to her fingertips. She couldn't get off the floor. All she could see, all she could hear, were the people at the first village of Caelin; the woman in the yellow dress, the preacher and his wife, then Thysirra and Thenysies from the second village. All of them angry, hateful and cruel, all wanting her blood.

Raemil was engulfed by a white light. Her veins bulged in her arms. She could feel the sting of energy flow through her. Her palms lay flat on the ground and from each finger, a crack wound its way through the bar-room floor. People leapt back as the ground quaked and the floor began to split and lift. People dived for safety as great splinters of floorboard shot up into the air, carried by the violently shifting ground.

Through the falling debris from the unsettled dust and the collapsing ceiling, Raemil saw Lestadt, crouching against the bar, his eyes wide with both shock and fear. The bottles of liquor vibrated off the shelves and smashed on the floor. The support beams around the room were cracking. One snapped and part of the ceiling caved in near the fireplace. People were screaming and diving for the exits.

Someone ran toward Raemil and kicked her hard in the ribs. She recoiled and the noise and the shifting floors stopped. All went silent again. Without wasting another moment, Raemil scrambled to her feet. Some people had regained some composure and were again rushing for her. Raemil became like a wild animal surrounded and trapped on all sides, instinct and desperation took over. She kicked a man hard in the stomach, at the same time bringing her elbow back hard and fast, hitting another man in the throat. He immediately dropped to the ground, gasping for air. Turning again, she tripped one man backward and punched him at the same time. He stumbled and landed heavily on his back.

Lestadt couldn't reach Raemil, there were too many people pushing and shoving. He watched in amazement as she fought her way toward the doors. She was brutal, kicking men and women here, punching and elbowing people there. She was a wild creature, let loose from the cloak that had contained her.

She was knocked to the floor but, undeterred, she kicked two men over, giving herself enough space to get to her feet. With a final, well-timed elbow to another man's nose, she shoved the door open and fled into the night.

Lestadt fought his way out too; he didn't want her to leave without him. He dived after her in time to see her coming from the side of the verandah with her belongings in one arm and Lylah tucked under the other. He tried to call out as she jumped over the small, white fence, but his voice was lost in the noise of the crowd as they burst from the bar.

Lestadt dashed around the corner and climbed in the window to their room, gathering his belongings. He whistled for Bonnie, who was standing there, torn between following after Raemil or following him. With an excited yap, she ran for Lestadt. He ran down to the stables and saddled Steel, ignoring the horse's biting and dodging his kicks. The cool air and the shock of the whole scene had at least helped to sober him somewhat.

Bonnie ran ahead of Steel. She seemed to know what was needed of her and she raced into the night, sniffing as she went.

23. A time for faith.

Isran stormed out of the chamber; she was so frustrated and tired. Reenah hadn't spoken to her since the truth about her mother was revealed. It had been three days. The king, queen and prince of Byrass stayed to help contact Kyler, but the task was proving difficult.

She began searching anew in the library. These particular books were passed down from generation to generation, some were over three hundred years old. Many told more about the history of magic and the ancestors of the sisters than about spells. Isran sat down at the big blackwood table and began the tedious search through yet another book.

Before the mages and mortals of Otowan fled to Iadron, Sirron was united under one ruling king and queen. When the king and queen died, their son had long been missing, presumed dead at sea, so the eldest daughter Oesyth became queen. Knowing that she would live a long life and caring little for marriage and heirs, Oesyth kept her sisters, Isran and Elyr, by her side. Over the years, the sisters had gained a reputation among their people, especially during the wars after the influx of mages from Otowan. They were fierce and protective of the people of Sirron, each equal in both rule and power. Eventually, their brother came home. He claimed the title of King of Sirron and by rights it was his for the taking. The people did not want to lose their sisters who had been so just and fair in their ruling.

In the end, it was bargained that Oesyth, Isran and Elyr would rule West

Sirron, and their brother, Koraldan, would rule the North, South and East lands of Sirron. They renounced the title of queens and adopted the much-preferred name 'the Sisters'. They met their half-sister, Kyler, when they were battling for control of Sirron in a desperate time when the fighting between mages and mortals seemed like it would never end. She came to fight for the sisters, earning her a place with them when their rule was diminished to West Sirron only.

Kyler was a wild thing. Living in the palace and governing a city was not for her. Once the battles were over and peace developed, Kyler said her goodbyes and left. The sisters had kept in contact with Kyler over the years, but hardly ever in person, as their half-sister never liked to stay in one place.

Isran remembered the last time they had seen Kyler in person. She'd turned up at the bridge-port, both frightened and bloody. Kyler held a tiny bundle wrapped in a bed sheet; she passed it to Isran. This tiny bundle was baby Reenah. She did not say who the father was or what brought her to their doorstep. She left baby Reenah with the sisters and disappeared back over the bridge and out of her daughter's life.

The last time they had all spoken more than a few words was through the stone. After her battle with Bascillium, Kyler requested to be forgotten. Despite their wayward sister's request, they tried to scry her out. That was when they glimpsed the other baby, the lost daughter. Sensing their intrusion, Kyler blocked them instantly. They had not seen or heard from her since. The sisters knew she was not coming back for her first born. They raised Reenah as their own. When Reenah was thirteen, they told her who her mother was. They made the decision to tell her that she was dead, rather than admitting Kyler had abandoned her.

Isran eventually found a spell she thought might work. She brought the book into the study where Oesyth, Elyr and the king and queen of Byrass waited.

'Where is Reenah?' Isran asked, ignoring the impatient looks from her sisters.

'She took the carriage into the city with Prince Tylon,' Oesyth replied.

'It mightn't matter. With the king and queen's help, we may not need her.' Isran placed the open book on a desk.

'Well? What have you found?' Elyr pressed.

'We have been looking for spells to commune with her, and have had no luck...'

'Get on with it, we don't need a speech about it,' Oesyth sighed impatiently.

'I am merely pointing out our mistake for future reference,' came the equally snappy reply. 'I have found something to bring her here to us. We must scry her out again. If we can feel her now, I think her spell to block us has weakened or even broken. With the king and queen's help, we can draw her back here.' Isran gave the book to Oesyth to read before motioning all to follow her to the stone room.

The sisters gathered around, placing their hands on the stone. Closing their eyes, they began to seek out their sister. Images of lands long forgotten flickered through their minds, smells and sounds, and even tastes, came to them and, suddenly, darkness. They had hit The Nothing before and made no progress. Isran could feel Elyr begin to pull back, to give up, but she stubbornly pushed through.

The king and queen of Byrass watched as the emerald stone flared into brilliance. They were feeling too, but not in the trance-like state the sisters were. They were waiting for the sisters to give them Kyler so they could lend their strength at the right time. Their presence in seeking would likely be more of a hinderance at this point.

Feeling a change in their path, distinct in its feel and sound, the sisters came through the darkness into blinding light. Their seeking brought them to an orchard. There were rows and rows of apple trees; their fruit was not red but golden. Isran was the first to imagine herself into something resembling herself, followed by Oesyth and Elyr. It was not truly them, only their spirits. Their physical bodies were still in the chamber in West Sirron.

A woman sat on the ground behind one of the trees. Her alabaster skin was bruised and scratched. She was covering her ears and rocking back and forth. Oesyth moved toward her, motioning for the other two to follow.

'Kyler?' Her voice was whispery. Already the sisters' hold on the place was weakening.

It took great strength to be so far from their bodies.

Quick as a flash, the woman leapt to her feet, her wild, golden eyes roaming their faces.

'You are not truly here, not here, not here... No, no, not you three. They cannot harm you... No, not them,' she was rambling.

Her red dress was in tatters and her hair was knotted into a dreadlock down her back. Without further hesitation, Oesyth grabbed the woman's wrists. Isran and Elyr rushed in to help. She struggled against the wraith-like sisters, biting and scratching, but she was not strong enough to harm them.

Urgently, they summoned the king and queen of Byrass, opening a passage to the strange orchard. The Byrassians reached for their power-stones on their necklaces. With their power combined to form a temporary coven, the mages dragged the deranged woman home.

Suddenly, the stone flared into blinding emerald, engulfing the whole room in its brilliance. The sisters snapped back into bodies that were previously slumped in chairs. Everyone in the room stared at the demented creature on the chamber floor. The woman writhed on the ground, giggling, then screaming and clawing at the floor.

'What now?' asked Elyr as she turned away, the sight of her sister too disturbing to watch.

'I've no idea.' Oesyth's hand trembled as she brushed a stray, golden lock out of her eyes.

'We cannot let Reenah see her mother like this. Let's get her into a room while we work out what comes next,' Isran added.

They were all exhausted from expending so much power, despite them all sharing the load. They still had much to organise and protection spells to cast. They didn't know what caused Kyler to be this way.

'Reenah...? Reenah?'

'Hmm?' She turned from the carriage window toward his worried face. 'Oh, sorry, Tylon. I was just thinking.'

They'd taken a ride through the city to help clear her head. It hadn't worked.

'What's on your mind?'

She frowned. 'What *isn't* on my mind?'

'If this is about Kyler, I don't see how it could be so bad. Yes, you were lied to, but it doesn't mean they don't love you. And as for your mother, her leaving you says nothing about you. It doesn't mean she didn't love you. You don't know why she left; she hasn't had the chance to explain. Shouldn't you at least give her that chance?'

'You're right, I know nothing about her. You must have thought about this a lot.' She smirked. 'You're getting wise in your old age.'

The prince laughed. 'I *have* been thinking about it a lot. When we were on the coast for my birthday, you were there for me when I needed it. I met a different Reenah then. She smiled a lot and she was funny. Now you won't smile and I can barely engage you in a conversation, let alone get you to make a joke. I just don't like seeing you like this.'

'I'm sorry, I'm not great company at the moment...'

'Any company with you is good company,' he said with a wink.

Reenah blushed and directed her stare out the carriage window again and silence fell between them. Tylon stuck his head out the window and motioned for the driver to stop. 'Stay in the carriage, Reenah,' he said nervously before climbing out.

'What's happening out there?'

She heard the murmur of many angry voices. She poked her head out the window to see an angry mob of city folk heading their way.

Prince Tylon ran his fingers through his pale hair in agitation. He wasn't getting anywhere with the people of West Sirron.

'One person at a time! I cannot understand you!' he shouted above the noise.

Again, everyone spoke at once. They clearly weren't an organised crowd.

'You!' Prince Tylon bellowed above the din, adding a touch of power to his voice to make it carry.

He pointed to a middle-aged man with dark brown, almost black, hair. He was standing at the front of the crowd, possibly the only one not trying to shout over everyone else.

'You. Tell me the meaning of this,' the prince demanded.

The man stepped forward and gave the prince a small bow. In his hands, he fiddled nervously with a black cap. Eventually, he looked up. His brown eyes were steady on Tylon's.

'Prince Tylon. I... we, the people of West Sirron, we want to know what's going on,' he said slowly, searching for the right words to do his tale justice.

'Go on,' said the prince, still utterly confused.

The Byrassians were well known to the people of West Sirron; they were respected amongst the West-Sirronese.

'Three days ago,' the man began again, his voice wavering with emotion, 'my wife was hanging our linen out to dry, carrying our eight-month-old daughter. I heard a terrible scream. I ran outside to find a creature attacking my wife...' The man paused, wiping tears from his eyes before continuing, determined to finish. 'There was blood everywhere. My... my daughter was on the ground, covered in blood. She was dead. My wife was screaming, struggling with the thing. I tried to help, but I was knocked out of the way. When I woke up, my wife, my daughter, my whole life... destroyed.' The man wept openly and faded back into the crowd.

'Half of my cattle were killed last night! Half! My family cannot live on half of a herd! Something ripped them to pieces!' a man shouted from the back.

'Prince! Prince!' A woman waved for Tylon's attention. 'Two nights ago my brother went out to check the fences. I've not seen him since... What happened to him?' She looked to the tall prince, pleading for answers.

'My son, he came home from tending our sheep last night. He was blinded. I asked him what happened, and you know what he said? He said he tore his eyes out to stop the monster from getting inside. He ripped out his own eyes! What are these things? What can make a person do that?' cried yet another man.

Prince Tylon stepped back from the crowd; his blood ran cold at what he was hearing.

'Gods,' he whispered, staring out over the crowd of West Sirronese.

He knew what was happening, but his lips could not speak it, not to a city that was not his. Then he wondered, what of his father's kingdom? They had left the trusted duke in charge. *How fared he if Byrass was hit with this horror?*

'We go now to the bridge's port. We must speak to the sisters; we'll stay there until we get some answers if we must,' called another voice.

Prince Tylon could do nothing to stop them; he turned his back and strode to the carriage.

Reenah was sitting close to the window when Tylon sat down inside. She gave him a shocked look; it was obvious she had the same thought, that they needed to get back to the bridge first. The crowd had already moved past the carriage. Tylon was about to open his mouth when Reenah called to the driver, ordering him to get them back to the palace fast.

Isran looked out the window. The sun was setting over the city. The sight took her breath away; soft pinks and purples reflected off the white rooftops in the city. She shuddered when she heard a screech from behind one of the doors, an ugly contrast to the beautiful dusk.

She saw a carriage careering through the streets of West Sirron. The grey horses were running wild, worked into a sweat she could see lathered around their harness. A mist formed over the lake, and then the white bridge appeared, connecting the palace to the city. Without stopping, the horses galloped across and onto the palace grounds; the bridge vanishing quickly behind them.

* * *

'They have been out there for two nights now, something must be done,' Elyr said quietly to Isran.

Though the sisters were considered equals, ultimately, they waited for Oesyth to make the decision.

'Oesyth?' Elyr turned to their eldest, receiving only a shrug from Isran.

'We cannot lie to our people, nor should we keep them in the dark.'

The sisters stood in a plain sitting room in front of the large arched window, staring down at hundreds of their citizens gathered at the bridge-port. They had pitched tents and as dusk fell they lit fires around and within the mob.

Reenah sat in an armchair at the back of the room, absently combing her long, black hair with her fingers. The last two days had been a nightmare. She had become too close to the prince. She would be disappointed when he had to leave, but he was not hers to keep. Worse, she could hear her mother's awful screams and ravings in the middle of the night and shuddered to think what lay behind those bedroom doors. She had promised Isran she would not go in there. The very idea repulsed her, yet late at night, she could hear and feel the insane woman beckoning.

'We'll hold a meeting in an hour, in the garden,' Oesyth said.

Prince Tylon and the king and queen of Byrass needed to return to their own city, but the crowd rushed forward as soon as the bridge appeared. The royals of Byrass were forced to abandon the bridge. A dozen or so people fell into the lake as the bridge disappeared from beneath them. The Byrassians were trapped until the crowd could be dispersed.

* * *

Chains ran from the bed to the furthest corner of the dimly lit room, where a pale figure leaned against the wall. She was like a sick rat, hunched in the corner away from the light.

The insane woman peered out at Isran from beneath a mass of Kyler's knotted hair. She giggled, her long yellow fingernails gently scraping against the wall. A dying bracelet of what looked like daisy-chains hung from her bony wrist.

'I've been waiting for you.' She smiled. Her lips were cracked and bleeding. There were sores around her mouth from licking her lips.

Isran said nothing. She sat just out of reach on the floor, should the mad woman rush at her.

'Did you bring the child?' she asked, her grin splitting her lips further.

Isran was determined to find Kyler. She knew she was still somewhere inside the demented thing before her. She had spent most of the last two days inside the dark room with the woman, projecting images and memories at her. The memories didn't seem to affect the woman at all. Strangely, she seemed only interested in Reenah. She just asked over and over, *'Where is the child?'*

'Give her to me,' the woman moaned and clawed at the wall, scratching the paint away.

'What child?' Isran asked innocently.

'The child, the child, you remember!' she cried, crawling toward Isran on her hands and knees, dragging the chains behind her.

Isran went as far into her mind as she dared, showing her memories of them together that had nothing to do with Reenah.

'Kyler's not here, she's not here, she's not here,' the mad woman sing-songed like a child.

Isran showed Kyler handing baby Reenah to her at the bridge-port.

'Fucking... f-fuck, give me the fucking child!' she screamed and leapt at Isran, but the chains pulled her up short.

Such profanity just didn't seem real coming from Kyler's mouth. Isran looked into her golden eyes. 'What do you want with Reenah?'

'Reenah...' She rolled the name on her tongue as if hearing it for the first time. 'Reenah! Reenah! Reenah!' She clapped her hands and giggled with delight. 'Give me Reenah?'

Exasperated, Isran left the room as the woman began to scream Reenah's name. She locked the door behind her and turned to see Reenah standing there, looking confused and tired.

'I heard my name.'

'She asks for you, Reenah. Listen to me. You mustn't go in that room, do you understand?' Isran pleaded, clasping Reenah's shoulders. 'Not now, not alone. Promise me.'

Reenah looked at the door behind Isran. As far as she was concerned, it was the gateway to hell and nothing would make her happier than to stay well clear of it. Yet something pulled at her, begging her to enter.

Reenah looked back to Isran and nodded. Isran placed the key in her pocket as she walked away. Reenah stared at the door a moment longer, resisting the urge to break through it, before turning away. She had not told anyone about the strange allure of the woman inside that room. She didn't want to worry anyone when there was so much already to worry about.

Torches flickered in the warm breeze; the stars shone brightly in the night sky. It would have been a pleasant evening had the meeting been for any other reason. The garden was packed with people. Some had brought their animals, not wanting to leave them unguarded in the threatening night. People wound their way through the garden maze, peering over the hedges, trying to get a glimpse of the sisters.

The guards stood between the crowd and the sisters, Reenah, the prince and king and queen of Byrass.

'People of West Sirron,' Oesyth began, extending her arms toward them. 'I wish that it were not such grave news that brings you all here tonight. I have heard of the attacks in the night, stock has been lost, people have been hurt, and people have died. We are indeed under a threat from across the Sapphire seas.'

There were gasps and some hushed voices complained from the back rows.

'Otowan will be first to fall in this terror, but Iadron will follow, unless...' Oesyth was cut short by the crowd erupting in panic.

'Unless!' Oesyth roared, silencing the people again. 'Unless we stand together to face the evil. We have time. This can be beaten.'

'What can be beaten? Exactly what are we facing?' a man asked, stepping from the crowd to peer over a guard at Oesyth.

'A sorceress in the land of Otowan, a full-blood,' Oesyth admitted as she looked over the sea of frightened faces.

'What sorceress?'

'Full-blood?'

'Why? Why us? Why come here?'

'How can they be beaten?'

'Who can kill a full-blood?'

The silver-haired mage stepped forward this time to speak. 'This threat is called Horsham, a survivor from the old days in Otowan before the earth goddess cursed the full-bloods with infertility with one another. She is possibly hundreds of years old and very dangerous. Her motive is revenge. She seeks revenge on mortals and probably anyone who stands to protect you,' Isran said, looking pointedly at her sisters, niece, and the Byrassian rulers.

People's faces were distraught, yet Isran saw them transform before her eyes. They understood.

Isran reminded them that the sisters and the Byrassians would protect their people, even if it compromised their own safety.

'Horsham will destroy Otowan, the land of the betrayers across the Sapphire Seas, first because that is where the original betrayal lies. Thousands died and Horsham was trapped in the mountains. But she will come to Iadron. She will not be satisfied until every mortal has suffered at her hands. And so it has begun. These creatures of the night, this is the first attack.' Isran stepped back and Oesyth stepped forward again.

'The good king, queen and prince of Byrass will help us. Together our kingdoms can form a barrier. We can try to stop her from coming across the Sapphire seas. We are searching for answers. We are looking for a way to defeat Horsham, but my good people, you must have faith in us. We must stand together or we stand to lose everything.'

The crowd stood silent. All that could be heard were the chirping cicadas and the hum of the willow moths' wings around the torches.

An old man stepped forward. Removing his cap, he placed his hand on his heart and bent on one knee. 'You stand for us, and so I will for you. You have my faith and my service always, great Sisters of West Sirron,' he said, bowing his head.

Slowly, the people followed the old man's example. The citizens bent their knees to the sisters and the Byrassians.

24. Hunger gully.

The Black skidded to a halt in a cloud of dust, visible in the moon's light. There was nothing but a few twisted trees and dark shapes on the ground. Raemil hoped they were only bushes. She had no idea where she was going; she couldn't even be sure she was heading toward Horsham.

Hearing a shout, Raemil turned to see the glow of torches flickering in the hands of her pursuers. They raced after her on horses and some on foot, carrying swords, pikes, axes, and some carrying rakes and brooms. Spinning the Black around again, they galloped away from the town.

The shouts were loud enough for her to hear a few distinct words, which she wished she hadn't. The Black was beginning to tire as he bound up a hill and the sound of pounding hooves grew louder behind them. Raemil put her hand on the hilt of her sword, her heart was beating wildly. Despite Lestadt's doubts about her ability to protect herself, she knew right now if it were a choice between some villager's life and hers, she would choose her own.

Raemil unsheathed her sword and twisted in the saddle, swinging furiously at an oncoming attacker. Her sword struck metal and stopped. Panting, she saw Lestadt deflecting her blow. She withdrew and veered away from Lestadt and Steel.

'Raemil! Wait!' he called, urging Steel up the hill behind the fleeing Black.

Something drove her to keep running, especially from him. Her mind was still muddled from the wine and the kiss, though the incident in the bar had sobered her considerably. As the Black began the descent on the other side of the hill, Raemil could see a gully below and directed him there. She could hear Lestadt on Steel right behind her.

The people of Vagamore reached the top of the hill. Their torches burned as brightly as their hatred of the witch. Looking around, they spotted a grey horse racing into the gully below. The people cried out for the witch's blood, raising their torches and weapons high as they sprinted down the hill toward their quarry.

As they reached the high walls of the cliff on either side of the gully, they stopped. A small group of people at the back of the crowd broke away and ran back toward Vagamore. The rest milled at the entrance a little longer. They were frightened of this place and teetered on the edge of indecision. The crowd eventually moved on, hoping the witch would die in the gully.

As she and the Black fled deeper into the dark, they could barely see through the twisting gorge. Lestadt and Steel tried to keep up with Raemil and the Black.

'Raemil! Stop!' Lestadt yelled frantically as he pulled Steel to a halt.

Raemil peered back into the darkness but there was so little light and she had no desire to linger. She urged the Black to keep moving, just as there was a loud hiss and the sound of a sword leaving its sheath.

Raemil spun the Black and he leapt into a gallop, back the way that they had come.

'Lestadt?!' she cried as she reached Steel, but Lestadt had vanished.

She put Lylah on the ground and slid from her horse's back, drawing her sword as she crept toward the grey gelding. Steel flared his nostrils and backed away. His muscles quivered as he shook his head and stomped his hooves in warning.

The cloud shifted from the moon and bathed the gully in light, revealing a gash on Steel's wither. It appeared to be claw marks. There was a squeal from behind and she spun to see Lylah racing toward her in wild panic. Two yellow eyes appeared in the darkness behind the little fawn as it bounded for Raemil. A large grey cat leapt toward Lylah. Without a second thought, Raemil raced to Lylah's defence. The cat bit down around Lylah's body, the tiny animal nearly disappearing into the cat's maw. With a jab and a slice, Raemil slit open the creature's belly, spilling its contents onto the ground and releasing Lylah from its jaws. Lylah had a few grazes, nothing more.

Raemil took a piece of rope from one of her saddle bags, looping one end over the Black's neck then the other over Steel's. She picked Lylah up and climbed back on the Black. Steel was strangely compliant at this point, taking comfort from his odd, new herd.

She discovered two dead cats and a dark pool of blood but no sign of Lestadt and she feared the worst. She studied the bodies of the cats, having never seen such creatures before. They were grey, with two stubby horns on the tops of their heads. They had short, stumpy tails and long bodies with short, powerful legs.

Fear and grief warred with each other and she didn't want to leave, but it was too dangerous to linger. Raemil's eyes burned with the threat of tears as she turned the horses away. Raemil called out to Lestadt again, hearing it echo off the cliffs, but there was no reply. She hoped Bonnie was with him and that they were keeping each other safe.

As the sun crept over the horizon, the cliffs still cast a shadow in the gully and everything was still, grey and cold. The cliffs were grey slate with caves that pocketed the walls, the rocks were mostly jagged and sharp. Raemil's arms loosened around the fawn as she stared blankly ahead. She was lost in another world. Her face was set hard, determined to keep from facing the possibility that Lestadt was dead.

Steel reared then began to buck and kick wildly, straining against the rope around his neck. Raemil was jolted from her morose thoughts. Steel's outburst caused the Black to panic. Raemil and the fawn were thrown from his back. The two horses charged off down the gully and out of sight in a cloud of dust.

Raemil stared after them in disbelief. She bent down to put Lylah on the ground and the fawn struggled, grunting and spitting. She ignored the tantrum and plopped her down anyway. Lylah froze with her front leg peculiarly raised. Raemil called her, but the fawn remained unresponsive. As Raemil approached, Lylah dropped to the ground on her side, becoming as motionless as a rock. With a chill running down her spine, Raemil realised Lylah was playing dead.

Out the corner of her eye, Raemil saw something move. She turned but could see nothing but the grey cliff. As she turned back to the fawn, something shifted again. Again, when she turned there was nothing. Raemil studied a smooth piece of slate sitting two feet higher than her head. She could have sworn something had moved near it. Great yellow eyes suddenly appeared and Raemil's mouth grew dry.

Raemil watched, stunned and immobile, as dozens of grey cats slinked down the cliffs toward her and the fawn from both sides. They'd been riding past cliffs that were heavily populated by dozing cats all morning.

He battled atop the cliff through the night and into the morning. His sword wavered in his tired hands. Blood trickled along his arm in rivulets and dripped at his feet. The shepherd fought bravely beside him. She, too, had been injured, but she would defend Lestadt as fiercely as he defended her.

Using all his strength, he hacked into another cat before two more came to replace it. Bonnie leapt at one, growling and snapping. She was caught in her side by a blunt horn. She flipped around, hackles raised and teeth bared.

During the night, the cats attacked suddenly, knocking Lestadt from his mount and clawing the grey gelding. Lestadt fought free and drew his sword to find the cats had taken Bonnie and headed up the side of the cliff. Lestadt chased them up the cliff to rescue the shepherd and that was when the cats had stalked by the dozens to the hunt.

Eventually, Lestadt dropped his sword and collapsed to the ground in exhaustion. Beside him, Bonnie whined and dropped too. Three more cats slinked out of the gully toward them. The shepherd moved to defend her master when something distracted her. She cocked her head, listening, scenting, and feeling the change in the air.

Bonnie began to howl; the cats became confused and scared. The felines advanced no further, listening too. The birds went silent, the wind dropped. Everything seemed to hold its breath in anticipation. The ground began to shift. The cats hissed and leapt down the side of the cliff as the earth heaved violently beneath them. Lestadt staggered to his feet, peering over the edge and down into the gully. Rocks tumbled and smashed into pieces as they bounced off each other. He couldn't see around the twists and bends, but he could hear cats roaring and screaming, and imagined they were getting crushed by the crumbling cliffs. He scrambled backward as the ground began to drop from beneath him.

Once the quake subsided, Lestadt and Bonnie climbed down into the gully and continued in the direction he presumed Raemil had gone. A cloud of dust and debris hung in the air, making visibility poor. Wiping the sweat and dust from his face with the bottom of his shirt, he scanned ahead. Through the haze, he could see shapes shifting toward them, too big to be cats. As they came closer, he could make out the shape of a black horse. He recognised Steel a few seconds later; his grey coat was harder to see in the shroud of dust.

Steel and the Black were tied together. They danced, both skittish and reluctant to come too close. He reached slowly toward Steel, running his hand over Steel's arched nose then carefully down his back. He watched the horse visibly relax. The gelding had come a long way since Lestadt had bought him at the market. He'd spent many hours trying to get the horse to trust him, but some things would take longer. Steel turned and bit Lestadt's shoulder hard. He spun around and prepared to run, but the Black wasn't interested in playing games. The taller horse leaned back, stopping Steel from taking off. Lestadt grabbed Steel's reins and removed the rope from their necks.

Lestadt refused to believe Raemil was in the gully when the cats attacked. He didn't want to think about the possibility that she could be dead.

Raemil opened her eyes and squinted at the glare of the midday sun. She was exhausted and could barely remember where she was or how she had gotten there. Sitting up, she could see she was on the bank of a river. The current was fast and carried twigs, leaves and small branches downstream. Far behind her was the mouth of the gully, a cloud of dust still hanging above it. She had caused it, she knew it now, and as grateful as she was, she also hated what she had done, what she could *do*.

She'd been knocked down by two of the cats, their claws dug deep into her flesh, a horn bruised her side, and a mouth of sharp teeth wrapped around her arm. She somehow found the strength to fight them off. She put her hands on the rocky cliff and concentrated all her energy into it, feeling power flow through her veins and into the stone. She ran from the gully with Lylah under her arm while boulders and debris crashed all around her.

She was completely drained of energy; she had felt this way before. There was no more denying what she was. She had caused the quake in the Caelinian village, she had entered the Black's mind, she had entered Gorran's. She killed the fish at Tagrahan Lake and she had caused two more quakes since. She had used magic; she didn't quite know what to call herself. She was too exhausted to think.

Lylah grazed nearby and Raemil gave the fawn a pat as she walked past. It was a beautiful river. Trees hung low over the water, their leaves dipping and swaying in the current. Raemil peered at her reflection and still couldn't believe that Lestadt had seen that face and that hair. She didn't want to believe she may never see him again, never look into those bright blue eyes or see his beautiful smile directed at her. Raemil turned away from the water and found herself wiping away tears.

'*It is early days to be crying.*'

Raemil jumped at the sound of a voice. She looked around wildly, but could see nothing.

'Who – who said that?'

'*I did.*'

A crow sat above her in a tree, looking down intently at her.

'I'm going mad,' she whispered.

'*Oh, do not look so surprised, we have spoken before,*' it said, fluffing out its wings.

'Was that you who attacked me?'

'*Yes and no,*' said the crow.

'You either did or you didn't,' Raemil snapped.

'*I did, but I also did not.*' The crow hopped onto a lower branch.

'Do all crows speak nonsense?'

'*Most of the time. I am sorry we attacked you. Sometimes it cannot be helped.*'

'We?'

'*We are many of wing, but one in mind.*'

'Really? No crow has its own mind?'

'*Some do, but we do and we don't. When the change happened, our mind was damaged, somewhat scattered, in fact. Some thoughts can no longer be controlled; thus, some actions cannot be controlled. So, I did and I did not attack you.*' He glided from the tree and onto the ground beside Raemil.

'The change?' Despite herself, Raemil was intrigued, eager for a distraction.

'*When I became us.*' The crow studied Raemil's confused expression, then fluffed out his feathers again, as if shrugging his shoulders. '*It is a long story and one I do not wish to share.*'

'Okay. Why speak to me at all?'

'*We find you fascinating. It has become a hobby to watch people, and we have not come across one like you in a long time.*'

'Like me...?'

'*I know what you are, Raemil, and I know what you face. I shall be watching you.*'

The crow spread his wings and prepared to fly away.

'Wait. What do you mean, you know what I face?'

The crow cocked his head at Raemil and squawked then hopped back from her as if suddenly afraid. She glimpsed pain and suffering, broken homes, maddened animals and people, hunger, war, and fallen kingdoms all in the crow's tiny black eyes before it took wing and flew away.

25. Where the madness lies.

Reenah wandered into the garden and sat by the fountain, running her fingers through the water. She was exhausted, but she feared sleep. In her dreams, her demented mother called her.

'Princess Reenah, I thought you would be with the sisters and my parents.' Prince Tylon startled her as he entered the garden.

'Well, I'm not.'

'Reenah, you look tired. When was the last time you slept?'

'Do not worry over me like I am a child, I am fine.'

Prince Tylon sat beside her on the fountain wall. 'I don't see you as a child at all, I just worry about you. You've had a lot to deal with. I just wish there was something that I could do.'

'You could leave me alone,' she said softly.

'What? Why?'

Reenah looked up at him and could see the hurt in his eyes. She wanted to fall into his arms and sob.

'Please, just leave me alone,' she said instead.

'As you wish.' He left without a backward glance.

Later, as Reenah came out of the garden, she saw Prince Tylon galloping past on his white stallion. He did not see her, nor did he look for her.

Reenah wiped tears away as the prince raced over the bridge and into the city. She could see his belongings tied behind the saddle; he was headed back to Byrass. She felt guilty knowing she had offended him, but she couldn't bear having to say goodbye. It was easier to push him away.

The king and queen of Byrass dined with the sisters in the open dining room. This meant that conversations went no further than the daily duties in their kingdoms. Reenah had lost her appetite. She was so miserable and unbelievably tired, so she poked at her food in disinterest. To make things worse, the queen couldn't stop talking about Prince Tylon's marriage to Princess Yaeli.

'Of course, Tylon is pushing for a castle on the beach,' she was saying. 'He was always at the beach when he was younger, you know. But we cannot expect poor Princess Yaeli to live at the beach, with the dreadful sand blowing into the castle and those noisy birds. It's just not proper.'

Reenah was seething. *Does she care nothing about her son? Who cares if poor little Princess Yaeli doesn't want to get her toes wet, or the gods forbid, a speck of sand in her hair!*

'... And the ceremony! My goodness, he wanted to have a simple wedding in Byrass in private! Now really, we are not talking about the boy next door wedding the farmer's daughter in the back paddock!' The queen chuckled, patting her husband's arm in merriment.

The king barely acknowledged her, his head bent to the task of eating. It was likely he had heard this line of conversation many times over.

'The wedding will take place in Thornbroke. They have lovely gardens and beautiful swans. We will be sending out invitations soon. There will be thousands of guests. Of course you will attend, won't you?' The queen eyed everyone at the table.

Before the sisters had a chance to answer, Reenah butted in. 'What of Prince Tylon? Does he not get a say in his own wedding?'

'Reenah!' Oesyth scolded from across the table.

Isran was trying hard to hide her smirk. She feigned a sudden interest in the intricate design on her goblet of wine.

'Well, I am sorry, but this is a *union* of two people. Surely Prince Tylon should not have to sacrifice everything he wants?'

'The way he wants things are impossible – they are not proper. We are royals. There is nothing simple about a wedding.' Crimson rage crept up Queen Loree's neck and coloured her cheeks.

'The wedding should be what they *both* want,' Reenah argued.

'Who are you to be giving advice on weddings? You are twenty and still not betrothed!' Queen Loree fired back.

King Herald and the sisters tried to intervene, but neither Reenah nor the queen listened.

'And I am glad of it! I would not want to be trapped into a marriage with a complete stranger.' Reenah shoved her chair back, leaving the table in an awkward silence over-shadowed by the queen's anger.

'I apologise, Queen Loree. This is unlike Reenah.' Oesyth tried to smooth over the damage, herself furious that Reenah would embarrass herself and the sisters like that.

'It's fine. I am sure she has been under a lot of stress with the events of late.' Queen Loree's face was still pinched with anger.

Reenah stayed well clear of the king and queen of Byrass the next day. She also stayed well clear of Oesyth, knowing how angry she would be. Reenah at least came down for a brief farewell to the royal couple in the evening as they climbed into the carriage, finally heading back to Byrass.

Reenah woke, gasping for air, her tangled sheets soaked with sweat. The mad woman beckoned, invading her dreams. She went downstairs to the kitchen and poured herself a glass of water, having knocked over her own when she woke up in a fright. Hearing light footsteps coming from the hall, she watched the double swing doors to the kitchen, expecting a kitchen hand to bustle in, but there was nothing.

There was a giggle, soft and sweet, the very sound of innocence to Reenah's ears. The princess crept toward the doors and pushed one open to peer out. The hall was large with stone floors; sound echoed easily in the space. There was a blue rug with gold patterns running in a spiral to the centre, it stretched to the doors that led outside. Six huge, white pillars supported the high domed ceiling.

Reenah heard laughter again and glimpsed a figure in white disappear behind one of the pillars. She walked out into the middle of the hall and stood on the blue rug; her bare toes sunk into the plush carpet. Another giggle, then sweet laughter, as a flash of white spun past her and disappeared behind another pillar.

'Hello?'

A woman seemed to float past Reenah like a wraith. She could not see her face properly and, out of curiosity, she followed. The woman skipped up the stairs, laughing merrily as she went. Though she seemed to merely glide, Reenah struggled to keep up.

'Wait! Who are you?'

Laughter was the only reply. The woman reached the top of the stairs and disappeared. Reenah raced up behind, trying not to lose sight of her. Despite her best efforts, when she got to the top, the mysterious woman was gone. Reenah turned left and walked slowly with her hand on the rail, hearing laughter to her right. She peered down a hallway and saw the woman in white disappear around another corner.

Reenah picked up her pace and suddenly came face to face with the woman. She was beautiful; her long auburn hair flowed down her back in soft curls and her eyes were golden. The woman smiled and put her finger to her lips before turning and dancing down the hall past rooms that had not been used in years.

'Mother?'

'Yes, my child,' the woman said, turning to flash a smile before skipping down the hall.

'Wait!' Reenah called, watching as she disappeared into a room. There was so much she wanted to know.

Reenah turned the handle on the door and rushed into the dim room. For a moment she thought she could hear ragged breathing, but she dismissed the thought as she caught sight of the woman in white. She stood with her back to Reenah, twirling a piece of auburn hair in her fingers.

'Mother, why did you leave me?'

'I am here now, child.' She turned to face Reenah.

With a startled cry, Reenah jumped back, landing hard against the wall.

The woman's beauty was marred. Her lips were cracked and bleeding and encrusted with scabby sores. Her eyes were sunken, dark ringed and crazy. Her hair was tattered and her dress was brown and stained.

'What is the matter? Don't you want to embrace your mother?' she said, reaching out pale fingers.

Her long yellow nails were almost curled into talons. She cackled and leapt at Reenah.

Reenah screamed as her ankle was grabbed and she was dragged toward the mad creature. She snatched for the doorhandle, but the door slammed shut and locked. All the while the mad woman laughed and screamed with Reenah as she dragged the princess into her clutches.

Isran started awake; someone had burst into her room in hysterics.

'What? What is going on?'

It was one of the maids. She was frightened and out of breath.

'Mistress, it – it's terrible... I heard her screaming, but I couldn't open the door. It's locked from the inside... You must come quick.'

'Who is screaming? What are you talking about?' Isran demanded, still confused and sleep-addled.

'Princess Reenah! She's locked inside Kyler's room!' the maid wailed.

Isran forgot all grace as she threw her sheets back and leapt out of bed in her nightgown. She raced down the hall, shouting for Oesyth and Elyr as she went.

As soon as Isran reached the room, she could hear Reenah's screams from inside.

'Reenah, I'm here!'

She tried to force the door down with her power, but it did not budge. She blasted the door with all that she had, terrified of what mad-Kyler was doing to Reenah. Nothing worked. Oesyth and Elyr arrived seconds later, and all together they tried to tear the door apart, but it held fast.

Oesyth stood back, distressed and frozen with indecision. Isran stared at her eldest sister in wild desperation.

'You cannot give up!' she shouted, not sure whether it was to Oesyth or Reenah. She pounded wildly on the door like she had gone mad herself.

'Kyler! You sick, twisted bitch! Let her go!'

There was a choked sob from inside then silence.

'Reenah?' Isran called, studying the door as though she could perhaps squeeze under it.

Moaning came from inside; they couldn't tell whether it came from Reenah or mad-Kyler. It turned into a deafening wail.

'Useless! Useless, useless! Damn you to the pits of hell!'

Isran leapt at the doorhandle, half expecting it to stay shut, but it opened with a soft *click* and she fell into the room. Reenah sat in the corner. Her back was pushed against the wall behind the door, as far away from Kyler as possible.

Her yellow eyes were wide, staring ahead. Her skin was as white as a sheet and her fingers were balled into fists by her sides.

'Reenah? Reenah?' Isran grasped Reenah's shoulders, trying to shake a response out of her.

Reenah slowly turned to stare wide-eyed at Isran. Suddenly, she screamed and crawled across the floor away from Isran. Mad-Kyler jumped up and grabbed Reenah by her hair.

'Useless! Useless! Useless!' she railed.

Reenah cried and twisted in the woman's grip. Mad-Kyler dragged her yellow claws across Reenah's face before letting her go.

Reenah pushed past the sisters and raced from the room. Isran went after her, and Oesyth and Elyr were left standing in the room, wondering what to do with their deranged half-sister.

Reenah sprinted down the hallway and out onto the balcony above the hall. Isran cursed as she nearly fell over her nightgown, trying to keep up with her niece. She watched in horror as Reenah approached the stairs as though they weren't even there. She stepped down, rolled her ankle, then tumbled down to the bottom. Isran came down after her, nearly falling herself more than once. Blood trickled down Reenah's forehead and down her cheek where mad-Kyler had scratched her. She was not moving.

26. Things left unsaid.

Raemil whistled again and, momentarily disturbed, Lylah looked up from her grazing. Raemil sat down as dusk settled, wondering if she would ever see the Black again. Lylah bounded over and Raemil pulled her into her lap, taking comfort from the fawn's warm, little body.

She shivered, feeling naked without her cloak. She was wearing only her white dress which was far too revealing and provided little warmth. The weather was turning. Raemil could smell rain on the cold wind that blew from the south. She thought of Caelin. The farmers would have sewn their crops weeks ago; they would be praying for the rain now. In the castle, they would be busy planning the winter ball.

She thought of her brother and felt a pang of fear. What if she couldn't find him? She sank into depression, wondering if, after all she had done and faced, he was dead. Now the sun had faded, the river looked haunted. Everything turned to shades of grey, as though harbouring dark and terrible creatures. She closed her eyes to the cheerless place and curled her body around the sleeping fawn.

Lestadt carefully manoeuvred Steel over the boulders. The valley exit was just ahead, but it was difficult to navigate the horse through the mess caused by the landslide. There were hundreds of broken feline bodies, and he guessed there were more beneath the limestone and slate scattered on the ground. The Black had disappeared, abruptly throwing his head in the air and galloping out of the valley.

As they emerged, he saw Bonnie put her head down and begin searching anew. He followed the shepherd, hoping she would find Raemil alive and well, but he wouldn't be upset if Bonnie found them something to eat either. Lestadt urged the grey gelding into a trot as Bonnie began to lope ahead. He could hear the sound of churning water and saw a river snaking through a break in the trees ahead. Bonnie reached the trees, wagging her tail like mad as she disappeared out of view. Lestadt broke through the tree line and rode into a small clearing. He was flooded with relief as his gaze fell on the woman sleeping on the ground.

Bonnie promptly curled up at Raemil's back, and Lestadt could see her arms were wrapped protectively around Lylah. He crouched, studying Raemil's face in the moonlight. A lock of her red hair had fallen over her eyes, and he gently brushed it aside. At his touch, she stirred but did not wake. He couldn't explain why but the thought of her waking right then made his heart beat wildly. He studied her features; her slightly rounded face, her red lips and her closed eyes, her brow furrowed, even in sleep. She was so different, yet he had to admit she was also beautiful. He wished he could hold her as fiercely as she held the fawn. He was sure she did not feel the same. He had stolen a kiss and blown it. Regardless, he felt so relieved to have found her, alive and unharmed. He curled up beside her, edging close enough to just feel her warmth.

Lestadt woke just after daybreak. He was uncomfortable and still felt exhausted. He could smell smoke from the fire that warmed his back. He rolled over, wincing as the stones he'd slept on, dug into his back. The pot was boiling over the fire, and his wooden cup sat on the ground beside some tea leaves. Raemil was nowhere to be seen. He made his tea and walked over to the river with his steaming cup in hand.

He was leaning against a twisted oak as he watched Raemil and the Black. They were wading in the shallows of the river, the Black's legs kicking up water as he pranced. Raemil laughed as she and the Black danced; she had a way of drawing him to her, just as she drew Lestadt to her. As the Black waded to her, Raemil waited for the opportune moment, before splashing him. The big horse snorted and stopped, then, tossed his head in the air, as though in disgust. He spun around and galloped through the shallow water, throwing up a fine spray of mist in his wake. Raemil laughed at the Black's antics.

Lestadt watched her intently. She was still wearing the white dress, and it clung to her shapely form, making Lestadt uncomfortable in a way he had been trying very hard to avoid. The Black trotted back to her, his head raised high and proud, and his tail raised in the air. Raemil turned away, grinning broadly, as the Black could not help but follow her, demanding her attention. She splashed him again, and he pranced to the side. When next Raemil put her hands in the water to splash him, the Black, with his gaze fixed on her, lifted one front leg high and pawed the water, splashing water everywhere: but mostly on himself.

Lestadt stifled a laugh. They were strange, the horse and his master, but they were both beautiful and compelling. He watched Raemil climb on the Black, and horse and rider danced in the water, both soaked and neither caring.

Raemil jumped down, beaming. She had missed her horse dearly. She climbed up the river bank, looking back to see the Black looking displeased that she had left him; she laughed and tried to call him. He twitched his ears back and turned away to sulk.

As she looked up, she caught sight of Lestadt leaning against an oak by the bank. He was watching her, his expression unreadable. She was instantly nervous and embarrassed, and he was just staring. Her embarrassment turned quickly to anger; she was not some curiosity to be gawked at.

'Why did you follow me?' she demanded, her green eyes burning into him with a courage she did not feel.

He opened his mouth as if to say something, then closed it again.

She glared at him a moment longer, then realising he was not going to reply, she walked away. Gathering her clothes, and in a rare moment of bravery, she left her cloak behind and headed further downstream to bathe.

27. The lion's den.

Reenah sat by her open window, a tendril of hair blew across her lips, but she made no attempt to move it. Her eyes were unfocused; the only movement she made was the steady rise and fall of her chest.

Isran watched her from the doorway. She was sure the unresponsive state Reenah was in had nothing to do with the fall. The sisters had tried to enter her mind, but it was like entering a murky lake. There was something blocking her memories. The sisters found their magic breaking like waves against a solid darkness.

The only other person close to Reenah that she could think of to help was Prince Tylon. Isran knew Reenah had feelings for him, *so how would she feel if he saw her like this?* They were yet to ask Queen Loree or King Herald. It was so soon after they had just arrived home from West Sirron, and so soon after Reenah's disrespectful outburst.

'What can we do?' Oesyth startled Isran from her thoughts.

'I don't know.'

'I cannot stand seeing her this way, but I just don't know how to find her.' Desperation escaped into Oesyth's voice.

'The Byrassians?'

'They would have only just arrived home; do you think that is wise?'

'No, but this is our niece.'

Oesyth only nodded and walked away, leaving Isran standing in the doorway, still watching Reenah.

Isran smiled a grim smile. Encouraging Oesyth to contact the Byrassians would give her just enough time to do something dangerous and stupid.

The mind was a treacherous place to enter, especially one as damaged as Kyler's. There were too many thoughts, both conscious and subconscious, that raced in their own pathways, some crossing over onto others. Those were just the thoughts. There were also feelings and senses and memories. It was easy for a mage to enter a mind and be caught in the person's busy thoughts. They could easily be trapped in an endless loop of chaotic impressions. Many skilled mages had returned to their bodies maddened by what they had seen and felt. Others never escaped, too weak to break free; they would stay blank of expression and lost forever.

Isran breathed deeply as she watched her half-sister in disgust. Kyler laughed and rolled on the ground, giggling then screaming. Isran knew the dangers of entering her mind, but she was desperate. They both might be saved if she could untangle Kyler's mind. Closing her eyes, she blocked all outside distraction, concentrating only on the demented woman before her.

Oesyth entered the room and visibly sagged at the sight of both Kyler and Isran unconscious on the floor. She should have known Isran would try something like this.

'No!' Elyr cried as she entered behind Oesyth to see what Isran had done.

'Elyr, we must leave her. If we intervene, we may make things worse.'

'How could she be so stupid? We are losing Reenah, and now Isran is gone too! This is the worst possible timing!' Elyr said angrily.

'I know, but Isran is not a child. She makes her own choices as both you and I do. She knows the dangers of entering someone's mind. Her chances are slim, but if she succeeds, we could have Kyler back and hopefully Reenah too.'

'But we are likely to lose both,' Elyr said grimly.

She opened her eyes and was faced with a huge serpent. She gasped and jumped back, her heart pounding wildly in her chest. The snake reared, exposing fangs dripping with saliva. Isran let out a frightened scream. She fell backward and grazed her elbow against the hard, gritty floor. Coming to her senses, she remembered where she was and why.

'Bitch,' she muttered as she studied the chamber she was in.

This was mad-Kyler's first line of defence. Though the snake was only in Kyler's mind, it could still cause Isran harm or kill her.

Isran could not imagine objects into someone else's mind. She was weaponless, unless Kyler gave her one, which was unlikely. The snake hissed and slithered out of one of many dark tunnels. Isran rolled out of the way as it tried to strike her. It missed and struck the brick wall behind. Bricks crumbled onto the dirt floor as the snake pulled away, rubbing its head on the ground, flicking off broken scales. Isran looked around, desperate for a weapon. The room was dimly lit, so there had to be a light source somewhere, yet she could see none.

'Light!' Isran shouted.

Slowly, around the room, torches appeared on the walls.

Because Kyler had imagined light without the source, it only took one reminder from Isran to trick Kyler's mind into considering the source. It was unlikely to work again. The snake hissed and lunged, as mad-Kyler realised the trick. Isran ran and jumped up to grab a torch as the snake tried to strike again. As its head whipped around, she stabbed the torch into its eye, causing the massive serpent to recoil.

Now blinded in one eye, it moved more cautiously, tasting the air with its tongue. Isran grabbed the next torch and ran at the serpent as it turned its good eye toward the sound. She felt the flick of its tongue and the whoosh of air from its next strike as she barely dodged. Isran twisted and jammed the torch into the remaining eye.

The snake was completely blind, but still it felt where she was and continued to hunt her. She ran to a pile of rubble at the entrance to a caved-in tunnel. She clung to the burnt-out torch, her only weapon against this monster. Narrowly dodging the snake's fangs, she thought she had bested it before it whipped her with its tail and she fell heavily to the ground.

Broken bricks lay just within reach. She grabbed one as the snake's head loomed over her shoulder. She threw the brick hard against the adjacent wall then froze. The snake's head snapped around, feeling the vibration of impact. Hesitantly, the snake began to slide away from her. She threw another brick to distract it from the sound of her crawling to her feet. She raced for the nearest tunnel entrance.

The tunnel was dark, but Isran's mage-sight helped her see. She darted to an opening on her right. The snake tried to follow, but the opening was too small;

it lodged it's head in the opening and was stuck. Isran smiled to herself and moved on through the dark tunnel. She never stopped to wonder why mad-Kyler would make the tunnel too small for the snake.

28. Falling.

The flames from the campfire licked at the night sky, while glowing embers flaked into the air and swirled away. There was a calmness in the air as dark storm clouds rolled in from the south. Winter would be upon them sooner than they had thought, and winters in Horsham were known to be savage and merciless.

Raemil and Lestadt had spoken little during the day. Tension lay thick between them and neither was prepared to clear the air. Bonnie and Lylah sat between them, Bonnie preferring to sit by Lestadt's side as his attitude toward the dog had changed drastically. He buried his hand in her thick coat, scratching the spot on her neck that caused a hind leg to thump the ground vigorously.

Raemil was staring at the fire, apparently deep in thought. Her red curls stirred around her face and she frequently brushed them aside. He could see the reflection of the fire dancing in her eyes. He wanted to bridge the gap between them, but he wasn't sure how. She was not the young girl he had expected.

The next morning, Lestadt woke early. The sun had not yet risen, but the birds were chirping noisily in the treetops. He was surprised to find Raemil sleeping beside him but not so surprised to find he had wrapped his arms around her. He enjoyed the feeling of her body against his, a little too much. He tried to shift subtly so his morning hardness was not pressed up against her. He lay his head back down beside hers, not wanting to let her go. His gaze wandered over her face, her lips, and the curves of her body. He closed his eyes and tried to think of something else.

He eventually forced himself to get up. He didn't want Raemil to wake to find him with his arms around her, nor was he sure at present that he could hide the erection straining against his pants. This was the first time in a long time that he had woken before her. He tried to distract himself with how he could take advantage of this.

When Raemil woke, she was cold and alone. She had hoped Lestadt would sleep late so she could move and he would not have to know she had been there. Waking in the middle of the night from a nightmare, she had needed the comfort of his closeness. Now her cheeks burned with embarrassment.

The wind was freezing. She wrapped the cloak around her and went to the fire. The water was already boiling, her cup and tea leaves were beside it. His cup sat a few paces away, the last mouthful containing the tea leaves was still inside.

She didn't know where he'd gone, but she was content to sit alone and drink her tea. The sky was dark, the clouds were heavy and ready to drop rain at any moment. The sky flashed with lightning, followed by a distant rumble. There was no point in breaking camp today.

A movement caught her eye as the first drops of rain began to hit the ground. Lestadt emerged from behind the trees, motioning for her to follow. She looked at him, puzzled, and a little afraid for a reason she couldn't quite define. She suddenly realised that all of their belongings were gone, save the pot and the two cups. After a brief and nervous hesitation, she followed Lestadt.

Raemil was impressed as she entered the clearing. Lestadt had been busy all morning. Sewing the two cow hides together, he had made a tent, using the trees to stabilise it. As lightning clapped overhead, Lestadt led the horses to a weeping willow nearby. He had cleared the lower branches, leaving an open area under the tree's foliage for the horses to keep relatively dry and warm.

Inside the tent their beds were already made, forced to be beside each other in the confined space. Raemil glanced at the real blankets, then looked back to Lestadt.

'I had forgotten about them, I bought them in Vagamore.' He laughed. 'To think it was so cold last night and we had blankets rolled up beside my saddle.' As though he read her mind.

Raemil sat down on one of the beds, noticing in the corner by the flap a small bed for Bonnie and Lylah. They lay curled around each other, intent on sleeping through the storm. Lestadt sat beside her on the other bed, listening to the wind outside.

'I have a feeling this storm is going to be bad,' he said, turning to Raemil, who sat with her head down, fiddling with her medicine pouch.

'I don't like storms. Are you sure it's safe to be near so many trees?'

'Don't worry, the lightning is far away and these trees are sturdy. It would take a cyclone to tear them out of the ground.'

'Don't speak too soon.' She smiled nervously.

Their eyes held for a moment. Raemil was the first to look away, pretending to be interested in her medicines, but she could feel him still watching her.

'What are you looking at?' she plucked up the courage to ask.

The corner of his mouth twitched up and he looked away momentarily. When he turned back to her, he laughed and looked suspiciously like *he* was nervous.

'You have no idea how incredible you are, do you?'

Raemil blinked. She was completely unprepared for that. Watching him grin at her, she suddenly wondered was he mocking her? She felt angry and hurt. *How could he be so cruel?* Spying the bow leaning against the side of the tent, she quickly snatched it up and stormed out, heedless of the rain.

The rain was pouring down and the thunder roared overhead. Raemil stood under the shelter of a tree, trying unsuccessfully to use the bow. Her shots went into the river, far off to the right, clattering against a rock, and way up in the air to be lodged in the top of a tree.

'Are you aiming for anything in particular?'

Raemil jumped at the sound of Lestadt's voice beside her. She turned to see him standing, drenched in the pouring rain, watching her with those intense and unreadable eyes. Droplets of water ran down his face and dripped off the end of his nose. His hair was soaked and dripping as he joined her under the shelter of the tree.

She tried to ignore him and continued to fire badly. She was aiming for a tree trunk across the river and directly in front of her, but the arrows were landing anywhere but there.

Lestadt moved behind her and grabbed her hand supporting the bow. Her body stiffened at his closeness. He turned her gently so she faced away from the river before closing his fist around her right hand and knocking an arrow.

He drew back and leaned forward over her shoulder, gently pressing his cheek against hers.

'How about we aim away from the river, so we can get the arrows back. We'll aim for that notch there, just below the lowest branch.'

Raemil nodded slowly, trying to relax against his body.

'The wind is coming from the south, so you want to consider and readjust, just so.' He adjusted her stance and aim.

Raemil found it impossible to concentrate.

When they released, the arrow was lodged into the notch just below the lowest branch, as promised; though Raemil didn't see how she could take any of the credit.

They stayed under the tree a long time. She wanted to learn to use the bow, and she wanted him close. Eventually, visibility became so poor they were forced to go back to the tent.

The horses stood close to each other under the willow, drawing warmth from each other, and Bonnie and Lylah were still asleep when Lestadt and Raemil came back. They removed their shoes as they entered, not wanting to trample mud everywhere. It was dark and cold inside the tent, causing Raemil to wrap the blanket around her, shivering as she sat down. She was frustrated and anxious, convinced Lestadt was only taking pity on her.

'Raemil, you look... troubled.'

'It's nothing,' she said, turning away and letting her damp hair fall like a curtain between them.

Lestadt picked up his blankets and sat beside her, wrapping them around her.

'You don't need to keep hiding your face like that,' he said, brushing her hair out of the way.

'It's easier.' Her voice was barely audible above the storm.

'Easier?' he repeated with a frown.

She was trembling. She didn't know how to react to his closeness, to him staring right at her and actually seeing her.

'I know what everyone thinks when they see me. You don't have to pretend as though it doesn't bother you.'

Lestadt became very still, watching her so closely that she wished she could shrug out of her skin and send her mind and soul anywhere but here. Instead, she froze as he wrapped his arms around her and drew her close. She made a feeble attempt to pull away, confusion and a desire to be close to him warred with each other.

Lestadt bent his head so close that his lips brushed against hers, teasing and torturing her. She wanted his lips on hers as much as she wanted to run out into the storm and let the rain cool her suddenly hot skin. He put his mouth close to her ear as he spoke softly. Raemil closed her eyes, feeling an unfamiliar thrill of pleasure run through her body at the warmth of his breath on her neck.

'Raemil, you are beautiful. The last thing I want you to do is hide yourself from me.'

Lestadt watched her intently.

She stared into the blue eyes she had fallen into the first time they had met. Finally, she realised there was no cruel intent or malice behind his words. She kissed him softly. A slow smile transformed his face and, needing no further encouragement, he pressed his mouth hard against hers, kissing her passionately. Heat suffused her body and she hardly had control, arching into him as they delved deeper into the kiss. Gradually, he eased her backward until she was laying across their beds.

Pulling away from her mouth, Lestadt began to slowly plant kisses down her neck while unbuttoning her shirt. She trembled at his touch but did not push him away. He made his way down her throat, torturously slow. Her shirt was open to the frigid air, and before she could adjust, his tongue encircled a nipple. She gasped and her back arched into him again, as though her body did as it pleased.

Raemil had never been intimate with anyone, but she felt herself wanting him, needing him. He slid his hand over her stomach and up to her breasts as his mouth found hers again and he parted her lips with his tongue. Raemil unbuttoned his trousers, then pulled his shirt over his head, letting her hands slide over his firm body. Lestadt lowered himself onto her so she could feel his hardness pressed up against her. Breathing heavily with desire, he forced himself to halt before it was too late.

'Do you want me to stop?' He watched her keenly. Her cheeks were flushed pink and she was breathing fast too.

She was silent for a moment, not sure how to respond or what exactly he was asking her. Taking her silence as uncertainty, he moved to ease his body from her, and in that instant, she knew she did not want him to stop.

'No,' she said, her voice had become husky.

She pulled him closer and parted her legs, despite her body trembling from a mixture of excitement and fear.

The storm raged, the wind lashed cruelly at the trees, shredding the leaves from the branches. The horses huddled closer to each other, frightened by the noise of the unrelenting wind, tearing at the trees around them. Beneath the brutal storm, Lestadt and Raemil made love, completely unaware of anything else but each other.

29. Deception.

Windfall was a strong horse; he was not so tall as he was well muscled. He was white with a light brown mane and tail, a distinctive and recognisable mount. He thundered through the Byrass city gates at Prince Tylon's urging.

Oesyth had appeared via spirit travel only hours ago. Prince Tylon packed his things without waiting for his parent's permission. Their friendship with the West Sirronese went back a very long way and despite Reenah's and his mother's recent falling out, he was sure his mother would understand.

He thought about the last time they had parted. Reenah had told him to leave, and he had, without question. He wished he had stayed, perhaps he could have prevented it somehow; maybe he could have kept her away from mad-Kyler. He felt an inexplicable guilt that was not perhaps entirely due to her condition and more do to do with why he was so terrified.

* * *

She still clutched the wooden torch tightly in her fist; her only weapon for what she would face next. As she stepped into the light, she scanned the room, first noticing the torches, high up on the walls and out of her reach.

Isran could hear someone weeping. A woman lay in the farthest corner of the room; she was curled into a tight ball, her dress in tatters, and her long auburn hair cascading around her face.

'Kyler.' Isran nearly wept herself, as she raced to her half-sister.

Kyler did not look up, she only continued to wail. Isran wrapped her arms around her sister.

'You are safe, I have found you,' she said softly.

Tears welled in her eyes. Poor Kyler, she had been through so much and kept it all to herself.

'My children,' she sobbed. 'I've lost them. I'm a terrible mother,' she wailed and collapsed into Isran's arms.

'You've not lost them, it's not too late.'

'I am a terrible mother,' she repeated. 'I don't even know where they are.'

Isran held her tighter.

'Reenah is with us... the other, she is somewhere across the Sapphire seas, in the southern lands of the betrayers. We can find her, Kyler, if you'd just come back to us.'

'The land of the betrayers?' she whispered in a hoarse voice.

Isran's grip loosened. There was something about her voice, something... not right. Mentally, she cursed herself for a fool, but it was far too late.

Oesyth peered out the large bay window. A man on a white horse was charging across the bridge. She recognised Windfall first and hurried down to meet Prince Tylon. The horse had been run ragged; he stood foaming at the bit and huffing as the prince leapt from the saddle.

'I came as soon as I heard. How is she?' Tylon asked, foregoing all decorum.

'I take it you mean Reenah? She is no better, and no worse.'

He visibly relaxed for just a moment, then asked, 'Who *else* would I have meant?'

'I'm afraid Isran has entered Kyler's mind. She and Kyler have been in a trance for days.'

'This is terrible, I'm so sorry, Oesyth.'

'Come, let us go inside. I will see to it that Windfall is taken care of.'

Elyr came across Prince Tylon and Oesyth in the foremost sitting room.

'How fares Isran?' asked Oesyth.

'She is much the same, a few more bruises, a graze on her elbow.' Looking defeated, Elyr sat heavily beside Prince Tylon.

'What happened to Reenah? Can she be saved?' he asked fearfully.

'We are not exactly sure; all we know is that Reenah went into Kyler's room and came out screaming with psychosis. We do not know what Kyler did, but Reenah won't talk. It seems as though she does not even know we are here. She just sits and stares out the window all day.' Oesyth paused to take a sip of water.

The small tremble in her hand did not go unnoticed.

'If Isran succeeds in bringing Kyler back, then we may be able to save her, but I am afraid that anything we do now could make it worse.'

Prince Tylon bowed his head in dismay. Isran was their only hope now, and if she could not get into Reenah's mind, *how could she save Kyler's?*

'Can I see her?'

'Of course, Prince Tylon. I think that if she knew, she would be glad to have you by her side.'

Before Isran could give it any more thought, Kyler's gaze snapped up to hers, her golden eyes insane. Kyler's face slowly twisted into a warped smile. Isran tried to shuffle back, but before she could escape, Kyler thrust a dagger into her belly. Isran's eyes went wide with shock. She gaped at Kyler, her half-sister laughed and twisted the knife. Kyler wrenched the blade free and Isran clutched her abdomen, disbelieving, as she watched blood ooze between her fingers.

As Isran watched with horror, Kyler's features twisted into that of an old woman. Her fingers long and knobbly, her haggard face framed by blue-grey hair.

'Horsham...?' Isran murmured through her pain.

'Fool!' she taunted. 'Horsham, Bascillium, I am both. You have aided me well, Sister Isran. I shall thank you by gifting you with death.'

Horsham cackled, then rushed at her again with the blade. Isran rallied and thrust the burnt-out torch into the evil woman's face. Horsham fell backward, but before hitting the ground, she vanished. The pain of her ruined stomach making her dizzy, Isran lay back on the hard-stone floor. Agony and shock prevented her from floating free of the prison that was Kyler's mind.

30. Awakening.

Prince Tylon held Reenah's hand, possibly for his own comfort, since she remained unaware of his presence. Elyr and Oesyth left the room, giving them some privacy. They made their way to mad-Kyler's room, though the very sight of the door had become a source of fear. They had been monitoring the situation but could do little but watch as Isran silently battled with mad-Kyler's mind.

Elyr pushed the door open and a thin wail escaped her lips. Oesyth brushed past her youngest sister and rushed to Isran's side. She lay on the ground, a large wound in her stomach and a pool of blood soaking into the carpet. Unable to bear the sight of her sister's blood, Elyr turned to Kyler's slumped body next to Isran's while Oesyth tried to stem the flow of blood from Isran's abdomen.

Elyr reached down to Kyler's incredibly pale wrist to feel for a pulse but paused, staring stupidly at the odd bracelet she wore.

'Is that a daisy-chain?' she whispered to herself.

'What?' Oesyth asked, looking up from Isran's wound momentarily.

'A daisy-chain. Was she wearing this the whole time?' Elyr asked.

Oesyth sat up straight, looking over to what Elyr was studying.

'That's no daisy-chain. Get it off her, get it off now,' she said through frightened tears. Sensing there was something sinister about the thing, she snatched at it and broke it away, ignoring the burning sensation that shot up her fingers and arm. She watched the thing shrivel and blacken on the carpet.

She stared at the dark smudge on the flooring as her tears blurred her vision. She couldn't bear to turn back to the scene behind her. She was sure Isran's life was slipping away and she was helpless.

Isran opened her eyes. She was still in the dungeon, her stomach throbbing with a dull pain. As the walls dimmed around her, she felt the pull of death, so very near. A being entered the dungeon; she was wraith-like and glowed with such power. She moved with grace toward Isran with an outstretched hand, smiling sweetly, though her face was creased with worry. Isran wondered if the woman was an angel, or perhaps a god, but she hadn't the strength to ask. The woman's smile faded as she looked on Isran's wound.

'I'll not let you leave me now. Come half-sister Isran, let us go home,' the woman said, her hand reaching for Isran's.

Isran smiled, not really comprehending the woman's words but drawn by the power of her presence, her tender smile, and her apparent concern for Isran's wellbeing. Isran reached up a paling hand, and the woman took it.

When next she opened her eyes, she was looking into Oesyth's grave face. She could hear Elyr weeping somewhere behind her.

'The angel, where... where is she?' she asked weakly.

Tears welled in Oesyth's eyes. Not many mages possessed the healing power, it was a power that few *could* wield. Neither Oesyth, nor Elyr, had been blessed with it.

'You! Stay away from her!' Elyr cried.

Oesyth looked up to see Kyler walking slowly to Isran's side. As she looked into Kyler's tired, but sane eyes, she waved Elyr off.

'You've done it,' Oesyth whispered to Isran.

Oesyth watched in amazement as Kyler bent down to Isran, and, placing her hands over the wound, she began to heal her.

The veins bulged in Kyler's arms, shoulders and neck, as though her very blood was pumping into Isran. The flesh began to mend, starting from the inside. Before the skin could fully close over, Kyler began to shudder and convulse before she collapsed.

Prince Tylon was completely baffled. One minute he was basically talking to himself, the next, Reenah had leapt up out of her seat.

'Reenah? It's okay, you are safe.'

'She tried to kill me.' Her voice was tight with panic.

'You are safe now,' he repeated.

'It's not okay! My own mother! She, she wanted me dead!'

He sat on the edge of the bed. 'Reenah, that woman was not your mother.'

Reenah watched the tired man before her, the man that she loved with all her heart. She visibly relaxed, remembering her mother had been crazy. There was still the fact that her mother had given her away, but that wound was harder to heal and she buried that hurt for now. As she began to cry with relief, Tylon embraced her.

'I thought we had lost you,' he said with a hint of emotion in his voice as he hugged her tighter to him.

Elyr stumbled into the room, then seeing Reenah and Prince Tylon embracing, she quickly closed the door and let them be. With her heart singing for joy, she went back to Oesyth.

Isran's wound was stitched by a doctor, and despite her complaints, she was given strict instructions to stay in bed.

Oesyth rolled her eyes at her sister's stubbornness. Even after such an ordeal, she still had the cheek to tell the doctor she knew best. Kyler was sleeping in a different room now. She was not harmed, only extremely exhausted. Kyler had used her last ounce of strength to save Isran.

For the next few days, Oesyth's and Elyr's attentions were divided. Isran insisted she was fine. Reenah spent much of her time with Prince Tylon.

Reenah stayed far away from Kyler's room. Even though she knew the woman slept, she was still uneasy. She visited Isran, who was immediately brighter after seeing the physical proof that Reenah was well.

Isran told her sisters that Bascillium and Horsham were one and the same, and that it was not Kyler they were speaking to all along. As that thought passed through her mind, she felt a pang of fear and suddenly realised the terrible motive behind Horsham's visit. Her mind raced as she pieced together the implications and she realised she had made a terrible mistake.

* * *

Horsham grinned wickedly. She nursed a split lip and a broken tooth, but it was worth it. While Kyler was an extremely powerful mage, there was one that was more powerful and could be of great use to her. Her battle with Kyler had proven that while she was strong enough to damage Horsham, she was not strong enough to defeat her, just as their first battle had confirmed.

Her daughter Tannagan sat beside her, not overly interested in Horsham's discovery. She knew not of her mother's full intentions. Tannagan wanted power, and she knew her mother could give it to her. They were planning to take control of everything and throw everyone, Iadronian and Otowanese alike, into a state of despair. The mortals would pay for their betrayal.

* * *

Isran paced the length of the room and back again. She always paced when stressed. It had also been the well-known trait of their father. Oesyth and Elyr insisted she stay in bed, but Isran was stubborn. Kyler had woken a day ago.

They waited for Kyler to arrive in the bright stone room while Princess Reenah, Prince Tylon, Queen Loree, King Herald, Oesyth and Elyr sat around the table. They watched with mounting irritation as Isran paced back and forth.

Kyler entered the hall, dressed in a cream and gold dress borrowed from Elyr. Left of the house power-stone was the large table where everyone sat, impatient yet hopeful. Kyler felt terrible to be the bearer of bad news. Her eyes swept the faces, noting the king and queen of Byrass were there in spirit only. Her gaze fell upon Reenah and she smiled weakly; her daughter had grown into a beautiful woman, and she had missed it all. She bowed, and silently took her seat. Isran quickly seated herself also.

'Sisters, Reenah and friend Byrassians, I bear grave news.' Kyler cut to the point. 'I am aware of why you brought me here, and I am afraid that I cannot help you. I fought Bascillium once, and was killed...'

'What do you mean you were killed? You're right here,' Queen Loree exclaimed.

'Yes, I am, but I *was* killed by Bascillium. When I blasted Bascillium with my power, it rebounded and I ended up in the underworld. This...' she said, standing and pulling up the sleeve on her dress, exposing her arm, 'is the mark of the Genrae, a walking soul. I am hell doomed. If I should die again, so too will my soul. I will never be reborn, I will never pass beyond, I will cease to exist, all memory of me will be erased.'

The mark on her arm was a black band of fire. She replaced the sleeve and sat back down.

'My point is that I did not have the power to defeat Horsham, as she now goes by; but she had the power to defeat me.'

'But you came back from the dead. Surely if you could do that, then you would have the power to defeat Horsham,' said Oesyth.

'No. There was a terrible price for my return, which I thought I had cheated, but not so, as fate would have it. I will do what I can to help, but I am afraid that I cannot do this alone.'

'Then perhaps with the lost daughter...' King Herald's voice trailed off as he read hopelessness in the room.

'I have some news...' Isran offered into the strained silence.

All eyes turned to Isran.

'While we thought we spoke to Kyler, we were truly talking to Horsham. For days, who I thought was Kyler had been asking for a child, asking where she was. I told her Reenah was fine. Then, we all know the night she took Reenah she was angry, saying that Reenah was useless.' She glanced apologetically at Reenah. 'When I went into Kyler's mind and was once again duped into believing I was talking to Kyler, she had asked where her children were, and stupidly, I told her.'

The blank expressions around the table proved her audience didn't quite understand the implications.

'Horsham was in Kyler's mind because she was searching for something. Reenah was not the daughter she was looking for at all. And stupidly, I have given Horsham the location of the lost daughter, or an approximation at least. We must ask ourselves, why would she go to such extremes for the whereabouts of the lost daughter? Obviously, she is of importance.'

Isran, as well as every other person in the room, looked questioningly to Kyler.

Kyler shifted uncomfortably on her seat. They looked to her for answers that she did not have.

'I know little of her. I gave birth to her across the Sapphire Seas in the land of the betrayers, and that is where she still is to this day as far as I know.'

'Where did you leave her?' asked Oesyth.

'I left her with a king in a castle to the north. She was to be a princess.'

'She is no longer there,' Isran said.

'How could you seek her out? Her powers are bound. I did so myself to keep her from harm, and I made sure the castle grounds would protect her,' Kyler said, dismayed.

'Well, your spell has weakened, because we have felt her several times, not strong enough for us to pinpoint her exact location, but still, it was her.'

'Impossible. As long as I live, that spell will be as strong as the day that I cast it.'

'Then she has grown more powerful,' said Oesyth in amazement.

'Is the king her true father?' asked Isran, trying to make some sense of it all.

'No...'

'Then who?'

Kyler remained silent.

'Damn it, Kyler! This is no time to withhold information,' Oesyth snapped angrily.

'Porlysius,' she said very quietly.

Heavy silence filled the room again. The existence of Porlysius was believed to be myth. Porlysius was the son of the earth god Misaria. It was said that he was not born, but made; he had no father and was purely of the earth. It was rumoured that he was created as a weapon. Should the mages ever rise again, he would be the destroyer of all. He would wipe the lands clean, and being of the earth, he would begin anew, without mage-kind. An unspoken threat to the survivors of the wars following the betrayal in Otowan.

'How? Why? Why would Misaria let something so powerful be created?' Oesyth stammered.

Kyler shrugged.

'I barely remember the night, but Porlysius could not be a weapon. While he is very powerful, I don't believe he could bring about such destruction.'

'If Misaria combined a full earth-god with a full-blood mage, she would get a powerful combination. While having the power of a mage, the power of destruction, there would be the power of the earth to recreate. What if Porlysius plays no part but to sire the weapon?' Reenah offered gravely. 'What if Horsham has learned of the lost daughter's existence and either just knows that she is extremely powerful, or she knows that she is the weapon, and she is the one to defeat Horsham... to defeat us all?'

'I'm afraid that Elyr and I also have bad news.' Oesyth grimaced as she added more grim information. 'We have reason to believe that Horsham, or someone, has released lesser-demons into our realm.'

'They've not wandered the mortal plain in hundreds of years,' Queen Loree exclaimed.

'We didn't notice right away, but when we pulled Kyler back to us, she was wearing a curse-chain. Similar to a daisy-chain, but one made by a lesser-demon. I think it was how Horsham gained access to Kyler's mind.'

Several people around the table hung their heads; there was just bad news on top of bad news. They discussed what could be done all through the night and into the early hours of the morning. Kyler was dismayed to find her daughter was on her way to her doom. Their hopes rested on Kyler's ability to find a more exact location. In her haste to protect her second-born, Kyler had made it difficult for even herself to find the lost daughter again. She was referred to as the lost daughter for a reason.

Prince Tylon left the morning after Kyler had addressed them in the stone room. He was to travel east to try to gain support from the other kingdoms and houses. Isran insisted on going to find the earth god, Misaria, despite Oesyth's and Elyr's protests. The journey would take Isran from West Sirron for some time. Kyler was to stay in West Sirron to help find her daughter. The king and queen of Byrass would search their library for anything that might help them face the battle ahead.

Though there were mages among the common people, many could perform little more than parlour tricks and street shows. The major houses and kingdoms housed the most powerful mages; unfortunately, the relationships between West Sirron and those houses was tense at best. West Sirron had been the first house to fight on the side of humans. The Byrassians declared not long after that humans seeking refuge from the violence and persecution from the other kingdoms could shelter in their kingdom. After Misaria had brought about the end of the wars, those kingdoms grudgingly accepted that humans were not to be enslaved, and technically, they weren't. Heavy taxes and heavy-handed border guards ensured that few could escape to the shoreline kingdoms.

West Sirron and Byrass were not well loved by the other kingdoms and houses. They had already attempted to discuss the fate of Otowan, and they were not well received, especially as many of those major houses and kingdoms were founded by people escaping their own persecution from the humans of Otowan. Byrass and Thornbroke, through the betrothal of Prince Tylon and Princess Yaeli, at least had a relationship, if not a delicate one.

Reenah sat in the garden feeling left out and unimportant. Everyone was busy, all set to task, save her. Hearing footsteps coming toward her, she looked up to see Kyler.

'We've not had a chance to speak, you and I.' She smiled and took a seat beside Reenah on the stone wall.

'Much is happening; something as small as the first meeting of a mother and daughter is unimportant,' Reenah said sourly.

'You are angry, and I can understand that...'

'How could you possibly understand? I was lied to and disowned. Do not presume to know how that feels,' she snapped, her angry yellow eyes burning into her mother's.

'Do not presume that giving up my child was an easy task! I loved you more than you could know, but I had to give you up. The sisters and I led different lives. I am not like them; my life is dangerous and unstable, not suitable for a baby. I took you to the one place I knew you would be safe.'

'Safe from what?!'

'Safe from me! I could not take care of a child! There were things that I had to do; it was too dangerous.'

'So why did you want everyone to believe that you were dead? Would it have been so hard to visit me via spirit travel?'

Kyler would not speak of what she had been searching for all of these years; she would not admit to her shame.

'It was safer that way. Look, I do not expect you to understand, I do not expect you to suddenly accept me as your mother. I am asking that for now, while there is so much to overcome, that we treat each other as friends. That is all.'

Reenah stared at the palms of her hands for a long time, not knowing what to say. When next she looked up, Kyler was gone.

Kyler did not follow the others to the library to begin poring through their volumes of books; instead, she came to the secret entrance to the stone hall. First, she had better try seeking out her daughter herself.

Her daughter was possibly still under the impression she was the princess of a palace in the land of the betrayers. Her true family were among the most powerful mages in Iadron.

There was much that rested on this one daughter, so much to overcome and it was all Kyler's fault. She had to make it right. She had kept her reasons for disappearing to herself. Her reasons were why she may not be able to make contact with the lost daughter as easily as the others might have thought. Kyler feared that while she had provided their saviour, she may have just as easily provoked their doom.

***

Prince Tylon had carefully presented his case to Koraldan the second. The King of Sirron NES turned him away, basically laughing in the prince's face. He was furious, but there was no point in arguing.

He then rode north on Windfall, heading for Thornbroke, the silver city. He was sure he could ask for support from the people of Thornbroke. If he was going to wed their princess, he would expect them to lend their aid. This was exactly what the prince intended to point out to the king and queen of Thornbroke.

As the prince rode through the high gates of the silver city, he looked past the houses and streets to the palace; a feeling of dread overcame him. He did not fear the king or queen; he did not fear Princess Yaeli as such, but he feared being trapped in not only a loveless marriage but a poorly matched one. He didn't want to be a doting husband and a king of a land in-between. It was true that this new palace would mean he would have his own land and he would be the start of its history. However, Prince Tylon did not want to be the start of a new line; he wanted to carry on his own people's traditions, his father's line and his father's father's line.

Taking a deep breath, in an attempt to refocus, he reminded himself there were bigger problems at hand. He squared his shoulders and sat straight in the saddle, knowing the streets of Thornbroke would come alive and be bustling with people at any moment.

There was one main cobblestone road that led to the silver castle's gates, the wealthiest people in the city lived in the houses closest to the main street. Smaller roads branched off the main road, winding far into the city to create the back streets of Thornbroke, where the poor lived in small houses and dark alleys. Brothels were hidden in dark streets under false business names and the taverns were always full of gamblers, whores and bounty hunters.

It was hard to imagine that Thornbroke's silver city could have such a dark side to it, but it was there. Thornbroke had the reputation of having the darkest and dirtiest of backstreets and illegal businesses in the north. It was hardly surprising, considering Thornbroke's size. All the rats of the human and mage race seemed to scuttle toward the silver city, willing to do anything to make a quick buck.

Windfall, being the well-trained royal horse that he was, began to prance prettily through the street as people emerged from their homes. Prince Tylon tapped his heels lightly to the stallion's sides to let him know he wanted no show. People began to line the streets as they recognised him. They were determined to please him; having waited so long for their princess to wed him. Prince Tylon gave a few nods here and there to keep the waving people happy as he rode through. A few carts and horses passed him by on the road, quickly detouring down side streets to give him right of way.

Prince Tylon looked down at their smiling faces, their waving hands, so happy to accept him, so willing to rejoice his coming. He hated them. The feeling surprised him and immediately he felt guilty; but they were not *his* people. He knew not one of their faces or names. He knew he would be marrying the people as much as their princess, his responsibilities weighed heavily on his shoulders but he tried not to let it show.

The castle was tastefully decorated in silvers and blues, with high silver and crystal chandeliers, beautifully crafted furniture, stained glass windows and solid silver handrails hugging the balconies. Carved into the wooden frames of the doors were cherubs holding small bows, horses and whispering angels. There had been a lot of money needlessly spent on the interior, beautiful though it was.

The king sat behind a solid oak desk in his private study. The quill in his hand scratched noisily on paper as he worked. There was a stack of papers pushed to one side on his desk and another bundle of papers on the floor. All around him there were books packed untidily into shelves.

The king looked up from his papers at the prince of Byrass standing before him.

'I find this hard to believe, there are no full-bloods, and there has not been a full-blood for over one hundred years. If we join you, we would be taking people away from important duties – not to mention we would be a laughing-stock,' the king said, after careful consideration of his social standing.

'What is more important? Hundreds of thousands of lives or dignity?' Prince Tylon bit his tongue; a bad choice of words could lose him the argument.

'I am sorry...' the king began, but was cut short.

'How can Princess Yaeli and I join in marriage when our people cannot even stand together? When you do not even trust the Byrassians and the people of West Sirron when we say that there is a threat?'

The king went silent and Prince Tylon knew a little persuasion was needed.

'All we need is your army when we call. That is all. No one has to know that you are involved at all until we have to fight, and by then, those houses that would not stand with us would be painted as the fools, not us. All I ask is the army be ready when we need it. What do you stand to lose?'

The king looked down past his bushy grey beard for the space of a breath, then he sighed heavily as he met the eyes of the young prince of Byrass.

'Then so be it. Should you need them, my men and I will be there.'

'Your men *and* you?'

'Well, if the world is coming to an end I am hardly going to stay at home and do paperwork, am I?' he snapped.

Oesyth was in the library when Prince Tylon's distorted figure appeared beside her. The distance between them made it difficult for the mage to maintain contact.

'Prince Tylon, what news?' she asked as she pushed yet another useless book back into the shelves.

'I have been to Sirron NES, and as we thought, Koraldan refused. I'm presently on the outskirts of Thornbroke; I have spoken to the king and he will fight with us should the need arise, albeit reluctantly.'

'How many men do we have?'

'Four thousand Byrassians are in training now, six thousand from Thornbroke – not yet in training. And you?'

She frowned.

'We have roughly three hundred men who haven't fought in years.'

'Well, put them in training. The more men we have, the better. But where to now? I do not think that 10,300 men will do against Horsham and her forces, especially if she has demons doing her bidding.'

'Well, it will have to do for now. It's all we have.'

Prince Tylon dipped his head in acknowledgment and farewell before fading out. It wasn't wise to leave his body devoid of spirit and unattended for too long on the outskirts of someone else's territory.

31. The weight of a truth.

After the storm, it drizzled lightly for five days. Raemil and Lestadt travelled ever south, the Horsham mountains looming above them. During the cold nights, the young couple could hardly keep their hands off each other.

Lestadt woke in the grey light of pre-dawn, smiling as his eyes wandered over Raemil. Their naked bodies were tangled around each other. He'd kept things light between them for the first few days to give her time to adjust, but they were both eager to take each other to bed again soon enough.

It was obvious she had caused the earthquakes, but he hadn't broached the subject yet. Her power had made him uneasy, but he was beginning to accept it; after all, they had been through so much together.

Shaking her gently, he watched her bright green eyes slowly open. He grinned. The last two mornings, they had promised each other to get up, but they made love instead. Outside, the rain had finally stopped and Bonnie and Lylah played, chasing each other through the long grass. The horses watched with mild interest.

When finally Raemil and Lestadt were dressed and emerged from the tent, it was nearly mid-morning. The climb was beginning to become steeper and rockier, making progress up the first of the mountains slow. Raemil replaced her hood as they approached the small village of Finigity, just north of Vercosin, where they would stop for the night. Spying children playing ahead, Bonnie raced toward the village, and of course, Lylah followed.

Lestadt was lost in thought. His dreams had come back to plague him again, putting him on edge, and further fuelling his need for revenge. Irramai was not so far now, he hungered for the blood of the Caelinians. They had brutally robbed him of his only family, and he would not be merciful to the king or his soldiers. He had not spoken to Raemil of his dreams. While he wished to share everything with her, there were some things that he was just not ready to talk about.

'I think Bonnie misses her family,' Raemil said, looking back to Lestadt, who had fallen behind.

Lestadt watched the dog play with the children. Keeping their distance, they pulled the horses to a halt. The children took particular interest in Lylah. They didn't have any experience with deer unless it was cooked and on their plates. Lylah bounced around them, just out of reach. The fawn was not quite sure of the human young. The children laughed and squealed, trying to touch Lylah's soft pelt.

A woman emerged from one of the small huts, and upon seeing the two strangers astride their horses, she called the children away. They had been wary of strangers since the Horsham men had begun to take their men, and there had been brutal attacks in the night.

Raemil called Bonnie and Lylah back before continuing through the deathly quiet village of Finigity. It seemed eerily deserted as soon as the children had been made to go inside. Doors were closed, windows were shuttered and the animals were penned in.

'Something haunts these people,' she thought aloud.

'Horsham looms above them. While there is still a distance between them, I've no doubt Horsham men have paid them a visit,' Lestadt said, urging Steel to catch up with Raemil. 'Do you not wonder what they build an army for?'

'No. All I want is my brother.'

'It doesn't worry you even a little that they would go to such extremes to build their army? That they would risk having men, who hated them, within their ranks?'

'Another war to be planned in a warring world. I shouldn't worry,' she said flippantly.

'Yes, you should. What is it exactly that you plan to do once you get to Horsham? Just knock on the door and politely ask for your brother?'

Raemil rolled her eyes. *Not this again.*

'I don't know what I'm going to do. I have no plan, no knowledge of Horsham or what is happening there. All I know is my brother is there and I will stop at nothing to bring him back.'

Silence grew between them on the shadowed track, only the sounds of stones sliding as the horses struggled for footing.

Lestadt was worried for her safety and wished he could talk her out of the whole idea. All things considered, he knew she would no more give up her quest than he would his.

'Perhaps you could use other means to find a way,' Lestadt said awkwardly, not quite knowing how to broach the subject. 'I mean, other than fighting your way in.'

He watched as Raemil's body tensed. She turned, her eyes searching his. He was careful to keep his expression neutral; he knew it was a touchy subject. Her expression softened.

'Lestadt, I know not who or what I am. I'm still only coming to terms with this... this "thing" myself. I was as surprised as you were at Vagamore.'

Lestadt's eyes widened. 'Surely you knew?'

'This was my first journey away from home. Many strange things have happened, even ones that I know for certain did not involve me. How could I know what was me and what was not? What was real and was not? I began to realise at Tagrahan Lake that there was something amiss.'

Lestadt was completely taken aback. 'What else have you done?'

Raemil began to speak slowly at first, not sure if she could tell him. Then suddenly the words all came tumbling out.

She told him about the quake at the first village she had passed through; she told him of the vision of her mother and that the Kannaks were afraid of her. She told him about the crows, about the dreams, what the wind had told her that night that he woke to find her apparently speaking to no one. She told him exactly what had happened at Tagrahan Lake and that she had meant to cause the quake in the valley that killed the cats.

When she finished, Lestadt was not mortified or afraid, he was only curious. A great load was shifted from Raemil's shoulders, she was so relieved. She knew now if she could tell Lestadt, of all people, what she had done and seen and felt, then she could survive anything.

Raemil and Lestadt rode into Vercosin in the early hours of the morning. It was still dark and the town was deathly silent, just as Finigity had been. The shutters and curtains were pulled closed on all windows, and fires burned outside every home. Raemil and Lestadt glanced at each other uneasily. The innkeeper questioned their motives and peered behind them into the darkness several times before letting them inside. There were no stables spare at this late hour, so the horses were tied outside, Bonnie and Lylah beside them.

The room was small and dusty. A rat scuttled behind a chest of drawers when they entered. They were so tired that neither of them cared. They undressed and collapsed into bed, falling asleep almost instantly.

Raemil woke first, opening her eyes to face Lestadt. She beamed, running her fingers along the prickly stubble on his chin. A slow grin caused his cheeks to dimple and her heart fluttered as his eyes met hers.

'I had meant to shave,' he said sleepily.

'Unless you grow a beard down to your knees, it does not bother me.'

'What's wrong with that?' He laughed, stroking an imaginary beard. Lestadt suddenly became more serious.

'Perhaps today we should find a place for you to practise your... powers.'

Raemil rolled onto her back, staring at the cobwebs and yellow stains on the ceiling.

'I don't think it's a good idea, it could be dangerous. Someone could see me, not to mention that I don't know what I'm doing.'

'You knew what you were doing when you created the rockslide.'

'I didn't know what I was doing when I destroyed a whole lake,' she countered.

'You will have to learn sooner rather than later,' Lestadt added.

He was gazing so intently at her that Raemil could barely think.

'Let's not worry about it now,' he said, and with a mischievous grin, he rolled over so he was on top of her.

'You, Lestadt, have a one-track mind.' She laughed.

'There is nothing wrong with that,' he murmured, bending down to kiss her.

He kissed her throat and pulled the blanket down, exposing her breasts. As he began to plant small kisses down her neck, he froze, staring at a mark below her right collarbone.

It was a small and faded thing, something easily missed in the throes of passion and in the dark of the night. It was a sword, the blade pointing down, and a snake coiled around the hilt. His heart felt like it had plummeted to the floor. He knew this emblem well; he despised it. He glanced at her, then back to the emblem, not wanting to believe what he was seeing.

'What's wrong?' she asked, confused.

They had made love many times before and he'd never looked at her like that. Lestadt couldn't find any words, his disbelief turning to anger.

'Lestadt? What is it?'

'That emblem...'

A chill ran down Raemil's spine. She'd never even thought about it, nor would she have ever thought that he would recognise it.

'Lestadt, it means nothing.'

'It means everything!' he shouted.

She flinched at the harshness of his voice; she'd never seen him so angry. She watched in dismay as he backed away from her. A look of disgust marred his face. It was her worst nightmare coming true. She could feel blood rushing to her cheeks, hot tears stinging her eyes.

'Lestadt, wait...' she pleaded as he began to snatch up his belongings and dress himself. 'Don't leave me,' she whispered, her eyes brimming over.

'You lying bitch! I trusted you, and you lied to me!' He hastily yanked up his trousers.

The harsh words cut deep into Raemil's heart.

'No... I...'

'You what?! Tell me the truth – is that not the Caelinian royal emblem? Given *only* to royal members? Fuck! You aren't just one of them, you *lead* them!'

Lestadt packed his things, violently stuffing them into his bag, not bothering to put his shirt on.

'It is, but...'

She was not given the chance to explain.

He opened the door, ignoring the protests of sleeping customers as he stormed out. Still holding the blanket to her nakedness, she raced to the window to see him urge Steel into a gallop and ride away. Raemil slid to the floor and sobbed into the blanket.

Raemil wandered in the dark night, thinking of Lestadt often, and she cried often. Loneliness overwhelmed her.

Her brother left her.

Her father had disowned her.

And now Lestadt.

She had been wandering for days alone and broken-hearted. She hugged tightly to the Black and drew in his warmth and love; it was all she could do to keep herself from succumbing to total and utter despair.

The weather was getting colder and Raemil often found herself lost in mist in the mornings. It had been days since she had fled the Vercosin inn. She had not eaten; she couldn't remember if she had even had any water. Raemil tried to think of something else and spent her days consumed by thoughts of what lay at Horsham. In the quiet of the night loneliness crept in, and too often, she cried herself to sleep.

32. A cloud from hell.

Raemil led the Black up a steep trail on the side of the mountain. She saw snow for the first time, and it wasn't a particularly pleasant experience. She felt queasy and wondered whether it was the rabbit she had shared with Bonnie in the morning. Unused to these heights or the uneven ground, the Black battled his way up the trail, puffs of fog erupting from his nostrils.

Raemil doubled over suddenly and vomited. It was the second time this week she had been physically ill. She breathed deeply and stared ahead, seeing that the ground flattened out again and she would be able to ride. Given the way she had to stretch her food and the onset of a cold-front she had never experienced before, she was unsurprised, but couldn't afford to get sick now.

Once they reached flat ground, Raemil stopped and made a fire, fixing herself some tea in the hopes of easing her stomach. As she sat by the fire waiting for the water to boil, she tried not to think of Lestadt, but to no avail. It had been five weeks since they had parted. She wondered where he was and hoped he was as miserable as she.

Interrupting her thoughts, high above her head she heard the cawing of a crow. She looked up to see the black bird spiral down toward her.

'Have you come to speak more nonsense?' Raemil asked the bird as it landed beside her.

'I have come at the bidding of another. Normally I am somewhat impartial to the goings on with you lot, yet I find myself reluctant to see you die so soon,' said the crow.

'Listen, crow...'

'Arramaou,' said the bird.

'Arramaou? I don't understand what you are talking about. Who sent you and why should I care?' she snapped testily.

'Horsham, Horsham wants to find you. I have been sent to locate you for her.'

'You should have just said so. Here I am, and I am not afraid,' Raemil said, casually stirring her tea.

The bird studied her with his cold, black eyes; there was much for her to overcome. She was being stubborn and he knew she would soon find out the hard way, what she was up against. He wondered briefly if she was a bit simple, perhaps there was nothing of interest for him in this girl after all.

'Very well,' he said before taking flight and circling once before disappearing.

Raemil shrugged off the brief encounter and finished the last dregs of her tea, immediately vomiting it back up. So much for curing her nausea. She extinguished the fire before mounting the Black to continue up the mountain.

All seemed to be in low spirits, even little Lylah. During the first few days, Bonnie wandered off, searching for Lestadt's trail, but Raemil called her back. Now, they had travelled so far and it had snowed. As skilled as Bonnie was, there was no hope of tracking him now.

By nightfall, heavy clouds swallowed the sky and it became too dangerous to travel in the poor light. She made a small camp on an uncomfortably steep part of the mountain. There were scattered rocks and boulders, half buried under dirt and snow. Above her hung a ledge, not overly tall, but big enough to provide her with shelter from the southerly wind.

Raemil left her fire burning as she dozed off. Bonnie and Lylah curled beside her, sharing her warmth. The Black rested beside them, his head hung low, resting a hind leg.

* * *

It broke away from the flock, a simple shift of his wings had him spiralling down toward the ground, like a nightmare on wings. While the others were content to fly south to the call, he was not. They had slept for hundreds of years. Naturally, he had awoken with an insatiable appetite, and would wait for no one.

In the village of Finigity, a woman chased a small tabby cat down past the houses. Everything was locked up tightly, and normally she would have been too, except her cat had raced out the door, just as she was about to lock it. It was just a cat, but it was *her* cat, and she loved him dearly, too much to let him be roaming in the night.

She stopped at the last house, where the last fire burned. It was too dark to see any further and the cat had disappeared. She called and waited. The woman looked up to the sky, it was all grey cloud. As her gaze swept north, she saw a huge black cloud rolling in fast, she hugged her shawl closer. The cloud was ominous, it would likely be a vicious storm.

He dropped lower, his keen night vision guiding him to what he knew would be a tasty morsel. Hearing the flap of wings behind him and turning, he discovered competition. He hissed as they crashed through the treetops and landed gracelessly in the middle of a human nest.

The woman gawked at them, glued to the spot by sheer terror, and perhaps stupidity. No sooner had one landed, with his green eyes fixed on her, another crashed through the trees and onto the road, hissing and spitting like a giant cat.

The first lunged for her. She turned to run and twisted her ankle. As it's huge, snake-like head lunged for her again, it screeched, high pitched and almost unbearable to human ears. Daring to look up, she saw the two dragons snapping and hissing at each other. Raising sharp talons, they grappled and fought ferociously. Using talons, teeth, tail and wing, they battered each other before both leaping at her. The woman, finally finding her wits, crawled to her feet and raced for the nearest hut.

She banged on the door as the two of them loomed behind her, still hissing and snapping. She screamed for help as the face of an aging man peered through the crack of the door. He took one look at the two creatures behind her, and, instead of heroically pulling her inside, he slammed the door in her face and bolted the door.

Backed up against the door, there was nowhere for her to go. She turned and began to claw at the wood in desperation, snapping her fingernails and bending them back until she bled. The dragons arched their necks then lunged, snatching her up between them. Her choking screams cut through the night as they each held onto one half of her, shaking their huge heads until they ripped her clean in half.

The black cloud in the sky shifted, banking low; revealing not cloud but a great writhing mass of bodies. They could hear and smell the frenzied feeding below, excited by the sounds and scents of feeding after hundreds of years without it. They landed in groups, perching themselves on huts and screaming their hunger to the night. People inside cowered and clutched their ears, the frequency of the call excruciating.

They peeled the roof tops back, revealing families of mortals huddled inside. The humans thought to hide under beds and tables and behind locked doors. It was almost too easy. One by one the beasts plucked screaming humans from their homes.

* * *

Raemil was restless. Lylah and Bonnie had long since found another place to sleep where they would not be disturbed. Her ears were ringing, melding into the background of her dreams.

The Black shook his head and flicked his ears; his skin writhing and twitching with anxiety. There was something out there. His nostrils flared wide, taking in the scent of something evil. He snorted and pawed the ground. He nudged his sleeping master with his nose, but she mumbled and rolled away. With a parting toss of his head, the Black headed for cover; Lylah and Bonnie followed.

Raemil shot bolt-upright, clutching her ears to block a piercing sound. Initially, she hadn't heard Bonnie's barking through the noise and pain. Beside her she saw Bonnie snapping and snarling, her hackles raised and her teeth bared. The shepherd was facing the ledge above them, where the noise of gnashing teeth and hissing was coming from. She felt sweat trickle down her temple and didn't want to turn around. She watched with dread as Bonnie went into a frenzy, barking at something above them.

Summoning her courage, she crawled to her feet to face the unknown threat. A huge creature stood perched on the ledge above her head, and as its green eyes locked on her, it spread its wings and stretched its neck, displaying its size. The wings were webbed like bat's wings, spanning roughly eight metres across. It's neck was long and there was no distinction between it and the head, like a snake. It was black, with a subtle red sheen to its scales. It's tail was long and thin, with a meaty bulge on the end, used for pommelling its prey into the ground if all else failed. The creature had three toes on each foot, equipped with talons sharp enough to shred flesh from bone.

It hissed, opening its mouth wide and revealing a fleshy red tongue and rows of serrated teeth. Raemil was frozen and staring into the face of a thirty foot dragon. Needless to say, she had not prepared for this situation. Not knowing what else to do, she grabbed Bonnie by her scruff and turned to run. She stopped dead in her tracks, as another huge dragon skidded to a halt in front of her.

There was nowhere to run, and there was nowhere to hide. Bonnie, either very bravely or very stupidly, was still growling and barking like she might just scare them off. One leaned forward, a sound vibrated from the back of its throat like the purr of an insanely huge cat; but there was nothing pleasant about the creature or the sound. Despite knowing there was still another one behind, Raemil scurried backward as it hissed and snapped.

A massive paw swiped her and she cried out, automatically releasing Bonnie as she toppled to the ground. The dragons were intent on playing with her. Bonnie started barking and snapping the air threateningly again, determined to protect her pack.

Raemil crawled to her feet and wrapped her arms protectively around the shepherd. She considered her magic, but she drew a blank. The second dragon swooped in, hissing as they began to circle Raemil and the dog. Their tails snapped back and forth, the bulbous end knocking Raemil from her feet again.

Raemil felt completely helpless. *What would Lestadt have done in this situation?* She quickly dismissed the thought, it didn't matter. What was *she* going to do? Perhaps another earth quake? It had worked in the past. She put her palms flat on the ground and tried to concentrate her energy into the ground. *Nothing.* She tried again, shaking with the effort, and again, nothing. One of the dragons lunged, Raemil rolled and put her arms up defensively, helplessly. The dragon took her by the arm and flung her sideways. If it had wanted to, it could have easily bitten her arm off, but the beasts seemed content with cruelly toying with their food.

Bonnie lunged.

'No!' Raemil shrieked.

Out the corner of her eye, Raemil saw the small fawn come out of the scrub, the Black materialising like a shadow behind.

'No.' Her voice was a hoarse whisper, tears beginning to sting her eyes.

Raemil grabbed her sword and recklessly ran at the closest dragon, stabbing at its feet while it snapped at Bonnie. The creature screamed its horrible high-pitched rage, turning to attack Raemil. She jumped out of the way, taking another stab at the massive beast as she went. They were big, but they lacked speed.

The other dragon edged closer, wanting in on the action. Bonnie turned her aggression to the new threat, the dragon only missing the angry dog by inches as it snapped back. Raemil watched the exchange, and while her attention was diverted, she was thrown backward into a rock by a flailing wing. Raemil's heart was racing as the dragon faced her. She could feel the sweat trickling between her shoulder blades. She could die this night.

Bonnie yelped as a huge tail battered her hard against a tree. Raemil leapt to her feet as a dragon head came at her with its mouth wide-open, razor-sharp teeth ready to tear her to shreds. She spun to the side and slashed her blade across the beast's throat. Blood sprayed all over her as the dragon's head shot up, roaring and gurgling.

Raemil watched in horror as little Lylah bounded over to Bonnie, who was limping toward the remaining dragon. The dragon was momentarily distracted by its screaming companion, until its head snapped towards Lylah's movement; its pupils became dark pools focused on her. Lylah ran toward the shepherd, her play mate and surrogate mother, not fully understanding the threat.

'Bonnie!' Raemil screamed and raced for her two companions.

The dragon she had just sliced open flailed, knocking her to the ground with its tail as it fell in its final death throes. Tears half-blinded Raemil; it had all happened in a split second, but it seemed to play out in slow motion. The dragon hissed and moved to kill the little fawn. Bonnie leapt in front, hackles raised, teeth bared. The dragon took the dog in one bite, shaking Bonnie until she fell limp, before tossing her aside. Little Lylah saw the dog's body thrown and her little legs took off after her.

Lylah raced to the shepherd's side, the dragon's head following with keen interest. With the beast momentarily forgotten, Lylah sniffed Bonnie's body. She snorted at the smell of blood coming from the dog's mouth. Lylah playfully pounced on Bonnie, thinking it was just a game, but the dog did not move. Looking up, her frightened brown eyes only found a huge dragon staring at her. She brayed, a pitiful, frightened sound. The dragon raised a massive paw and stomped on Lylah, crushing her tiny body with ease.

The dragon roared triumphantly as its companion slowly bled to death beside it. Raemil stared at the scene, stricken with grief and shock, her face deathly pale. Nothing could have prepared her for this.

The slopes were quiet, as though the mountains mourned with her. The wind gently ruffled the grass and seemed to touch her cheek softly in understanding, but the quiet provided little comfort for the loss of Bonnie and Lylah. She closed her eyes as tears slid down her cheeks; they were not mere animals, they had become family and she had loved them dearly.

Raemil knelt beside a patch of turned over soil. She had made a wooden marker and etched their names into the wood. She buried them together, a sentimental part of her rationalising that they still needed each other. She covered the grave in small pink flowers, though she knew the wind would sweep them away or they would die when she was gone. She cried so hard that her body shook. Raemil curled into a tight ball and mourned.

* * *

The woman was wrapped in a white cloak. She walked with a shepherd and a fawn and her black horse. The woman's hair was curly and red like fire. From the bird's eye view that she was watching, this woman looked just like Kyler.

Horsham grinned evilly as Arramaou perched himself on the balcony rail. So, she was heading straight to her, and not far away, as the crow flies, so to speak. It had only taken a few days for Arramaou to come back. Horsham laughed ecstatically, clapping her gnarled old hands together with glee; she would have to do nothing but wait for the lost daughter. The girl was key to her next move.

33. Dog army.

As Lestadt descended the slopes of the last foothill, he caught sight of Irramai. He breathed in deeply, *the free lands*. It was dark and he could see torches burning around the guard wall. As he came closer, he could hear shouts from the walls. The city of Irramai was surrounded and protected by high walls. In the torch-light, Lestadt could see figures moving at the top, the faint sounds of orders in chaos.

Steel became skittish beneath Lestadt and suddenly broke into a flat gallop toward Irramai's high gates. Lestadt tried to pull him back as he saw the dark shapes shifting through the night, but Steel charged on. An impossibly large dog moved out of the shadows of the wall. It snarled and its crimson eyes seemed to bore right into Lestadt's. Lestadt finally managed to pull Steel to a skidding halt in front of the brindle dog that stood at least chest height on the horse. Arrows rained down from the wall but seemed to miss the dogs by inches every time. It was difficult to see, but there were over a dozen dogs that he could make out.

'Halt! Rider on the west side!' came a shout from somewhere above.

Steel screamed and reared and Lestadt drew his sword, and, touching his heels lightly to Steel's flanks, they charged.

The dog snarled and leapt for Steel's throat, but at the last most, Steel twisted, giving Lestadt the opportunity to strike. Lestadt didn't hesitate but with surprising speed, the dog leapt up and grabbed his wrist, pulling him from the saddle. The dog and Lestadt fell to the ground. The canine instantly moved to tear at his throat, but Lestadt thrust the sword into its belly. He crawled to his feet, dripping with blood. He turned to face the wall, seeing dozens of crimson eyes fixed on him.

'Open the gate!' Lestadt yelled as he ran for Steel, who stood vigilant to one side.

Titan stood at the top of the wall, his men rushing around him trying to fight off the huge dogs with little success. He had been a soldier, a pure killing machine, and he was good at it. Now he led Irramai – the free lands. He was protector of the survivors and commander of his men. They were a small resistance to Horsham, but they grew larger by the day.

He could hardly see the man at the bottom of the wall, but he was sure that he was *just* a man. Titan nodded to the soldier beside him and the gates were heaved open on heavy chains. Titan watched with interest as the gates came up halfway and a grey horse thundered into the yard. The man had to duck as he came in, and as he did so, he swung the sturdy grey around to meet the onslaught of hellish dogs. With a great swing of his sword, the man cut a dog's head clean off. Three more rushed in to replace it and as he tried to defend himself from one, he was pulled to the ground by the others.

'Close the gates and get down there,' Titan said.

Lestadt rolled onto his feet, only to be knocked down again. The dog bit into his side and Lestadt felt a rib creak before grasping its jowls and wrenching it away. His grip shifted to the dog's ears, but its powerful jaws began to slip towards Lestadt's face, reminding him of the lion that nearly killed him not so long ago. Pain shot up his leg where another dog joined the attack and bit hard. Lestadt was forced to shift his grip again. Freeing his legs briefly by shoving the dog off with a swift kick to its face, he managed to scramble out from beneath the first one.

Lestadt rolled out of the way, picking up his sword as the dogs launched at him. He stabbed one through the throat, then sliced one across its chest before the other was on him. He kicked and thrusted his sword, until both dogs were maimed. One was dead and the other was clearly dying, but still, it padded toward Lestadt, determined, despite its own fatal wounds. Bleeding and in shock, Lestadt staggered to his feet to meet the attack when an arrow whizzed by and lodged right into the dog's heart.

Looking down, he gawked at his wounds. He hadn't realised how badly they'd injured him until now. His leg was torn up, he had long scratches down his stomach and there was a gash on his head above his eyebrow. He suddenly began to hurt all over as the adrenaline wore off. Lestadt stood, lingering on the edge of consciousness, before his sword slipped from his bloodied fingers and clattered to the ground. He dropped to his knees in the dirt, his hearing muffled as blurry shapes drifted toward him, then he toppled over.

The castle was damaged and the top floors were out of bounds due to the danger of collapse. The roof was missing in much of the upstairs area; it wouldn't be long before the old stone building came down around their ears.

The courtyard was bare, the soil was packed hard after a century of training drills that had taken place there. The twenty foot stone walls made it look more like a prison. Against the north wall stood a large stable, housing fifty horses for use against immediate threats. The rest of the horses were stabled on the other side of the brass gates that separated the city from the courtyard. Behind the castle, the city of Irramai was growing.

Titan turned away from the window. He was in the map room with his most valued men. Yezimar, who had been by his side for years, stood nearest to him. There was Neximus, a hard man, but trustworthy and their best archer. Neximus had no family in Irramai; they were murdered before he reached the free lands. Parleans was an older man, known for his intelligence as an advisor. And there was Rem. His full name was Remmador, but everyone called him Rem. Rem was second in command and a good soldier. Titan couldn't think of anyone else he would rather have at his side in a battle. Rem had only recently married, finding his wife amongst the hordes of refugees that came to Irramai during the last sixteen months, and they already had a baby daughter together.

'I've been informed they are digging under the wall. Parleans has looked over the old maps,' Titan said, gesturing toward sketches of the castle that lay on the desk in front of them. 'It seems the walls extend only a few metres below the soil. The dogs will be in the city within a day, sooner if they all start digging in the same place.'

Titan rubbed his tired eyes and slumped into a chair.

'Why aren't the archers hitting them?' asked Yezimar, looking accusingly at Neximus.

'Have you seen these things move? They're near impossible to hit.' Neximus defended himself and the other archers.

'Well, *near* impossible is not impossible, now is it? Why aren't your archers out there now?' Rem demanded.

'Because I called them in,' said Titan. 'The men are wasting their arrows. They move too fast. Within a blink of an eye they could have moved twenty paces away. We are not dealing with normal dogs here.'

'They can be killed, we saw last night. That man killed them with only his sword. We *can* stand against them when they come in under the wall,' suggested Neximus.

'Can we? There are at least two dogs for every man out there now.'

'What? That's over one thousand dogs! Last night there was less than two hundred!' exclaimed Rem.

'It's obvious they've been sent by Horsham. I've been looking through the archives in the upper levels and found this,' Parleans said, dumping a dusty, open book on the table.

It was a sketch of a large dog, bearing a resemblance to the ones that were currently digging under the castle wall.

'They are the Carlemn hunting dogs, once owned by the mage-king of Carlemnia. He used them in the battle on the Huddington plains, where, legend has it, several mages worked together to destroy them. Before the mage-king of Carlemnia, it is unknown who owned them or where they came from.'

'It seems they reproduce rapidly. Gestation for a bitch can be only hours, taking anywhere between a day and a week for the pups to mature. It's extremely rare for a male to be born, but one had been right before the battle of Carlemnia. There wasn't enough time before the battle for the numbers to get high enough to contend with a coven of mages bent on their destruction.'

'There is magic within them, and as the numbers grow, so too does their power. So, it seems to me that this new-found speed is the result of their breeding. They are highly intelligent animals and will stop at nothing to obey a master's orders.' Parleans finished, looking at the grave faces around the table.

'But if they are so intelligent, then why do they dig separately instead of together?' asked Neximus.

'I do not know.'

The men sat around the table in silence. They had not enough fighting men to face them, and so much at stake, should the dogs succeed in getting through the walls. Titan sighed. Soon he would have to address the people, soon he would have to admit to just how much danger they were all in.

He opened his eyes to a dark room. Beside him on a small table was a glass of water and a bowl of cold soup. His head was throbbing. He touched his head and winced, feeling rough stitches through his eyebrow. His leg was bandaged tightly and there was a sharp pain in his side. He remembered feeling a rib possibly fracture under the force of one of the hell-born dogs.

Lestadt propped himself up on one elbow and scanned the dim room. The dark green curtains were drawn closed, there was no other furniture save the bed and the small table that his meal sat on. He had no interest in the food. He wanted to speak to the leader of Irramai; the sooner he could prove his worth, the better.

As if on cue, the door swung open and a tall man entered. At first, he could only see a dark shadow of a man and for a split second he felt very vulnerable. Stepping into the light, the man was no less intimidating as he loomed above Lestadt in the bed, his face set like stone as his eyes fell on Lestadt. Lestadt was surprised to see the man's hair was the colour of dry wheat fields, a colour foreign to Otowan. At first glance his eyes could almost pass as normal, but they held no break in colour, no lines or detail as most people's iris had. When the stranger moved into shadow, his eyes looked like grey stone, but when the light hit them, they were like polished steel. He probably wouldn't normally notice such details, but the man had a face set like thunder; Lestadt wondered if he had done something wrong.

'Who are you?' he demanded, stepping out of the shaft of light that the open door cast and Lestadt could see him better.

'I am Lestadt of Hewter. Who are you?'

'Neximus.' His facial expression remained unnerving and unchanging.

'Are you in charge here?'

'No. I've come to ask if you know anything of the dogs?'

'Only that they're fast and they bite hard. What's going on?'

The man turned and left the room, assuming Lestadt was of no use to them.

Lestadt was annoyed by the dismissive treatment, but he had to remind himself these people didn't know him. He'd been lucky enough to be allowed in at all, given the mood of the people in the villages he and Raemil previously passed.

Thinking of Raemil left him feeling as though someone had stabbed him in his gut and twisted the knife, but then he *had* been torn up by the dogs. He pushed thoughts of her aside. She was irrelevant, a distraction he did not need.

Swaying with dizziness, he hobbled from the room, using the doorframe and then the walls for support several times. He moved down the hallway of a house and out into a living area. Scanning the room, he almost looked past her twice before spying an aging woman sitting on a chair and knitting. She looked like a pile of old rags amongst more piles of rags.

'Oh, you're up. You mustn't be up, much too soon,' she said, placing her eye-glasses on the table and her knitting beside it.

'Where am I?'

'Irramai,' she said cheerily.

'I know I am in Irramai. I mean – what is this place?' He hadn't meant to sound so frustrated, but he was.

'Well, there's no need to take that tone with me, young man. You are in my house; I am a carer. I triage all the refugees that come to Irramai.'

'Who is in charge here?'

'I am. It's my house.'

Lestadt bit back a sarcastic reply. He was in pain and had no patience for this old crone.

'Who rules Irramai?' he asked slowly, biting off each word.

'Well,' she said, standing with her hands on her hips, 'we've not a king, as such, but if you want someone in charge, Titan is your man.'

'Where can I find him?'

'In the castle, I suspect, but you really shouldn't be going anywhere right now. You've two broken ribs that I can feel, a bump and a gash on your head and nasty bites all over.'

Lestadt limped out of the house. He was thankful she had taken care of him, but he found her dim-witted answers insufferable.

He was surprised to find himself in a large city bustling with life – he hadn't known that Irramai was so big. He called a man in his cart to a halt in the street and asked for a ride as close to the castle as possible. The driver smiled cheerily and took him to the castle gates.

Lestadt went right into the castle. There were no guards barring his way or locked doors. He was astounded that the people were so trusting.

He bumped into a soldier in a corridor.

'Can you tell me where to find Titan?'

The soldier nodded and silently led the way. It was unusually simple.

Titan, Parleans, Rem, Yezimar and Neximus had been in the map room for hours and still had no solution.

'We need to kill the male before one thousand becomes two thousand,' Neximus said, pacing the length of the room.

'How can we possibly tell from such a distance which one is the male? And how do we kill him once we know which one he is?' Parleans asked as he scanned the maps again with renewed frustration.

'It will be the one with bollocks swinging between his knees,' Neximus mumbled under his breath and continued to pace.

There was a knock at the door and they all looked up, dreading more bad news. It was only a soldier presenting the man from last night. Titan had an open door to the public at this point. Survival was their goal and anyone willing to help contribute to that was welcome. He did not fancy himself a king, rather just a man like any other.

'My name is Lestadt.'

'What business do you have here, Lestadt?' asked Titan, only very briefly looking up from the mounds of scrolls both rolled and unrolled on the table.

'Are you Titan?'

Titan nodded.

'I have come to offer you my services.'

'Are you a soldier?'

'Not as such.'

'Then what bloody help are you going to be?' asked Yezimar in his frustration.

'I can wield a sword and a bow as good as any other,' Lestadt said with confidence.

'What do you know of these dogs?' asked Yezimar.

'I already asked him, he knows nothing,' said the blonde-haired man Lestadt met earlier.

'Well, why don't you tell me what is going on, and perhaps I can be a pair of fresh eyes at the least.'

Parleans looked up at Titan's tired face. They needed all the help they could get. Titan nodded, no one else was coming up with anything ground-breaking.

Lestadt rubbed his head, wincing as his hand brushed over the stitches through his eyebrow, again.

'Have you got men out there watching the dogs?'

'We have two men standing post,' replied Titan.

'Any change?'

'Originally they were digging in odd places around the entire fortress, now they have gathered at the front, all in a line and focused on the gate.'

Lestadt sat back, his eyes roaming over the maps in front of him. Inspired, he eased out of his chair and started flipping through a dozen maps that were on the table.

Lestadt grabbed the map he needed. It was old and yellowed and showed the structure of the wall. The wall was pretty standard, save that it had been reinforced with another layer of bricks to keep it standing strong. There was a code in the top right corner of the page: HL4S12P4.

He looked up to the men. 'What does H-L-4-S-1-2-P-4 mean?'

Titan looked to Parleans who shook his head in confusion. Surprising all the men in the map room, with the exception of Lestadt, who didn't know anything about any of them, Neximus approached the table.

'Let me see.'

Lestadt offered him the map. Neximus studied it for a moment then he looked to Parleans.

'History log four, section twelve, page four.'

Both Yezimar and Rem gave Neximus a suspicious glare, but Neximus ignored it. He pulled a stool up to the table while Parleans hurried from the room.

'What significance do you think the map has?' Neximus asked.

Lestadt looked around the room. Seeing hopeful faces, he wished he could provide more.

'I don't know how we can defeat the dogs. You said they were intelligent, so why were they digging in separate places along the same wall until now? I think maybe there is something about that wall. Why not dig at the back of the city, where they can get to the people faster?' Lestadt sighed, tired and in pain. 'We need to find out what they are doing, or at least how much time we have before the city is breached.'

'This is pointless,' Yezimar said, throwing his hands in the air.

'We have no way of defeating the dogs, and you are worried about finding out how they are going to get in and kill us all?' Rem snapped, mirroring Yezimar's anger.

Titan ignored it all, staring blankly at the maps on the table. He was so tired. He had not asked to run Irramai, it just happened; now he felt the burden of too many lives in his hands.

'We are trying to save a city, and you two are having a tantrum! What do you do when you are planning an attack on an enemy?' Neximus demanded, his steely glare pinned Yezimar.

'Do not patronise us, you are nothing! You're just an archer...'

Ignoring the barb, Neximus continued, 'You find out all you can about the enemy, the most valuable information being how the enemy thinks, its weaknesses...'

'I cannot believe my ears, the dumbest man alive is giving us a lecture!' Yezimar said, throwing his arms in the air in a theatrical gesture and storming out of the room, Rem following after him.

'What a time for my best men to have a second childhood,' Titan mumbled.

'How many people in this city?' Lestadt asked, ignoring the bickering behind him.

'Including the soldiers, less than two thousand, but we cannot expect them to fight. Women cannot fight, and most of the men have never been trained to wield a sword.'

'Women can fight, I've seen it. When your life is threatened, it's amazing what people can do. Give them an inspirational speech, remind them that they have their freedom to fight for, and they will fight for Irramai.'

Lestadt took his leave of the men shortly after, to give them space to think.

Titan looked up at Neximus, who was staring at the maps in front of him.

'Why must you fight with everyone, Neximus? The world is not against you, we are not against you.'

'What would you know, Titan? You have a city at your feet, you command an army of hundreds of men who would give their lives for you. And as always, I stand alone.'

'You are not alone. If you would stop being so damned difficult, then the men would like you.'

He knew Neximus was a good man, he had spent enough time with him to be sure, but the hostile façade he showed the world pushed people away more often than not.

'The men will never like me; they will never respect me. You know it and I know it, so just let it be.'

Titan shook his head.

'Fine, if you are determined to be a prick, then so be it, but I will not have you disrupting my men.'

Neximus gritted his teeth. Titan could be a fool sometimes; he didn't want to see that his precious friends were the arseholes.

Yezimar's comment had angered and humiliated him. Neximus wasn't stupid, but a failure to read aloud a letter from a messenger, in front of half of the army, left him with a reputation. Neximus had never been taught to read and the men, who already didn't trust him because of his appearance, had not let him forget about it. He could understand the letters and numbers, but he didn't understand how the letters came together and formed words, especially if he was under pressure. Once, Titan had offered to have someone teach him to read, but Neximus wasn't about to let them humiliate him further.

They reconvened in the map room, Lestadt amongst them. Parleans opened the book to the page that was indicated on the map, skimming over the writing in silence. After a few minutes, Parleans looked up at the men in defeat.

'It just mentions the history of the wall, nothing of use.'

'A waste of our time,' Yezimar said sourly.

'What does it say?' Lestadt asked, annoyed he'd given up so easily.

Parleans sighed.

'The wall was built when the threat of war came, then, in peace-time, the king ordered his men to knock the front wall down to open Irramai to the world again. Twenty years later, the king's successor ordered for the front wall to be rebuilt as the world warred against the mages. That's it, basically.'

'Basically? Let me see,' Lestadt said, reaching for the book.

No one seemed to question the stranger's lack of deference to the men in charge. As Parleans handed the book over, a folded piece of paper slipped into Lestadt's hands.

'What is it?' Titan asked as Lestadt folded the page out.

'Another map of the wall; this is how it was rebuilt.'

Lestadt placed it on the table beside the new one.

'It's all the same wall, how is this relevant?' Rem complained.

The others showed no interest either, only Titan still held out hope. Lestadt looked over the map while Titan leaned over his shoulder, searching for any small detail that could help them.

'Here,' Titan said, pointing to the new map where the west wall and gate met the adjacent walls. Everyone suddenly looked interested again.

'You see where the walls meet on the old map, now look on the new map. On the old one, the walls are interlocked, the stones fitting together to hold strong, but on the new one, the front wall stands alone.'

He interlocked his fingers to make his point.

'What does it mean?' Yezimar asked.

'Neximus, you logged where all the dogs were digging originally, right?' Titan asked the tall man, who had been leaning against the wall and watching everyone.

'Yes.'

He came back to the table and fished around for his scrap of paper with his hasty drawings scrawled across it. Titan scanned the parchment, then the map.

'These are places that are likely the weakest parts of the walls.'

Titan pointed to the corresponding places on the map, looking pale as he dropped the paper back on the table.

Lestadt still held the map, staring as though it were a puzzle he could solve.

'The dogs will dig out under here,' he said, pointing to either side of the gate, 'because the front wall is not supported by the adjacent walls. With no earth beneath its middle, it will fall fastest and more likely in one hit. The dogs would get in all at the same time, instead of trickling through one after the other from a tunnel, essentially making it harder for us to cope,' Lestadt said as Titan stepped back so the others could hover over the new map.

'They abandoned the surrounding walls after *you* came in,' Parleans said accusingly, hinting that Lestadt was the reason they were attracted to the weakest part of the fortress.

'They may get in faster, but at least we will be facing them on one side, instead of spreading ourselves thin throughout the city,' Neximus said, coming to Lestadt's defence. Whether on purpose or by coincidence was unclear.

The men's faces fell. If their wall came down, the city of Irramai would fall too. They didn't have the forces to fight these things whether they were all in one place or not. All that was between the front wall and the city was the castle and high brass gates. The full force of that number of dogs could easily break it down, leaving the common folk exposed.

34. Five warriors.

Despite the torches burning in pale and shaking hands along the great walls, the city was plunged into darkness. Their hearts were heavy with dread as dusk fell, the crickets and cicadas fell silent as apprehension grew. The air was thick and tense; there was little hope in any heart as the people clung to the brass gates that shut them off from the courtyard. They watched with fear in their eyes and in their hearts, for any sign, any warning that their time was nigh.

Atop the walls the shouts and orders had long since fallen silent. The soldiers, and a whole city, waited in darkness with bated breath. The torches flickered, licking at the darkening sky as a gentle breeze coaxed them to burn brighter. Less than one hundred archers were lined along the stone wall, their bows trained on the lower half of the front wall. They waited and listened, as the whole city did. A further six hundred men were backed against the castle walls and along the front of the brass gates. They had swords at the ready, waiting for that terrible moment when they would rush forward to meet their foe.

Five men stood at the very front; their eyes held fierce determination. Each thought of their pasts, the needless deaths of their loved ones, the sorrow, the humiliations, everything that had brought them to Irramai. They turned the pain into anger, and they directed that anger at the wall. Swords were clenched tightly in fists, keen eyes watching the wall.

The five consisted of very different men, but they stood together nonetheless. In the middle, stood a broad-shouldered man. He had long dark hair that was tied back at the nape of his neck, his brown eyes set under a heavy brow. His skin was dark bronze and the very look of him cried war. He was Titan.

On Titan's left stood a slighter man in build, with lighter coloured hair that was pulled back in a braid. His eyes were also brown, but again, lighter than Titan's. He had a goatee that was shaped almost squarely to join with his short moustache. This man was Yezimar. Beside Yezimar, stood the third man. His hair was dark brown, nearly black in the fading light, and long, but hung loose around his face, his eyes were grey. He was shorter than the others, but what he lacked in height, he made up in brawn. On the battlefield he was known as a maniac, and rightly so. His name was Remmador and he currently stood with a sword in one hand and a sharp hatchet in the other.

On Titan's right, stood a tall man, his golden hair cropped short and his eyes the colour of steel and as hard. He had two days' worth of stubble on his jaw. He wore only a thin singlet, baring his muscular arms as he stood ready with a long sword in his left hand and a dagger in his belt. He was Neximus, both a feared and hated man among his peers.

Next to Neximus was a stranger, only just slightly shorter and of similar build to Neximus. He wore long sleeves rolled up to the elbows, still adjusting to the colder climate of the southern lands. He had dark brown hair that was also cropped short, his eyes were as blue as the Sapphire Seas. His name was Lestadt.

Children had been locked away in the houses; their eerie muffled howls could be heard echoing in the deserted streets. Mothers' hands shook as they feared for the safety of their children, who they had forced behind locked doors to keep them relatively safe from harm.

The wall groaned. The five stood stock-still as it shuddered and debris sifted down between cracks.

'Here we go,' Titan said quietly to his men.

The middle wall sagged forward as though it were elastic. The sound of stones rubbing together was now all that anyone could hear. Huge cracks snaked down the centre, then with an almighty *crash*, the wall folded in on itself and dragged the rest of it down as a huge ball of dust rose into the air.

Some of the soldiers rushed forward past the five as the dust billowed into the air. Perhaps overly keen for a fight, or startled into running like a frightened flock, or just plain stupid; it didn't really matter. The five held fast, waiting for the dogs to come to them. The first soldiers stopped, realising their mistake.

The dust was too thick, obscuring the enemy. They glanced nervously at each other and peered ahead but could hardly make out a shape, or breathe for that matter. High up on the remaining walls, the archers, even with their keen sight, could not make out the dogs. Their brindle coats were camouflaged perfectly into the veil of dust and debris.

Slowly, small specks of crimson began to appear through the haze. The men that had been foolish enough to rush into the dust met their end screaming horrifically, but no one saw.

The dogs had lost some of their pack when the wall fell, but the rest were undeterred. As the tall dogs slinked into view, the remaining soldiers ran forward to attack, the five joining their comrades in a battle for their very lives.

Behind the brass gates, women clung tightly to each other and their pitiful weapons of firewood, kitchen knives and heavy rolling pins and pots. They watched as their husbands, brothers and friends were viciously mauled by the hell-born dogs. The soldiers were tasked to keep the dogs away from the brass gates and the city for as long as possible. They hoped it would not come to the women having to fight, but the odds were not in their favour.

* * *

Her gaunt face twisted into something resembling a grin, laughing as she watched the battle unfold with her mage sight. She watched through enchanted water in a bowl shaped from a particular stone that naturally concentrated her power. Both Horsham and Tannagan watched the men battle with the Carlemn hunting dogs. Horsham enjoyed showing off her newly gained strength to her daughter.

Arrows rained down on the scene; the archers seemed to be shooting blindly. Beside Horsham, Tannagan laughed as she watched an archer accidentally shoot one of his own. The dogs leapt, tearing at faces, ripping open stomachs and throats. Blood splattered on the paved courtyard, making it slick with red mud.

Horsham scowled as she saw five men fighting away from the main horde. They fought in a semi-circle with their backs to the grey castle wall. They struggled with the dogs' speed to begin with and a few of them suffered injuries, but they'd since found their rhythm. They were formidable together.

'Who are these warriors?!' Horsham snapped as she watched one of them cut down a dog with a hatchet.

'I don't know, Mother,' Tannagan replied dismissively, entertained by the battle and disinterested in anything that wasn't dead or already dying.

Someone threw a torch soaked in flammable liquid from over the brass gates, hitting one of the dogs.

Amazingly, the dog burst into flames and ran off screaming into the battle, setting men on fire as it went. Tannagan burst into laughter again at the sight of frantic Carlemn hunting dogs setting men ablaze. *What a disaster!* she thought, as she struggled to gain her composure in front of her scowling mother.

* * *

'Gods!' Titan exclaimed as he glanced up to see a few of his men rolling on the ground in flames. Black smoke billowed into the night sky.

The stables against the north wall had caught alight. Horses screamed in terror as the smoke threatened to choke them and flames licked at their stalls. Titan and the other four men were surrounded. The dogs were so fast as they zipped around them, trying to find the weak link in the group.

Lestadt heard the terrified screams of the horses and struggled to keep focus. Steel was in that stable. Taking advantage of his distraction, a dog leapt at him, gripping his arm in its jaws like a vice. He viciously kicked its legs out from under it. The dog landed on its back, exposing its belly and giving Lestadt his opportunity. He jammed his sword into the dog's gut. With a final twist of his sword, the contents of its stomach spilled amongst the rest of the gore at Lestadt's feet.

'I have to get those horses out!' Lestadt shouted above the din of battle.

As Lestadt fought his way toward the stables, the group stepped backward to close the gap in their defence that the dark- haired warrior left behind.

* * *

Horsham's knuckles turned white as she gripped the stand her bowl rested in, while Tannagan watched eagerly as blood spilled in the courtyard of Irramai.

The younger mage scanned the pitiful faces of the women and men that were locked behind the brass gates. *Such despair, such anguish, such horror!* She thrived on such things.

There were many more dogs than there were men in the courtyard, but the five warriors were killing them at an alarming rate. Horsham watched as one of the five broke away to run into the burning stables. *Fool*, she thought bitterly, *hearts have no place in war.*

Moments later, ghostly shapes galloped out of the flaming building and into the thick, choking smoke. Dozens of the beasts ploughed through the courtyard, knocking both man and dog to the ground in their pursuit of freedom. The horses screamed in panic, the whites of their eyes showing as their eyes rolled in their heads.

Horsham glowered as she watched the dark-haired warrior re-join the other four. Tannagan grinned as she watched the terrified beasts plunge through the chaos. *Idiotic creatures*, she thought. Only one horse had brains enough to go over the ruins of the front wall, and even that one snapped a leg in its desperate attempt to flee.

Tannagan's triumphant thoughts were interrupted as she heard her mother growl beside her.

'They have killed him!'

One of the five warriors had just hacked the male Carlemn hunting dog's head off. Now she had no male for breeding. She'd had great plans for her pack of ruthless killers, and now their numbers and powers were at stake. In a fit of rage, she screeched like a feral animal and overturned the stand, scattering the image into a million pieces.

* * *

The women and men behind the gates could take it no more. Together they forced the brass gates open, stupidly rushing out into battle.

'Get back!' Yezimar shouted hoarsely.

The split second he turned to see the gates forced down cost him dearly. Two dogs leapt on him, ripping open his chest and legs. He let out a single cry of pain before his voice was smothered by the huge hunting dogs.

Perhaps a dozen citizens had ploughed into the full force of the battle and were killed before the dogs suddenly retreated. Titan, Rem, Neximus and

Lestadt stood for long moments, still in their defensive semi-circle. They surveyed the horror before them, not one of them feeling they had won.

The carnage in the courtyard was brutal as they began the body count. They found discarded arms and legs around the space; it was a gruesome task to clear the area. Half covered by a canine body, one of the soldiers pulled Yezimar free. He was deathly pale, horrifically wounded and barely conscious. His torn chest revealed three ribs, smashed and bloodied. Yezimar was slowly bleeding to death when he was stretchered to the old healer in the city.

The grey morning revealed a bloodstained courtyard and hundreds of human and dog bodies strewn on the ground like leaf litter. Beneath the ruined wall poked brindle tufts of hair and occasionally a dog leg or head poking out from beneath the rubble. There was nothing to rejoice here. The city still stood, but for how long? And at what price?

They sat in the tiny, dust filled map room of Irramai's castle. Parleans was now sitting with the four exhausted men as their wounds were dressed. Titan had suggested Parleans stay with the men and women behind the brass gates. The older man had lamely insisted that he stay with Titan, but in the end, he knew he was no soldier and no longer had youth on his side.

They had all been surprised by Lestadt. Despite his injuries and his claim he was no soldier, he had fought well. They had made a good team, the five of them.

'Any news on Yezimar?' Rem asked.

'Not yet,' Titan said forlornly.

There was a knock on the door and without much pause, a soldier entered the room.

'One hundred and forty-three dead, sir. One hundred and twenty-eight soldiers and fifteen civilians.'

Titan thanked him, though he didn't feel particularly thankful.

Out of the thirty horses stabled in the courtyard, eleven had been severely injured and had to be killed, and most were traumatised. Steel was found unscathed and was cheekily foraging for unburnt bits of hay amongst the ruins.

Lestadt was not cold-hearted; he felt sorry for the men that had been killed and the people that grieved them. He also knew an opportunity when he saw one. After all, he would be looking after Irramai's interests as much as his own.

35. Nights of the damned.

Drawing ever closer to Horsham, she considered a million different things she could have tried or done. The night the dragons attacked her, her heart felt broken all over again. She could barely remember how she had escaped the jaws of the ghastly dragon. *A piercing whinny, a flash of thundering hooves kicking up clods of dirt and snow in the beast's wake. Snorting and nervous stamping of hooves.* Somehow, Raemil had found the courage and strength to get on.

She hugged the Black now as he struggled to keep his footing going up a steep incline. Going against his natural instincts, he had raced to her that night. He had been her strength in her weakest moment.

Ahead there was another deep gully where the mountains seemed to both end and begin at once. The white snow made everything appear clean and pure, any foot prints of human or animal or other had been covered or swept away by the icy winds. She was so close to finding Serrin.

Raemil touched her hand to her belly and her heart fluttered like a trapped bird. *But could she go to Horsham now? Could she risk it? Risk herself?* The hammering in her chest grew fierce as guilt plagued her soul. The Black shifted nervously under her weight; he was not without scars from the dragon night. Her nervousness flowed right to him and he pricked his ears and sniffed the crisp air, expecting to see a great winged beast spiral out of the sky.

Raemil hadn't been physically ill for a while now, but she was certain of what had caused her sickness. She'd dreamed of a tiny child wrapped up in her arms, and to Raemil's surprise when she awoke, she discovered that her belly was slightly swollen. Here she was, in the Horsham Mountains in the freezing winter snow, riding to a deadly place, and she was with child.

Could she raise a fatherless child? Could she raise a child at all? She wept as she wondered what Lestadt's reaction would have been, had he not fled from her. Her a mother, and he a father. It didn't seem real, but at the same time, it felt terrifyingly real. *How and where could she raise a child?* She had nothing to offer a new life in this world. This was the last piece of Lestadt she had, and it was hers. *He* was hers. She was convinced it was a boy; she didn't know how, or why, she just knew.

Glancing one last time up at the black smudge on the peak of the highest mountain, with a sadness constricting her heart, she turned the Black away from Horsham. As much as she longed to see Serrin and though it seemed that it was only just out of reach, she dared not go. She could hardly go to Horsham pregnant.

Raemil didn't want to think about how she could go to Horsham with a baby in her arms if she couldn't with a baby in her womb. Using her cloak, she shielded herself from the wind. She could just make out a cave ahead. She would stay there as long as she needed to decide what she was going to do with herself and a baby.

The wind howled and viciously whipped the snow in and around the small cave. Raemil could see nothing but white beyond the mouth. It was freezing and she was so hungry, but there was little she could do until the storm subsided. She lit a small fire at the back of the cave, but the wind found a way in and was threatening to snuff out the already guttering flames.

Beside her, the Black shifted uncomfortably. He disliked both the storm and his confinement beneath it. His ears were flat back against his skull as he listened to the screaming winds beyond. He was also terribly hungry; food was scarce this time of year and he hadn't eaten for a day.

They had been in the cave for nearly two weeks now. There was hardly any food for her or the Black and her pregnancy was advancing at an alarming rate. She longed for human company, someone to tell her it was all going to be okay, and that it was perfectly normal, but she knew this was far from normal. Pregnancy in humans lasted for nearly ten months. It had scarcely been two months since Lestadt left and already her stomach was huge, her breasts were swollen and the child had begun to move. Her unborn child was taking a toll on her body: her arms and legs were bony and she had dark rings under her eyes. It seemed the child was sucking the life out of Raemil. Each day she felt just a little weaker than the day before. The lack of food didn't help.

Raemil walked to the tiny fire and stirred a pot of watery broth that simmered gently above. It consisted mainly of water and very few herbs. Removing the broth, she sat back down while it cooled, resting her hand on her belly as she felt the baby kick. She wondered what it would be like to be a mother and wondered what he would look like. She hoped he would look more like Lestadt than her; Raemil wouldn't wish her appearance on anyone.

Raemil's grip tightened over her belly as she heard strange whisperings in the wintery night. The creatures of the night often haunted her from just outside the cave. She could see shifting forms of dark demons and deformed creatures through the snow, but they never stepped over the threshold. She trembled with fear as she watched a pair of yellow eyes peer into the cave at her. Beside her, the Black snorted and shied away from the cave's gaping mouth.

A chill ran down her spine as she heard the yellow-eyed demon speak.

'Come and play,' it whispered.

'Leave me alone.' Raemil's voice was hoarse. She had no courage to face a demon.

'Come sorceress, we will eat of your flesh and bathe in your blood.'

'Leave!'

'We will devour your unborn child and feast on the flesh of innocence.'

Raemil whimpered and curled into a tiny ball over her stomach.

'We rule the night and feed on the people.'

'Go away!'

'You will die, and they will die.'

'Come, sorceress, play with us,' it whispered. 'Your time has ended; our time has begun. Come, Raemil! Mage of the earth, heir to Caelin!'

Hatred stirred within Raemil. How dare this creature threaten her so!

'Be gone, creature of the night! Leave this place! You are not welcome here!' she shouted with a strength she did not feel, glaring all her anger and disgust into the foul creature's yellow eyes.

Within an instant, the eyes, and the creature they belonged to, vanished. The whispering remained, promising her death, but they were just whispers, nothing more. Raemil wondered what kept the creatures of the night from coming into the cave. It was obvious she was not fit to defend herself, so why linger outside? Raemil drank her broth and lay down beside the Black to share his warmth. She thought of Serrin and wondered how he fared. Was he even alive?

***

In villages far and wide, all around the land of the betrayers, it would seem that hell had woken and the creatures of the night fed. Many demons had been released on the land. In the village of Witchgrave, the demon of torment devoured children in front of parents. She fed on their anguish, their heartache, *their torment.* In the deadlands, the demon of pestilence plagued the desert rats, reptiles and insects. In front of him a centipede writhed and twisted in agony until it tied itself in a knot and struggled so hard that it ripped itself in half. The pustule covered face split into a hideous grin as he watched the small insect writhe in agony while it slowly died.

Many demons waited in dark woods, caves and boles. After countless millennia of banishment, they were back on the mortal plain. They had been called home. Among the demons was Murott, the Devourer of Souls. His grey, knobbed fingers twisted ugly daisy-chains in the night while he waited for his victims.

***

High on the Horsham mountains, there perched the army of winged beasts. They waited patiently for their caller to address them. They stood as statues around the courtyard, their eyes focused on the west tower where *she* dwelled. *Soon*, they mused as one, soon they would feed as did the demons outside. Their time had begun, now they waited for the words, the words that would set them to their task.

Then it was done. A black cloud spiralled above the crumbling castle on top of Horsham. It whirled higher and higher, then suddenly it seemed to explode. Fragments of the cloud darted off in all directions. They were released into the night, to feed on anything they could catch. A group of five broke away together; they had their own task to perform before they too could scatter across the land. These five headed north-east where a feast awaited them.

* * *

Raemil slept fitfully, dreaming of her baby and the demons that threatened to kill him, unaware of the other things that haunted the night. Outside her cave alone, there crawled dozens of crazed and warped people. They had been mothers, fathers, sisters and brothers, but now they were twisted by the demons and the creatures that plagued the lands at night. They moved with one thought, one feeling, one mind. They were there to create madness, to slaughter any who remained what they once were.

Beside Raemil, the Black trembled, he could feel the prickling unease of a demon's touch in his mind. He could smell their stench of rotting flesh and festering wounds. Standing up and careful not to harm his sleeping master, he began to pace nervously around the small cave. There would be no peace for him or his master in this cave; but was there any plain, hill or mountain that was safe now?

36. Pink aunts and blue princes.

Prince Tylon rode Windfall into the city of West Sirron in the late afternoon. The streets were strangely deserted and he could feel his chest tighten with unease. Windfall pricked his ears and scanned his surrounds; he had seen enough cities in his time to sense that something was amiss. He could feel it in the air. *Where were all of the people?*

The prince gave Windfall a gentle nudge and they trotted through the side streets. As they approached the lake, Tylon's jaw almost dropped. He couldn't believe all that had happened since he'd left. Where the enchanted bridge would normally meet the shore, there used to be two watch-towers either side, but only one tower remained, which had been built higher to peer beyond the city. In the cleared space, there was a group of soldiers by a tall tent, and in front of the soldiers, there lined hundreds of civilians. The soldiers were taking down information. These people were joining the army.

The soldiers saw him approach and bowed, as did most of the people that recognised him. Prince Tylon gave them a quick nod before he urged Windfall on, whispering an enchantment, along with a few quick hand gestures for the bridge to appear. Windfall's hooves clattered on the bridge as he galloped toward the castle. It felt like coming home.

Reenah sat in the library. Three dusty books sat in front of her on an old pine desk. She sighed and turned the page of the biggest book in front of her. It seemed like there was something missing. They had tried everything to reach the lost daughter, but nothing worked. It was as though she weren't a mage at all. But of course, she was a very powerful one. So why was it so damned difficult to reach her?

They hadn't explored potions as an option. Most mages were more used to using their minds or spells, coupled with hand gestures. Potions were a difficult thing to master; one missed ingredient could have disastrous effects. Reenah hadn't studied potions herself, but she knew Elyr had in her youth. She stood and rolled her head on her neck to work out the tension. She'd been bent over that desk for hours. Oesyth and Elyr were in the library somewhere amongst the many dark and dust filled aisles.

Reenah wandered through aisles filled with ancient books and scrolls. Occasionally she would brush aside a cobweb that hung from the ceiling or a shelf. It was a long walk before she found what she was looking for. She filed through the books in front of her and picked up a small, green handbook called *Peering into present*. Reenah began to flip through the pages as she walked back to the desk. There were so many potions for so many seemingly useless things.

Behind her, a tall, blonde-haired man stood watching her intently. He went unnoticed as a cloud of enchanted mist smothered the scent and feel of his power and being. He smiled, entertaining the thought of scaring her, then decided it would be in poor taste while everyone was on edge. He shadowed her movements, watching as her brow furrowed in concentration.

'Tylon, do you know what a level three potion mage is?'

Tylon jumped and let the enchantment fall.

'How did you know?'

'You slipped, I could feel the moisture in the air.' She laughed at his disappointment, then added, 'Don't let the sisters catch you using water-magic amongst all their books.'

He grinned sheepishly. 'I don't know what a level three is. Perhaps you should ask one of the sisters?'

Reenah nodded. 'I thought you went home to Byrass?'

'I would probably be of more use here than in Byrass, besides, the company here is much better.' He smiled and escorted her from the library.

'Why are the sisters drafting civilians into the army? Surely we could find more soldiers before we had to resort to that?' he enquired as they strolled through the hallways and out into the foyer.

'Well, that is exactly it. If we have to resort to that, then our people must be ready. They are volunteer reserves. Oesyth wants the willing men to start light weapons training this week.'

'It's really happening, isn't it?' the prince sighed.

'We have known for a while now...'

'But then it was just speculation, it wasn't so ominous. On the bright side, I could be killed before I have to marry Princess Yaeli,' he tried to joke.

'Don't say that. I – we would rather you alive and married than dead.'

'Well, thanks, I'm glad to hear it.'

Elyr interrupted them as she rushed down the main stairs.

'Prince Tylon.' She bowed in greeting. 'Reenah, Prince Tylon, would you join us in the stone room?'

In the stone room, Kyler and Oesyth sat in front of the dark green stone, a shallow dish of water on the floor in front of them. Beside Oesyth, there sat a large open book. Elyr, Reenah and Tylon sat beside them, forming a semicircle around the stone and the dish. Oesyth and Kyler had their eyes closed, whispering a spell. The dish of water clouded, foamed, then cleared again, showing nothing but the reflection of the brightly coloured ceiling.

The other three mages picked up on the spell, then, closing their eyes, they joined Oesyth and Kyler in their chant. In front of them, the stone flared and the water clouded. At first, the murky water was green, but, as it became denser, it lost the colour, and soon became white. They peered into the dish. Long moments of silence passed before Reenah spoke.

'What is the spell?'

'To show us where the lost daughter is,' Oesyth replied, not taking her eyes from the dish.

'She's in a cloud?' Elyr asked.

Kyler shook her head in frustration.

'Why is this not working?'

'It is!' Tylon said, leaning forward eagerly.

They watched as the whiteness roiled and shifted, and suddenly, a fearsome face peered through the water at them. Beady black eyes stared at them from a sickly green face. The creature grimaced, revealing tiny, yellow, pointed teeth. White shrouded its disfigured body as it stepped away, extending its arm toward them and inviting them to follow. The mages watched as the scene altered and revealed a woman lying on the ground. Her naked body was covered in oozing scabs and welts. The stranger looked up and shrieked, raking her long fingernails down her own face. She left deep gouges down her forehead and cheeks; blood pooled into her eyes.

Reenah shuddered. *Was this the lost daughter? Was all hope gone?* She watched as the creature grabbed the woman by her hair. He pulled her roughly to her feet, and she made no sound of protest as she stared ahead through blood-filled eyes. The creature forced her to look into its eyes and as she did, her face twisted and she screamed horribly. Bloodied tears streamed down her tortured face. The image of the woman and the creature disappeared, and the murky water showed them more. Children dying alone in the streets, animals turned mad, people gone insane, some suffering unimaginable wounds. One man was shouting aggressively at a tree, his flesh was gangrenous, but he didn't seem to notice. Figures roamed the land, not human, not animal, but odd twisted creatures that could have once been men and women.

Reenah swallowed. She knew it was Otowan, the land of the betrayers. It had already fallen into despair and this was what awaited Iadron. She glanced back into the water to see the horrible creature staring at them again. A malignant creature should not be able to see them fully while they were in the protection of the stone room, but Reenah felt as though it was staring right into her soul. An ugly diseased hand shot toward them and before anyone could react, it reached out of the dish and wrapped it's disgusting hand around Kyler's throat.

'Demon!' Elyr shouted in terror.

Kyler choked as the demon's hand closed tighter around her throat.

'Join us, earth mage! Or you shall suffer in madness!'

The demon's face twisted into a mixture of anger and surprise.

'What trick is this? You are no earth mage – you are nothing! Give me that bitch of a mage!' the demon squeezed harder.

Kyler was about to lose consciousness. The other mages were impotent against the demon. Less powerful, they could not affect it as it could clearly affect them from beyond.

Using her last ounce of energy, Kyler focused inward, she closed her eyes and let it take hold. The energy burned inside. It crept forward and out of her body until it reached the skin around her throat. The demon recoiled, letting the mage go and pulling his arm back into his own land. Before the demon could retaliate, with a flick of his wrist, Prince Tylon forced the water from the dish and the image sloshed onto the ground.

They sat in shocked silence, letting Kyler regain her breath.

'What was that about?' Elyr asked, breaking the silence and staring wide-eyed at Kyler.

'I don't know. The demon was mistaken, perhaps looking for the lost daughter also.'

'So, this is what is to become of our home – a cesspool of pain, madness and disease?' Reenah asked.

'Not if we can help it,' Oesyth said firmly. Her lips were pursed and she had a look of determination on her tired face.

'Well, that was yet another useless attempt,' Kyler croaked bitterly. 'We already know she is in the land of the betrayers. One would expect the spell to be a little more specific.'

'Elyr, Reenah has found a book on potions. Do you know what a "level three" potion mage is?' Prince Tylon ventured.

'It would be a very powerful and skilled potion mage. Mages have in the past studied for years and never reached that level. All those books were written centuries ago, they mostly apply to full-bloods. I doubt that any of us, save Kyler, would be able to use them.'

'I thought that you studied potions?'

'I did, and although knowledge is a powerful tool, great power itself is required for much of the magic. I could only master the basics.'

Prince Tylon looked questioningly to Kyler. She shook her head.

'This has all been so useless. What good is a saviour if we cannot reach her when the world is falling to pieces?' Kyler snapped, before storming from the room.

'We must not give up,' Oesyth said to the remaining mages. 'It is only the beginning. We have armies that can hold off the darkness for now. We'll have to go back to the library.'

* * *

Isran walked through a field on the edge of Ulamnia's borders, leading her horse to give it a break as much as to give her backside a break from the saddle. She stumbled on a stone and habitually she looked around to make sure no one had seen, though the place was quite obviously deserted.

'Curse Misaria for living so damned far away,' she said under her breath.

Just as the curse left her lips, a branch snapped above, crashing in front of her, mere inches from hitting her head. Isran eyed the limb suspiciously and continued, mindful that the place seemed to have ears.

As day turned into dusk, Isran mounted her steed and rode him at a flat gallop across the fields of Ulamnia. The Shenkar Forest was just ahead. Isran knew she would have to find her way to the heart of it to reach the earth goddess. She was entering a place that was dangerous even in the day at nightfall. As she reached the first group of trees, the horse snorted loudly and pigrooted before coming to a sliding halt.

'Move on, you stupid beast!'

The horse's ears flattened against his skull and he spun so sharply that he dumped Isran on the ground. She landed with a thud in the leaf litter on the forest floor. The horse reared, wrenching the reins from her hands and galloped back the way they had come, followed by a stream of abuse from Isran.

She picked herself up and dusted the twigs, leaves and dirt from her gown, then turned to give the horse one last glare. The trees were tall and straight, reaching far into the heavens. A low cloud hid their true height, but Isran had heard a rumour that these trees, should they ever be climbed, had no end and the roots no beginning. The floor was dappled with shade, and as the sun sank lower, the shadows grew long and sinister. Isran shuddered. There could be any number of terrible creatures lurking within.

Fog seeped through the trees toward her, making the awfully silent place even eerier. The trees turned black and the low hanging leaves grey. A loud, crashing noise startled her and she leapt behind the thick trunk of a tree. She peeked out to see a huge beast lumbering her way. Its massive head swung from side to side, supporting five long tentacle-like appendages around a gaping mouth. It made a low rumbling noise in its throat as it stopped and searched the forest. From its tough skin black hair sprouted in tight curls. It stood much taller than her; its legs were long and thick and its tusks were long and sharp. The stench of the animal was almost unbearable. The creature paused, as though it were waiting for something.

Eventually the beast seemed to tire of standing around. It put its long tentacles to the ground and began to pick leaves, twigs, rocks and dirt up and put them in its mouth. As it noisily crunched and gurgled, it wandered closer to where Isran hid, as though it were tasting her trail. She held her breath, hoping it would wander away, but it continued to taste around the tree, wrapping its tentacles around and scraping bark off to sample. Isran stepped around the tree as the creature moved to where she had been. A few whispered words and a quick gesture of hands summoned a wind, blowing her hair back from her face and sending the leaves eddying around her feet.

Adding more urgency to her words, the wind blew harder, effectively picking up the forest floor and scattering it around the beast. Now her taste was spread around the clearing. Satisfied, she crept away, and once she was sure she was out of earshot, not that it appeared to have ears, Isran broke into a run.

After putting some distance between herself and the odd behemoth, she shivered and rubbed her arms, wishing her belongings had not gone with the horse. She looked up to the mist-shrouded tree trunks as she heard a shrill cry from above. Isran shuddered; there would likely be no sleep for her in this place.

* * *

After a potions disaster that turned Elyr pink, Reenah and Prince Tylon found themselves in the potion storeroom, searching for a cure for Elyr and to make sure stock wasn't running low. Reenah rolled the old wooden ladder across the shelves and began to climb. Prince Tylon, admitting that he wasn't comfortable with heights, checked the lower shelves.

'You've been quiet this morning, is there something the matter?' asked Reenah.

Prince Tylon looked down for a moment, fiddling with the cork in a bottle of boxthorn juice. He sighed, placing the bottle back on the shelf.

'My mother came to see me this morning. She was very brief, and the vision faded before I could say anything at all. She wants me to wed Princess Yaeli.'

'We already knew that.' Reenah chuckled, but the humour left her face, realising the prince was distressed.

'No, she wants me to marry Princess Yaeli ahead of schedule. She wants me to be married within months, weeks even.'

As Reenah looked down at the dismay on the prince's face, she couldn't help but feel relieved. He did not want to marry the Princess of Thornbroke! That wasn't to say that he could or would marry Reenah, but it did give her a small pleasure nonetheless.

Reenah climbed from the ladder and placed a hand on his shoulder, staring up at his blue and yellow eyes that seemed dimmer than she remembered.

'Perhaps you should speak with your father. I don't know what advice I could offer you; I know nothing of marriage.'

Prince Tylon laughed. 'To tell my father! Do you honestly think he would help me? This union means everything to my parents *and* the king and queen of Thornbroke. This isn't just a marriage; it is a peace treaty. Voicing my fears to my father will only make things worse.'

'I wish I could help you, Tylon, I really do.'

'It doesn't matter, nothing can stop this marriage, short of my disappearance.'

Reenah gasped. She had not known this melancholy side of him.

'But of course, I wouldn't,' the prince stammered, seeing her expression.

Reenah turned away from him.

'Are you telling me the truth?'

Tylon remained uncharacteristically silent, not quite knowing what to say.

'You are not the prince that I thought you were.'

'Oh, come now. We have both joked about getting away, living the simple peasant's life.'

'Yes *joked*, but never did I seriously consider such a thing – such a reckless and irresponsible thing!' Reenah turned toward him in anger, surprising herself that she felt so strongly on the matter.

'What would *you* do?'

Reenah's mouth snapped shut. *What would she do?* She couldn't marry someone that she didn't love and the sisters would not force her into such a situation; a reason she was still unmarried to this day.

'You are right.' Tylon sighed. 'It is a reckless and irresponsible thought, but that's all it is, just a stupid thought.'

Reenah nodded, still unsure if she truly believed him. She couldn't bear it if he just disappeared, yet when he married he was unlikely to be able to spend time with her; either way, she had lost him.

Reenah suddenly realised these were her last few precious moments with the man that she loved with all her heart, and she was wasting them by arguing.

'No, it isn't stupid to want to be free. I'm sorry.'

He smiled, though it never quite reached his eyes.

37. Trumpets.

He sat with his chair tilted back on two legs and his feet up on the desk as though he owned the castle. The map room was in disarray. Books, maps and parchment lay strewn across the floor and desk. Titan sat opposite, then Rem on his right, Parleans on his left, and Neximus stood in the far corner, eyeing the man suspiciously.

'It is not possible, Lestadt, it cannot be done,' Titan said firmly.

'It must be done. Do you not understand?'

Lestadt removed his feet from the table, letting all four chair legs thud to the ground.

'I, for one, will have no part in this madness,' Parleans declared.

Lestadt walked over to the window facing the courtyard. The burnt ruins of the stable had been piled into a heap against the northern corner. The smaller rocks from the fallen wall were piled against the remaining walls, and the bigger boulders remained scattered at the entrance.

'Look out this window. The courtyard is in ruins; we have no wall to guard the city. Horsham men will likely be here by the hundreds in a matter of days! You can no longer defend Irramai. We *must* leave.' Lestadt turned, studying their faces. 'Would you risk your families for this crumbling castle and city?'

'That is ridiculous! Have you not noticed the madness out there? I would rather contend with the likes of Horsham men than with whatever the hell is out there! To leave would be suicide!' Rem argued, looking to Titan for support.

'Rem is right. It's far more dangerous out there; we would have a whole city to move and protect out in the open if we left. And where would we go? We would be hundreds of homeless people at the worst possible time,' Titan reasoned.

Lestadt rested his hands on the table, studying the dark cracks that snaked up its length. He sighed, exasperated with both Remmador and Titan.

'Then will you send scouts? Irramai has resisted Horsham for so long, I doubt it will be long before they're back.'

Titan nodded. 'I'll be sending men out tonight. In the meantime, we will have to try to repair the wall.'

'Perhaps the city folk should be taught to wield weapons,' Neximus added.

He had stood silently at the back of the room for the majority of the conversation, weighing up the arguments and scrutinising the newcomer.

'And what weapons shall they wield? Yours?' Remmador asked sarcastically, going out of his way to make the blonde man feel inferior.

'We make them: clubs, spears, garden tools – whatever. As long as they cause injury to our opponents, they will suffice.'

'That's a good idea, I want our people prepared for the worst. Neximus, you're in charge of training them; you can have half the army to assist you. The other half will rebuild the wall.' And with that, Titan strode from the room.

With Titan gone, Rem and Parleans followed closely on his heels, leaving Lestadt and Neximus alone. Neximus pulled a stone from a pouch on his belt, then made his way to the door.

'Neximus?'

Neximus turned to face Lestadt, not quite knowing whether he was to expect friendship or hostility. From personal experience, he was sure it would be the latter.

'Perhaps I could help you? I'm not much of a builder.'

Neximus dipped his head once. Lestadt wondered if the stone he gripped in his hand might contain more personality than the tall warrior.

Neximus casually leaned against the brass gates, the city of Irramai before him. Small sparks jumped from his sword and swirled away in the wind as he sharpened the blade. Two men stood in front of him, a little apprehensive. It was obvious they did not trust Neximus. He pocketed the stone, and resting his sword on its tip, he absently spun it as he spoke.

'I want you and the other soldiers to gather all the abled men and women in the city, no one younger than… sixteen and no one older than fifty. I want them gathered in the courtyard by sunset.'

'Yes sir,' the two men replied in unison before hurrying toward the city to do his bidding. Though they may not have liked Neximus, they knew he spoke for Titan.

'You wouldn't have to sharpen that so often if you didn't do that,' Lestadt said, his tone light, trying to sound more conversational rather than condescending.

Judging by the flat stare he received from Neximus, he hadn't pulled it off.

'What exactly are you planning to use for weapons?' Lestadt tried again, once the other two men were out of earshot.

'Exactly what I said.'

Lestadt had been told that he tended to have a cold disposition, but he had nothing on this man.

'Garden tools?' Lestadt asked doubtfully.

'You would be surprised how easily a head can be prised off with a well-made shovel.' He didn't even look at Lestadt, his expression unchanging as he scanned the city.

'What about the women? I hardly think the Horsham men will be frightened by a woman brandishing a rolling pin.'

'Was it not you that so nobly pointed out women can fight? And now you're telling me they could only wield kitchen utensils?' he retorted, finally turning to regard Lestadt, giving him the impression he was under close scrutiny.

'That was before I knew Irramai was in such short supply of weapons. Shovels, rakes, pitchforks and even axes are awkward for men to use, I cannot imagine a woman lasting long trying to swing a shovel.'

''Tis true. I thought we could find some black-slate to make spear heads, even short daggers, for the older people. I don't think they'll have the strength, nor the stomach to bludgeon a man to death with a lump of wood – or a shovel for that matter,' Neximus added, sheathing his sword.

'A little primitive, but it could work. We could make hatchets, they can be swung well enough,' Lestadt thought out loud.

'Whatever cuts yer throat,' Neximus drawled, half grinning.

Lestadt returned the smile. So, the man had a dark sense of humour. He seemed like he might even be friendly once he was coaxed into talking. Lestadt could see why the other men might struggle with him. Neximus was hardly approachable, yet Lestadt sort of liked him. Neximus' low social standing did make him wonder if it was wise to become too close, given Lestadt's own ambition. Yet he felt inexplicably drawn to Neximus, perhaps even because he looked the way he did.

They left for the main stables to fetch their horses. As soon as Lestadt entered, he knew where Steel was. Neximus gave Lestadt a questioning look as he saw, and heard, the stocky grey brute kicking the sides of his stall. Steel wasn't overly fond of being stabled. Lestadt and Neximus saddled their horses and left via the ruined wall, picking their way through the scattered boulders.

As they rode silently away from the city of Irramai, Lestadt wondered how he could convince Titan to leave. It was not just that Lestadt needed the army, it was also clear to him the now exposed city lay vulnerable to attack by both Horsham and the creatures of the night.

He felt sorry for Titan and the other men. Their friend Yezimar was dying and it seemed that none of them had had much sleep. Lestadt looked over to Neximus, who silently rode a big roan gelding, his eyes firmly fixed ahead. Lestadt didn't blame him for seeming the least upset about Yezimar's fragile state. There was a lot of hostility between the other men and Neximus. Now he understood Raemil's behaviour. It had been easier for her to hide her differences rather than face hostility from everyone. Lestadt couldn't help but feel some respect for Neximus for facing the world and appearing to be unaffected by their taunts and obvious distrust.

The hum of hundreds of voices drifted up from the courtyard as the sun sank out of sight. The crowd of people was restless, wondering why they were there. They broke off into small groups of families and friends, whispering of sightings of bizarre creatures beyond Irramai's walls. Soldiers milled at the front and back of the crowd, tight-lipped and careful not to speak of their dire situation until Neximus arrived.

Lestadt turned his back to the courtyard and leaned against the balcony rail, folding his arms across his chest. They'd been back a few hours now and had gotten a good stack of sharp rock for weapons.

'How many did you send?'

'Six. Four spreading out toward Horsham, one heading north east, and the other heading west. They're on well rested horses. I told them to ride hard for two days and expect them back in no more than five,' Titan said wearily.

He was grateful for this man's help. He had proved his worth, but he resented the fact he had sometimes found himself feeling like a soldier answering to his commander around Lestadt.

Lestadt nodded.

'And what if there is danger heading to Irramai? Have you a plan?'

'We will defend Irramai to the best of our ability; there is not much else we can do.'

'There is a whole city at stake. I know a place that would be safe for the people. The castle is built much like Irramai, only it's not crumbling to ruin. Give it some thought, Titan. We could have this city packed and ready to leave in twenty-four hours if you said the word.'

Before Titan could reply, Lestadt turned and left. Titan watched the man leave. *What was he up to?* This stranger rode into Irramai out of nowhere one night, and already he seemed to have some sway with him and his leading men. Furthermore, he seemed to be so worried about a city he had never met, wanting to move them out in the open. Titan turned away from the courtyard as Neximus walked through the crowd of people to the front. Was he even running things anymore? Neximus was rallying the people, Remmador and Parleans were planning the new wall, and the stranger was hatching plans to move the city.

Lestadt stood on the north wall, looking down at the people, half listening to Neximus' speech. His mind wandered off as he studied the daunting peaks of Horsham. Raemil should have reached her destination by now. He thought of her often at night, unable to push the thoughts of her away. He longed to have her wrapped in his arms, but then he thought of who she really was, the Caelinian Princess, the heir, if her brother was dead. His blood boiled.

How could she have lied to him like that? Her people had killed his family! Gods! The hands of her brother himself could have killed his mother and sister! Lestadt bit down on his lip in anger, his blue eyes turned icy as he glared at the mountains. The Caelinians would pay, he thought bitterly.

The people down below in the courtyard began to cheer, and Lestadt realised the speech was over. All it took to get the mob moving was a few carefully chosen words and they would do just about anything, he thought as he watched them slowly move off. So what words, what speech, would get these men to follow Lestadt?

As the sun set on the second day of training, the crowd of people dispersed, rubbing tired muscles and placing makeshift weapons in a pile against the castle on their way out of the courtyard. Neximus was the last to leave, checking the weapons and stacking them neatly since the people had failed to do so. He had worked hard. In just four days, the weapons were made and the people were in training. Though the people were full of complaints of sore muscles and bruised limbs, they were generally good students.

Neximus entered the castle and made his way to the front balcony toward the map room. He could see Titan, Remmador, Parleans and Lestadt leaning over the rails, they'd been watching the training session. As usual, as he approached the men, he was greeted with an unfriendly stare from both Remmador and Parleans.

'It seems to be going well with the training then?' asked Titan.

'They are learning, the weapons seem to be holding together. Any news?'

Neximus was referring to the scouts. One had returned late in the morning and another had returned only an hour ago. None so far had returned from Horsham and they were due back this day.

'No. Nothing.'

'Give them time, the day is not over. It would be hard to push the horses to get to Horsham's borders in just two days,' Lestadt said, eager to lift their gloomy spirits.

'And how is Yezimar?'

'Don't even pretend like you care – arsehole!' Remmador snapped.

'Fuck you!' Neximus stepped forward to challenge Rem.

'Enough!' Titan moved between them.

Rem backed down, muttering something under his breath as he turned away. Neximus remained where he was, glaring past Titan's shoulder.

'Both of you can put your petty differences aside, this is not the time. Stay the hell away from each other – is that clear?!' Titan growled, though he was staring directly at Neximus.

'Is that clear?' Titan repeated, low and between clenched teeth.

Finally, Neximus turned away, his jaw set firmly in anger.

Over the last few days, the tension between Neximus and his companions had grown. They were all tired and worried about Yezimar and worried about the safety of the city.

Despite the tensions, much had been accomplished in just five days. The people were training, the weapons were made, and a defence drill was planned and practised. Using three trumpets, the people would be warned of danger and they would gather their weapons and go to the courtyard. One trumpet stayed with the guard on watch duty on the wall, another was given to a second soldier stationed in the middle of the city. As soon as the first trumpet was blown, he would then blow his so the soldier at the back of the city could hear and he too would blow his. It was effective and as good as a warning system could be when created in a matter of days.

Things were not going so well for the rebuilding of the wall; they lacked the tools to move the boulders and they lacked the mortar to repair the wall. The world outside of Irramai was hostile. They had already lost one man to the madness outside; he'd been sent to the markets of a nearby village to find materials and hadn't been seen since.

The next week was busy. Since the wall could not be rebuilt, all efforts were turned toward preparing the city people as best they could for a fight. Though none spoke of it, they were all on edge. None of the scouts had returned from Horsham. They'd plenty of time, something had obviously gone wrong. Titan ordered for Yezimar to be moved into the castle. Though it was no safer, he did so on his friend's request. The man was still quite sickly and the prognosis was poor.

Neximus worked night and day. If he wasn't training the city folk, he was training his archers, and if he wasn't training them, he was training himself. Lestadt often joined Neximus. They fought in the courtyard as the sun set over the city, preparing themselves for the unknown threat that was sure to come. They returned to the castle with bruises, grazes, cuts and often grins. Lestadt and Neximus grew closer as they retreated from the constant bickering in the map room. Neither needed to say anything to the other. Nothing but the smooth sound of a blade leaving its sheath, the sharp clink of metal on metal and the occasional grunt as one was knocked to the hard-stone floor.

Titan had insisted Neximus take a break; he was worried that he was over-working himself. Neximus laughed the suggestion off, but when it became apparent that he had not slept in days, the suggestion became an order and Neximus was relieved of his duties to train the people. Lestadt hadn't taken particular interest in Neximus' sleeping habits, not until Titan had expressed his concerns. Titan was often with Yezimar, and Remmador had gladly taken charge of the city people. In the end, Neximus continued to work. His archers were training themselves now, so he and Lestadt trained together frequently.

'Hah!' Neximus cried, looking down at Lestadt who lay sprawled at his feet. 'Your form is shit today.' He puffed, wiping sweat from his brow.

Lestadt grinned, then from his position on his back, he kicked Neximus' feet out from under him. Using his blade, Lestadt flicked the sword from Neximus' hands as the tall warrior crumpled heavily to the ground.

He rolled up onto his feet and stood over Neximus.

'Say again?' He laughed.

Neximus rolled backward and up into a crouching position, retrieving his sword at the same time.

'Again.'

The two men fought atop the south wall, enjoying the thrill of balancing along a narrow strip of partition, twenty feet in the air, whilst each trying to best the other.

Neximus swung hard at Lestadt, but his attempt was blocked. He twisted, thrusting his sword out and catching Lestadt's shoulder. Lestadt returned the favour and sliced across Neximus' ribs, then knocked him backward. Neximus hit the ground, but recovered quickly, turning and kicking out in an attempt to knock Lestadt from his feet, but Lestadt was quick. He leapt over the kick and brought his sword down to crash against Neximus' blade.

'Neximus! Lestadt! What is going on?!' Titan barked from the balcony adjacent to them.

They turned guiltily toward their commander, then looked back at each other. Lestadt was standing over Neximus, who was crouched on the ground, their swords still locked.

'Practice,' Lestadt offered lamely, knowing Titan had specifically told Neximus to give it a miss for a few days.

'Neximus,' he snapped, approaching the two men who'd instantly thrown down their swords. 'I told you to stop. What the hell are you to doing atop this wall? Using *real* swords! We cannot afford to lose good men to accidents during practice! What are you thinking?!'

'Lighten up, Titan. I'm not a child, I can take care of myself.'

'No one has seen you in the castle for a week! You have worked day and night; this obsession has got to stop! I won't have you endangering our people with recklessness. You disobeyed a direct order.'

'There is nothing wrong with me, I just want to...' Neximus paused, his keen eyes scouting out over the southern horizon. 'There's a rider approaching.' He pointed.

Titan's eyes narrowed in suspicion, but the blonde man did not move or take his eyes from the south. Titan reluctantly turned to see.

'Where?' both Titan and Lestadt asked, struggling to see that far, their argument now forgotten.

'Just out there,' Neximus said, pointing again in the same direction.

'You must have eyes like a hawk,' Titan said, still searching.

Moments later, the rider was clearly visible at a gallop. There was a dip before a small hill, then it was a flat plain before reaching Irramai.

The man rode at breakneck speed toward them. By the time the scout reached the slope, dozens of people were watching from the wall. The rider never slowed his horse as he descended, briefly disappearing out of sight.

'Did anyone see that?' Neximus leaned dangerously close to the edge of the wall.

'What?'

'A dark shadow following him? Did no one see that?' he repeated.

Lestadt shook his head. He too never took his eyes from the scene, waiting for the rider to reappear.

The rider galloped the horse hard up the hill and every soldier that watched went pale. A huge black creature flew up from behind, giving the illusion of bursting from the ground. It flapped its great black wings, looming above the rider on his terrified mount. As they neared Irramai, the sweaty foam on the exhausted horse was visible and so too was the blood on the rider. No one moved. All watched on in horror as the rider tried desperately to escape the winged monstrosity above him.

As the horse began to falter, the beast swooped down and plucked the rider from the saddle. The horse's horrible rasping breaths could be heard from the wall before it stumbled then went down, dropping dead from exhaustion. A bone chilling shriek echoed off Irramai's walls as the beast seemed to snap the man in half in its talons. Tossing the body aside, it kept coming.

'The trumpet! Someone sound the trumpet! Men – to your weapons!' Neximus' voice boomed across the courtyard.

Suddenly the top of the wall was alive with panic as the soldiers rushed past each other to collect their weapons. There seemed to be a surge of confusion and chaos as the men raced to their positions in a writhing mass of bodies, but just as quickly it died down to eerie silence. All that could be heard were the haunting sounds of the trumpets echoing across the city of Irramai as its people stood quaking in fear.

Titan, Remmador, Lestadt and Neximus moved down into the courtyard to stand with weapons drawn. Neximus' archers lined the top of the north wall with their arrows trained; they could see the black creature approaching from their vantage point. The air was thick with apprehension as a crowd of city folk filed into the courtyard, silently taking up their tools and home-made weapons and moving to stand behind the soldiers. On the other side of the castle, Parleans was busily herding the rest of the civilians into the castle.

There was a loud whooshing sound and a piercing screech as a huge black-red dragon landed on the south wall. There were gasps and even a few frightened whimpers. They had been preparing, but not in their wildest imaginations did they think they were preparing for this. Their puny weapons were almost laughable in the face of the massive creature.

'Archers, take aim,' Neximus cried.

'Soldiers, hold your ground,' Titan ordered.

Before any more could be said or done, a horrific, high-pitched screech came from the south and bounced off Irramai's walls. The sound forced most of the people to drop their weapons and clutch their ears.

'Archers! Fire!' Neximus shouted above the noise.

And then the courtyard broke out in utter chaos.

38. Blood lust.

The wind buffeted her cloak around her legs, threatening to topple her as she edged her way along the narrow ledge. The Black plodded below, facing into the wind, his head low as he shifted through knee-deep snow. She stood on her tip-toes and reached above her head, hugging her body to the cliff face; a difficult feat due to her protruding stomach. She felt along the top of a large rock until she felt a brittle, leafy plant. She carefully plucked it out and stuffed it into her pocket.

Hunger had driven Raemil from her cave. She worked out it was safe to go out during the day as the creatures seemed to only come out at night. A few days ago, she had passed a gibbering, half-crazed man, his flesh was black from frost bite. Raemil was sure if he'd tried to harm her, he'd have likely fallen apart just attempting to stand. Raemil had caught herself a lost bear cub using the bow. She was sorry she had to kill the helpless thing, but couldn't afford to be picky. Now she had to find the Black some food.

Raemil descended awkwardly to where the Black was trudging along. She caught up and walked beside him, not wanting to burden him with her weight. He was already carrying her belongings and now there was a dead bear cub slumped across his back.

She patted his shoulder.

'I am sorry Black, I know you're hungry and tired.'

The Black pricked his ears and glancing at her, blew softly out his nose, as though he understood.

It had been a long time since either of them had eaten, they were both looking thin. Raemil's stick-like arms and legs seemed to protrude from an awkward-looking belly.

It finally stopped snowing, and through some trees she could see what looked like a small house. She hoped someone would be kind enough to give her some food for the Black, while pulling her hood over her hair.

It seemed to take forever to reach the house and Raemil's legs ached from pushing through the deep snowdrifts. As Raemil and the Black approached the front door, a movement caught her attention. She turned to see a little girl skipping around the trunk of a large tree. She was laughing, before stopping abruptly to stare at Raemil. The little girl looked to be around five. She had short, brown hair that was tied back in pigtails using white ribbons. She wore a little red dress with white frills around the sleeves and the skirts. She smiled and ran to Raemil with her arms outstretched. Raemil smiled back, glad to see a friendly face.

With her hands tucked neatly behind her back, the girl stopped in front of Raemil.

'Are your parents home?'

The girl shook her head.

'Who is taking care of you?'

'We take care of ourselves. Come, play with me,' she added.

Raemil studied the child, inexplicably she was suddenly reminded of the creature outside the cave.

'I'm sorry, I cannot.'

'Come play,' the little girl repeated, and before Raemil could respond, the girl pulled a huge kitchen knife out that had been tucked into her ribbon at the back of her dress.

She lunged at Raemil. Raemil stumbled backward, tripping over a loose rock. She fell with a grunt and looked up as the child, now laughing madly, loomed above her, brandishing the knife.

Raemil kicked out her legs, knocking the murderous child to the ground. The girl dropped the knife as she fell and Raemil quickly snatched it up. There was blood on the blade and she realised with horror, that the knife had already been used on someone else. The child was crying now, as Raemil climbed awkwardly to her feet and stood over her.

'Bitch,' the girl spat, dashing her tears away with the backs of her grubby hands.

Raemil was shocked, she didn't know what to say or do.

The little girl kicked Raemil in the shin and pushed past her, skipping off into the wilderness, laughing and shouting, 'Bitch, bitch, rotten bitch.'

Raemil stood outside the house, holding the knife in her hand and watching as the girl disappeared out of sight. *What was a little girl doing on her own, running around with a bloodied knife? Where were her parents? And who is 'we'?* Raemil suddenly thought, remembering the child had said, *'we' take care of 'ourselves'*.

She looked around, suddenly realising she was alone and very exposed. She hadn't noticed the Black had shied and bolted when the little girl approached. She whistled for her horse as she approached the front door, knocking loudly, just in case there was someone else home. She waited a few seconds after her second knock, before reaching for the handle. The door swung open, revealing a dark and messy house.

Raemil cautiously stepped inside. 'Hello?'

The house smelled awful. She held her hand up to her nose as she picked her way through the mess. Dirty pots and pans lay around the kitchen, papers, books and clothes were thrown on the floor, chairs, tables and bookshelves were overturned. There was something dark smeared on the floor and up some of the walls. Raemil kicked something and it went sliding across the floor ahead of her. She walked over to a window and pushed the shutters open, letting light flood the dining area. It was blood that was on the floors and walls. It was someone's severed index finger she had kicked across the floor. Smeared on the wall in blood was a message:

We are no longer alone. Shed your blood and shed your skin. Join us my friend.

Raemil turned to run, but stopped, sliding to a halt on the tiled floor. Frozen in front of her was a young boy. Blood was smeared around his mouth; in his hands he held the remains of a black cat, a gaping wound in its side. The boy glared, baring his bloodied teeth like a wild animal. He dropped the dead cat and ran out the back door. Raemil's heart was pounding as she looked down at the half-eaten creature. *What was going on?* She felt an urge to throw up, so she ran outside, not that her vomit could make things any worse inside.

She found the Black standing patiently outside and wrapped her arms around him, taking deep, steadying breaths into his neck. She and the Black continued past the house to find cattle-yards and a large barn at the back.

It was getting dark and Raemil didn't want to be caught without shelter. She and the Black snaked their way through the cattle-race to take shelter in the barn. It was divided into two sections, one had pens for the cows, the other was stacked with feed, both of which had no apparent use, as there was not a cow in sight. Raemil was relieved, she had somewhere to stay and food for both her and the Black, though she was uneasy being so close to the house.

Her feet seemed to move of their own accord as she strode steadily toward the cloaked figure. She wore a long, black, sleeveless gown that dragged on the floor behind her. She felt her lips move into a smile – but she wanted to do anything but smile. The hooded figure ahead of her reached out a long, cloaked arm and a hand sprouted from inside.

'Come to me Raemil, my bride.'

And as she took his hand in hers, the walls bled, the sea bubbled and boiled. Strange creatures spilled onto the banks, and the souls that witnessed, they did weep.

Raemil jolted upright in her makeshift bed from the ominous dream. There were horrid scraping noises running along the sides of the barn. Something was out there. Raemil wished she could go out with sword drawn and challenge whatever haunted her, but she would not endanger her baby.

Though it was still dark outside, Raemil guessed it was in the early hours of the morning. Soon the things outside would disappear, she hoped. Terrible things haunted her when she was awake, and something equally as terrible haunted her sleep. *Was there no peace for her?* The days were safe enough she supposed, then she thought of the frost-bitten man, the child with the knife and the boy who had eaten the cat. *What is happening?* She thought back to the body she had found just outside of Witchgrave and the message she'd found carved into the tree. *Was this all linked? Was this what was to begin? And what of the dragons that killed Bonnie and Lylah? The mysterious deaths outside of Verramoi? Were people falling to these creatures even then?*

Raemil ate her breakfast as the sun rose and the noises outside the barn ceased. She wanted to escape this sinister house, so she had to make the most of this day if she was going to find shelter. She filled two small sacks of grain and a bigger bag of hay to bring along. Opening the doors to the white wilderness outside, she scanned the area before deciding it was safe.

The Black was looking more and more like a pack-animal, Raemil thought, as she walked beside him. He was carrying her food, which at least was much less of a burden now that it was in pieces. He carried his food, and he carried Raemil's clothes, blankets, hides, utensils, and various other objects she had brought with her. She carried her medicines and her weapons, and the weight of her pregnancy.

They were heading east, though Raemil did not quite know what she would do with a child. As soon as he was born, she had to continue on toward Horsham. *Perhaps she could leave the child with someone?* But as soon as the thought came to her, she dismissed it. She could not leave her child with a stranger, *but what could she do?*

Raemil was bleak as she marched. Perhaps it was time to think about giving up on her brother, *how could she do anything so dangerous with a babe in arms?* But then, her whole terrifying journey would have been for nothing: the heartache; the humiliation; the suffering – could she really just turn around and leave after all she had overcome?

It was noon when Raemil stopped under a small cluster of trees. Though they weren't heading directly toward Horsham, they were still in the mountain ranges and the trek was exhausting. There was a slight breeze that swayed the trees above them as the Black and Raemil scoffed their food. Raemil smiled and rested her hand on her stomach. Her thoughts were finally far from the troubles at hand. Feeling her baby's movements, she wondered what it would have been like if she had met Lestadt under different circumstances.

The Black snorted, he pricked his ears, listening as a warning seemed to still the air. He stomped his hoof impatiently, *what was this?* He sniffed the air, a strange smell drifted around them. *I know this smell!* His senses shouted, but it was too late. The Black squealed as a huge black beast crashed through the treetops above them.

Raemil leapt to her feet with great difficulty, struggling onto the Black's already crowded back. They raced away from the dragon as it snapped at the retreating horse and rider. In his terror, the Black stumbled and fell to his knees. Raemil gripped tight with her thighs and urged him to get up. Huffing, and his eyes rolling toward the threat above them, he struggled. The load was so heavy, and the ropes were tangled around his legs. He managed to heave himself to his feet as the dragon swooped over them and snatched at Raemil, just missing. The

Black spun, no longer secure against his back, the bags were swinging around his legs, causing him to over-balance. Raemil tried to swipe them out of the way, unwittingly adding to the problem.

The dragon lumbered toward them as the Black stumbled awkwardly away. It reached out one massive taloned paw and swiped the Black, gouging deep wounds along his right flank and knocking him to the ground. Raemil was thrown from his back, landing hard, with the Black half rolling over the top of her, striking her shoulder with a hoof as he struggled for footing. Rolling to his feet, he was about to take off, when the dragon approach again, its mouth gaping wide. Raemil crawled to her feet, but a sharp, hot pain in her abdomen forced her to drop back down, clutching her bulging stomach in pain.

The Black reared and screamed, rushing in front of Raemil. As terrified as he was, he understood she needed to be protected. Raemil forced herself to her feet and struggled onto his back, and the Black leapt into a gallop. She glanced back once to see all her belongings scattered on the ground, the grain, the hay, her hides, her clothes. She gripped her stomach as more pain raked her insides. She had lost everything. The dragon screamed above their heads and the Black darted back under the safety of the trees.

Dizziness swayed her. Looking up she could see darkness descending. The Black was walking through a thick cluster of trees on a mountainside and there was no longer a dragon pursuing them. Where she sat, the Black was moist with sweat. Raemil was gripped by another sharp pain and she cried out, doubling over. Once the worst had subsided, she touched her hand to where she sat and lifted her fingers to the fading light. It was not sweat at all, it was blood. Raemil looked up at the sky and wailed, her heart breaking as she realised she was losing her baby.

39. A price to pay.

Argané watched the prisoner from the shadows, a cold glint in his eyes. This one had been in isolation for a week, and while he seemed to be pretending he was unaffected, Argané was sure he could crack him.

The Horsham man turned to one of his men. 'No food or water for this one. I want to see him break.'

The prisoner stared after them as they left, then he looked to the bracelet around his wrist. Anger and hatred burned like a fire in his belly. Sweat trickled down his back and dripped from his forehead as he trained, building his strength with sit-ups and push-ups, since he'd been denied the training yard. He rolled onto his back on the hard stone floor and stared up at the ceiling. Momentarily, he let his fatigued mind take him home to the courtyard where an old oak tree reached into the pavers. Where the stables were always busy and bustling with life, smells of sweet hay and horse sweat drifting through the air. He thought of his little sister, dressed in one of her many hooded cloaks, playing with the black colt. It was once his home, but he wondered if it would ever be again.

Serrin lay, counting the minutes and the hours as they passed. There was nothing for him to do but wait. He was feeling light-headed, living out of sheer stubbornness and will, but he tried to not let Horsham's men see that. He contemplated feigning collapse; he was sure the lead Horsham man would want to see him nearly dead before he would give Serrin sustenance. He needed to speak with the others as they needed reassurance now more than ever.

Someone had to test the strange apparatus that was forced onto his wrist, so he volunteered. Everyone now wore the foreign bracelets; they were doomed if they didn't find a way around the devices. Serrin chose a Horsham man to fight and attacked him unprovoked, with only a wooden sword. He lunged with all he had and jammed the wooden practice sword into the soldier's eye.

Serrin felt the bracelet working the moment he chose violence against Horsham's minions. He tried to fight the burning fire inside, the pain almost unbearable, his heart struggled. It felt as though his heart was going to burst at one point and Serrin nearly blacked out. He had broken out in a sweat and could barely breathe, but the pain had reached its pinnacle and he managed to only just stay conscious. He was carried from the courtyard, his dismayed men watching with doomed expressions. Serrin needed to see one of his men, so he could tell them they had to fight through the pain, that they may be able to beat it. He was sure with some conditioning it could be possible.

He feigned unconsciousness after the incident, just to reinforce their belief the bracelets would keep them safe from the slave-soldiers. A plan was slowly forming between the men, but they still had no real idea what was going on outside. The presence of the dragons had frightened them and put doubts in their minds. The bracelets on their wrists had not made it any easier. It was important Serrin be with his men now. They needed their General now more than ever.

'Craiden, keep your sword up,' Bennagon growled at the young man as they practised.

'If the General couldn't do it, then no one can.' Craiden panted as he thrust his sword at the big man, who stepped aside easily.

'We know nothing, we've not seen him, so shut up and keep practising,' Bennagon hissed as he knocked the sword from Craiden's hands.

'We're worried, that's all – no one wants to accept defeat, not now that we have been given hope, but...'

'Craiden,' Bennagon reprimanded sharply. 'One more word out of you...' he snarled, leaving the threat hanging in the air.

Craiden picked up his sword, sighing in defeat. Bennagon nodded toward where Galten and his opponent fought.

'Switch,' he simply said and Craiden obeyed.

Moments later, Galten and Bennagon were fighting against each other.

'Craiden seems to be getting better,' Galten said as he watched a Horsham soldier move past them out the corner of his eye.

'Yes, but he talks too much. He's easily distracted.'

'So most young men are.' Galten smirked.

Between the three of them, Serrin, Galten and Bennagon had chosen the weakest fighters amongst the slave-soldiers and taken it upon themselves to train them. They were building their army within Horsham's army.

'What news?' Bennagon asked in a lower voice, once the Horsham men were out of earshot.

'None.'

'You don't think he could be dead?' Bennagon's voice dropped even lower.

'The General? Are you kidding? The man is simply too stubborn to just die,' Galten replied. He too was conscious of the burning ears all around them.

'That may be so, but stubbornness doesn't mean a thing when there is a sword piercing your heart.'

'I doubt they would give him a clean death; besides, they seem reluctant to kill any soldiers now. The supply of men from the outside must be starting to dry up.'

'Not even one that has blinded one of their own? They may decide...' Bennagon paused as a guard passed by. 'They may decide that he's too dangerous to keep alive. What if they know something?'

Galten and Bennagon threw down their swords and walked over to sit at the benches, drinking from a waterskin.

'Bennagon, he is not dead. He can't be to the soldiers right now, anyway. We are supposed to be keeping the men's spirits unbroken and you are panicking more than they are. Just sit tight, okay?' Galten said, before taking a swig from the waterskin and placing it back on the bench.

'I hope you're right.'

Serrin was still laying on the floor on his back when he turned his head to watch the Horsham men as they unlocked the door. They dragged him to his feet and none too gently pushed him into the hallway, chaining his wrists and feet. He was shoved along in front of them until they reached a hooded figure at the end of the hall. Serrin baulked. *Was this Horsham?* The person turned and removed her hood. Her flesh was grey and her hair was blue. Bright orange eyes stared at him from a decomposing face.

'Bring him this way,' she said to the Horsham men behind him, her disturbing eyes never leaving Serrin.

The blue-haired woman strode through the corridors with an air of confidence. The Horsham men seemed to cower away from her. Serrin took note that the one he had blinded a week earlier had now joined them in their march through the halls. The woman stopped in front of the huge double doors to the courtyard. She shoved the heavy doors open with apparent ease as they flung back, banging against the outside walls.

In the courtyard, the men fought restlessly; tension was thick in the air and the silence was heavy. Usually, they would have been forced inside an hour before dusk, but the Horsham men were standing closer than usual around the slave-soldiers, and it was dusk now. They dared not speak whilst being watched so closely, but the fear was evident in their eyes and the way they fought.

Every slave-soldier's head shot up as the doors to the castle burst open. They saw the blue-haired woman and gawked. They watched in strained silence as three Horsham men forced the General out into the courtyard to follow the disturbing woman. Bennagon and Galten noted their fellow prisoners were not taking enough care to mask their outrage. If they were not careful, they would give the Horsham men reason to believe Serrin was of some importance to them.

They led Serrin to the west tower and disappeared inside. Galten and Bennagon exchanged a troubled look. They realised the Horsham men were not making them fight, proving this little show was for the benefit of the slave-soldiers. Still the question remained, *what did they know?*

Serrin was on his knees, his wrists cuffed behind his back to his ankles. He gaped at the dead-looking woman before him, wondering who and what she was. Off to the side, he could see the flickering light of a fire burning. Two Horsham men were standing behind him, and the one he had attacked was nowhere to be seen. The room was otherwise empty.

'You continue to defy us mortal. Whatever shall we do with you?'

Serrin said nothing.

'You simply won't die, although we had hoped that would not be necessary.'

She stepped forward and grasped his chin in her cold, clammy hand. Serrin supressed his urge to shudder.

'We will just have to find other ways to control your little outbursts.' She studied his face, turning it this way and that. 'Such a pity.'

The third Horsham man appeared from the darkness, his eye socket empty and raw. In his hands he held a red-hot poker. Serrin turned his head and he felt a pang of fear starting as a sharp stab in his chest and sinking like a cold stone in his stomach.

'We would simply like to return the favour,' the blue-haired woman grinned.

Serrin felt hands restrain his head from behind. Rough fingers pulled his eyelids up, forcing him to watch. The Horsham man was grinning sadistically as he approached. Serrin struggled as he felt the heat of the poker warm his face, but he could barely move in the grip of the two Horsham thugs behind him.

Their apprehension grew with every second they waited in the courtyard. Did they know that Serrin led them? Did they know that they planned and schemed every night against them? Were they going to kill the General? None of them knew the awful extent of Horsham's power. They only guessed and their imaginations ran wild, thinking of what Horsham would do to them if she found out.

A tortured howl erupted from the west tower, echoing around the courtyard, drumming the fears deeper into the slave-soldiers. And then there was complete and utter silence. The men stared at the west tower, hoping and praying for some sign that all was not lost, but there was nothing.

40. Freefall.

There were screams, shouts and bubbling, choked cries as people died. It was complete mayhem. In the face of the beasts, the people forgot all training; nothing mattered but escape. The archers hit the dragon on the wall but failed to significantly harm it. Four more dragons descended on Irramai.

Neximus and Titan shouted orders left, right and centre, but it seemed to make no difference. Their army, their city, had scattered like ants in the rain. Half the people surged toward the castle, scrambling over the top of each other to get inside. The few hundred that stood with Neximus, Rem, Titan and Lestadt were struck dumb and frozen with fear.

'Hold your ground!' Titan shouted futilely. It seemed the mob of frightened people were hurting each other more than the dragons were.

Lestadt watched as three dragons swooped toward the mass of people swarming the castle's front doors. One snatched up several people in its talons and mouth, the other two perched themselves on top of the castle. There was a loud groan as the castle's walls protested the weight. The rooftop sagged and a few bricks tumbled to the ground, causing more injuries to the crowd below.

Neximus pointed to the dragon that stood in front of the group of soldiers, ready to feast on them. 'Archers, take aim!'

He glanced at the north wall, discovering that his archers were gone. The fifth dragon was currently chewing on his second commander.

'Fuck!' Neximus shouted in anger and hopelessness.

'Surround him!' Titan ordered and the group of two hundred or more men that were left rushed forward with Lestadt, Titan, Rem and Neximus at the front.

As they surrounded the dragon, it snapped up three men, swiping several more off their feet with its bulbous tail. The men stabbed at its sides, hacked at its feet, and as its head came down, they slashed its throat. Its distress call was heard over the noise and the fifth dragon glided from the north wall at the group of soldiers. The first dragon was overwhelmed by the soldiers, but as its blood spilled, the next dragon killed a half dozen or more men as it landed. While the soldiers battled to overwhelm the next dragon, Neximus slipped away.

Lestadt and two other men began to hack off one of the dragon's taloned toes, but it flung them off into the crowd. Roaring and swinging its tail at them, it scattered the men to all corners of the courtyard. It lifted its head and screamed its piercing cry, and the other three took up the call. The noise was deafening and the soldiers cried out in pain with them. The screeching stopped and a tremendous crash sounded through Irramai. The men looked on in horror as the castle's roof gave way and began to collapse in on itself under the weight of the three dragons.

The dragon in the courtyard shook its great head, alternating between hissing and screaming. There was now an arrow protruding between its eyes. Soon enough, two more arrows pierced both eyes and blinded the creature. It roared and blundered forward to where Neximus stood on the north wall. Neximus fired again, but he missed as a huge head loomed above him. It opened its mouth wide and tried to snatch him up. Neximus rolled out of the way, slipping in the blood of his archers and barely escaping the dragon's maw.

Lestadt could see Neximus struggling to keep his footing on the blood-slicked wall. He picked up a brick and threw it at the dragon, hitting it in the back of the head. It's head shot around to hiss a warning, and as it turned fully to attack, it opened its mouth wide and rushed at the crowd of soldiers. Lestadt immediately regretted throwing the brick.

Titan, Lestadt and Rem stood their ground, trying to show bravery where they felt none. The dragon fell suddenly and slid along the ground toward them. They jumped back and the dragon's body came to a halt, an arrow protruding from the back of its head. Neximus stood on the wall with another arrow ready, but the dragon was dead.

Their attentions turned toward the dragons on the castle. The remaining monsters did not seem to care that two of their kind were dead, they were busy further destroying the castle. They sifted through the ruined top level and plucked screaming people from within. The castle groaned again and the top floor collapsed, dropping to the next level. They hovered above the wreckage for a moment before settling back down to continue their feasting.

There was a shout from Neximus and the soldiers in the courtyard turned as he began to toss the bows and arrows down from the wall.

'Aim for the back of their heads!'

Most of them were foot soldiers, but they did what they could. For a few moments there were arrows whizzing in all directions. When another dragon fell to its death, the weight of it smashed against the castle and the whole thing shuddered then collapsed almost completely to ruin. The two remaining dragons took flight, hovering above the crumbled castle, before they too were shot down. One crashed into the courtyard, the other smashing into the south wall. The whole wall toppled, destroying the houses beneath.

The remaining two hundred men stood in shocked silence as they looked on the ruins of Irramai. Many wept, for their wives, children, brothers, sisters and fellow soldiers were crushed beneath the rubble of the castle. Titan looked on this disaster, tears welling in his eyes. His dream, their freedom, was literally crushed. He threw down his weapons and ran to the ruin, shifting rocks and boulders out of his way. As he blindly pulled rubble from the broken castle, he did not notice that every abled soldier was behind him, also picking up the debris.

By morning, the city of Irramai was still shrouded by a thick cloud of dust from the fall of an ancient castle. Sorrow lay heavy in many hearts as they worked in absolute silence, pulling rocks and bodies from the ruins. By now there were sixty corpses lining the courtyard, but there were many more to follow. The city lay open like a wound, and while many physically died, each and every soldier that worked to pull his friend's and family's bodies from the wreckage let their hope die with them.

41. Innocence.

She screamed again. The sound of her pain bounced around the mountain range. Pain wracked her body like long talons dragging through her insides. For hours she had been suffering. She longed only for death now, to slip into the comfort of the darkness where nothing could touch her. She sat with her knees up and slightly apart, her back pushed against the trunk of a tree. The Black had long since disappeared into the forest around them, unable to bear the smell of blood and fear.

Raemil's contractions were close. She knew he would come soon, though she wished with all her heart he would not. Tears of pain and frustration trailed down her cheeks as she braced herself for another wave of agony. Panting heavily, she began to push, screaming so loud that it seemed to shred her throat.

Beyond the flickering flames of her small fire, there were strange, warped creatures watching as the mage struggled. Raemil was oblivious to them now; she cared not if they stole her soul. Nothing mattered now. Her mind grew fuzzy with dizziness as she struggled on into her sixth hour of labour. It seemed to her the pain and torment of her child's damning birth would go on forever. The whispering and hungry noises of the twisted creatures beyond the light of the fire went unheard by Raemil as she cried.

Hours later, using all the strength she possessed, Raemil gave one last push and her baby was born. She was in a pool of crimson snow that had melted to slush beneath her. She was utterly exhausted and had lost more blood than she thought possible. She barely had the strength to sit up and see the baby. Finally, a small, choked sound made Raemil pick up the tiny body. Gazing at it in wide-eyed wonder, she saw the small chest move up and down. Suddenly her heart began to beat wildly in her own chest. He was alive. She turned him on his side and removed the mucous from his mouth and he made a quiet sound of protest, before falling silent again.

Raemil removed her tattered cloak and wrapped him inside, holding him firmly to her chest, determined that nothing would harm him. She tried to stay awake but exhaustion took her and soon she was asleep. The Black returned sometime during the early hours of the morning and he stayed by Raemil's sleeping form until dawn broke.

Raemil woke with the weak winter sun on her face. She had been sweating during the night, but she felt so cold. She held her baby tighter to her. Pushing the cloak back to peer at him, she noticed the fine fuzz of dark hair on his head. She ran her finger beneath his tiny hand. His hand fell limp, back into the folds of her cloak. Murky blue eyes stared up at her as she peered at her tiny miracle. She had thought babies were noisier, but he was so quiet. Not once had she heard him cry. Her milk had come through in the night, and she tried to feed him, but he seemed disinterested. Raemil stayed close by the fire, not daring to put him down as she prepared her food.

It was near noon when Raemil finally admitted to herself he was too quiet. He hardly moved at all and she was sure he should be hungry by now, yet he still would not feed for a sufficient amount of time.

42. Guardians of the forest.

S he mentally cursed the earth goddess again, deciding not to let the words leave her lips this time. After collapsing from exhaustion, Isran was instantly attacked by a strangler vine she'd not noticed growing around the base of the tree she was leaning against. Normal strangler vines attacked other plants. In the Shenkar Forest, they weren't so fussy, killing anything around it that was not already dead, including tired travellers looking for a place to rest. Isran quickly cut her way out of the murderous plant and, after stepping on a rather prickly creature buried under the leaf litter, she sought refuge in one of the giant trees. So now the mighty mage, Sister Isran, was perched indignantly on a branch, several feet in the air.

Sometime during the night, she let her guard down and dozed in the tree. When she woke, a very weak light was filtering down to the forest floor. The forest was dense and still fairly dark despite the sun having risen. Isran assumed this was as light as it was going to get. She climbed out of the tree, absurdly checking no one was there to witness her disgrace. Reaching the bottom, she brushed her hair out of her face, immediately discovering a horrible sticky substance stuck to the side of her head. Holding a long strand of her silver hair up to the dim light, she discovered tiny blue eggs in yellow goo stuck to her hair.

'Wonderful!' she grumbled aloud. 'That is just splendid. Some hell-born insect has decided to start a family on *my* head.'

She kicked the trunk of the tree in anger and startled a strange, long-necked bird from its roosting place.

As the day drew on, the forest became thicker, but each tree or bush she passed looked much the same as the next. She felt she was getting nowhere and wondered if this was some trick of the forest or perhaps the earth goddess. Isran had always been an impatient woman, and she was beginning to get very impatient with the Shenkar Forest. She passed many bizarre-looking creatures on her travels, often catching glimpses of a strange, cat-like creature with a long body, huge, pointed ears and short little legs. She saw weird little feathered dragons, sunning themselves in the pools of light, but as soon as she turned to get a better look, they would vanish.

Eventually, Isran's patience wore out. She sat on the ground to meditate, letting her senses leave her body and seek out Misaria. Her mind meandered through the forest, feeling and listening, but all was quiet, even the creatures seemed shy of her seeking mind. Isran opened her eyes again, staring at the dark trees, at the damp leaves on the ground, at the prickly bushes that somehow managed to find space to grow down here.

'Misaria!' she shouted angrily. 'I call upon the mighty earth goddess Misaria! I have come a long way to speak with you!'

Isran listened, but the forest was silent.

'Do not abandon us now! Your people are in need! Will you hide in cowardice while your precious earth is dying all around you?!'

The wind rustled the leaves in the trees and the forest began to whisper in a language that Isran could never comprehend, despite her innate power to understand languages.

There was a movement between two trees ahead. She looked up, expecting to be attacked by another of Shenkar's creatures. Her eyes locked with what seemed like the sad eyes of a deer, but he was more than that. More shapes drifted out of the trees, between a dozen and twenty of them. She could not see the ones behind her, but she could sense them. They simply separated out of the shadows of the forest, as though they had always been there.

She glanced around briefly before turning her attention back to the one directly in front of her. His long legs moved forward delicately but deliberately, showing no fear of her. His head was crowned with antlers that could easily cut down a predator. Stopping at arm's length, he gazed down at her, flicking his tail as he did so. He crossed his arms across his muscular torso then dipped his head. His gaze never leaving Isran, as though he was constantly assessing her for signs of a threat.

'Great Sister Isran, we are the stag-people, brothers to the centaur. My herd and I are here to escort you.' He nodded his antlered head to several of his herd members before turning his back on Isran.

Isran was completely astounded. She had never seen nor heard of such people. The stag-people were men with bodies of deer from the waist down. They had four delicate deer legs with cloven hooves, short tails that would twitch now and then, and their pelts were dark brown. Their bellies where white and so too were the undersides of their tails. Their torsos were bare to reveal the chest of a man. They had arms and hands and fingers like any other human, but their faces were the strangest combination of man and deer. Their jaws jutted out and their foreheads sloped back slightly. Their noses were human-like, but seemed to be flatter and sloped outward with the jaw and mouth. Their mouths and lips were slightly wider than most men. Their ears were human, though slightly pointed and tipped with the lightest layer of brown felt. The eyes were deep brown and shaped like a human's but much larger.

They walked in silence and the forest grew darker around them; the stag-people didn't even speak amongst themselves. They followed their leader, keeping a watchful eye on Isran. She didn't know which direction she was going anymore. The lead stag-man reached a clearing where the trees seemed to arch over like some sort of formal entrance. He turned to face Isran and the rest of his herd.

'We will rest here this night.'

He stepped aside, sweeping his arm invitingly toward the entrance. Isran stepped into the clearing and saw in the centre a massive tree, looking as though it were dead. Its limbs were gnarled and bent and there were black hollows in its trunk. Isran shuddered to think what might live there. Around the tree hung orbs of white light – they were just a little bigger than a man's fist. They seemed to float in the air. Isran was intrigued and she moved closer to study them.

'Here, things of beauty are often bait,' the stag-man said while his herd settled beneath the trees on the outskirts of the clearing.

Isran turned to him puzzled then watched as the stag-man dropped to his knees and picked up a stone. Nodding toward one of the orbs, he threw the rock at the light. Just before the rock hit, spindly black legs shot out of the orb and it flipped over, catching the rock and curling its legs over the projectile. She gaped. They were not lights, but spiders; they hung from webs, giving them the appearance of floating lights. Their backs glowed and they folded their heads and legs in, until prey disturbed their web.

Isran backed away from the tree and its deadly inhabitants, now understanding why the stag-people took refuge elsewhere. She settled on the ground and eventually felt safe enough to fall asleep under the watchful eyes of the stag-people.

The Shenkar Forest was alive with birdsong at first light. It was difficult to sleep through some of the odd noises. Isran woke, feeling a presence beside her. She looked up to see the stag-man standing watchful.

'I have not come here to cause you or this forest harm; I came only seeking the earth goddess Misaria.'

The stag-people seemed unmoved by her declaration.

'Tell me, stag-man, do you know of the current state of the world? Does this evil haunt the forest too?'

The stag-man seemed to look past Isran as he spoke.

'I shall soon know you as friend or foe, only then may you know me.'

'It is I who you have come to see,' whispered a voice from behind Isran.

The mage turned slowly to face the tree that had previously housed freakish spiders. At first, she saw nothing but the tree and for a fleeting moment she thought Misaria *was* the old tree. When she studied it hard enough with her mage-sight, she could, in fact, see the shape of a woman in the bumps and knots of the trunk. The woman's face was delicate with fine cracks woven through it. The deity's eyes flew open to reveal they were completely white with no pupil or iris. The tree creaked and groaned as Misaria stepped forth. The tree shifted and writhed until it filled in the empty space the goddess had left.

Misaria remained the colour and texture of the tree as she stood before Isran. She wore no clothes, unconcerned by her nakedness. Her movements were fluid, as though she were made of muscle and tissue, despite her wooden appearance.

'What say you now, oh powerful mage? Do you dare call me a coward to my face?' Misaria's voice whispered on the wind.

'Perhaps I spoke in haste,' Isran admitted.

'Indeed.' Misaria's expression changed from fierce to grim. 'You've questions to ask me?'

Isran nodded.

'Yes, I want to know about your son and why you let a full-blood live?'

'I cannot give you those answers.'

Isran glared at the goddess.

'You have brought me here to tell me this? To raise a hope only to crush it?'

'Sister Isran, I never raised your hopes; you have done this on your own. And I certainly did not bring you here. Some journeys must be taken, some truths are best left untold, and some wonders must remain mystery. You mages have often taken your human sides for granted, and so your gifts have led you astray. My hand is not the only one to touch the hearts and minds and lands here, you must know this. Your future is unknown to all at present. We can but only tamper with such events. I can tell you one certainty: your end will come, but it is up to all of you as to how you will meet it and what will become of your souls.'

'Are you telling me there is no hope? That we have no saviour? Should we just stand aside while innocent people and creatures are murdered?' Isran was incredulous. They had worked so hard to find a way to defeat Horsham and it was all for nought.

There was a pause and the forest seemed to draw in a breath.

'You must save yourselves. I will tell you this: the lost one you seek could very well be your doom. It is you, Sister Isran, who must know my words, do with them what you will. I know your heart is just, your mind is sound, and your will is strong, and I do wonder what you would tell your waiting family at home when you see the hope in their hearts. This is truly where the mystery awaits us all.' Misaria turned and started for the tree.

'Wait! I don't understand,' Isran admitted, shaking her head in frustration. 'Your words are contradictory. If we will meet our end without a doubt, how can we save ourselves?'

Misaria turned again to face Isran.

'When you journey home, would you snap your fingers and say your words and be home with your defiant answer, or do you walk it and see the land for what it is? Do you choose to see a farmer's wife being beaten by her husband in front of their son and to know the son will become that man and his son become himself? Do you walk the journey and ask yourself what you are searching for? The one who will save a putrid and rotting land must surely have a heart to match.'

Misaria smiled sadly. 'Walk the journey, Isran, and your heart will know. You are who you are and my words cannot change the truth in that.'

And with that, Misaria stepped back into the tree, and the trunk shifted to conceal her once again. Isran turned her back on the tree, noticing the stag-people had gone. She was dismayed, but a part of her was angry. The goddess had told her practically nothing. Despite the goddess' words, she wished she *could* just snap her fingers and be home and be rid of this place, but it was not a power she possessed.

Isran walked back the way she had come, not really knowing whether she was heading home, but her thoughts were distant as she considered the goddess' words. When darkness fell on the Shenkar Forest, Isran had to rely on her mage-sight to guide her. Her thoughts circled back to the same conclusion, that the goddess was cruel to say anything at all. Her angry musing was interrupted by a movement in the shadows and she tensed.

It was only the stag-man. He came alone this time.

'Greetings, stag-man. I'd not expected to see you again.'

'Greetings, Sister Isran,' he said, bowing his head. 'My name is Kriard. I have seen you walk past this same place three times now and can only assume you are lost or insane.'

Isran thought for a moment he had made a joke, but his expression remained unchanged.

'Lost in thought, perhaps.'

'The gods have always confused the minds of mortals and mages alike. They have too much time. They will never understand the way we live nor the way we feel. They know not what it is to be fragile, to be temporary.'

'Perhaps it was unwise to seek council with Misaria,' Isran said, frowning.

'The goddess has indirectly told you some useful information, but to truly understand it, you must be a god. No matter what you are told, you decide whether you believe it or not and anything that you see or hear from now on will colour your opinion and therefore your actions. *You are who you are and nothing anyone says can change that,*' Kriard quoted.

'So, it's true. Not even the gods can know the outcome?'

'In a way, however, some things are for certain. Fate has orchestrated many events, but as the goddess said, many gods tamper with the world. While one god may create a storm that will pass in three weeks, that is for certain, they may not know that another god has inspired a man to spend his life's savings on a herd of sheep that now perish in that storm. Our lives are a mixture of luck and fate, and the outcomes affect us in different ways. That farmer who lost his sheep may despair and never try again, resulting in an unhappy life – counting every penny. Or he may be determined and try again and triumph; it just depends on who we are.'

'So now, I must return home, and decide what to tell my family, and what course of action to take, if any at all. That is my burden.'

'Yes, but your home is far. Tonight, I would like to welcome you into my herd to share a meal with us.'

'I would be delighted.'

Isran spent the night with the stag-people under the shelter of the Shenkar Forest, which somehow felt like the safest place in the world now that she was a friend to the stag-people. She listened and watched as they laughed and talked. She was trusted enough to be taken to their place of rest, where their mates and their children resided. She found herself completely in awe. They seemed much like the forest in the way that they had seemed fierce and hostile the night before, and now she couldn't think of a gentler community.

The food was not terrible, but it was lacking in something Isran could not put a name to. Perhaps it was just the lack of meat and salt and pepper and sauces and gravy and wine and all things civilised meals consisted of. They danced and they sang and they laughed and they joked; even Kriard seemed cheerful.

It was morning before Isran knew it and it was time for her to take her leave. Not before saying a farewell to Kriard who had shared his world with her for just one night.

'Misaria is wrong. You and your herd have shown me there is still something to fight for. If not for the people, then for this,' she said, spreading her arms wide. 'For all of the families like this one, for all of the love and vibrant lives like yours.'

'Then fight you shall,' Kriard said, bowing his head in acknowledgement of her compliments.

'Will you not fight with us?'

'No. We will stay here and protect the forest as we have always done. This is our home and these creatures are our friends and our family. Most of them know no such thing as war and fighting and death and torture, and I will not stand to let them discover it.'

'But surely you cannot hold this place alone. This forest will die and you with it. We have more in number than you and still I fear it is nowhere near enough,' Isran argued.

'Though Misaria claims to have little love left for the world and is quite prepared to let it go, I doubt very much that she will let the forest fall.'

Isran nodded her head in dismal understanding.

'Thank you for the meal and the company, Kriard.'

Kriard made a small noise that seemed to rumble from the back of his throat. It echoed across the forest with an unnatural quietness that yet seemed loud enough for all to hear. Isran gave him a questioning look – both amazed and puzzled by the magic he had so clearly just used.

'I shall offer you a guide, a close friend of mine. He is a shy creature and will not take kindly to mistreatment. He often comes and goes from the forest as he pleases. In fact, he would be the only creature of the forest to have ventured beyond the borders in many, many years. He knows the forest and its creatures well; he'll not lead you astray. His name is Mallacad and he will guide you and see that you come to no harm at the border.'

As if on cue, a small cat-like creature came slinking out of the undergrowth around them. It looked around with suspicion at first, knowing something was amiss. Looking from face to face before its gaze fell on Isran, it made a small noise that sounded like a cough before looking to Kriard in askance.

'Greetings, old friend. The lady, Sister Isran of West Sirron, will need guidance out of Shenkar. Would you do this?'

Mallacad looked from Kriard to Isran and seemed satisfied as his violet eyes searched the mage over. The long-bodied cat slinked ahead, looking back when he knew Isran was not following, as though he were impatient with her already.

'Thank you again, Kriard,' Isran said, realising the cat was waiting for her.

'Sister Isran.' He stopped her again, and the cat, still some distance away, flopped onto his side and ticked his tail as he waited.

'Our brothers, the centaurs, they live in Agdongren. If you tell them my name and give them this' – Kriard said, removing an amulet from around his neck – 'their leader will know you as friend. They may help you in your quest. Take it,' he said, pressing the amulet into the palm of her hand. 'And be well.'

With that said, Kriard turned and faded into the forest. In a split second he was gone, leaving no trace. Isran suddenly found herself wondering if he had ever existed, but the amulet in her hand and an angry mewl from Mallacad reassured her. She rubbed her fingers across the surface of the amulet, finding it completely smooth. It was just a plain, flat disc with a hole at the top for an equally plain string. Placing the amulet over her head and around her neck, Isran turned back toward the cat to see him staring at her through half-closed eyes, his tail still ticking in annoyance.

As she started toward him, his eyes opened wide to reveal a flash of violet brilliance and he leapt to his feet. His long body and short legs made him look like a giant caterpillar as he ran. He had a small head and fine features, with the exception of his two massive, pointed ears that sat ever alert on the top of his head. There were several black stripes down his spine as well as a mohawk that started between his ears and continued down his back, diminishing in length as it reached the tip of his very long tail. Mallacad's overall colour was a dusty grey, suited to the daytime shades of the forest.

The cat was quick on his feet and knew the exact direction to take Isran, though she could see no difference between one tree and the next or one clearing and the next. Mallacad ran ahead, forcing her to quicken her stride as she caught glimpses of him in the distance. It was as though he wanted to get this business over with, as though he had some other pressing task to attend to. Isran found herself thinking very ill of the little creature before long, as she tripped over a tree root and stumbled onto her hands and knees. When she stood and brushed herself down, Mallacad had already disappeared far ahead of her. She walked on grimly grumbling to herself and only assuming Mallacad had not changed direction.

Eventually she decided it would do no harm if she slowed just a little. For the first time she could see the beauty in the dark green and grey shades of the silent forest. She found peace in the still warmth of the air and in the powerful presence of the giant trees.

Just as she noticed the beauty of the forest, she heard a strange sound, like a song with no music or words. It was a haunting yet beautiful wail that brought tears to her eyes and an ache of longing in her heart. It seemed to come from everywhere, above and below, left and right. She spun in a full circle as the forest was engulfed in a white light that bleached all shadow from its darkest recesses. And suddenly, there before her was a great white horse with a mighty silver horn on his head. He danced and the soft fall of his silver hooves was like a sweet melody to her ears. With a flick of his long white mane and a swish of his star-filled tail, he pranced from her, in dreamlike slow motion. Thinking of nothing more than the longing in her heart to touch the mighty unicorn, Isran followed the unearthly creature as it danced ahead wailing its sad song, just out of the mage's reach.

The forest grew dark around her, but Isran followed on in a trance-like state. Ahead, the brilliant light streamed from the unicorn's pelt and her eyes seemed to drink in the brightness, wanting more. The unicorn hesitated before her and its song grew louder; she reached out, yearning to touch him, and he sprang away from her, seeming to float gracefully from one place to another. Isran tried to follow, when a sharp pain tore at her leg and her gaze shot down. She saw Mallacad with his teeth and his claws set firmly into her calf.

She swore and shook her leg furiously. Mallacad instantly let go. The peace immediately dropped from her heart as she looked up and realised the unicorn had vanished. She felt dismayed at the thought of never seeing such a creature again, when she came to her wits and studied her surrounds more carefully. Her clothes were torn from rushing through a thicket of tangled thorns, but more astonishing was that she now stood on the precipice of a great chasm. She would have stepped right off to follow the unicorn to her death had it not been for Mallacad. She eyed the cat, who stood beside her, and could have sworn she heard 'Fool' slip into her mind as though he had thought it for her. He gave her such a look that made her believe it was so.

With a sharp mewl that turned into an angry growl, Mallacad turned and trotted off again, and when he flicked an ear back to hear her following, he began to lope ahead. There was no further incident in the forest after that for Isran, though she found as she marched the unicorn was often not far from her thoughts. She wondered at the power of such a creature that could dupe a mage.

The forest seemed to be as ugly and frightening as she had thought in the beginning, now that she had met yet another beautiful, deadly creature of the Shenkar Forest. She eyed her guide suspiciously from then on, even though he seemed to have saved her life. She found little comfort in thinking he had spoken in her mind, which was an insult at that.

43. Rise the damned.

Some were too badly injured to be identified. Beyond the courtyard was fast becoming filled with unmarked graves. There was a cross or a stone here and there where someone had been alive to bury their family member or friend. The men worked tirelessly by torchlight to unearth the remaining corpses. The dust had mostly settled by night, leaving a clear bright sky, aiding in the retrieval of the dead.

Lestadt spotted Titan amidst the rubble, pulling down boulders and debris. Irramai's leader had not stopped since the dragons destroyed the castle; it was now heading toward dusk on the second day. The survivors were passing a waterskin around so Lestadt stood from his brief resting place to take it to Titan.

He could see pain and defeat in so many soot and dust covered faces as he walked by; it was hard to believe this was the same city. He heard a pitiful wailing to his left, and as he wandered closer, he looked down to see a huge, muscular man on the ground weeping. His beard was covered in saliva, his dusty face streaked from tears as he rocked back and forth on his heels, clutching a deceased child not more than five. Lestadt stood for what seemed like an age, staring at this weeping warrior. Suddenly, after all he had seen and done on his journey, this was the most confronting yet. He knew the pain of losing family, but a small defenceless child was something else.

'Lestadt... Lestadt, come, leave him to mourn.'

He was jolted from his thoughts and realised he was still standing and staring stupidly at this poor man. He turned to see Neximus at his side, his hand on Lestadt's shoulder and his face touched by pain.

'We cannot stay here. I don't know where, but we cannot stay in Irramai, or what is left of it,' Neximus said quietly in Lestadt's ear as he pushed him toward Titan.

'I have already stated this, you know?'

'I know, and perhaps it is time that you suggest it again,' Neximus replied, climbing the rubble toward Titan.

'You know, Titan trusts you better than I. Why don't *you* suggest a move?'

'That may be true, but it's not my intelligence that he trusts. You're the one with ideas.'

'Well, he *should* trust your intelligence; even so, now is not the time,' Lestadt said as they neared where Titan was working.

Neximus shrugged, but continued up the mound of rubble.

Though Lestadt was surprised at the suggestion, and relieved. He wanted to keep some integrity. He knew the city was still in danger and the sooner they left, the better, but he could see they were not ready to leave their dead behind.

'Titan...?' he called, proffering the water skin.

Titan barely looked up as he tossed debris aside; he shook his head in refusal.

Seeing Titan was intent on ignoring anyone around him, Neximus gave Lestadt a meaningful look, indicating he would take over. Lestadt stepped back and turned to help a young man who was struggling with a large piece of splintered furniture. Though he had his back to Titan and Neximus, he listened as best he could.

Neximus squatted beside his leader as he dug through the debris.

'Titan... was it not you who recently warned me of the dangers of over-taxing one's self?'

Titan only stopped to glare at Neximus in annoyance before continuing.

'I am expressing genuine concern. You've not stopped, this is madness...'

'I wouldn't expect a man such as yourself to express concern, and I don't expect you to understand. These were not your people,' Titan said harshly, glaring up at the unusual-looking man.

'I lost all of my archers and I knew these people nearly as well as you. It is a terrible thing, but it does not mean you have to sacrifice yourself for the dead,' Neximus said, trying to hide his hurt.

'You cannot begin to understand. This is my responsibility. I'll not let them lay like this, they deserve to be mourned. Just leave me be,' Titan snapped.

Neximus stood, looking down at Titan and slightly angry now.

'You think me heartless and cruel? I would not wish this on anyone, and I *do* understand that you mean to give the dead the proper respect they deserve. But I also realise that right now, the living have more need of you than the dead. *These* are your people and they look to you for leadership. Who will they turn to if you drive yourself into an early grave?'

Titan turned away, looking down at the fallen castle beneath him.

'Better they turn to someone else; I failed as their leader,' Titan said softly, fiddling with a broken piece of slate.

'Wars are fought and lives are lost, this is no failing on your part. Look down there...' Neximus indicated the courtyard. 'Just you try telling them that you have failed. I doubt very much they would believe you, and neither do I.'

Titan saw the men resting. Every now and then, they glanced up at him, and though their eyes were pained and they were wounded and depressed, they still looked to him.

'They wait for you.'

Titan was silent as he looked at the people of Irramai and at Neximus, who he never seemed to give enough credit to. But so many people had perished here beneath the rubble, people that he had led.

'You look exhausted, you need to rest,' Neximus persisted.

'I cannot. I can still hear their cries for help, wailing, children crying, every time I close my eyes. They all died here, Yezimar and Parleans among them. The least we can do is give them a proper burial.'

Neximus offered the large man the waterskin, and finally Titan accepted it. No words passed between them for a few moments. Titan eyed Neximus, noticing his odd expression.

'What...?' he began to ask, but was silenced as Neximus put his finger to his lips.

Titan watched as Neximus' eyes became distant.

'I hear them too,' Neximus suddenly said, turning to Titan in amazement before kneeling and heaving a large rock out of his way.

'What...?' Titan repeated, disbelieving.

Neximus began frantically heaving rocks and bricks out of his way, tossing them carelessly down the side of the mound of rubble.

'Gods! I can hear them! People calling for help! I can hear the child sobbing!'

'I meant figuratively...' Titan started.

'I'm bloody telling you, I can hear them!' Neximus was already breathing heavily from hurling debris out of his way.

Though Titan had his doubts, he resumed his digging.

People were beginning to notice the cascade of debris tumbling down the side of the ruins and drifted closer, curious of what was afoot. Lestadt had worked his way down the other side of the castle with a few of the younger soldiers when he heard the excitement. He and the other men soon dropped their loads of rubble and moved toward where he had left Neximus and Titan. Even Remmador stopped digging one of the many graves to see what all the commotion was.

'What's going on?' one of the soldiers asked, peering down at Titan and Neximus, who had dug themselves into a pit.

Titan looked up, shaking his head. 'Nothing.'

'How can you not hear that?' Neximus demanded, looking up briefly before throwing a broken piece of floorboard out of his way and ignoring the protest from the soldier he'd thrown it into.

'Hear what?' asked Rem.

'The voices, there are people trapped under here.'

Rem looked to Titan for verification, but Titan shook his head. The people were already moving in to help though. Some were still missing their loved ones and now they had hope of finding them alive.

'Wait,' Rem said, holding up his hand. 'This man is fatigued; he's not slept properly in a week or more. No one make a sound. Let's hear these voices.'

The whole crowd grew silent, holding their breath, and praying to hear sounds of life beneath the ruin. The wind blew softly around them. Far in the distance a hawk cried and a horse snorted, but there were no voices, except perhaps in the captain of the archers' mind.

'There... did you hear it? The child...?' Neximus looked wildly from face to face.

'I heard nothing,' Rem said, turning away and pushing through the crowd.

Some people milled around the site, still hoping, but many moved on, annoyed and more upset than before. Lestadt hesitated only a moment before he was in the pit beside Neximus. He wasn't sure he believed it either, but he couldn't abandon his friend now. He didn't believe Neximus was delirious, perhaps a little tired, he admitted, and who could be sure of anything in a time like this?

Some people stayed to dig. They were glad of any sort of hope, but as the dawn of a new day broke, only Titan, Neximus and Lestadt were left searching. The others' hope had left them ten feet of rubble ago. Titan and Lestadt never believed there were survivors from the beginning and now were even more certain.

'Perhaps we should take a break,' Lestadt finally suggested, noticing how tired Titan looked.

'You can rest if you'd like, but these people won't survive much longer. Already they have gone quiet,' Neximus said, now looking more determined than Titan had been.

Lestadt stared at the man, thinking this hope was like a contagious obsession. He turned to Titan and nodded toward their exit in a silent question. Titan was defeated. He and Lestadt began climbing their way out of the pit.

Though the morning sun was weak and the wind had a slight chill to it, sweat dripped from Neximus. He wiped his brow and groaned as he pushed a large chunk of rubble aside; barely acknowledging that Lestadt and Titan were leaving. They had uncovered two more bodies in their search for life, but that had done little to dishearten Neximus. He was determined to find someone alive. He uncovered a half-crushed corner of a door frame and beneath that Neximus could see a small, bluish coloured hand. He touched it briefly, finding it cold. He prepared himself for another grisly sight of a corpse, and this one was quite obviously a child's. Neximus brushed some of the dirt away and uncovered part of the arm that was pinned under what looked like a chest of drawers. A gap between the drawers and the rubble yawned into darkness.

He reached past the limb and began to lift the heavy oak drawers, but something clasped his arm and he jumped in surprise. He looked down in amazement at the small hand curled around his wrist. He unclasped the fingers and cupped the hand in both of his large hands, squeezing gently and waiting for a response. There was a weak squeeze from the child, then, from the dark gap beneath the drawers, there came a wracking sob. This was what Neximus had heard.

'It's alright, you are safe now. I'll have you out in a moment. What's your name?' he asked to distract the child as he let go to move the drawers.

'Don't... don't go, please,' the little boy pleaded, sobbing even louder and searching for Neximus' hand for reassurance.

'I won't leave you.' Neximus grabbed the small hand again, noticing the boy's grip was much stronger now as he clung to Neximus.

'Tell me, what is your name?'

'I'm – my name is Hector.' He sniffed.

'Okay, Hector, my name is Neximus. Can you tell me, are you injured? Is there anyone else with you?'

'Just my arm, sir. My sister, she is next to me.'

Neximus loosened his hold on the child for just a moment and the boy became hysterical. He was trying to tell Neximus something, but the force of his sobs made it impossible for Neximus to understand.

'Hector... Hector? Is your sister hurt? Can you both be moved?'

'My sister is dead,' Hector said through his sobs.

'Okay, okay... I'm just going to move the drawers that are pinning your arm, then I can have you out of there.'

The boy held Neximus' hand in a fierce grip and became hysterical again. Neximus looked around him, not knowing what to do. He didn't want to let go of the boy, he was so terrified, and though Neximus had no intention of leaving him, he didn't want to give the child reason to think he might.

'Titan! Lestadt!' His voice echoed off the rubble around him.

Titan and Lestadt were sitting with Remmador and a dozen more soldiers. Understandably, there was not much conversation. Lestadt didn't feel it was the right time to bring up the fact they were still in danger and should be moving on. They were all still dealing with their grief. Some women and children were spared from the disaster since some had stayed home to take care of the little ones and there were the elderly that could not fight. Many houses had remained relatively untouched, save the few crushed by the south wall. The soldiers had searched the areas affected for survivors and brought back the wounded.

There was a tent in the centre of the courtyard, currently full of sick and injured civilians. Luckily, Irramai's healer had refused to leave her home and had subsequently been spared injury. The old woman fussed about the patients and some of the women were there to help her. The horses, though frightened, were safe in the city stables. They had minor cuts and scratches that were mostly self-inflicted. Steel remained unscathed by the whole ordeal. Nothing seemed to faze him.

Lestadt was lost in thought for some time. The conversation around the fire hadn't been overly stimulating. He picked up on a hushed conversation between Rem and Titan that sparked his interest again.

'... even if we do, we are still wide open to whatever is out there. We would be sitting and waiting...' Rem was saying.

'I know this, Rem, but we can hold this position and wait for it to come to us, or we can march right out there into it on unfamiliar terrain. Do you understand the difficult decision we are going to have to make here?' Titan replied.

'I'm sorry for eavesdropping, but I have to say, staying here when we had a wall didn't help us nor did staying here when we had the castle standing. And now all we have is a giant pile of rubble. Clearly, staying here is not working.' Lestadt was acutely aware he was way out of line and being quite rude.

He figured he was making a valid point, and under the circumstances, he felt every opinion mattered – especially his.

'Well put, Lestadt,' Rem said, validating him.

Before Titan could oppose, they heard Neximus' call.

'Is that fool still hearing voices?' Remmador growled with more than a hint of venom.

'Mind your tongue, Rem. Neximus deserves more credit than you allow him,' Titan snapped, painfully aware of his own recent treatment of the former captain of the archers. 'Best we see what the matter is.'

He couldn't wait any longer. Neximus let the child's hand go, and though it pained him to do so, he ignored Hector's frantic screams and sobs. Neximus just wanted to get the boy out. As he began to lift the drawers, he heard a loud creak, and the boy screamed. He paused momentarily then began to lift the drawers yet higher. There was another groan and the boy screamed louder as his arm began to slide down into the darkness below. Acting quickly, he lowered the drawers onto his own foot so he did not hurt the boy. He grasped Hector's arm, holding it tight.

'What's going on?' Neximus heard Titan's voice from the top of the pit.

'There is a boy trapped down here,' Neximus said between clenched teeth as the pressure of the heavy drawers on his foot intensified.

A rock rolled down into the pit, barely missing Neximus, then there was a spray of dirt as both Titan and Lestadt came sliding down the sides. Immediately they were beside the tall warrior, staring in amazement at the tiny hand fiercely gripping Neximus'.

'Hector, can you tell me what just happened?'

'I... I don't know. All the dirt came down behind me and something slipped beneath me. There is a hole down there. I might fall,' the boy said in a rush of words the three men could barely understand.

'Okay,' Neximus said, thinking, 'Lestadt and Titan, can you slowly lift the drawers enough so I can get a better grip on the boy?'

Titan and Lestadt both moved to either side of the drawers and began to lift on Neximus' command. Neximus laid flat on his stomach and reached further down into the hole now there was enough room and his foot was free.

He grasped beneath Hector's elbows. 'Lift now!'

As the drawers were heaved aside, he heard a small gasp from the boy and then felt the child's full weight dangling in his arms. Neximus pulled and eased up and back onto his heels as he dragged the boy out. He hadn't noticed until now the putrid stench coming from beneath. Now revealed was the full horror of the situation. He quickly pulled the boy into his arms, pinning the boy's head to his chest so he could not see what lay behind him. The boy was eager to accept the contact and desperately clung to Neximus.

A small pocket had saved the boy's life, but inside also lay the bloated body of his sister, who had a splintered support beam piercing her ribcage. Incidentally, that support beam seemed to be the only thing keeping everything else from crushing the boy. The girl looked to be about twelve years of age; the boy was barely half that. Hector had been standing on a slanted piece of board that had now fallen, wedged part way down into the hole beneath.

'There could be more people down there. They would be running out of time. We have to get them out,' Titan said, peering into the darkness below.

They waited, but only silence met them.

'There *are* more people. I could hear their voices last night. Now they are but murmurs, they are getting weak,' Neximus said.

'You take the boy to the healer. Lestadt, go with him and get every abled man and woman down here. I will see if I can figure out a way to get down there without causing a collapse,' Titan instructed.

As the two men climbed from the pit and descended the mound of rubble on the other side, the men at the camps looked up, squinting into the sun. When they realised Neximus was carrying a small boy, a cheer went up through the crowd. Lestadt began ushering them toward the rubble.

On his way to the healer's tent, Neximus passed Rem. He looked at him past the boy's head, now resting on his shoulder and could see Rem still held nothing but contempt for him. Remmador gave Neximus a brief nod and mumbled some form of praise, but his eyes were still hard and hateful as he followed the rest of the survivors to the pit.

44. Visions.

Her eyes flitted open as the damp cloth touched her head, but her awareness faded moments before her eyes closed again.

The old woman shook her head slowly. She and her assistant stood over the impossibly small bed that was in what used to be a pantry full of food. Now there was not a morsel of food to be seen since 'it' began.

Darkness took her where she was only aware of a floating sensation that seemed to be pulling her down as much as it was lifting her up. She made a weak effort to find herself again, but as the black turned to grey, there was a crushing weight that would not let her escape. Soon she drifted back down into the dark. The darkness was not so bad, there was a peace in knowing nothing. In the rolling black sea of her unconscious mind, she let her grip go just a little more.

Unaware that time had passed at all, voices stirred her from her peaceful nothing, yanking her into reality for just a bright and painful moment before she slipped deep into herself again. This time there was no comfort. It was as though a doorway had opened inside her, and though she wanted desperately to drift again in dreamlessness, she could not.

Awful things held her mind hostage. *A man hanging from a tree by his gizzards. A family murdered and strung up on display outside their home. A grinning, bloodied man, four heads dangling from his hand. A sweet little girl brandishing a knife. An insane man burned black in the snow.*

She tried to push the terrible images from her mind, but they rushed back in waves. Bleak and twisted images assaulted her, and for a moment she was aware she was going insane.

A woman trapped inside a burning house. Succumbing to defeat, she presses her hands against the window and sobs as she watches people watching her die – no one cared. A woman running to save her child, only to be grabbed and pushed to the ground – moments later she is screaming as she lifts a bloodied stump in the air where her hand once was. Dead children wake to lay slaughter to their sleeping kin in the night. A huge black beast materialises from the sky, biting a man's head clean off. An insane woman buries her child alive in the night. An insane woman buried her child alive – this night. She was suddenly awake in the painful and bright world she had tried to forget.

The young girl leapt back as the woman sprung upright in bed, her eyes wild and searching.

'She's awake, it's too late for her,' the girl cried, as the old woman shuffled into the kitchen.

For a brief moment, Raemil remembered nothing and it would have been blissful had she known that soon she would remember everything. The woman, withered and bent with age, shuffled closer, a wary look in her eye that made her seem hard. Raemil's fever had not cleared and her eyes were still bright and red. She was confused and half-crazed.

'My baby... where is my son?'

'Hush now and rest,' the old woman said, reaching for Raemil's forehead.

Raemil ducked away and, gripped by panic, she leapt out of bed in a flurry of sheets and seized the old woman by her throat. She dizzied and the dark swept toward her, but she fought it back, knowing only one thing. She had given birth to a son and she didn't know where he was.

'You came to us in the night, covered in blood from the birth, but no babe... no babe.' The old lady repeated the last with sorrow.

Raemil pushed her away and fled. She ran past a young woman who sat huddled against the door frame, staring up at her with wide, frightened eyes. Raemil hardly cared that she was the source of this girl's fear.

Dozens of beds lined the walls of the passages. Most of the people were either dying or should have died. They lay in their chains, screaming insanity at each other as she ran by. Her sword caught her eye, leaning carelessly against the entryway wall. She snatched it up on her way past. Raemil burst out the front door, and, wearing only a thin, white undercoat and her sword, she fled into the night.

Losing track of all time as she ran through the snow, she was unaware of the rising sun and of the Black following at a distance. She didn't know where she was going, but her feet seemed to take her to a place she had been before, as though her body remembered, but her mind had not caught up yet.

Raemil dropped to her knees in the snow under a lone cypress tree. There was a tiny mark that could have been a partial print from an animal or just a shape the wind had blown the snow into, but a sick feeling in the pit of her stomach told her that it was not so. Something told her it was the impression her palm had left on the snow. She had knelt in this very place the night before, but what was she doing? She was afraid to know, yet she was already digging.

* * *

The men were terrified. Galten and Bennagon could only do their best to reassure them and keep their hopes alive, but without the General, it was proving difficult. It had been three unbearable days since they had briefly glimpsed the General and the strange blue-haired woman. Both Bennagon and Galten feared the worst but tried to keep the rest of the men hopeful. They heard no news of Serrin, the two men figuring they had left the poor prince's body to rot in the tower.

Only the women had brief wanderings in the night as they were escorted from their quarters to the Horsham men's, but that was less often now. Only a few women took their fancy, the rest had succumbed to the illness that was spreading through their filthy quarters. The slave-soldiers had their contacts within the women's camp, stealing brief conversations. They traded food rations and scraps of real sword tips, nails and material found around the yards, for information on one thing or another. For the most part, the men and women were worlds apart from each other, though only a mesh fence separated the two exercise yards. Bennagon and Galten had asked most of the regularly used women if they had seen the former Caelinian Prince, but none had.

It was noon on the fourth day when the doors to the west tower swung open. Every slave-soldier's head shot up as they heard the unmistakable sound of the doors squealing on their rusted hinges. Out of the darkness within the doorway, a form stumbled into the dirt as a pair of rough hands shoved him aside. Two Horsham soldiers stepped past the fallen man and walked away. The man lay for some time, face down in the dirt. He didn't bother wiping the blood from his nose or the dirt from his face as he eventually stood, squinting his one eye at the bright sun.

'Filth!' a Horsham man spat.

The man did not respond, nor did he react when a wooden sword was hurled and struck him hard in his back.

'Train,' the Horsham man commanded.

He didn't respond. His eye gazed over the yard dispassionately. The Horsham soldier stormed over, raising his hand threateningly.

'I said train!' He backhanded the man across the temple.

The man stumbled before bending and gingerly picking up the sword.

Bennagon and Galten were at opposite ends of the training yard from each other when they saw him and neither could control their shock, letting the façade of their indifference drop for the first time. The General was barely a shadow of his former self, like a dog with all its bite beaten out of it.

Serrin's nose bled unchecked down past his lips and dripped off his chin. His clothes were filthier than usual. He was bruised from beatings and his shoulders were stooped. Worst of all was the exposed socket where his right eye used to be. His remaining eye was downcast, unable to meet anyone's gaze.

* * *

Somewhat amazed, Arramaou the crow swooped down toward a tree that stood apart from the others on the hillside. He landed quietly on a branch above the familiar figure, wishing his presence to remain undetected for now. He cocked his head, wondering what she was doing and whether she had finally fallen at the hands of... what...? He did not know, but indirectly one would suppose only Horsham was to blame.

Curiosity made him lean out just a little further to see past her sprawled form in the snow to see that before her was a tiny, shallow grave. Inside lay the body of an infant, only days old, he could guess. The last time he had seen her, she had been with child. *How sad,* he thought to himself, though he felt no real emotion, only recognising that once he would have thought so.

He was a little disappointed she had met such an end, but watched with interest as he saw two Horsham men approaching in the distance. They were on a routine check of the borders, not often done this far north, but on occasion it was required of them.

'Raemil... are you sound of mind? Are you ill? Such a disappointment to see you this way. You had been my hope, pathetic as you are,' he crooned.

She rolled onto her back and her shocking green eyes stared up at him from a dirt-smudged face. Some form of awareness glimmered beneath that unnerving blank stare. Raemil's brow furrowed, perhaps trying to remember. Her black horse stood not far from her. He nodded his head and whickered as he saw her move but failed to gain her attention.

Arramaou watched as a dragon flew in from the east and screeched as the approaching Horsham men came into view. Suddenly, Raemil's eyes became deadly aware. They flared with such rage that even Arramaou was a little afraid, as safe as he was in the tree. As the dragon landed before the two Horsham men, Raemil rolled onto her stomach, half crouching as though she were a lioness on the prowl. Arramaou squawked, lapsing into the nervous habit of a flock-bird, and the horse below snorted, his nostrils flared as the scent of the dragon carried to him. Both noises failed to disturb Raemil. She only had eyes for the exchange taking place before her.

The dragon swooped, ready to attack, but incredibly, it seemed to recognise the Horsham men as allies. Landing before them, it scrutinised the soldiers, lest it make a mistake and pass up the opportunity for a meal. One of the men tossed the ominous creature a hunk of goat meat and the dragon, satisfied, took wing, heading west to wherever it had been going.

Raemil stared between the retreating dragon and the two Horsham men, obviously just as confused as to why they were still alive. Suddenly and amazingly, Raemil sprang into action. Arramaou could only watch in complete and utter delight as Raemil, crazed as she was, vented her rage.

45. The bane.

She was consumed by hatred and disgust and fear and hurt and loathing. Raemil cast it all at the two Horsham men that had just made some form of dealings with a dragon; the very creature that had taken everything from her. She unsheathed her sword and bore down on them, roaring like a wild animal. By the time the Horsham men turned toward the sound, she was already upon them with sword swinging.

The blade flashed once, twice, then, in a river of dark blood, it was over, or so it seemed. Arramaou watched as Raemil collected their heads from the stained ground and mounted her somewhat reluctant horse, urging him into a wild gallop south. Arramaou took flight, intent on following her mad dash, wondering just what she would do once she got to where he knew she was headed.

The Horsham men preferred to complete weapons training away from the slave-soldiers' yard on open ground. There were thirty or so participating in drills in the afternoon, practising with sword, lance, mace and an assortment of blades and daggers. Argané was among the fighters. They would move out soon and he wanted them to be ready.

There was a gruff shout from one of the northernmost groups of men, followed by more cries of alarm. There was some sort of commotion and a knot of men surging toward a rider. The rider cut down several men as – *she* –

continued toward the main group. She held in her bloodied fist, by the hair, two heads of the soldiers who had been sent to patrol the northern border.

'Stop her!' Argané shouted, pointing his sword at the rider cutting her way across the field.

There was deadly focus on her blood-streaked face. Her wild red hair streamed behind her in the wind and her once white undergarment was stained copper with old blood.

Raemil was beyond all rage now. An eerie calm had taken its place. She had felt it before, the calm before the storm. She was determined to annihilate any soldier that prevented her from reaching the castle and strangling the life from whomever this Horsham person was.

A horde of men surged forward with weapons drawn, enveloping her and the Black. She was quick to use her own sword, hacking at limbs in long swoops. She impaled one man through his open mouth and had difficulty dislodging her sword from the back of his head. As she used her foot against the remains of his face, wrenching her bloodied sword free, she herself was caught between the ribs by a small dagger. She cried out and turned on her attacker, but in the rush of bodies pressed to her mount, the Black reared and someone caught hold of her hair and dragged her to the ground. Her sword was lost somewhere below in the swarm of bodies.

There was nothing to do now but fight like she had never fought before; she had nothing to lose. She kicked legs out from beneath some of the men around her, clearing enough space to scramble to her feet. She took up the curved blade of one of the fallen Horsham men. She kicked, elbowed and slashed. Whatever it took to get through the horde. She was covered in small wounds and finding it harder to push back, but still she fought on.

In the confusion of the scuffle, the soldiers were hacking at each other more so than the elusive woman. One knocked her stolen sword from her hand and elbowed her in the back of her head, sending her sprawling. She rolled onto her back and tried to get to her feet when a booted foot pressed down on her throat. He pointed his curved blade at her face as others began to circle.

She was yanked to her feet and her arms were pulled behind her. One of the burly men came at her with sword drawn. She hooked her foot behind her captor's leg and pitched her weight backward, throwing them both off balance.

They both fell, her landing hard on top of him. Climbing to her feet, she saw the shadow of a soldier come at her, sidestepped and grabbed him by the throat. He stopped dead in his tracks and his features contorted in pain. His face flushed and sweat began to break out on his forehead. Suddenly a crow flew overhead, squawking madly and diving at one of the Horsham men, then someone hit her hard in the back of her head and she knew no more.

Arramaou watched as Raemil fought her way through the field, killing several men, leaving many more wounded. From above, he could see she used unnatural speed and strength. He intervened when he realised Argané was getting impatient and would likely kill her.

They took heed that he was Horsham's bird and perhaps was not just an ordinary crow. He witnessed Raemil seizing a man's throat, nearly killing him, before she was struck from behind. Arramaou glimpsed the mark she left on the man's thick neck. His neck was so stout she could hardly have fit her hand around his windpipe, but she hadn't needed to. The soldier's neck now bore the print of Raemil's hand, burned into his flesh.

She was at first aware of a dull thud, growing steadily louder as she came to her senses. With a sharp intake of breath, she realised the thudding came from the base of her skull. She reached up with her trembling hand and touched the mass of knotted and bloody hair stuck to her head where she had been clubbed. She could hear shuffling feet, the wailing of a woman, quiet mutterings, and a slow, constant dripping coming from somewhere behind her.

Raemil opened her eyes slowly and, as they adjusted to the dark and the pain, she could see she was in some kind of dungeon. She crawled back as a barefoot suddenly stepped past her head. It was covered in oozing blisters and cuts.

Raemil's head reeled as she took in the sight. The floor was slick with slime. By the smell she could only guess it was human filth and blood. There were women walking around the cell or huddled in groups. Their clothes were mere rags, filthy and torn. Their hair matted, and most seemed to be coughing or wheezing. Their skin sickly pale and their wounds festering. Chained above the floor to the stone walls were at least a dozen more women, badly emaciated, horribly wounded and some had long been dead.

Disturbing as the sight was, Raemil felt no emotion toward them. As she sat staring in the dank, dark cell, she felt nothing at all. She was all out of tears, all out of compassion, all out of anger and all out of caring.

The other women in the cell sat well away from her, terrified of the strange-looking woman that had been thrown into their cell a day ago. Raemil sat for hours, a vague expression on her face, as she looked over the walls and the floor. There was a grate in the middle of the floor that she assumed was to be the toilet. A wall jutted out and past that she could see a dim source of light, where the barred door was to the cell, peering out into a dreary hallway. On the floor was also a large bowl of water, turned brown from the filth coming from the women's hands. There was no ladle or cup for them to drink from.

Raemil ventured over to look out into the hallway. The women glanced up at her and either scuttled away or quickly looked away again. Raemil barely noticed them. She held onto the bars and stared at the opposite wall. There was a slight flicker in the light that came into the cell. If she pushed her face hard enough against the bars, she could see a torch mounted on the wall in the distance. She assumed it was night time.

'It won't get any brighter during the day. Little light is shed into the cells of any slave of Horsham,' said a deep but beautiful voice from the shadows behind Raemil.

Raemil slowly turned her head as a woman stepped out of the darkness, as though she saw no difference in Raemil's appearance to the other women's.

Her skin was quite dark and her shoulder length hair was jet-black, tied back in a messy braid. She studied Raemil with an unwavering gaze. Her left eye was swollen and murky, as opposed to the deep dark brown it should have been. The woman seemed to know Raemil was taking note of her blinded eye.

'It is a cruel fate to come to these dungeons. There are no cures for your hurts, no one shall come for you when you are sick, and no one shall come for you when you are dead. We are all rotting down here, dead or alive,' she said, sweeping a scarred arm toward the corpses hanging on the wall.

'How do I get out?' Raemil asked, turning her gaze back to the hallway.

There was a low, humourless laugh. 'You don't.'

'Most of these women are dying, not only from their infected wounds, but they look as though they've not seen light for weeks. Yet you and a few others seem unaffected by the lack of light. One would assume you are either not human or have seen the sun at least this month. Now tell me... how do I get out?'

'Those are the ones that aren't so crippled from their wounds they can be escorted into the exercise yard once a week or so. Others, such as myself, have other ways of seeing the outside more often.' She shrugged. 'Not by choice, but it is a small mercy to feel fresh air, if you can erase the memory of the reason you are allowed it.'

Raemil cocked her head at the cryptic reply, but the woman didn't elaborate. The two women said no more to each other as they stared longingly out of the cell.

Raemil found a place to sleep with her back against a wall and away from the other women, who huddled together like livestock. Eventually, exhaustion took her and the last thing she saw as her heavy eyelids fell closed was a dirty rat scampering across the floor.

46. Fury.

Her head itched and something tugged her hair. Raemil woke very quickly to find a rat tangled in her curls. She snatched up the balding creature and squeezed its spine until there was a squeak and a snap and the rodent went limp. Raemil looked up to see the women in the cell all staring at her in fear and disgust, all save the dark-haired woman whose expression seemed unreadable. A tall and heavily-set prisoner stared at her in a particularly hostile manner. Raemil stared back, and much to Raemil's surprise, the woman stood, and, slowly raising her right hand, she pointed at Raemil.

'Serlyn.'

Raemil's eyebrows rose, and she strode with purpose toward the larger woman. She vaguely remembered being a princess. She'd had beautiful dresses, neat hair and apartments within the castle. She had been taught that it was necessary for her to avoid dirt and to be afraid of rodents, snakes and insects. She had perfect speech and perfect manners, no matter the occasion; this had been her life, and it had been all she knew. She remembered all of this as she seized the woman's throat in one hand and lifted her from the floor with unnatural strength. She was no longer a princess.

The large woman kicked her feet hopelessly and squeezed Raemil's wrists, but Raemil's hand was wrapped firmly around the woman's throat. The other women scuttled away in fear, none brave enough to come to the other woman's aid.

'Say it now,' said Raemil, her gaze unwavering.

A choked sound came from the woman.

'If I hear that name again, I will tear your heart out.' Raemil dropped the woman and she fell heavily at Raemil's feet, coughing and spluttering as she crawled away.

There was no further incident during the day after Raemil had made it very clear she would not tolerate their hostility. There was very little the women could do in the cell to amuse themselves, but some had managed to find small items around the yards to keep them busy. They found sword tips and pebbles, some carved small bits of wood. This kept some of the prisoners relatively sane.

Raemil sat alone in a dark corner, with dark thoughts consuming her. Often small snippets of conversation would break her reverie and she would listen with half interest. One common name she heard was 'The General'. As the day drew on and the women had little else to talk about, Raemil began to gather more interest in the person they spoke of.

Apparently, the captured men were not just soldiers but men who had been abducted from fields, homes and small villages that were raided. This explained the fearful looks from the villagers Raemil had passed. None of the women seemed to know which category the General fell into, or if they did, they weren't going to say so; but one would assume he had been a general at some stage.

What interested Raemil the most was the man was so well liked, and so well respected, that even the women held him in high regard. She wondered if he knew of Serrin and wondered if she could speak to this man to discover his whereabouts. If the man had been a general when he was caught, it could only mean he was either the Korranian general or Serrin's general. In either case, he would know the Caelinian prince and likely know of his fate.

* * *

He had spoken to no one, and any attempt at communication with him had been met with either hostility or a blank stare from his one eye. Galten and Bennagon continued training the other soldiers, trying to keep their hopes alive, but it had come to the point where the men seemed to worship the General, especially the younger men. Spirits were rapidly dropping.

Bennagon was beginning to feel the loss of their leader himself. He knew the General had once been the Caelinian prince, weeping and cowering in his cell.

He was just one man, the same as any other, yet Bennagon thought because Serrin had become the General, it had made him stronger. They all started to think he was invincible, until now.

Serrin wore a patch over his eye, made from a circle of leather from the tongue of his boot and the boot lace threaded around his long, straggly hair. The man sat staring across the yard at nothing, it seemed. It was the same bland expression he had worn a week ago, when he was tossed back into the yard.

Distracting Bennagon from his study of the General, he heard a Horsham man shouting and cursing as a hooded woman ran toward the men's training yard. She clung to the fence and Bennagon stood his ground, for the men rarely received the punishment for such encounters. The woman clung to the mesh and her shocking green eyes pinned Bennagon, startling him.

'I must see the General. He would know Serrin. I am…'

She was thrown roughly to the ground and the Horsham man raised a whip to her. He cracked it across her wrists as she flung her hands up to protect her face. She fought back but was subdued by several Horsham soldiers.

Bennagon retreated, but he was intrigued. He'd heard mention of a woman they called the Bane and it was easy to assume it was her.

That night in his cell, Bennagon carved a message into his bowl to ask the General about the woman then thought better of it and scratched it out. He couldn't help wondering if the man would even bother scratching the message out after he read it.

For her disobedience, Raemil bore whip marks on her wrists. Minor wounds could prove fatal since chances of infection were high, and she had so many cuts. One small comfort was Raemil had managed to find a cloak to keep her warm. She ignored the repulsed looks she received as she pulled it from a nearly dead woman hanging in their cell.

The dark-haired woman claimed there was little hope of speaking to the General now. The odd woman did inform her that the men trained most days from sunrise until dusk. The women were due an outing soon; they never knew exactly when. It was hard to tell when one day ended and another began. Raemil barely spoke to the only woman that had at least made some effort to extend something akin to a friendship. She noticed that, sometimes, the half-blind woman sat alone, with a frightened expression, and speaking to no one. This place took its toll on even the strongest.

It was several days later when the women were woken from their sleep at what they assumed to be night time. Three Horsham men escorted them through the dark hallways and into the broad daylight of their exercise yard. There were several women that could not drag themselves out and some had attempted the short journey through the halls that shouldn't have bothered. The weakest collapsed in the hall before being dragged back into the cell by their filthy, matted hair.

The yard was bare dirt and snow packed firm by the shuffling of many tired feet. There was little to see but barren land and the half collapsing castle. Raemil squinted, surveying the yard; the weak winter sun was harsh after being confined in the darkness. She studied the mesh fence separating the two yards, disappointed that there were no slave-soldiers.

Many of the women wandered aimlessly or talked in small groups. Raemil walked the perimeter of the yard over, looking for a way out. Eventually two of the Horsham men that had escorted them out left the yard, leaving just one on guard. Raemil could see there were possibilities for escape, but only if she could get out of her cell first.

The dark-haired woman, who had rediscovered her tongue, said every so often the women were left alone in the yard whilst there was a guard change. Sometimes the guard would wander a distance away to relieve himself and that was generally when she grabbed her chance to speak to the slave-soldiers. It was roughly noon when there was movement at the far end of the men's yard and Raemil could see them shuffling out in single file.

She completed another lap, trying to feign disinterest. By the time she was circling around to the fence again, the men were in clear view. She searched their faces, looking for Serrin. She could not see him amongst the one hundred or so men. Circling the yard yet again, she came back to scrutinise the faces once more. She heard a man call to the General. At first, no one responded, and Raemil recognised the prisoner from several days ago that had been standing at the fence. The large man was addressing a fellow prisoner with an eye patch, whom Raemil had previously overlooked, partially because of the patch. Now, as Raemil studied him more closely, her heart skipped a beat.

'Serrin!' Raemil cried, clinging to the fence and completely forgetting the guards behind her.

The one-eyed man did not respond.

'Serrin, it's me... Raemil!'

At this, the man visibly tensed, then turned directly toward her, staring in confusion. She pulled the hood back and let her messy, red hair tumble free. The hard expression melted from his face as he pushed past the others to get to her.

Raemil wept as her brother fell to his knees on the other side of the fence, reaching up and holding her fingers through the wire. His shoulders began to shudder and she realised she wasn't the only one crying.

'I have found you...' she whispered as she sank to her knees.

He looked much older than he should have. His once cropped hair was now long and matted, hanging over his eye in greasy ropes. He also had a dark beard that hid yet more of his sad face. A new wave of emotion hit her as she looked upon the patch, wondering what hardships he had been made to suffer.

Before anymore could be said, her head was snapped back by a rough hand entwined in her hair and she was dragged from the fence. She could hear Serrin's curses and the rattle of the fence, guessing he was trying to climb, but she could only see the sky. She struggled, twisting and writhing and clawing at her assailant's wrists to no avail.

'Let me see him!' she shrieked.

Serrin was halfway up the fence when he was tackled by the guards on his side. He tried to kick them off and was initially succeeding, but he could hear reinforcements coming. He suddenly stopped, staring wide-eyed at his sister. Every soul in the yard seemed to pause and stare in bewilderment.

Raemil convulsed, veins bulged in her arms, and a gust of wind suddenly whipped her hair back from her face. Initially, the wind seemed only to affect the men holding her as they were thrown backward by the force. Raemil fell to the ground and with her arms spread and her back arched awkwardly. She remained pinned there by an unseen force.

What started as a small gust soon turned into a large whirl-wind. It picked up snow and filth and soon a dirty off-white wall of wind was blown in everyone's faces. Serrin, and the guards that had been trying to restrain him, were blown from the fence. People had to shield their eyes and hunker down against the force. The west tower groaned and shuddered and debris began to peel off and fly around dangerously.

From where Serrin lay, trying to protect himself from flying pieces of the tower and general debris, he could see Raemil caught in the middle. It was difficult to see, but Serrin thought he could make out the shape of one of the women approaching. She leaned over his sister, partially blocking Serrin's view. Suddenly, Raemil's body went limp and the wind died. Items that had been airborne dropped suddenly out of the sky and all was silent and still again. The Horsham men recovered quickly and both men and women were promptly forced back into their cells.

Raemil woke back in the cell. Her throat was bruised and she had the impression that someone had strangled her. She felt weak and tired. The dark-haired woman was sitting beside her but said nothing for a long time. She wore an odd expression and Raemil assumed she was having one of her peculiar episodes.

The first few times, Raemil wasn't aware of how she did it or how it began. Now Raemil remembered the feeling of air between her fingers. It almost felt solid to her, as though they were all suspended in the stuff. She moved her fingers, feeling *it* move, and knowing she could manipulate it, or that perhaps it could manipulate her. She had been gripped by a massive force as the wind seemed to gain momentum, building speed as it whipped around the courtyard like some monster unleashed. Then a shadow had loomed over her, seized her throat and choked the very wind from her.

'Why did you come here?' The dark-haired woman broke the silence between them.

'I came for my brother.'

'You came here willingly, knowing what you would find here?' She emphasised her point with a sweep of her arm toward the dead bodies on the chamber wall.

'Knowing that I would find my brother.'

'And then what? Live happily ever after in the prison camp with him?'

'Then I shall take him home.'

The other woman laughed. 'Where is home, Raemil?'

A cold shiver ran down Raemil's spine, followed by a wave of numbness. 'Home is North to Caelin, for my brother, at least.'

'And where is *your* home?' The other woman leaned closer, her interest intensifying.

Raemil didn't notice; she wanted to sleep.

'I am disowned, I have no home.'

Raemil's head dropped back down and she let her exhaustion take her.

Serrin was not taken back to his normal cell, nor was he taken to the solitary cell, where he guessed he had spent just as much time. The room was perhaps the bedchamber of a servant, not so lowly to be sleeping in the kitchen with the rest, but not so highly valued that they were afforded any luxury, save a small fireplace. Serrin was cuffed to iron rings set in the floor in the furthest corner from the door. There was a tiny window in the wall opposite him and adjacent to the fireplace.

As he watched the day leak out of the room, he thought of Raemil, both shocked and saddened by her appearance. Although she had wept at seeing him, there was a certain hardness in her eyes that had never been there before. He didn't know what evil had befallen her in the courtyard and thought perhaps Horsham had attacked her with her awful magic.

Serrin had a cold feeling he was no longer alone in the room. A quiet voice came whispering to his ear, causing his body to tense.

'Serrin, silly Caelinian prince, you should have stayed home.'

'Who are you?'

'That is no matter to you.' There was a sickening laugh. 'You had to come rushing to the Korranians' aid,' the voice chimed, and Serrin had the distinct feeling it was feminine. 'The Korranians were already ruined before word was sent to you. Did you notice they seemed surprised to see you come to their aid?'

'They had thought we would not come,' Serrin said, trying to keep his fear in check.

'Nay, little Prince. The Korranians never called you.'

'You lie. I saw the messenger with my own eyes.'

'Did you? Or did you see what I wanted you to see?' There was more laughter. 'The fact is, little Prince, your sister is here because of you. You, rushing off to war with no experience, nor the intelligence to strategise or to question the Korranians' need of you, has caused much of the suffering and sorrow that is to come. As you walk as a *free* man, I hope you will know this and despair.'

'What do you mean?'

'Oh yes, you shall go free. You will know the shame of leaving your men to rot while you return to your home.'

'Why are you telling me this? Who are you? Are you Horsham?'

Serrin felt the presence leave and knew he was alone again.

47. Linvar's fire.

The cool wind swept across the yard where the final preparations were underway. Survivors milled about in groups of family and friends; some had been lucky enough to be reunited. Their work was done, but they were not likely to sleep this night with the uncertainty of the next day looming.

Twenty cart horses stood impatiently in the courtyard. They were loaded to the brink with supplies. Even so, much would be left behind. The courtyard was crowded with little space for a private conversation to be held and remain private. Most were in good cheer, considering the events of the past months, and though many were apprehensive about the coming day, they were also relieved to be moving on.

It had taken several days to rescue the 120 soldiers and civilians from the castle. When almost everybody, dead or alive, had been accounted for, Titan finally agreed with Lestadt. They could no longer stay.

Steel being the build that he was would be put to work pulling a cart. Though he was standing relatively still now in the harness, as Lestadt adjusted it to ensure its fit, one could easily see the big grey gelding was none too pleased. Lestadt gave the straps one last jerk to ensure nothing slipped then left Steel as he was, hobbled to another horse.

Lestadt made his way to the group of men standing in the far corner. Small fires bloomed in the descending darkness. He headed to Titan's fire. The mood was more sombre. They were mourning the deaths of Parleans and Yezimar.

Both men were killed in the fall of the castle.

'Everything is set for first light,' Lestadt said, joining the men.

'Thank you, Lestadt. We should all try to get some rest before we leave, there's a lot of ground to cover tomorrow before we reach our first camp.' Titan excused himself from the semi-circle that had formed around him.

Lestadt and Neximus retreated to their own private space to speak.

'I'm surprised you got your way in the end, Lestadt. I have to hand it to you, for a while I thought you would be cast out.' Neximus' thoughtful expression was revealed by the firelight.

'So did I.' Lestadt grinned, catching the half smirk from Neximus out of the corner of his eye.

'I know it is far north, but where exactly is this "safe place" that we are going to?'

'Caelin castle.'

'Do you personally know the king? Does he owe you a favour?' His voice was thick with sarcasm, but not without warmth for his friend.

Lestadt remained silent.

'Oh, come on, Lestadt, you don't strike me as someone who has friends in such high places.'

'Are you not my friend, Neximus?' Lestadt eyed him, a little annoyed with the probing.

'Of course, but if you think I'm in a high place, then I *know* you don't know the king. From the beginning you've been secretive and have pushed for us to leave Irramai – but why? Why come here because you want to leave? It strikes me as odd, and it has not escaped the attentions of Titan or *Remmador*. You have proved too useful to be confronted about it just yet. Furthermore, one does wonder where you gained these skills to be so useful to Irramai.'

'These sound like the answers that Titan would have of me. Tell me... do you speak on his behalf, or yours?'

Neximus paused, staring at the fire as he scratched the stubble on his chin. Lestadt could see the flames reflect in his cold, grey eyes and for just a split second thought he had something to fear of this man. Then Neximus turned his gaze back to Lestadt and he could see only friendship lay there.

'I ask on my behalf, but yes, Titan did approach me. He knows that you and I are close, but I suppose he believes I owe my loyalty to Irramai first.' Neximus smiled bitterly. 'I don't owe them all that much. I would have these answers of you because you have always been on my side. I feel now the tables are sure to turn, I would return the favour; if only I knew what it is you want.'

'What do you mean?'

'Rem hates me, and seeing you have allied yourself with me, has, of course, earned you disfavour with him. Rem is close to Titan. Especially now Yezimar is dead, Rem is his closest and most trusted friend. They will not follow you to their deaths, and they will not risk this city any more than it already has been. They are watching you closely, Lestadt.'

'I mean no harm to these people if that's what you think. But you're right, I do have ambitions of my own. I have had my own agenda with Irramai since long before I arrived. Tell me, in a time like this, where will a whole city seek refuge? Perhaps splitting up will guarantee one quarter of the population shelter and safety *in servitude*. The rest, perhaps, will die as beggars. This city needs another fortress, just like Irramai, but away from Horsham.' Lestadt paused, choosing his words carefully.

'Caelin is the nearest fortified city. No town or village could, or even would, help these people. I have seen it out there, doors close very readily in a stranger's face, and that's only if the door is opened at all. The only way to find refuge for over three hundred people is to take it by force and I know we could. We have survived a horde of evil dogs and an attack from dragons. Seizing this castle will be easy for us.'

'That's a pretty speech, Lestadt; you should have saved it for the people. Your answer to this city's woes is logical but flawed where numbers are concerned. Three hundred soldiers are nothing. Three hundred citizens are merely refugees, but what I really want to know is why it is that *you* care? What exactly is your agenda?'

Lestadt sighed, rubbing his hand through his hair at the nape of his neck. He'd hoped his 'pretty speech' would have saved him from having to be honest. He should have known it wouldn't work on Neximus.

'I came to Irramai after the people of my village were raped and pillaged by Caelinian soldiers, my mother and sister amongst the dead. I'd heard Irramai was led by a rebel army that had fortified a broken kingdom and created the "free-lands". I came because I wanted the army. I want Irramai to take Caelin and her spoils and I want to feel the satisfaction of sliding my sword into the heart of the king for what his men did to my family.' Lestadt's voice turned hard and bitter.

Before Neximus could respond, a shadow leapt toward them, toppling Neximus and landing him flat on his back. Neximus sat up and Lestadt managed a half grin at the sight.

Yet again, the little boy Neximus had rescued, Hector, had come seeking the tall warrior's comfort. This was a ritual for Neximus and the boy. Neximus would spend the next hour comforting the boy, then the next half trying to convince him to go back to sleep in the village healer's tent with the other orphans. By then, the boy would be pretending to be asleep in Neximus' arms, and Neximus would inevitably give in.

Discussions were now over for Neximus and Lestadt, but it was clear Lestadt's story had left Neximus troubled. Whether it was because of the manner in which his family had died or because his cause was flawed with bloody revenge, Lestadt couldn't tell.

As dawn broke on Irramai, the courtyard was bustling with activity with horses being checked and people adding last minute items to already heavy loads. The orphans were gathered and counted and people chatted excitedly over hastily eaten breakfasts. There were also last-minute briefings for Titan's closest men. Their first camp would be just outside of Linvar, a large village northwest of Irramai. They could not hope to find refuge in the town for so many people but thought to find more supplies in the village, especially grain, which they were particularly short on.

No one had really ventured beyond the walls of Irramai for a long time and survived to return, not since the dogs had come. The city had a decent stock of food, but that was another reason Titan finally agreed with Lestadt – the food wouldn't last forever.

Beyond Irramai, the world had changed. The bonds of winter were finally beginning to break and the great melt had started, which meant there were many slow-moving streams carrying blocks of ice away. Run off from the Horsham Mountains created temporary streams that joined the larger rivers and waterways, making travel hazardous.

Much of the day consisted of picking their way across slushy fields then trying to avoid crossing streams whilst dodging drifts of ice threatening to crash into their carts and horses. Fortunately, they did not have to cross the main river before reaching Linvar, but many small streams of run-off had to be conquered, without getting the narrow cart wheels stuck in muddy snow.

Lestadt walked beside Steel, looking around in wonder. He had never properly experienced snow melt before. Normally, the coming of spring was a joyous occasion in any village, but this line of refugees were scared and exposed in a land they no longer recognised. Though the experience was fascinating, he couldn't help but notice the awful quiet that enveloped the world. There was something missing, and for a long time, he could not figure out what it was.

The people seemed disquieted, as though a thick cloud of tension hung above them. Lestadt eventually realised what was missing. There was no birdsong, no wind, the air was heavy. Even the horses seemed quiet and flighty. Their dark eyes rolling occasionally, catching a movement of what they thought could be some demon but was only one of the many travellers. The people themselves stopped communicating with one another, as though unconsciously conforming to the strange new quiet.

'Halt!' a shout shattered the oppressive silence around them.

Lestadt could see Titan, several carts ahead, his hand raised to signal the people further back in the line. On this soundless day his voice should have rung clearly, but the air seemed to catch and muffle his voice. The silent spell broke and general chatter began as food rations were passed around for their first and only break before sundown. There was no shelter from the wind or early spring rain until Linvar's forest. It was the only small amount of shelter they were going to find this close to Irramai and Linvar.

Lestadt hadn't the opportunity to speak to Neximus again; he was behind him walking with Hector, who seemed to have become Neximus' shadow. Lestadt found it odd to see the emotionless man so attached to the boy, as much as the boy was to him. Neximus had been especially attentive after noticing a peculiar rash on the boy's neck, discovering that at least half of the people rescued from the ruined castle had also broken out in the rash. The healer thought it was an infection caught and spread while they were trapped in the rubble.

They saw smoke rising ahead and reached Linvar an hour before dusk. Linvar was surrounded by fires but seemed completely deserted. Again, the eerie silence distracted Lestadt and did not go unnoticed by others. He felt a presence behind him and turned to see Neximus.

'I don't like the look of this. I passed through Linvar on my way to Irramai, it was full of people. They should be out tending their fields and sheep and thronging the streets. There have been no birds or animals for the whole of our journey.' Neximus gazed ahead with his hand instinctively on the hilt of his sword.

Lestadt was surprised to find his hand had also unconsciously strayed to his weapon. He handed Steel's reins to a young man, as Neximus gave the reins of his big roan horse to Hector. They moved up the line of people toward Titan. Lestadt heard the indignant snort of his gelding, followed by the curse of the young man holding him in check. He glanced back to see Steel standing on the man's foot. He was leaning his weight onto that leg and refusing to budge, causing Lestadt to grin, despite his unease.

They found Titan with Rem at his side, toward the front of the line.

'I see this unnerves you both too. I'm going to go in with a small group of men, to see if anyone is still here and willing to sell us some supplies. Rem will stay here.'

'I would feel better if I came with you,' Neximus said, stepping forward.

Titan nodded then looked at Lestadt, who stepped forward also.

'Good. Let's keep our hands away from our weapons right now, we don't want to startle anyone.'

Several other men, seeing him move, fell in behind the three. As they passed the first fire to enter the village, huge flames leapt up, higher than Lestadt was tall. The orange flames licked at the sky like a hungry demon, unnerving Lestadt further. Nothing moved nor made sound and the village seemed as though nothing had lived there for years.

'Hello?' Titan's voice bounced off the walls in a lonely echo.

Lestadt strayed from the group and approached the first house, followed by Neximus who, despite Titan's instruction, had his hand ready at his weapon.

Lestadt knocked on the door loudly enough to rattle the hinges. There was a noise from within like a sharp intake of breath that was cut short. Lestadt put his ear to the door but heard nothing more.

'Hello? We mean you no harm. We are travellers, seeking to purchase grain if you have any to spare.'

There was no reply and he banged on the door again.

'Kick the door in,' Neximus said quietly into Lestadt's ear.

'No. We need their trust. We cannot simply barge into their homes and demand hospitality of them.'

Neximus shrugged his shoulders as though he didn't mind either way.

'I don't think more violence is going to help us here. Irramai was born out of need to protect the people.'

'Irramai is dashed to the ground – what...' Their hushed argument at the door was cut short.

'Sirs?' questioned a timid female voice by the door.

'Hello...'

'You passed the fires, but some can do that and still harm us.' There was a yelp of pain from the girl.

They heard a rough male voice speaking in another tongue, followed by the sounds of a struggle.

It was Neximus who pushed past Lestadt with sword drawn. He booted the door so hard there was a loud snap and one of the hinges ripped loose from the frame. The door swung back, bounced off the wall and threatened to slam shut in their faces again, but Neximus was already shouldering past the splintered entry.

'See what you have done?!' the man shouted, using common tongue.

Seeing Neximus coming at him, he turned to the cowering girl at his feet and began to hit her, blow upon blow.

He tried to get as many in as he could before the tall blonde-haired man was upon him. Neximus brought the hilt of his sword crashing down on the man's head, and the man crumpled to the floor in a heap beside the cowering girl. Titan and the rest of the men followed Lestadt and Neximus in shortly after.

'We did not come here to hurt you.' Neximus hadn't thought his statement through as he stood beside the unconscious man.

She peeped up at him with a mixture of fear and awe from behind a scrap of messy, dark hair.

She did not accept his offered hand. She began speaking hysterically in her own tongue before sidling herself across the floor until she had significant space to get to her feet and run to the back of the room. Lestadt and the other men lowered their swords and Neximus sheathed his blade.

Neximus advanced slowly, reaching out to toward her. 'We...'

He was cut short by a savage shout, and she spun around fast. Lestadt caught the glint of a dagger as she lunged for Neximus. He leapt forward as Neximus stumbled to the side, receiving a glancing blow off his hip as the dagger jarred into bone. Lestadt was on her in an instant, wrenching the bloodied dagger from her shaking hands. He pushed her face first into the ground and twisted both her hands behind her back. He pressed his knee into the small of her back so she was well and truly pinned. She was speaking frantically in her own tongue again, and Lestadt pushed his weight into her back harder, forcing her to cry out.

'You spoke the common language before. Do so now or I shall inflict much more pain,' he threatened.

There was a commotion beside him and Lestadt turned to see Neximus had seized a young boy who was also armed with a dagger. She had been trying to convince her brother to come to her aid. The boy looked more terrified than threatening.

'Useless coward!' she shouted in common tongue.

'You let them in, you fool,' he fired back, suddenly finding courage now that Lestadt had his sister pinned.

'How dare you – you little wretch!' She struggled beneath Lestadt's weight.

The two adolescents seemed more determined to fight each other rather than the people who had just invaded their home.

'Father will have you cast out now for sure! You will be at the mercy of the night-crawlers this time!' the boy taunted.

Lestadt was standing with his foot still pinning the girl, and Neximus had confiscated the dagger from the boy and set him loose. Neximus stood to the side, pressing a hand to his wound.

The two youths were taken from the small hut. The older man, who they assumed was the father of the boy and girl, was bound and left sitting outside where they could keep an eye on him. Dusk was descending, and the boy and girl looked nervous as darkness crept toward their village.

'Why do you have these fires burning?' Titan asked the girl, but she looked away, refusing to answer.

Titan turned toward the boy instead, seeing his hostility only seemed to be directed at his sister.

'The fires keep the demons back, but sometimes some of the deadheads come and try to put them out. We have a night-watchman, but he won't come out now that you're here.'

Titan turned to one of the men beside him. 'Send for the rest of our people. I want everyone within the boundaries before nightfall.' He turned back to the boy to say more, but the girl cut in.

'You idiot, now they bring more!'

'You let them in first! Besides, they're not deadheads, you heard them, they are afraid too.'

'What is a "deadhead"?' Titan asked.

'I don't know exactly. They rarely come out in the day.'

'They were normal people, like you or I, but Murott, the soul devourer, got them.'

'Don't be stupid, there's no such thing,' the boy cut in.

'How can you disbelieve now? How is this idea so absurd, yet you have seen other demons roaming outside the fires?' the girl snapped.

'We also know tales of Murott, born soulless...' Titan said, and the girl finished for him.

'... and hungry for everyone else's, taking people's souls and turning them to his will. The deadheads are his gatherers of fresh souls; they trap you and call him to your soul. The night-watchman doesn't let them in, but they fear the fires too, and only come near enough to douse the flames. The night-watchman shoots them, then someone else finishes them off. The bodies are dragged away in the night by some beast or other.'

'What about the demons? Surely they have no fear of fire. Is that not where they live? Surrounded by the fires of hell?'

'Yes,' she said, her gaze serious and unwavering, 'surrounded and trapped. They fear being captured and imprisoned within the fire again. Someone, or something, has set these things free – a witch, I would suppose.'

She looked at Neximus briefly, but only Neximus thought he caught the meaningful glance. He had been indirectly accused of witchery because of his hair colour on several occasions.

'You are a witch! How else would you know such things? You speak of demonry and witches. We should burn you and see if you're afraid of the fire!' the boy sneered.

Their people were filing into the main street, causing a welcome distraction. Others gathered in the street behind the group of foreigners. Neximus nudged Lestadt, nodding toward the strangers at their back. They were poor, frightened people, seemingly harmless.

Most were women, some holding swaddled babies or standing protectively in front of their children. There were few men amongst the one hundred or so people in the village. Many were quite old or around the age of the boy, caught between adulthood and childhood.

Once Titan was alerted to the situation unfolding behind him, he turned to face the villagers but found himself speechless. He was suddenly reminded of the first day he entered Irramai. There had been just a small rabble of unorganised and frightened people. Refugees ravaged by poverty, wounds and loss of their loved ones, a feeling of hopelessness emanating from them.

The two groups of people studied each other. As the last of the light seeped away, thunder rolled above them, and seconds later, came a massive downpour. They all quickly realised the danger of their situation. The rain was already running in small rivulets down the muddy main street. The wood on the fires would get wet and extinguish the flames. It was night time, the time when the creatures and demons came hunting.

48. Prince Deserter.

She woke to the sound of faint tapping on the stone floor of the dungeon. Despite her malnourishment, the lack of sunlight and the disgraceful conditions that she was at present living, she felt refreshed after her long sleep. Looking around, she momentarily forgot the sound that had woken her and noticed first that the room was darker than normal. Even the torches on the walls outside had guttered out. The other women were fast asleep. The tapping began again, bringing Raemil's attention back to why she woke. There was a dark lump on the ground. Her eyes adjusted and she realised it was, in fact, Arramaou the crow, tap-tap-tapping on the floor to get her attention. He ruffled his feathers and made a quiet sound, studying her with his little black eyes.

'How did you get in here?'

'Who are you talking to?' a familiar, rich voice whispered close to Raemil's ear, startling her.

'No one, go back to sleep,' she said, trying to shoo Arramaou away.

She settled on throwing a blanket over him, making him squawk in distress.

'Where did that thing come from?' the dark-haired woman peered over Raemil's shoulder.

'That is what I would like to know,' Raemil said testily.

Arramaou flopped around indignantly beneath the blanket before managing to struggle free.

'You would treat me kinder if you knew my business here, Raemil,' said the bird,

337

regaining his composure and dramatically preening his feathers.

'It talks!' the other woman squeaked and tried to swat him with a hessian sack that had been made into a crude pillow.

Arramaou fluttered out of the way, and taking wing, he swooped her. She ducked, throwing her arms protectively above her head.

'Stop this nonsense. Why are you here, Arramaou?'

'*I came to lead you to your freedom.*'

'I came for my brother. I'll not leave without him, and you know this.'

'*Indeed, I do,*' he said flatly. '*I will lead you all to freedom.*'

'All?' asked the dark-haired woman.

'*Well, the three of you. Since you've interrupted us, I can hardly stop you from following.*'

'Why?' Raemil asked, her excitement and suspicion at odds with each other.

'*You do not trust me? I am hurt.*'

'Of course I don't trust you.'

'*Nevertheless, you will follow me.*' Arramaou cocked his head before taking wing and flying straight through the wall behind him to both of the ladies' astonishment.

'It seems the bird has talents other than speaking,' Raemil mumbled as she moved to follow.

A quick examination of the wall revealed that only a very small portion could actually be walked through, or crawled through, as it turned out.

The two women found themselves in a crawlspace in the wall. The way behind was blocked as soon as their bodies left the cell of sleeping women. It was dusty, cold and filled with cobwebs stretching across their path. Mice darted out of their way as they came crawling past.

They crawled to a junction and Arramaou turned right instead of going straight on ahead where there was a strong wind whistling down that passage to blow dust in Raemil's face. After following Arramaou for another short distance, Raemil found herself faced with another wall. The bird was now gone, so she put her hand out, feeling until she found the wall that could be crawled through. Finding herself in a small room, she glanced back to see she'd crawled out of a fireplace, thankful it was not lit.

The room was dim, but she could clearly see a body shackled to the floor. He seemed to be sleeping. Arramaou dropped a key at her feet and hopped back through the fireplace. With involuntary tears welling in her eyes, she reached out her trembling hand to touch her brother. She was startled to find he was not sleeping. As he looked up at her, she realised in that one moment he would not go with her.

'Raemil.' He reached out and touched her cheek lightly where a tear had escaped.

'Do not say it, brother, do not...'

'I cannot go with you.' He ignored her request. 'I think I have done something foolish. I cannot go free with you and leave my men here; I could not bear the shame. I know what it is to suffer and despair, I know what it is to know no hope. I can't leave them like this,' he pleaded for understanding.

He saw her lovely green eyes harden, instantly realising he no longer knew her.

The hurt and her own shame, everything he had hoped she'd been spared from, lingered quietly between them. Before he had a chance to understand what caused the sudden merciless expression, he watched her pick up a length of the chain he was shackled with. The chain thumped into his head and he crumpled to the ground and knew no more.

Dragging Serrin out through the tiny passages behind the walls was not Raemil's idea of a perfect escape, but she had little other choice. She was not prepared to even listen to the rest of Serrin's plea, let alone actually consider it. She had come too far and endured too much; she was not prepared to let anything get in her way.

Both the dark-haired woman and Arramaou were surprised at Raemil's brutality, but neither said a word as they watched the scene unfold. The two women dragged Serrin through the passage leading out of the compound. When they were free, they barely spared a glance for the prison. They hurried to follow Arramaou. He knew where the horses were, though he mentioned apprehensively that it would be difficult to seat an unconscious man.

The stables and horses were in a pitiful state. There was no warm feeling or sweet smell of hay and horse. It was cold and damp and draughty. The horses were skinny and unfit; it seemed these were the confiscated horses of the imprisoned soldiers. According to Arramaou, the Horsham men were unfamiliar with horses and were somewhat shy of them. They kept them mostly for meat.

They tried to select horses that seemed the fittest to make the long journey. The dark-haired lady selected a chestnut mare who sported many battle scars, and Raemil chose a grey mare with flecks of black on her white coat. The two women fitted the horses with appropriate tack, piled in no particular order and with no apparent thought to preserve the life of either the metal bits and buckles, which had mostly rusted, or the leather, which had stiffened. Raemil mounted first and with the aid of her companion, awkwardly dragged Serrin into position in front of her. It was not ideal, given that the horse was in no condition to be carrying one rider for a long distance, let alone two, but Raemil insisted they would not need to burden themselves with another horse.

By the time they were picking their way along the narrow track, zig-zagging down the mountain, the sun was creeping over the horizon. Looking over her shoulder, Raemil could see the peak of the mountain was still shrouded in mist and shadow. With a shudder, she urged the horse faster down the precarious path.

Raemil simply could not bear to be captured again, as it was, she was suspicious of Arramaou's loyalty. He did get them out of the compound, and at present he was flying ahead to scout for them – that was enough for her for now. It was Arramaou's job to make sure there was no threat behind the foothills of the massive mountain range.

Raemil was desperate to get to the flat. It was where she had last seen the Black and she could barely keep her fear and excitement in check when she finally urged the horse off the steep trail and onto the tablelands. She raced the horse at a flat gallop across the snow toward the line of trees near the drop off, whistling a piercing call across the ranges.

Her companion hung back, clearly baffled at Raemil's actions. Half-way down, they'd switched Serrin onto her horse so Raemil's mount could rest. His body was still slumped against her. Arramaou was silent and watching, perched on a jutting rock further back on the last stretch of path. Raemil pulled the horse up at the trees in a white spray of snow as the animal skidded to a halt.

Minutes passed in silence. Her gaze fell on a lone cypress tree, and her heart skipped a beat and she went cold. A vision seized her – of a tiny mewling baby.

His breaths irregular, her desperate and confused, she wants him to stop hurting. In her insanity and her desperate need to hush his painful wheezing sobs, she places him in the snow while she digs. By the time she picks him up again, he is cold and quiet, barely moving.

With a gasp, Raemil pulled herself from the awful memory and cruelly wrenched her mount's head away and kicked it on toward the nearby village.

Arramaou was quiet. He alone knew the reason for Raemil's sudden and savage need to escape this place.

Raemil was moody and silent. Dark, heavy clouds were rolling in fast, matching the mage's mood. They'd switched Serrin back behind Raemil again; the half-starved horses were struggling to cope. By dusk it was snowing lightly and they had reached below the tablelands, not far from the villages.

She was finally on her way home with her brother, but where to then? She could not live with her father. She loved Serrin very much and wanted to stay by his side, but could she? What would she do with herself now that she had travelled so far and seen and experienced so much? She was restless – *what if Caelin has fallen to ruin in this time of chaos?* There were dragons on the loose, strange and twisted creatures and people.

Even *she* had doubts about the soundness of her own mind since her journey took a turn for the worst. Would she and Serrin have a safe place to go home to? Was she really rescuing him or taking him to a far worse place?

Her thoughts were interrupted by a high-pitched whinny that Raemil immediately recognised. Her heart lurched in excitement and she whirled the mare to find the Black.

He had suffered long without his master. The twisted people in the night had tried to catch him, manipulate his mind and tried to hunt and eat him. Perhaps by a long association with his mage master, he was protected from their probing. He survived by finding stores of hay in old barns and sometimes finding small shoots of grass beneath the snow on the lower ranges where winter's grip was beginning to weaken.

She felt Serrin's posture straighten behind her and realised he was awake and hadn't said a word. Raemil dismounted and without hesitation handed the reins of the mare to an indignant Serrin. She ran to the Black and wrapped her arms around his neck, like she had done so many times before. He pulled her in close with his head in an equine embrace.

They made camp in a small cluster of trees. They were freezing and hungry, but dared not light a fire in case they drew attention to themselves. Raemil couldn't sleep, and after much tossing and turning, she sat up, pulling her knees to her chest and tucking her arms behind her calves to keep warm. Arramaou was perched in a tree above her head. His own head was tucked over his shoulder, presumably asleep.

She suddenly wondered why everyone had been so silent; even the dark-haired woman had not spoken a word since they left. Raemil had noticed on several occasions that she looked frightened. Raemil supposed it was because they could be pursued. She likely didn't have a home to go to either. The strange woman possibly had no other choice than to follow Raemil or face this new and terrible world on her own. She knew Serrin was upset with her, she could see the hurt expression on his face every time she glanced in his direction. Raemil wasn't proud of what she had done, yet given a chance to do it over, she'd do it again.

An hour later, Serrin woke from his fitful slumber to see Raemil was awake too. He studied her for a while. The light from the moon reflected off the snow, making it bright enough for him to see her clearly. She was disconcertingly beautiful; he had always thought so. Her's was a face that he had always known and loved, but it was not the face of an innocent little girl anymore. She had the face of a hardened woman and it saddened him deeply to see she had grown up while he was gone. He was still angry she had taken him by force and ashamed that his men were left to suffer while he went free.

He jumped at the sound of her voice, unaware that she'd known he was watching her.

'I am sorry, Serrin, truly, I am, but there was no alternative.' Raemil didn't turn to face him.

'What do you mean there was no other alternative? How about *not* bashing me over the head and taking me by force?'

'Precisely. There was no alternative. You would not have come of your own accord, and there was no way I was going to leave you behind, nor stay with you in that rotting hell.' There was a cold glint in her eyes.

'My men need me. I'm nought but a coward for leaving them like I did.' His voice was low and angry.

'Then so be it.'

'How dare you! I am your brother and I deserve some respect. You are treating me as though I am your prisoner!' he practically shouted in anger. 'I suffered greatly to get to the position I was in when you stole me away. I owe them!'

'*You* have suffered greatly?! Do you think you are the only one?'

'No, but I have a responsibility to those men. I was a stupid, proud prince dragging them off to war. I was not a man; I was a foolish boy and a coward.

When I came to Horsham, I wept every night like a babe. Every night my men heard me cry, their prince, their leader, crying like a spoiled child in the cell beside them! What right had I to lead them into someone else's war? What right had I to weep when they watched their brothers and fathers die? When they were pitted against their loved ones to fight to the death? What right had I to weep, when most of the men in the camps had witnessed their wives and daughters being raped and murdered?' He fidgeted angrily with the bracelet still on his wrist as he spoke.

'I became their leader not because I was their prince, but because someone had to lead them and I realised I could. For once in my life I could be something other than a snivelling coward, and I was. I was something to those men; I was their hope. And you snatched me away. I may as well be that same snivelling coward in their eyes,' he finished angrily.

'I am sorry, Serrin. You are not a coward; you have never been a coward to me. You have always been someone I looked up to, that I love. King Farramand would not send soldiers to your rescue; he'd have let you rot and die in Horsham! You, his son, my brother, to be disregarded as though your life was nothing at all! You were something to me! Who else could I talk to? Who else would love me?' she finished quietly with a sob, remembering Lestadt's painful rejection.

She quickly wiped her eyes before her tears could spill; she had cried enough already. Serrin studied Raemil, her familiar green eyes, her pale skin and rosy cheeks, her long red curls. She had changed, but she was still his little sister. He leaned over and embraced her, timidly at first, but she clung to him fiercely and soon he was holding her harder. It had been so long.

49. The nameless thief.

G et those women and children inside – lock the doors! You, you, and you – get to those fires, keep feeding them dry wood!' He pointed his finger at two startled civilians.

For a second, they couldn't decide whether they were more afraid of the large man shouting at them or the threat of the fires going out and admitting demons into their village. The latter, they decided as they scurried off to do the warrior's bidding.

Titan ran a hand through his dripping hair as he stormed toward Lestadt and Neximus, who were still guarding the young girl and boy.

'Take the boy back into his hut – you'd better get *him* back in there too,' he said, gesturing toward the man they had left bound and gagged.

'What about the girl?' Neximus asked, shooting an irritated glare at his captive.

She was still bound, mostly because he wanted to punish her for inflicting the knife wound on him.

'She can stay here; I don't want her disappearing on us. She seems to know a lot about the demons,' Titan said before marching off, then he whirled around. 'Get her to point out who this night-watchman is.'

Lestadt set off to get the boy and his father into the hut. The young boy was, of course, complaining.

He left Neximus to tend with the girl, much to Neximus' disgust, Lestadt noticed with a grin. Neximus looked down at the girl and she glared back at him steadily. She barely reached his shoulder, but he suspected she might be older, and wiser, than she looked.

'Well, come on then, show me where the night-watchman is.'

'It would be easier if I weren't bound, you know,' she snapped.

'Oh, would it? It would be easier for me if you hadn't stabbed me, but here we are. Now get moving,' he said, giving her a small shove in the back.

The people worked together, despite the language barrier for some. There were still enough people that spoke the common tongue to translate. Many Irramainians had passed through Linvar on their way to the free lands.

They fed dry wood from stores and damp hay bales into the fires, but Titan didn't know what to do when they ran out of supplies. He glanced up at the black clouds. They weren't going anywhere anytime soon. The sun was almost set and they would be forced to rely on the dying fires for light. He turned back to where Lestadt was standing with a group of young men. With a pang of jealousy, he noted most of the young soldiers seemed to look to Lestadt for leadership.

Neximus was unimpressed by his new charge and the girl seemed far from impressed by his brutish behaviour. Finding the night-watchman was proving difficult in a time of chaos, and Neximus was beginning to suspect the girl was leading him on a wild goose chase. She eventually led him to a large barn at the back of the main street. Neximus pulled her back as her bound hands reached for the door.

'Wait a minute – why would he be in here?'

'This is where he normally is if he isn't at his house. He was Linvar's blacksmith before his apprentice took over. He's a bit odd, but I like him,' she explained before tugging his arm that held hers.

Neximus relented and followed her into the dark building.

There were tools and equipment hanging on the walls and on stands, including swords, horse tack and old shoes and new. The massive furnace was still burning brightly, adding light to the large area. He noted the fire and the pile of kindling. This could be the place for their last stand if necessary. The girl pulled Neximus toward a ladder leading up to another level, a hay loft that appeared to be converted into a blacksmith's quarters.

The girl went up first and Neximus was uneasy about letting her loose, but he had no other choice. He didn't want his back to her for a second, so he insisted on her climbing first – in a gesture she knew better than to mistake for chivalry. Neximus was quick to climb up behind her and was already freeing his hands from the rungs before she had fully turned to face him. Much to her annoyance, Neximus grasped her wrist tightly again, as he saw she meant to keep moving. They went to an open window and she stepped out onto a small ledge, moving to climb another ladder.

'What? Surely he's not on the roof?'

'I don't know, sometimes he is. He's not anywhere else.'

'Fine, but if he's not up there, I'm not searching any longer. I don't see the point, anyway.'

'You're probably right. He's only the night-watchman because no one likes him and he was the one person that nobody would miss if he were to be slain in the process of protecting the village, other than me,' she said under her breath, but he heard.

'You *are* popular in this place, aren't you? Is that why you like the man so much, he's just like you?'

'Don't think that the lack of friendly glances for you or the treatment from your people has gone unnoticed either!' she snapped.

Once they reached the top, they found an old man sitting in the rain, next to a large crossbow mounted on the roof.

'You brought that damned thief up here?'

'I can assure that you are mistaken – you cannot possibly think...' Neximus was cut short by the scruffy man.

'Of course I don't bloody know you. I was talking about the wretch of a girl, and who the hell are you anyway? I don't trust you. You've funny coloured hair.' The man squinted his dark eyes in suspicion at Neximus, all the while making quick glances at the girl.

It was as though he was making sure she wasn't stealing anything. Perhaps he thought she might make off with the giant crossbow at any moment.

'Gauldrad, Linvar is in peril. The people of Irramai are here, they wish to speak with you.' The girl was unaffected by his distrust.

'Not only that, did you see? The fires are going out!' Gauldrad whined.

'I know, I meant that is why we are in peril. The Irramainians are here to help.'

'Is that what you call them now?' he asked, giving Neximus a disgusted look. 'Filthy, stinking and evil is what I'd call 'em.'

'Do you think so?' Neximus took a threatening step closer.

'Since when did the Serlyn help us?'

'We were passing on our way to Caelin – we can *not* help, if you'd prefer.'

'Damn you and your people, we don't need your help. Get out, and take the little sprite with you.' Gauldrad turned away, focusing on the fires below in the village.

Neximus yanked the girl back toward the lower level. Anger radiated like heat from him.

He was mostly angry that he had been sent on the stupid errand in the first place. He supposed he was meant to find out about the creatures and their behaviour from the night-watchman, but he wasn't going to waste another second on the demented old man. He considered taking the time to hurl the old bastard from the roof, but it wouldn't be received very well by the people below.

'You said you were going to Caelin. Why?'

'Mind your own business. I thought the man was your friend. I couldn't decide who he hated more – me or you,' Neximus snapped.

'I never said that. I said that I liked *him*. Are you meeting someone at Caelin?'

'Why would you like someone who doesn't like you? And why do you want to know about Caelin?' As he climbed down, he absently helped her from the ladder.

'So, there *are* manners in there somewhere! People don't have to like you for you to be able to like them. And I was just curious about Caelin, that's all.'

'Why did he call you a thief?' Neximus ignored her comment and pulled her roughly toward the door.

'I don't know, he's confused, I guess.'

'Well, I'll be keeping watch...' Neximus patted himself down. 'Empty your pockets.'

She stared at him innocently and emptied her pockets, revealing a thimble and an old button. He grabbed her roughly by her other hand.

'You know, in some places, people cut off the hands of thieves and wear them as necklaces.' As he yanked her forward, from the voluminous sleeve of her coat fell Neximus' coin purse.

'Just a confused old man, was he?'

She looked away guiltily.

Once they reached the bottom, Neximus made a bee-line for the furnace to warm himself.

'Shouldn't you be helping your friends?' asked the girl, apparently impatient.

'Shouldn't you be minding your own business like I told you?'

'No. Stupid Serlyn.'

She thought she had spoken under her breath.

It took Neximus less than a minute to have her bound again. This time, he tore off the hem of her skirt and gagged her with it before binding her feet together so she could only shuffle behind him. Neximus left the barn with a smile on his face as he dragged the girl out behind him. He began to whistle, relishing in her fury as the gag muffled her curses.

As they walked toward the main street, Neximus began to slow his pace. He touched a hand to his ear briefly before falling to his knees, covering both ears. He closed his eyes and grit his teeth against pain. It ended suddenly and Neximus swore, then sprung to his feet and ran off. He left the girl alone and bound on the ground where she had knelt in an attempt to comfort *him*.

Titan was on his way to find Rem when he saw Neximus charging though the crowd like a streak of lightning. The former captain of the archers looked to be in pain. He said something to Lestadt and Lestadt's face dropped in what looked like sheer dread. Titan need not have bothered making his way to Lestadt to find out what was said as his ears began to ring. Moments later, a dark and massive shadow swept over the main street.

A loud screech was echoed by the screams of people before a dragon swooped and plucked a woman from the crowd. The Irramainians, being no strangers to the devastation wrought by dragons, were not afraid to barge into homes for shelter. The street was in chaos. With people scattering in every direction, there weren't many places to hide. Titan charged through the fleeing crowd while the dragon sat on the sagging roof of a house, gulping down its first victim. He found Lestadt standing by his ill-tempered horse, strapping his quiver on his back as Titan approached.

'Has anyone gone for the weapons? Have you seen Rem? Where did Neximus go?' Titan asked, all in one breath.

'I've not seen Rem, but I suspect he's gone for the weapons. Neximus went to make sure Hector is safe,' Lestadt said, slinging the bow over his shoulder.

Since Neximus' archers had been eaten in the last dragon attack, the bows and quivers had no owners. They were piled amongst various other weapons from the weaponry of Irramai that weren't used from day to day. Titan jogged toward the weapons cart. Lestadt moved into a comfortable position between two huts, leaning against the wall to watch the dragon around the corner.

The village of Linvar fell silent, save the few shouts from the rallying soldiers sneaking between huts and the steady pelting of the rain. The dragon screeched, sitting upon the sagging roof of the house and looking out over the village, content with the idea of slowly eating them all. Lestadt gave a nod to Titan as he saw him across the street, moving between huts to get closer to the perched monstrosity. Rem was not far behind; he didn't spare a glance for Lestadt. Minutes passed and the dragon had not moved. None dared to fire while the dragon was motionless, afraid to attract the creature's ire.

Lestadt heard a scream and was aware that at that moment the dragon had taken flight. The person who screamed came from the opposite end of the village. Peering around the corner to see what was happening, Lestadt saw the fire had died down to little more than the size of a small campfire. A soldier stood with his back to Lestadt. He appeared weaponless and was transfixed by something on the ground.

At first, Lestadt refused to believe his own eyes. On the ground before the soldier was a disfigured woman. She was missing one leg, cut off below the knee. Her right arm was twisted at an impossible angle and was dragging uselessly behind. She used her left arm to pull herself forward. Her head was slightly askew and a bone seemed to be protruding from her neck. She should have been dead, yet she was making her way toward the soldier who stood frozen. *What is wrong with you? You fool, why aren't you moving?* Lestadt thought. He had no idea that across the road, other soldiers were directing similar thoughts toward Lestadt.

A gust of stinking, hot air brought Lestadt back to the situation at hand. While he had been preoccupied watching the disfigured woman, he was about to become the dragon's next meal. He turned to find the dragon staring at him intently and close enough to blow his hot, putrid breath in Lestadt's face. Lestadt had no time to reach for an arrow as the dragon lunged. It's hideous, snake-like head split into a massive tooth-filled maw. He dived forward and rolled under its body.

Titan watched as Lestadt rolled under the dragon. He reached back and knocked an arrow, but before he could release, the dragon screeched and fell forward, dead, with an arrow in the back of its head. Titan looked back to see Neximus squatting on a roof-top, slinging his bow back onto his shoulder as he hopped onto the ground.

'Nicely done, Neximus. Is young Hector safe?'

'He's in that house with the other orphans and the healer.' Neximus gestured behind them.

'Where did you send the girl?'

'Shit...! I left her!' Neximus went pale and was gone in a flash, running between the huts toward the barn.

No one had thought to see if Lestadt was safe. He was pinned beneath the base of the dragon's heavy neck as it fell on him. He lay unconscious between the two huts as the 'deadheads' slowly crept into the village and two more dragons swooped in from the east.

He was crippled by a foot that twisted backward. Bone was mashed into the flesh, making his step rubbery as he wobbled toward the girl. She whimpered and hopped away from him as far as she could, but she had backed herself into a corner. Having bound feet was proving to be more of an impairment than a backward foot, apparently.

The deadhead was filthy and his body was covered in scabs. He smiled, blistered and oozing lips stretched wide to reveal blackened teeth. Seeing her exposed legs where Neximus had torn her skirts to gag her, he began to move faster, reaching to unbuckle his trousers. She could see the lust in his mad eyes as they roamed up and down her. She screamed; though it was muffled by the gag, her fear leant volume to her terror. She wept and tried to hit him. Her bound hands, balled into little fists, did nothing to deter him as he tore at her skirts and his filthy trousers dropped to his ankles. She struggled and twisted and screamed and nearly choked on the gag, but she didn't care. Nothing could be worse than the end she was about to meet.

Suddenly the deadhead went limp and fell forward on top of her, toppling her backward and spraying her with dark blood. She realised she had squeezed her eyes shut only when she opened them again. Her would-be rapist was now headless and properly dead. The filthy, half-naked body was hauled off her.

She was trembling, only just keeping herself from retching because of the gag. She looked down to see her skirt had been yanked off and she sat in the mud in her undergarments. A large, black cloak was gently laid over her lap, then she was gathered into a man's arms and carried away like a child. Only once did she look up to see Neximus' ashen face as he removed the gag from her mouth before she buried her face in her shaking hands.

Lestadt woke in the darkness and could hear the sounds of battle around him but could not move. For a moment he was confused until he reached behind him to feel the scales of the dragon. He couldn't see what was going on, but he could mostly hear swords hitting flesh with sickening thuds. There were no clashes of metal to indicate armed assailants. A dragon dived into the ground and died not far from where he lay. He could see numerous arrows protruding from it and spotted the fatal arrow in the back of its head. Hearing a cheer go up, he realised the fighting was over and he'd missed all of it.

'Ho – Lestadt! We wondered where you'd got to,' said a young lad, popping his head around the corner to see Lestadt's predicament.

Lestadt thought for a moment, several names running through his mind, before he remembered.

'Henry – thank the gods! I thought I would die under this thing.'

'Nah, you're as tough as old boots – the boys told me you fought your way into Irramai when the dogs attacked! Those things were beasts,' Henry said as he lifted the neck enough for Lestadt to wriggle out from beneath.

Lestadt had made many friends both young and old within the ranks of Irramai's soldiers; often drinking with them and sharing tall-tales.

While Lestadt rubbed the feeling back into his legs, Henry filled him in. The young man told him of the deadheads and the civilians that were killed before anyone realised that Linvar had been breached. Lestadt asked where Neximus and Titan were, but Henry hadn't seen Neximus since he slew the first dragon, and Titan wasn't far from them.

Lestadt found Titan addressing the people from Irramai and Linvar. The rain had died down to a drizzle and the fires were small but holding.

'We go on to Caelin for safety. You may pack up your belongings and follow us or you can stay here. It is your choice, however, we will be moving out at first light and will wait for no one,' Titan was saying to the gathered crowd.

Lestadt looked around to see so many frightened faces and realised their group of travelling refugees was likely to get bigger every time they stopped near a town.

He spied Neximus past the crowd, emerging from one of the huts. He carried

Hector in one arm; the boy rested his head on Neximus' shoulder. Behind Neximus, Lestadt could see the young girl trailing. She was wearing Neximus' large black coat and was so small that it covered her entire body.

Lestadt made his way through the crowd toward Neximus, and as he came within speaking distance, the look on the man's face stopped him from saying anything. He looked at the girl again and barely recognised her as the feisty brat that brow-beat her brother for being a coward. Her face was pale and her eyes were downcast. She glanced in his direction, but couldn't meet his eyes.

'It would seem that we all go to Caelin, as you wished,' Neximus said.

Lestadt shook his head, indicating they should speak later. Neximus shrugged, ignoring Lestadt.

'I think your mission more foolhardy than noble, but would that I had the chance for revenge for such a thing, I would do no less.'

The girl watched Neximus walk away, as though she didn't know whether she wanted to follow or not. Instead, she stared blankly into the crowd with a dismal expression on her face. She fingered a pendant around her neck absently, as though it brought her comfort, or at the very least, distraction.

Only some of the men were lucky enough to get one or two hours sleep in the hours of pre-dawn that followed. Most Irramainians, including Lestadt, Neximus, Rem and Titan, were busy helping the people of Linvar pack up their lives. The most difficult task was finding room amongst the overloaded wagons for more blankets and clothing. Horses and wagons waited at the northern end of the village, but there weren't enough for everyone. Many Irramainians already faced the journey on foot. The horseless people would join the others in the middle of two ranks of mounted soldiers.

As the sun rose, Lestadt and Neximus shared the warmth of a fire, both holding steaming mugs of tea. They allowed themselves some rest before leaving; Hector had found him quickly and was asleep in Neximus' lap already.

'I'm sorry; I haven't been the nicest of late...' Neximus began.

'Have you ever been the nicest to anyone?' Lestadt chuckled.

'Of course, I'm delightful.' His face stayed expressionless. 'Lestadt...'

The hesitation alarmed Lestadt. He waited patiently while Neximus seemed to choose his next words carefully.

'My family was killed by bounty hunters. They shot an arrow through my wife, through my son and into me. They said we weren't worthy of more than one arrow.' Neximus' solemn eyes lifted to Lestadt's. 'I know your motive here is revenge and Irramai is a means to that end. I get it. If I had the opportunity to destroy those men, I would do no less. Just don't let your need for revenge lead us all into doing something stupid.'

Lestadt only nodded.

'Otherwise, I am with you no matter what, my friend.' Neximus reached over and clasped his hand over Lestadt's shoulder.

Lestadt returned the gesture, the only physical contact he'd seen Neximus receive that was not from the small boy or from violence. They didn't say anything for a long time. There were no words that could ease that kind of pain.

Something nagged at Lestadt, and eventually, he had to ask.

'Neximus, why was there a bounty on your head?'

'I did something stupid for the sake of revenge,' Neximus said flatly. His tone invited no further discussion on the matter.

They stopped for the night in the next forest beyond Linvar. Everyone slept in tents or out in the open. They were banked by small fires for safety as well as warmth. Insane people roamed, jabbering to themselves in the night. They rarely ventured close to the fires, much to the relief of the guards on duty.

Neximus sat by a small fire with Hector asleep in his arms, but the man did not sleep. He watched too. Lestadt slept not far from him. He was snoring softly and seemed undisturbed by the mad people that stalked the outskirts.

Neximus noticed the crazies beginning to scuttle away and he realised it was morning. A heavy fog had settled around them and he could hear people being woken up by the guards. Neximus nudged Lestadt with the toe of his boot and heard him grunt. He laughed and nudged him again.

'Wake up, darling,' he teased and saw Lestadt roll over and glare at him with bleary eyes.

It was late in the night when Lestadt had fallen asleep and he was clearly exhausted. 'Did you sleep?'

'Sure.'

'I think you are one of them, it's not normal,' Lestadt said, narrowing his eyes and gesturing with a nod of his head toward the outskirts of the camp, where the deadheads had been.

'Maybe *you* are. You're starting to look like one of them!' Neximus laughed and tossed Lestadt two empty cups. 'You find the tea; I'll boil the water.'

'You're a bastard,' Lestadt said as he rose slowly, reluctant to move away from the warmth of the fire where Neximus was still enjoying the heat.

It wasn't long before they were mounting up again.

There were a few people whose tents were still up, but Titan was adamant they be out just after dawn. The first soldiers were moving out now to give people more room to pack up. Neximus and Lestadt were a part of the first group and they had just mounted their horses when Titan rode past telling everyone to hurry up, for what seemed like the millionth time. Hector was mounted behind Neximus now. The boy refused to leave the man's side, which was fine by Neximus. He was still concerned by Hector's spreading rash.

'Oh, stop fussing like an old woman, Titan, they will come,' Neximus said as Titan rode past yet again.

'Someone has to get them to see sense! And I don't see *you* moving yet,' Titan pointed out.

Neximus turned in the saddle toward Lestadt to see if he was ready and then stopped, an odd expression on his face.

'What is it Neximus?' Lestadt was familiar enough with that expression by now to know he was either seeing, or hearing, something.

'A horse galloping this way... maybe two...'

Lestadt couldn't hear it but trusted Neximus. He turned his horse in the same direction and looked over the top of the tents into the fog. It wasn't long before he could hear the dull thud of hoofbeats, then he could see a dark shape moving fast toward the camp.

A horse squealed, then two riders materialised out of the fog. A small bay leapt to the side of a grey gelding that was pursuing them. They both thundered into a tent and collapsed it before galloping through the camp at breakneck speed. They were followed by a string of curses from the people who had been trying to pack up. The rider of the little bay horse was cloaked and hooded, carrying a black bundle. The bay's reins were seized by the rider of the grey gelding and the horse reared.

Neximus immediately recognised the man on the grey and the girl, whose hood fell back in the struggle. She kicked the man hard in the shin and snatched the reins away then spun the little bay around fast. Seeing Neximus, she saw safety ahead. She manoeuvred her horse in behind Neximus' big roan and

Neximus blocked the girl's father as the man's horse came skidding to a halt. Neximus drew his sword, and beside him he heard the slither of Lestadt's sword and a half dozen others behind them.

'I come to get my property,' the man said angrily, his cheeks flushed red.

'People are not property. Now leave,' Lestadt said.

'Not her – she could rot for all I care. I want her clothes and that horse. They belonged to my wife.'

'Well then, they are hardly your property, are they? Now go,' Lestadt retorted.

Neximus moved his horse closer to glare down at the man, his hostile gaze never leaving his face. As if noticing for the first time, the girl's father took in the sight of the handful of soldiers that stood with hands to hilts. He scowled and rode off into the fog.

Neximus turned his horse to see the young girl staring at him, round-eyed and frightened. She held out the black bundle to him.

'Your coat. I–I thought you would want it back,' she offered.

He pushed her hands back. 'Keep it for now,' he said and urged his horse forward. They were already running behind.

Lestadt waited to let the girl and her little bay fall in behind Neximus, then he manoeuvred Steel around to follow them.

Lestadt couldn't help but notice that the girl looked different. She looked more like a little lady than she had the day before. A red jewel on a chain around her throat caught his eye. It seemed out of place; he realised that had been what she was gripping so tightly the day before.

Looking down the long line of refugees, he realised just how close he was to gaining his revenge. He thought about how far he had come, the things that he had witnessed and done to get here. Soon he would reach Caelin and sink his sword into the king's heart. He wanted to watch the light fade from his eyes, like he had watched the light fade from his mother's while his sister's body dangled from the ceiling in the background.

The long line trudged on, hopeful to find sanctuary from the horrors they witnessed. They would never know they marched only for Lestadt's ambition; pawns in his twisted fantasy that led only to more death.

END BOOK ONE.

Epilogue...

S taring up at the ceiling, she reflected on the decisions that led her here. Guilt after the fact wasn't overly helpful, she mused. Her eyes roamed over the naked and passed out body of her latest conquest. It was hot and sticky; she had thrown the sheets from her body and his. She tossed his limp arm off her and lay spreadeagled to get some relief. Unsatisfied with the room allotted to her in the bed, she gave the man a shove and he rolled off the edge with a thud.

'What the...?'

'Get out,' she simply said, waving her hand toward the door, causing it to swing open.

The bewildered man gaped. He was handsome, but stupid. The look she gave him invited no negotiation on the matter and he snatched up his clothing and hurried out.

Now more comfortable, she went back to reflecting on her past mistakes. It was difficult for her to acknowledge she had made mistakes, but unfortunately there were many. Her biggest had led her to this forsaken armpit of the world, in Agdongren of all places. She had no idea why anyone sane would come here.

She had come seeking to gain back her power to travel. As it was, she had to travel by land and sea like a commoner; it was a large inconvenience and took up far too much of her precious time. What she sought was the key. There was only one with the power to open the way into the place known as the Hall of Realms. This travel was different to how she had once travelled in spirit, going to the Inbetween and then to people or places she was connected to. To travel with the key was to take your body with you, to only travel a few hallways and be in another country all together. It was rumoured that one could even travel to other worlds.

She had lost the right of spirit-travel when she negotiated for her life, not realising that if she ever stepped back into the Inbetween, it would be forfeit. If she had the power of a coven, she might do such a thing, but it would leave her and her companions weak and vulnerable. Not exactly a desirable state to be caught unawares in and on a regular basis. If she had the key, she would expend little to no power to reach her destination; she could come and go as she pleased, or so legend had it.

The problem she faced was, by all accounts, the key had disappeared a long time ago, precisely around the same time Eldantez met his demise. She couldn't be sure if the two were linked, but if he'd had the key when he was trapped, he would surely be free by now. She followed leads to Agdongren to find her old friend Stah, who was rumoured to be living out her life in the wildlands. She discovered her friend had been long dead. Any information she had died with her.

All the powerful mages were either dead or had no idea what the key was. So much knowledge had been lost to the wars following the exile of mages from Otowan. The sisters could travel without needing the Inbetween only because they used their stones and only very short distances to places and people they already had a connection to. From what she had learned on her own, the stones had a connection to the key, but she couldn't work out what it was exactly; her findings were sketchy and incomplete at best.

She rolled out of bed and put on her loose dress before heading to the hidden garden. She was in Carlemnia, one of only three populated cities on Devil's Tooth Bay on the southern edge of Agdongren. The castle lay in ruin, a reminder of the destruction mages wrought on the world during war-time. People still lived there, but there was no king; it was governed by a council now. People lived in and around the ruins of the old stone castle for protection. The jungle was a deadly place and even now she could see it trying to creep in and claim the castle. Vines grew up the cracks in the stone work, animals peeped out of deep and dark holes created by the rubble. Small trees sprouted through the cracks in the pavement of what was once a courtyard.

She spent the previous day wandering the ruins of the castle. It was dangerous and falling apart – the whole western side was uninhabited due to the fact. In her wanderings, she had crawled through a crack barely big enough for her to fit to find a forgotten garden. It was taken over by vines like everything else, but the old foundations and some of the pretty flowers still thrived. A crack high above let some light in.

She sat down at the pond as she had done the day before and stared at the statue in front. It too was crumbled and she'd had to pull vines away to get a good look. It was the statue of a man, or a god, it was difficult to be sure. The size and the posture made her think it was a god. It was just how those pompous bastards enjoyed being displayed. The face was worn off, but she imagined from the jawline and the muscular build that he would have been handsome, whoever he was. What intrigued her the most was the carving on the base of the statue. The rest of the statue was smooth and worn with time, but the carving looked as fresh as if it had been carved just hours ago, though she knew it had not. The carving was stained with a blood-red circle in the palm of a hand, fingertips pointed to the sky: the symbol of the key.

She had searched all around the base of the statue and climbed every surface of the ruining garden walls, to no avail, the day before. The thought of doing it again today left her feeling less than enthusiastic. Sighing in resignation, she bent to the task, vowing to leave no stone unturned – literally. She tried to find passion for the task by thinking of her reason for all this searching.

She was not welcome in Otowan and travel for her kind had only become more dangerous. While she could mask her features, the power it took was exhausting, and again, left her vulnerable. Her reason to want to come back to Otowan was also a part of a bargain struck for her life that she thought she could cheat. Living out a boring life in King Farramand's castle was not the mewling baby she left behind several years ago, but the red-headed young girl that she could only dream of but never touch.

To know that her second daughter bore her resemblance so much more so than her first was like a knife in her heart. She could not raise her and know her, not without the key, not without the means to visit her safely. She wasn't even sure her daughter's safety was granted. She had hidden her, yes, and bound her powers, but she could not be confident it would keep her from an untimely death.

She was promiscuous by nature. Luckily for her, being a mage left her free to be so, without becoming a broodmare of sorts. She, as most mages, could control such things with simple measures prior to the act. She had been stupid and thought that she was in love when she met her first daughter's father. As it turned out, she was just in a week long stupor due to enjoying too many pixie herbs.

It was too late when she emerged from under a pile of naked bodies with a blinding headache and a desire to stab each and every person that so much as breathed too loudly. She was already pregnant. If left unchecked, perhaps by a drugged mage on a week-long bender, pregnancies in mages advanced very quickly. A mage foetus was an aware one; the selfish little leeches used the mother's power to their advantage to be born faster if left to their own devices. She had woken with a blinding headache and a suspicious pot belly that wasn't there previously.

The second daughter was never going to happen, not ever. So it had been an easy bargain to make in exchange for her life. She had the power to prevent it and the previous experience to learn from – which was to avoid being stupid. She had not counted on meeting the Earth Goddess and her son in the Shenkar Forest. Though she couldn't be sure about the consent, the experience was exquisite; she enjoyed it so much that flocks of birds erupted into the sky in fright and blacked out the sun when she gave voice to that pleasure. The encounter led to her second daughter; the one who was never meant to be.

While mage-babies could selfishly speed up their births for their own ambitions, she, having some talent with healing, could slow down the impending birth. Not knowing what else to do other than hide the baby as best she could, she took herself to Otowan. She found herself a king, charmed her way into his pants, then allowed the baby to grow to be born into a more convenient and believable timeline. When the girl was born, she named her to the king. She bound her daughter's powers and the castle around it to protect her, for the castle was built in a very powerfully significant place. It was a place she had sworn to forget, a place she had lied about, and a place she therefore knew the lost daughter would stay lost.

Now, if she could just find the key, she would be able to visit her daughter without detection. Most importantly, she could make sure that whatever powers her daughter had remained bound as she grew. She couldn't imagine what her little red-headed girl was capable of if she happened to gain anything from having a father born of a goddess.

She searched full circle back to the statue and the pond, realising the only place she hadn't looked was at the bottom of the pond. Peering over the edge, she could see the water was black and stagnant. It didn't seem as though anything could be living in it, yet something moved in its depths. She leaned yet further over the edge, and before she could react, a gaping maw shot out and swallowed her whole.

She struggled inside the thing, feeling cold seep in around her. She felt the blackness press in on her until she could no longer keep it out. Darkness leeched into every part of her and settled deep into her soul. She saw not death himself, for she had already met him, but she saw and felt the deaths of millions.

Manipulations, beatings, rapes, torture, mutilation, half-living people forced to prey on others. Horrific creatures that had not walked the world in hundreds of years, demons; she saw them all. Her family torn apart, scattered to the wind and defeated, murdered. She could do nothing as vision after vision assaulted her. This was what was to become of the world. Mages and mortals enslaved alike would become nothing but beasts of burden, play things for the grotesque demons who danced to the tune of the one dark lord.

He would rise from his prison and his vengeance on the world would be nothing short of mass genocide, but not before every sick, torturous fantasy was dealt to the people that betrayed him. Not before he witnessed every act of depravity carried out before him and for him. Not until he could find her and destroy everything that she held dear. The lands literally bled, Otowan, Iadron and Agdongren all. Nothing was safe from this horror.

She woke in an orchard, hidden away and useless. The things she had foreseen caused her to go stark raving mad.

Acknowledgments

Thank you to my wonderful partner, my best friend, Scott Kerrisk. You always believed in me, even when at times I didn't.

Thank you to Vanessa Barnes and Shane Heritage for transferring my early works from a DOS compatible floppy disc to something remotely Windows friendly. I would have lost so much groundwork without your help. Thanks to the tiny caterpillar that crawled out of the back of the ancient computer. We know it was your hard work keeping things running smoothly behind the scenes.